P9-CZV-337

*continued . . .*

# Murder on
# Mulberry Bend

Victoria Thompson

BERKLEY PRIME CRIME, NEW YORK

**THE BERKLEY PUBLISHING GROUP**
**Published by the Penguin Group**
**Penguin Group (USA) Inc.**
**375 Hudson Street, New York, New York 10014, USA**
Penguin Group (Canada), 90 Eglinton Avenue East, Suite 700, Toronto, Ontario M4P 2Y3, Canada
(a division of Pearson Penguin Canada Inc.)
Penguin Books Ltd., 80 Strand, London WC2R 0RL, England
Penguin Group Ireland, 25 St. Stephen's Green, Dublin 2, Ireland (a division of Penguin Books Ltd.)
Penguin Group (Australia), 250 Camberwell Road, Camberwell, Victoria 3124, Australia
(a division of Pearson Australia Group Pty. Ltd.)
Penguin Books India Pvt. Ltd., 11 Community Centre, Panchsheel Park, New Delhi—110 017, India
Penguin Group (NZ), Cnr. Airborne and Rosedale Roads, Albany, Auckland 1310, New Zealand
(a division of Pearson New Zealand Ltd.)
Penguin Books (South Africa) (Pty.) Ltd., 24 Sturdee Avenue, Rosebank, Johannesburg 2196,
South Africa

Penguin Books Ltd., Registered Offices: 80 Strand, London WC2R 0RL, England

This is a work of fiction. Names, characters, places, and incidents either are the product of the author's imagination or are used fictitiously, and any resemblance to actual persons, living or dead, business establishments, events, or locales is entirely coincidental. The publisher does not have any control over and does not assume any responsibility for author or third-party websites or their content.

MURDER ON MULBERRY BEND

A Berkley Prime Crime Book / published by arrangement with the author

PRINTING HISTORY
Berkley Prime Crime mass-market edition / March 2003

Copyright © 2003 by Victoria Thompson.
Cover art by Karen Chandler.
The Edgar® name is a registered service mark of the Mystery Writers of America, Inc.

ISBN: 0-425-18910-4

BERKLEY® PRIME CRIME
PRIME CRIME Books are published by The Berkley Publishing Group,
a division of Penguin Group (USA) Inc.,
375 Hudson Street, New York, New York 10014.
The name BERKLEY PRIME CRIME and the BERKLEY PRIME CRIME design are trademarks belonging to Penguin Group (USA) Inc.

PRINTED IN THE UNITED STATES OF AMERICA

13  12  11  10  9  8  7  6

# I

"I HOPE YOU ENJOYED THE EVENING."

Sarah Brandt turned toward her companion, even though he was merely a shadow in the dark coach beside her. "It was lovely. I can't remember when I was last at the opera."

Indeed, she felt more than a little like Cinderella. Dressed this afternoon in finery borrowed from her mother. Dinner at Delmonico's. Then the theater, with its glittering performers singing soul-shattering music and the magnificently garbed patrons who were more interested in being seen than watching the performance. Now she was riding home in a carriage that was going to deliver her, if not back to her place among the cinders, at least back to ordinariness again.

"There's no reason you couldn't go out like this frequently," Richard Dennis said, amusement in his voice.

They both knew her present life on Bank Street, working as a midwife, usually allowed little opportunity for an evening like this one. "Ah, I see it all now. My mother bribed you to tempt me back into the world of the idle rich, didn't she?"

He sighed theatrically. "I thought I was being so discreet. How did you guess?"

"Because she tries it with everyone," Sarah assured him without rancor. Her mother only wanted what she thought was best for her child, and Sarah's birthright entitled her to a life of leisure. The kind of life Richard enjoyed. "What did she offer you as a reward for rescuing me?"

"Why, your hand in marriage, of course. Nothing less could have satisfied me."

Sarah smiled in the darkness. "Then you should be grateful that I am proof against your charms. My last suitor came to a very bad end."

"I'd be faint-hearted indeed if I allowed that to deter me," he insisted. "Most men would only consider it a challenge to be overcome."

"I hope you're more sensible than most men, then," she said.

"No one has ever accused me of that," he replied with mock outrage, making her laugh. "And how about you, Sarah Brandt? Are you more sensible than most women?"

Her amusement faded. "I'm afraid I am. Too sensible to marry again, at least."

Although she couldn't see his expression in the darkness, she sensed the change in him. As the coach continued bouncing gently over the cobbled streets, they sat in silence for a few moments while they both remembered their lost mates. The three years that

Tom Brandt had been gone seemed like only as many days. Her companion's wife had been gone longer, but she was just as sorely missed.

"How do you bear the loneliness?" he asked finally.

"I don't. I just try to fill my days so I'm too busy to think of it."

This time his sigh was weary. "But we still have the nights, don't we?"

Yes, they did still have the nights. The darkness that sometimes seemed endless when you had no one to hold you. Sarah wanted to reach out to him, to tell him she understood, but that would be a mistake. Lonely people could make terrible mistakes if they weren't careful. She'd been careful for too long to risk it now.

"Richard," she said, calling him by his given name in spite of their brief acquaintance, "you don't need to be lonely. You must know you're attractive, and you're certainly eligible. You could have your pick of women in this city."

"And what about you, Sarah?" he asked, taking the liberty of using her first name as well. "You could have your pick, too, starting with that policeman. What's his name?"

"Malloy?" she asked in astonishment.

"Oh, well done!" he teased. "Anyone would think you had no idea how he feels about you."

Sarah had no intention of discussing Malloy's feelings for her. "I'm happy with the life I've chosen, Richard, even though I am lonely sometimes. But you don't seem happy at all, which is why I don't understand why you haven't found someone else."

"I've been waiting for you," he tried, but she

wasn't fooled. She could hear the wistfulness in his voice.

"Your wife would want you to be happy, Richard."

"Is that what you tell yourself, Sarah? Do you really think your husband would want you to be with another man?"

She almost said it was different for men, but she caught herself. She had no idea if it was or not. "I never knew your wife. What was she like?" she asked instead.

"Was she jealous, do you mean?"

"I'm not sure what I mean," Sarah confessed. "You were obviously devoted to her, so you must have loved her very much."

"Is that what you think? That I was devoted to her?"

She couldn't quite read the expression in his voice. "You still miss her," she reasoned. "And you haven't been able to find anyone who could take her place in your life."

"So you assume I'm still grieving for her."

"Aren't you?" she asked, although she was no longer certain she wanted to know the answer.

"Grief isn't the only emotion that keeps people in mourning."

Something Sarah knew only too well. She thought of her parents, who still mourned the death of her sister Maggie, although they rarely spoke her name. Their guilt would never allow them to forgive themselves enough to truly let her go. "You can't think you were responsible for your wife's death," she said. "She died of a fever, and even the doctors couldn't do anything for her. You told me that yourself."

The glow from a passing streetlight briefly illuminated his face, and Sarah saw the kind of pain felt only by those suffering the torment of the damned. He must have seen her reaction, because he turned away quickly.

"I have no right to burden you with my sins. I never should have . . ."

"You never should have what?" she prodded when he hesitated.

He didn't reply, but she was afraid she already knew. "You didn't invite me out just because you wanted the pleasure of my company, did you?"

"You *are* very pleasant company, Sarah," he insisted. "I consider myself extremely fortunate to have met such a charming lady as yourself, and —"

"Stop that nonsense," she snapped. "I know exactly what I am, and charming isn't exactly the word I would use to describe myself. Something else drew you to me, and if you don't tell me what it is, I shall never speak to you again."

"How heartless you are, Mrs. Brandt," he tried in a feeble attempt at levity.

"I have many other undesirable qualities, too, and if you wish to see them, then by all means continue lying to me."

"I've never lied to you," he protested.

"There are lies of omission," she reminded him sternly.

"You are a hard woman," he said. "I wonder if even a policeman could tame you."

*"Richard,"* she warned.

"All right." He lifted his white-gloved hand in mock surrender. "I was hoping that . . . that you could help me understand."

"Understand what?"

"Hazel. My wife. She . . . Oh, God." His voice broke, and Sarah was instantly contrite.

"I'm sorry, Richard! I can be so stupid sometimes. I warned you that I have bad qualities. Please forgive me. I didn't mean to —"

"No, stop," he said, clearing the emotion out of his voice. "It's not your fault. It's mine. Just like it's my fault that Hazel is dead."

Sarah wasn't sure she'd understood him. "Do you feel responsible for your wife's death?"

"Of course I do."

Now Sarah understood. "We always feel responsible when a loved one dies," she assured him. "We blame ourselves for not loving them enough when they were with us, and we feel guilty for being the one still alive and —"

"But do you feel *responsible* for your husband's death, Sarah?" he challenged.

"I've wished a thousand times I'd stopped him from going out that night," she admitted.

"But are you *responsible* for his death?" he insisted desperately. "Do you blame yourself for *killing* him?"

Sarah felt herself grow cold beneath the many layers of her fancy dress clothing. "Did you . . . Did you cause your wife's death, Richard?"

"As surely as if I'd plunged a knife into her heart!"

Sarah gasped, instinctively recoiling from him. Over the past few months, she'd heard several confessions of murder, but she'd never expected to hear one riding in a luxurious carriage while returning from the opera.

He muttered something that might have been a curse and slapped his thigh in anger, making her jump. "That's not how I meant to tell you," he said. "Why does nothing ever go the way I plan?"

Now Sarah was sliding her gloved hand over the side wall of the carriage, trying to find the door handle. Even if she found it, would she be able to get the door open and escape, hampered as she was by her borrowed finery? Once on the street, where could she go? Would the carriage driver help her or be loyal to his master? And where were they? She might actually be in more danger outside the carriage than inside with a confessed killer, depending on the neighborhood.

"Sarah?"

She started, instantly alert and ready to scream bloody murder, if necessary. She waited, holding her breath beneath her tightly laced corset.

"Oh, God, I've frightened you," he said in despair. "I didn't mean . . . Please forgive me. I just . . . Sometimes I get so angry when I remember . . ."

He lifted a hand to his forehead, and his whole body seemed to sag in the shadowed darkness of the carriage.

Sarah forced herself to take a fortifying breath. "How did you kill her, Richard?" she asked softly, wary of angering him again.

"What?"

"If it was an accident, no one will blame —"

He groaned, causing her to recoil again, but this time she had no farther to go because the carriage wall was against her back.

"How did I manage to make such a hash of this?" he asked of no one in particular. "Maybe I should let you think I killed her and turn myself in to your policeman. I've often thought I should be punished for what I did to her. Would your Mr. Malloy punish me, Sarah?"

"Richard, I don't think —"

"Enough of this," he said, interrupting her. "I can't allow you to be frightened anymore. I'm not a killer, Sarah. Not the way you think. But even still, I'm responsible for Hazel's death."

Sarah felt the knot in her stomach loosen just enough that she could breathe without conscious thought. "What do you mean?" she asked, glad that her voice sounded perfectly reasonable.

He sighed, and she heard the anguish that came straight from his soul. "I didn't mean to make you think I'd taken her life," he explained. "She did die of a fever. The doctors came, but they could do nothing for her. It was a fever she'd caught from those people."

"What people?"

"The people she went to help. At the mission. You know what they're like. Filthy and diseased, little more than vermin. All she wanted to do was help them, and they took her life instead."

Sarah didn't know how to reply. There was some truth to what he said. "How did she get involved with this place — what was it called?" she asked in hopes of finding a way to help him.

"It's called the Prodigal Son Mission. A friend of hers had been approached for a donation. She and Hazel went down to see what kind of work they were doing. The next thing I know, she's going down there every week to help."

"I take it you didn't approve."

She expected an explosion of frustrated anger, caused by his guilt at having allowed his wife to do something of which he didn't approve, but he made no response at all for a long moment.

"It's worse than that," he said at last. "I . . . I didn't care."

Now Sarah was thoroughly confused. "If you didn't mind that she went, then you can't blame yourself for what happened."

He sighed in the darkness. "No, you don't understand. It's not that I didn't mind. I didn't *care*. I didn't care what she did or how she spent her time, just so long as she didn't bother me."

Sarah recoiled instinctively, this time out of aversion instead of fear.

"You see," he accused. "You hate me from just hearing about my behavior. I'm despicable."

"Oh, no!" she tried. "I don't hate you."

"Don't try to spare my feelings. You can't hate me more than I hate myself. I was a selfish cad. I didn't know how fortunate I was to have the love of such a wonderful, selfless woman. I would have bought her anything she wanted, but all she wanted was a family — the one thing my money couldn't buy. When the children she wanted didn't come, she tried to find other things to fill her life."

"That's only natural," Sarah assured him. "I know many people think women should be content with managing their households and visiting their friends, but that's not enough for some of us."

"It wasn't enough for Hazel. She was too restless, too . . ."

"Intelligent?" Sarah supplied when he hesitated.

She could feel his sharp glance. Few men acknowledged that females could be intelligent.

"Yes," he admitted after a moment. "I think that

may have been it. She was bored with the things women usually do. After she . . . was gone, I remembered things she'd said. She'd tried to explain it to me, but I was too busy to listen. Too busy to care. And then it was too late."

"Are you sure it's too late?" Sarah asked softly.

"What do you mean?"

"I mean you admitted that you sought me out because you wanted me to help you understand her. That is what you were saying, isn't it?"

"Yes, it is," he said wearily. "I had this insane notion that if I could figure out what drew her to that place, I might be able to understand . . ."

"Understand why she died?" Sarah guessed.

"I know it sounds foolish."

"It doesn't sound foolish at all." Sarah had experienced the same need after Tom died. If only she'd known what he'd been doing the night he was killed, and who he'd seen, and who had killed him and why . . . It *was* foolish. Knowing all that wouldn't bring Tom back. It might, however, bring her some measure of peace. "How can I help you?"

"I don't think you can," he said sadly. "I'm sorry I burdened you with all of this. Please forget we ever had this conversation, and forgive me if you can."

"Nonsense. Your wife sounds like someone I would have liked to know, and now I'm curious about this mission myself. They must do wonderful work there, or she never would have continued to support it. Perhaps they need our help. We owe it to her memory to find out."

"You don't need to involve yourself in this, Sarah. I'm perfectly capable of making the necessary inquiries myself. It will be my sackcloth and ashes."

"You forget that I owe you a favor, Richard," she said, reminding him of what he had done for her neighbor, Nelson Ellsworth. He hadn't been entirely willing to perform this favor, but he still could have refused outright and ruined an innocent man. Sarah felt he should be encouraged to continue on the proper path. "I will consider it my duty to help you learn everything you can about the Prodigal Son Mission."

Detective Sergeant Frank Malloy grumbled as he pulled his coat collar up against the early morning chill. Any sane man would be home in bed, enjoying his Sabbath rest. Trouble was, on certain subjects Frank Malloy wasn't exactly sane. He'd been forced to acknowledge that recently. That was why he'd left his warm blankets and trudged out into the deserted city streets this morning. He knew the early daylight hours of a Sunday were the best time to catch miscreants unawares — not only with their pants down but completely off as they slept away their Saturday night revelries.

He walked down the filthy alley behind a row of tenement buildings. He'd been here twice before and found no one in residence, although the place was clearly occupied on a regular basis. He'd received a tip from a drunken prisoner that he would find the answer to an old mystery here. The drunk had been interested in being released from jail in exchange for this information. Frank had been happy to oblige him, figuring Ol' Finnegan would get picked up again within the week anyway. The favor he had granted was little enough, even if the information proved worthless. And if it wasn't worthless . . .

Frank stopped and looked around for any signs of life. Even in daylight the alley was dark, shadowed by the five- and six-story buildings looming over it. The sun's rays would reach it for only a brief period during high noon before moving on to warm other, more deserving parts of the city.

Above him stretched a cat's cradle of clotheslines, strung between the two buildings that backed to either side of the alley. Most of the laundry had been removed in honor of the Sabbath, but here and there a lonely pair of drawers or a tattered sheet hung limply. The porches that stretched along the backs of each building on every floor were cluttered with bundles of belongings and stray pieces of furniture that wouldn't fit into the cramped flats or had been removed for the night to make room for sleeping. More clothes hung over a railing here and there, forgotten.

The alley itself was littered with the debris of many people living tightly packed together. Garbage was piled next to a crudely constructed children's "fort." A reeking outhouse stood beside wooden washtubs. The cobbled ground was stained with decades of discarded waste, human and otherwise. A mangy dog lay in the shelter of an overturned crate, but Frank's arrival hadn't disturbed him. Either he didn't care or he was dead.

Nestled in the midst of the alley was a compact dwelling of sorts, made of an odd assortment of materials obviously scavenged from many different locations over an extended period of time. Some tin here, some brick there, and many sizes, shapes, and colors of wood everywhere. The window holes were shuttered from within with what appeared to be crudely constructed wooden planks. The door had been scavenged from an old building and seemed as solid as it was scarred. A bent and battered stovepipe extended above the ramshackle roof, but no smoke drifted from it. If anyone was inside at this early hour, he wasn't stirring yet.

After taking one last look around for lurking danger, Frank strode up to the worn door and pounded on it. "Open up, Danny!" he shouted.

He knew this would draw as many of the neighbors as could raise their aching heads out onto the surrounding balconies to see what was going on. Entertainment was at a premium in this section of town, and free entertainment was always a draw.

Without waiting for a response, he tried the door, putting his shoulder to it when it didn't open immediately. To his surprise, it wasn't a lock that prevented the door from opening but a sack of rags lying on the floor in front of it. One good push sent it rolling away, allowing the door to swing wide.

Even though the alley was deeply shadowed, he still needed a moment for his eyes to become accustomed to the darker darkness within. For an instant, he had the impression of having disturbed a rat's nest. The floor seemed to come alive. Piles of rags — including the one that had blocked the door — and dirty blankets trembled and rose up, becoming children of varying sizes, shapes, and genders. They were groaning and cursing, and a dozen pairs of eyes glared at him murderously in the morning haze.

"Danny's the one I want," Frank bellowed, using the voice that turned hardened criminals to jelly.

A girl screamed, drawing Frank's attention to the far corner. A young fellow, a few years older and much larger than those sleeping on floor, had pushed himself up to a half-sitting position from where he'd lain on a thin, straw mattress. The girl who had screamed was one of two sharing the makeshift bed with him. Neither of the girls wore much in the way of clothes, and Danny didn't seem to be wearing any at all. From what Frank could see of the girls, which was quite a bit, he knew they couldn't be more than twelve, if that.

"Danny, it's the cops!" one of the other children yelled.

"I don't want any of you guttersnipes," Frank shouted. "Get out of here before I run you in!"

He didn't have to warn them twice. As quickly as little hands could snatch up belongings, they were out the door and gone, off to find a doorway or a drain pipe or a stairwell in which to hide. The two girls sharing Danny's bed were a little slower because they had to throw on enough clothing to make their dash for freedom somewhat decent, but in another blink of the eye, they were gone, too.

"Good business you've got here," Frank remarked as the young man rose, cursing, from his stinking mattress and looked around blearily for his clothes. "How many kids you got working for you?"

Not bothering with drawers — perhaps he didn't own any — Danny stepped into a pair of trousers that were clean enough to indicate they'd been recently stolen off someone's clothesline. Buttoning his fly, he glared balefully at Frank. "I pay my protection money to the captain regular, so don't try to shake me down for more. I got friends."

"I'm sure you do." They both knew even honest businessmen paid a fee to the police for the privilege of being allowed to operate unmolested. Danny would have to pay a hefty percentage of his income. "I'm not here to give you any trouble."

"Then get the hell out." He stepped forward belligerently, and Frank had to resist an urge to laugh at his feeble attempt at intimidation. The boy was probably no more than sixteen. His hairless chin and bony chest were those of a child. His eyes, however, were older than hell itself. Cleaned up, he'd be a handsome lad. His hair, beneath the dirt and grease, was fair and curly. His eyes were blue as a cloudless sky. His nose gave evidence of having been broken, but it lent character to an otherwise merely pretty face. He twisted his full lips into a snarl, revealing that he'd lost a few teeth along the way. The look he was giving Frank probably terrified the urchins who stole for him in exchange for the protection of living in his shack. Frank merely returned it tenfold.

To his credit, the boy hardly flinched. "I ain't afraid of you. I've taken beatings before."

"I really don't want to get blood on my suit," Frank said reasonably. "So if you'll tell me what I want to know, you can go back to sleep none the worse for wear."

The boy rubbed his head, which was probably aching. Frank reached into his pocket and pulled out a flask.

"Here, this should help."

He looked at the flask suspiciously for a moment before snatching it unceremoniously from Frank's outstretched hand. Still watching Frank, he pulled the cork and took a swig. He gasped as the liquor burned its way down his throat. "Mother of God, b'hoyo," he said hoarsely. "You shoulda warned me it was the good stuff! Are you trying to poison me?"

This time when he showed his missing teeth, he was grinning with delight.

Frank grinned back, although it wasn't from delight. "Now, tell me what you know about Dr. Tom Brandt."

"Who?"

Frank knew he wasn't being coy. It had, after all, been three years since Dr. Brandt had died. "Tom Brandt," Frank repeated. "He was a doctor. Used to treat people in the neighborhood. Didn't mind if you couldn't pay."

Most physicians who ministered to the poor insisted on being paid before even examining a sick person. Some people were forced to forgo food for treatment, and those who couldn't pay at all were left to suffer. Consequently, doctors were universally mistrusted and despised by their patients in this part of the city. Dr. Tom had been different, however.

Frank watched Danny's face as he forced his aching brain to work. It took a few moments, but the light of recognition finally brightened in his blue eyes. In the next instant he must have remembered what happened to Dr. Brandt, though, because the light vanished, replaced by wary fear. "Never heard of no Dr. Brandt," he insisted. "Here, take your whiskey and be on your way."

He tried to give the flask back to Frank, but he didn't take it. "Have another drink. Maybe your memory will improve," Frank suggested.

Danny shook his head violently, then instantly regretted the motion. He almost dropped the flask in his haste to grab his head and stop his brain from rattling around inside of it. Frank glanced around and saw one rickety chair leaning against the wall. He grabbed it and forced Danny to sit.

"I don't know nothing," the boy insisted, looking up at Frank beseechingly. "I was just a kid when it happened."

"If you never heard of the good doctor, how do you know something happened to him?" Frank asked mildly.

Danny's eyes darted wildly as he searched for some means of escape, but Frank stood between him and the only door.

"No one will ever know you told me," Frank said.

That challenged his manhood. Danny stuck out his chin defiantly. "I ain't scared of nobody! Not even you, lousy copper!"

Frank simultaneously took hold of the flask that Danny still held and hooked his foot around the front leg of the chair. When he jerked his foot, the chair fell over backward, slamming Danny into the floor along with it. Frank still held the flask safely in his hand.

As soon as he got his breath, Danny started cursing and howling with pain. The chair hadn't survived the fall, so Frank kicked the pieces out of the way and gave Danny a slight nudge, too, just to get his attention.

"Ow! Whadda you want from me? I told you, I don't know nothin'!" the boy protested.

"And *I* told *you* I didn't want to get blood on my suit, so if you make me do it, you're going to be real sorry. Now just start talking, and I'll let you know when I've heard enough."

Danny protested only once more, so Frank had to nudge him only once more before he started talking.

"I was a newsboy then," he said through gritted

teeth, resentment darkening his too-old eyes. "I had a real good corner, right by an El station." Newsboys fought each other regularly for the best corners. Most of them were homeless, and having a good corner might mean the difference between eating regularly and not. A spot by a station of the Elevated Train would be prime. Having such a spot proved Danny had been a tough kid even then.

"Go on," Frank said.

Danny sighed with resignation. "This swell comes along. He buys a paper from me. He asks me do I want to earn some extra money. I say sure."

"What did he look like?"

"I don't know. A swell. You know, fancy suit, silk hat, walking stick with a big silver handle."

That could describe half the men in the city. "Was he old or young? Tall or short? Fat or thin?" Frank asked impatiently.

"I don't remember. I wasn't paying much attention!"

Frank had to give him another nudge of encouragement.

When he stopped howling, he said, "Old, I guess. Older than you."

"What color was his hair?"

The boy screwed up his face in the effort to remember. "He had on a hat." Frank drew back his foot again, but Danny quickly recalled, "He had some gray around here, I think," he said, pointing to his temple.

"You're doing better, Danny. That's the kind of information I'm looking for. Tall or short?"

"A little taller'n you, maybe. Not fat, not thin."

"How much did he pay you to kill Dr. Brandt?" Frank asked mildly.

"I didn't kill nobody! I swear!" He was genuinely frightened now. Most cops wouldn't hesitate to solve a case by arresting the most convenient suspect, and Danny was certainly convenient at the moment. "I told you, I was just a kid. All he wanted me to do was take a note to this Dr. Brandt."

"What did the note say?"

"I don't know. I can't read!"

This, Frank knew, was probably true. "What was Dr. Brandt supposed to do when he got the note?"

"I told you, I couldn't read the note. I don't got no idea."

Frank shook his head in disapproval. "You're trying my patience, Danny. You were supposed to take him someplace, weren't you?"

"Who told you that?" Danny demanded, the fear in his voice just a little stronger than his feigned outrage.

"Never mind who told me. Where were you supposed to take Dr. Brandt?"

A shadow darkened the doorway, and Frank looked up to see another boy about Danny's age peering in.

"Are you pinched?" he demanded of the boy on the floor.

"Yes, he is," Frank replied, "and you will be, too, if you don't get the hell out of here."

"You come here alone, copper?" the boy asked incredulously. He was bigger than Danny, stocky beneath his ragged clothes. "You should know better."

With the light behind him, Frank couldn't make out his features, but he saw the glint of the boy's teeth as he grinned, and almost too late he saw the flash of the knife.

He threw up his arm to block the blow, and the blade slashed through his coat sleeve. Danny was scrambling to his feet, and Frank shoved the boy with the knife, sending him sprawling out into the alley. The knife clattered on the cobblestones, but before Frank could turn to deal with Danny, the boy barreled into him, knocking him to his knees. Frank made a grab for him, but the bare flesh of Danny's skinny arm wrenched from his grasp as he darted out of the hovel.

By the time Frank pushed himself to his feet, both boys were disappearing down the alley in the direction of the street. Cursing his carelessness, Frank checked his coat sleeve and was furious to see blood already staining the fabric. It wasn't bad enough that the coat was ruined, but he'd probably need stitches. He pulled out his handkerchief and awkwardly tied it around his arm as he made his way quickly back to the street. The creatures who occupied the tenements around him could sniff out weakness like a pack of jackals. He needed to get to a safer part of town as quickly as possible.

His mother would howl like a banshee when she saw the damaged coat, and now he was staining the handkerchief, too. The worse part, however, was that he'd let Danny get away. At least the old drunk hadn't been lying. The boy did know something about Tom Brandt's death. Something more than that he'd been beaten and left to die alone in an alley one dark night three years ago. Someone had hired him to lure Dr. Brandt to his death, which meant his murder hadn't been a simple robbery as the police had determined at the time.

Frank had known the minute he read the account of Brandt's death in the police files that robbery hadn't been the motive. Brandt's black doctor's bag hadn't been taken, nor had his wallet or watch. Even if a thief had been frightened off before being able to gather his loot, the poor of the city wouldn't have hesitated to relieve a dead man of his valuables. He wouldn't be needing them anymore, would he? Yet no one had touched Brandt's body until the beat cop found him the next morning.

No one on the force had cared to investigate further, however. Sarah Brandt hadn't understood then that she needed to offer a "reward" for finding her husband's killer, and apparently her wealthy family hadn't either. Without such a motivation, the detective on the case had simply concluded Brandt had been killed by an unknown assailant and closed the case. Many people got away with murder every day in the city. The chances of finding who had killed the good doctor after three years were worse than slim.

But miraculously, Frank had located someone who knew what had happened that night. True, he'd foolishly let the boy get away, but that was just a temporary setback. The boy would surface again. Danny knew no other life, so he wasn't going to be leaving town. And just as someone had betrayed the boy once already, someone would again.

Frank cursed and hurried his steps. His arm was beginning to ache. He needed to see a doctor, and he didn't want to waste his time with any of the sawbones in this neighborhood, assuming he could even find a sober one.

Sarah Brandt was causing him a lot of trouble. If he had any sense, he'd forget what he'd heard today. She'd never know what had happened with Danny, so she'd never be disappointed in him for giving up the search for her husband's killer.

Then he thought about his son. Brian was getting his cast off in a few days, and he might be able to walk for the first time in his life. The best surgeon in the city had operated on his club foot — because the surgeon was a friend of Sarah Brandt's.

No, Frank wouldn't forget what he'd learned today. Danny and he would meet again soon, and this time, he'd find out exactly what he needed to know.

# 2

"GOOD MORNING, MRS. BRANDT!"

Sarah waved a greeting to her neighbor, Mrs. Ellsworth. In spite of the Sabbath being a day of rest, Mrs. Ellsworth was out sweeping her front porch. This enabled her to keep an eye on all the activities on Bank Street. She had the cleanest porch in New York City.

"Is that a new hat you're wearing?" the old woman asked.

Sarah reached up to touch the hat in question. "As a matter of fact, it is."

"Very stylish," Mrs. Ellsworth said in approval.

"It should be," Sarah replied with a grin. "It was my mother's."

"Your mother's?"

"Yes, she decided I needed some more presentable clothes, and she made me take my pick from her closet." The gown she'd worn to the opera last night had been only one of her new acquisitions. Mrs. Ellsworth hadn't noticed that her suit was "new," too.

"That was very nice of her. Now I suppose you're taking your old things to be laundered, but where are you taking them on a Sunday?" Mrs. Ellsworth asked with a puzzled frown at the bundle Sarah carried. "Or are you taking something to poor Mr. Prescott?" Webster Prescott was a newspaper reporter who had been injured while investigating the murder Sarah had just helped Malloy solve a few days earlier.

Sarah glanced down at the bundle. "No, this isn't for Mr. Prescott. His aunt is taking very good care of him, and she assured me he doesn't need anything. And it's not my laundry, either. I'm paying a visit to one of the missions on the Lower East Side, so I thought I'd take my old things down to them as a donation."

"Oh, my, what a nice thing to do. I do hope you have included some shoes in your donation. Giving someone a pair of shoes is very good luck."

"I'm afraid I —"

"No, wait, I'm wrong about that," Mrs. Ellsworth corrected herself, frowning in concentration. "It may only be *new* shoes that bring good luck. I'm not sure what old shoes bring. Oh, yes, I am! They're good luck for the bride and groom, aren't they? To tie behind their carriage. Yes, so they must be good luck for everyone, don't you think?" she asked, satisfied she had solved the problem of the value of old shoes.

"I'm sure I don't know," Sarah said diplomatically. She never bothered to argue with Mrs. Ellsworth's superstitions. "In any event, I didn't have any shoes I could donate, so I'm only giving away clothes."

"Oh, well, I'm sure those poor souls at the mission will appreciate whatever you can spare. And how is Mr. Prescott doing?"

"I saw him yesterday, and he seems to be improving. He's fortunate his aunt was able to look after him. If I have time, I'll stop by the hospital again today to check on him after I visit the mission."

"I'm glad to hear he's better," Mrs. Ellsworth said. "But you aren't going down there to that mission alone, are you? An unescorted woman isn't safe in that part of town."

Sarah didn't bother to point out that it was broad daylight, and that as a midwife, she was accustomed to going to all parts of the city unescorted, at all hours of the day and night. "No, I'll have a gentleman with me."

"Mr. Malloy?" she asked, brightening instantly. For some reason, Mrs. Ellsworth had developed a fondness for the gruff police detective. Sarah would attribute her warm feelings to Malloy helping clear Mrs. Ellsworth's son of murder charges, except that the old woman had liked Malloy long before that.

"No, not Mr. Malloy," Sarah said, disappointing her. "I'm meeting Mr. Dennis."

"Mr. Richard Dennis?" she asked, instantly wary. "Nelson said he thought it was Mr. Dennis's carriage that picked you up last evening. We couldn't help noticing," she added, lest Sarah think her nosy.

"We went to the opera," Sarah said, relieving Mrs. Ellsworth of the need to inquire.

"Did you enjoy yourself?" the old woman asked, still not certain how she felt about her friend seeing Nelson's employer socially.

"Very much."

"Mr. Dennis is an honorable man," Mrs. Ellsworth said, although Sarah heard the echo of a question in the words. "He was very kind to Nelson during the . . . the unpleasantness."

Sarah saw no need to mention that Dennis hadn't *voluntarily* been kind. "He didn't want to lose a valuable employee," she said instead, the soul of tact. Dennis *had* done the right thing, after all, no matter what his motivation.

"He certainly won Nelson's undying loyalty," Mrs. Ellsworth assured her.

"Then Mr. Dennis is fortunate indeed," Sarah said.

"And speaking of Mr. Malloy, how is his son doing after the operation?" the old woman asked, returning to a subject nearer to her heart.

"He'll be getting his cast off on Wednesday. I guess we'll know then."

"Please tell Mr. Malloy I'll be remembering the child in my prayers."

"I'm sure he'll appreciate that."

Mrs. Ellsworth looked around expectantly. "Is Mr. Dennis calling for you?"

"No, I didn't think it would be a good idea to take his carriage into the Lower East Side. People might get the idea he was trying to flaunt his wealth."

"Oh, yes," the old woman agreed. "The poor should be allowed to keep their pride, at least. But how will you get there? A Hansom won't want to go there, either."

"I suggested we ride the El," Sarah said with a smile.

Mrs. Ellsworth smiled back. "Mr. Dennis on the El. That should be an experience."

"I'm sure it will be."

Sarah wished her neighbor good morning and set off to the nearest train station at Eighth Street on Sixth Avenue.

She really hadn't expected Richard Dennis to ride the Elevated Train down from his home on the Upper West Side, but she smiled when she spotted his carriage sitting near the station. Dennis must have been watching for her, because he alighted from the carriage and hurried toward her as she approached.

He really was a fine figure of a man, and his clothes were tailored to accentuate his lean figure and height. He smiled as he reached her and removed his silk top hat. "Good morning, Mrs. Brandt," he said. "You look lovely this morning, as usual."

"Thank you," she replied, wondering how many times he'd said this meaningless phrase to women who looked far from lovely.

"I've been thinking about your plan to take the El and then walk over to Mulberry Street, but I really don't see any reason why we can't go in my carriage. You have this bundle, after all, and —"

"I really think we should arrive unannounced, Mr. Dennis," she reminded him. "Your carriage would attract a crowd, and believe me, we'd make very slow progress surrounded by hundreds of curious children." Besides, she thought, I want you to walk through the neighborhood and see for yourself "How the Other Half Lives," as the reporter Jacob Riis had tried to do for the entire city in his book by that name.

"But I'm not sure it will be entirely safe," he protested. "While you're under my protection —"

"I don't need your protection, Richard," she said kindly. "I travel the city every day without it. But if you prefer, you can go in your carriage, and I will meet you there."

"Certainly not!" He was outraged at the very suggestion. "I will, of course, do whatever you think is best." He glanced uncertainly at the driver, who was watching for a signal. After a slight hesitation, he waved the man on. Then he turned back to Sarah with a strained smile. "Allow me to take your . . . your package." Plainly, he thought it odd she'd chosen to carry such a thing as a bundle of clothing on a public street, but he was too gentlemanly to mention it.

Sarah surrendered her burden, then took the arm he offered her.

"I'm afraid you will have to instruct me," he said, looking uneasily at the tracks that ran over their heads. "I'm embarrassed to admit I've never ridden on the Elevated."

"I'm sure you'll find it a superior method of transportation," Sarah assured him, and led him to the covered stairway that would take them to the station, two stories above the street.

"The stations have always reminded me of the chalets in Switzerland," he remarked as they climbed the stairs amid the crowd of other travelers.

"Many other people have noticed the same thing," Sarah said. "I'm sure they were designed to be as attractive as possible."

"It's a pity the trains themselves can't be more attractive."

He was right. The trains rattling overhead sent a shower of dirt and debris down on the streets — and pedestrians — below, and the noise rattled the windows, making everyday life a strain on the four avenues where the trains ran. On the other hand, they were the only means of speedy and reliable transportation in the city.

They waited only a few minutes for a train to arrive. Dennis quickly figured out how to pay the fare, and they settled into their seats. Fortunately, Sunday morning was not a busy time for the trains, so the car wasn't even quite full. During busier times of the day, Sarah had seen the conductors cram the cars so tightly that passengers could hardly move before allowing the train to leave the station.

Dennis had settled her bundle on his lap. "What have you brought?"

"Some clothing I no longer need. I thought perhaps someone at the mission might be able to use it."

He frowned. "I hadn't thought. You're right, of course. I should have my man check my own wardrobe and see to it."

Sarah figured his "man" probably appropriated all of Richard's castoffs for himself, but she didn't say so. The train was pulling out of the station, and Dennis glanced around a little apprehensively. She had to admit the crowd was of a much lower social class than Dennis would be accustomed to, although no one appeared to be truly disreputable. Then the train cleared the station, and Dennis was distracted by something else entirely.

"Good heavens!" he cried before catching himself. Lowering his voice, he leaned closer to Sarah and whispered, "You can see right into those people's rooms!"

The train tracks had been built over the sidewalks on either side of Sixth Avenue, within a few feet of the tenement buildings that lined the street and on the same level as the third-floor windows. If the train had stopped, the passengers were close enough to reach out and shake hands with the residents of those third-floor flats.

"Sometimes I'll catch a glimpse of someone and try to imagine a life for them," Sarah said. "It helps pass the time."

"But . . . but . . ." He was speechless with horror. Finally, he managed, "They have no privacy!"

"That's why the rent for those flats is lower than for those on other floors. Many people gratefully sacrifice their privacy for the economy."

Plainly, he could not imagine such a thing.

The train picked up speed, but it would be stopping again soon, so it never went very fast. The people at home on this Sunday morning presented a tableau to the train passengers.

"Shocking," Dennis murmured, unable to turn his gaze from the passing scenes.

"The poor endure much more shocking indignities every day," Sarah said. "I'm sure your wife understood this and wanted to help."

Dennis only shook his head in amazement. This trip was supposed to help him understand his wife better. Sarah began to wonder if he would be able to absorb all the lessons he would learn today.

They left the train at Bleeker Street, the next stop. Dennis protested that his carriage could have come this far, at least, and saved them this much of the journey. Sarah ignored him and led the way out of the station and down the steps to the street.

Sunday morning on Bleeker Street was little different than any other day, except perhaps to be busier. Because the men who would normally be at work the other six days of the week were home, their voices and bodies were added to the bustle and the din. The cobbled street was clogged with the carts of the street vendors who were hawking their wares.

"Don't those people have any regard for the Sabbath?" Dennis asked, nodding toward a cart loaded with shoes of every size and description.

"They're Jews," Sarah said. "Their Sabbath was yesterday."

Although the air was still cool, the sky had cleared after an early morning shower, and many of the windows in the tenement buildings were open so women could lean out and talk to their neighbors. Never mind that the neighbor with whom they were conversing lived on the other side of the street. Shouted conversations in several languages went on over their heads as children, still barefoot even in the chill of October, darted in every direction, heedless of their elders or their right of way. Some of the children played a game of stick ball in the street, using piles of horse manure for bases. Others chased each other in tag, while still others jumped rope or played hopscotch on a pattern scratched into the sidewalk.

Young men clustered on corners, passing a bottle while they ogled young girls who passed in pairs or small groups, dressed in their Sunday finery and pretending to ignore them. Old men squatted on stoops and complained to each other in their native tongues. Old women bartered with the vendors, scolding and screeching incomprehensibly.

At night these streets were deserted and the buildings were packed with humanity crammed into every corner to find rest. During the day, the life could not be contained, and it spilled out into the streets and onto the fire escapes, exploding with an energy that made the very air electric.

Could Dennis feel it? She glanced up at him, but he simply looked bewildered and anxious. He was probably worried someone would pick his pocket.

They were certainly attracting more than their share of attention. Dennis's tailor-made clothing and aristocratic bearing set him apart. The only reason they hadn't been approached or intimidated yet is because so many people knew Sarah. Several in every block greeted her by name, and when anyone made a move toward them, either to beg or to steal, someone else would warn them away with shouts and curses.

"That's Mrs. Brandt, the midwife! She saved my daughter's life!" was a common theme, repeated in many languages.

"You have a lot of friends here," Dennis marveled after they'd gone several blocks.

"The poor are very sensitive. They know when someone is patronizing them and when someone treats them with genuine respect."

"Respect?" he repeated as if he'd never heard the word. Plainly, he could not imagine having such a feeling for these people.

"Yes, and their loyalty is the reward for that respect."

At last they reached Mulberry Street. Police Headquarters sat on the block between Bleeker and Houston, and Sarah thought of Malloy as they passed. He would be at home today, spending time with his son. She'd see them both on Wednesday, when Brian went to the doctor's office to get his cast off. Malloy had invited Sarah to be there, and she would be. She told herself the thought of seeing them made her stomach flutter only because she was excited for the boy.

The buildings across the street from Headquarters were quiet today. The rooms there were rented by newspaper reporters who spent their time watching to see who came and went at Headquarters in hopes of getting a story. Only a few cub reporters would be on duty on a Sunday, and they were probably sleeping until the next Black Maria full of prisoners arrived.

"Is that a saloon?" Dennis asked in surprise, pointing to a building located half a block away. "It's practically next door to the police station!"

"I've heard that the owner justifies it by saying 'the nearer the church, the closer to God.'"

Dennis frowned in disapproval. Sarah wondered if he disapproved the sentiment or of hearing her express it. "That's blasphemy."

"Yes, it is." Sarah managed not to smile. "The area farther down, where the street curves, is known as Mulberry Bend," she added. "It contains the worst slums in the city."

"There are worse slums than this?" he asked in amazement, looking around.

"Indeed, although they aren't as bad as they used to be. Just a few years ago, the police would only go in there in large groups," Sarah said. "The Italians have settled there now. So many of them live here, they call it Little Italy."

"The real Italy is nothing like this," he informed her, making no effort to conceal his dismay. Sarah could imagine the inhabitants of Little Italy would agree with him.

The Prodigal Son Mission was located in the next block. Sarah had never paid much attention to it before. Missions and settlement houses had started appearing in various locations in the Lower East Side as society developed a social conscience.

This mission was in an old Dutch-style house that had once been a large and comfortable home to a well-to-do family. That family had long since moved farther north, leaving the house to be divided into flats for the flood of poor immigrants currently invading the city. Now the house had changed character again. Someone had hung a large cross over the front door, and a sign identified the mission to anyone in the neighborhood who could read English.

When she glanced at Dennis, he was frowning.

"Isn't it what you were expecting?" she asked.

"I'm not sure what I was expecting," he said. "I was just trying to imagine Hazel coming here, walking down these streets and seeing these people." He turned to her. "She wasn't like you, Sarah. She wasn't brave or strong."

Sarah didn't consider herself particularly brave or strong, either. "Perhaps you misjudged her."

He wasn't prepared to admit such a thing.

They'd reached the front stoop, and Sarah walked up the steps and knocked on the door while Dennis waited on the sidewalk, still holding Sarah's bundle. In a few moments the door opened. A young woman stood there, and she smiled uncertainly at Sarah.

"You want something, yes?" she asked with a lilting accent. She was an ordinary-looking girl, but her smile brightened her face and her light brown eyes, making her almost pretty.

"We'd like to see Mrs. Wells, if she's available," Dennis informed her from his place at the bottom of the steps.

The girl looked down in surprise, and her smile vanished. Richard Dennis was used to intimidating those he considered his inferior, and he'd certainly intimidated this girl. "*Sì, Signore,* I mean, yes. Please to come in, *Signora.*"

She stood back hastily to allow them to enter. Sarah recognized her accent as Italian, but unlike most of the Italian immigrants, she had light hair and a fair complexion. Sarah knew from her dealings in the neighborhood that this meant she was probably from Northern Italy, although Northern Italian immigrants were much rarer than Southern ones.

"You will wait here, please," the girl asked, still wary of Dennis, since he hadn't done anything to reassure her. In fact, he was practically glaring at her in apparent disapproval. Sarah couldn't imagine why he would disapprove of the girl.

She wanted to chide him, but she didn't know exactly how to make him see how rude he was being. Instead, she looked around while they waited for the girl to return. The entrance hall was remarkably clean and virtually bare of furniture and decoration except for a cheap picture of Jesus on one wall. The floors had been painted brown and scrubbed until they were spotless. From another room, Sarah could hear young voices uncertainly singing a hymn.

The girl had disappeared into that room farther down the hallway, and after a moment, the singing stopped and a woman came out. The girl made as if to follow her, but the woman said, "Thank you, Emilia. Please stay with the girls and have them continue with their Bible lesson," and came down the hall alone to meet them.

"Mrs. Wells?" Sarah asked as she approached. She

was a small woman of middle age. The years had thickened her figure and put silver streaks into her dark hair, but her face was remarkably unlined. Her dark brown eyes glowed with the confidence and serenity of someone very confident of her place in the world.

"Yes, I'm Mrs. Wells," she replied. "Welcome to the mission. Have you visited us before?"

"No, we haven't," Sarah said. "I'm Sarah Brandt, and this is Mr. Richard Dennis. His wife used to —"

"Mr. Dennis, of course," Mrs. Wells said, her intense gaze instantly on him. Sarah saw a flicker of emotion cross her smooth face. She must have been amazed that Richard had suddenly turned up on her doorstep after five years. "I'm sorry I didn't recognize you. We met when I visited your wife during her last illness."

"Oh, yes, I'd forgotten," Dennis said apologetically. "That was a difficult time. I'm afraid much of what happened then is a little unclear to me, even today."

She nodded with understanding. "No need to explain. It *has* been a long time. Your wife was a remarkable woman, so dedicated to the work we do here. You must feel her loss deeply. I know we still do."

"Thank you," Richard murmured uncomfortably. Sarah knew he didn't want to discuss his wife's death, particularly when they were standing in a corridor.

Mrs. Wells obviously realized it, too. "Now tell me," she continued briskly, as if as eager as Richard to move on from the unpleasant thoughts of Hazel's death. "What brings you here after all this time?"

Sarah came to Richard's rescue. "Mr. Dennis and I were wondering if you would mind telling us a little about the work you do. He's interested in finding out why his wife was so devoted to your ministry."

She seemed to be considering Sarah's answer, almost as if she were trying to judge the truthfulness of it. But perhaps Sarah was only being fanciful. The woman probably had to be careful her visitors were sincere and not just curiosity seekers wanting to have an experience they could tell their wealthy friends about later. "Well, it is the Sabbath," Mrs. Wells reminded them, "and usually I'm leading the young ladies in a Bible class at this hour." Sarah wasn't sure if this was meant as a reprimand or not. "But they can get along without me, I'm sure," she added kindly, taking away the sting. "It's much more important for you to find the peace you're seeking, Mr. Dennis."

Her eyes were filled with sympathy, as if she understood completely the pain Richard had felt and his need to assuage it. Sarah could easily see why she had been successful with this ministry. Such kindness would draw the children of these streets like a magnet.

"Please, step into the parlor," Mrs. Wells said, "and give me a moment to instruct Emilia."

The parlor was almost as austere as the hallway. The mismatched furniture had to be the result of donations or rescues of salvageable pieces from the trash, and the décor was uncluttered with the assortment of knickknacks and doilies most people felt was fashionable. Sarah took a seat on an ugly sofa. She was glad for the layers of her petticoats, because they cushioned her against the protruding horsehair stuffing which would make sitting on it feel like sitting on a hairbrush. Dennis chose a chair that seemed reasonably sturdy, if a little the worse for wear. He set Sarah's bundle self-consciously on the floor beside him.

After a few moments, Mrs. Wells returned, closing the parlor doors carefully behind her and taking a seat on the sofa beside Sarah. She moved with an unconscious grace that drew the eye while at the same time giving the overwhelming impression of modesty and humility. She was dressed in black bombazine unrelieved by any adornment. Even her pierced earlobes were bare. Sarah judged that she was in mourning.

"Now, what can I tell you about Mrs. Dennis?" she asked when she was settled on the sofa beside Sarah, her back perfectly straight and her hands folded properly in her lap.

Sarah looked to Richard, but he sent her a silent plea to begin.

"As I said, Mr. Dennis is interested in finding out more about your work here because of his late wife's involvement," she began. "Perhaps you could begin by telling us how the mission got started."

Once again Mrs. Wells studied Sarah for a moment before replying. Sarah had the impression that Mrs. Wells was once again weighing her words to see if they were truthful. "I would be happy to," Mrs. Wells said, her smooth face settling into a small, sweet smile, making Sarah think perhaps she had only imagined Mrs. Wells questioned her sincerity. "My dear husband started the mission more than seven years ago. It was his dream and his calling. He'd worked in this part of the city for a long time, preaching on street corners and ministering to the poor wherever he could find a place, before he was finally able to purchase this house." She turned her gaze to Dennis. "He was only able to do so because of the generosity of a wealthy benefactor."

"How . . . how fortunate," Dennis managed, somewhat nonplussed at what might have been a very broad hint that his generosity would also be appreciated.

"Fortune had nothing to do with it, Mr. Dennis. The Lord provided," she corrected him gently.

"Of course," Dennis murmured, properly rebuked.

"Is your husband busy?" Sarah asked to save him from more embarrassment. "I would love to meet him."

"I'm afraid that won't be possible, not in this world, at least," she said with another of her gentle smiles. "My husband passed away less than a year after we opened the mission."

"I'm sorry," Sarah said, responding as good manners dictated she should, even though she hadn't known the man.

"No need to be sorry," Mrs. Wells informed her. "Although I miss him dreadfully, he's in a much better place now. If the Lord took him, He must have thought his work here was done, and that we would be able to continue without him."

"So you took over the work here after he passed away?" Sarah asked, amazed that so unassuming a woman would have been able to make a success of a ministry in one of the worst neighborhoods in the city.

"I did what I could," Mrs. Wells clarified. "My talents are very different from his, of course. He was a gifted and dynamic preacher. I am merely God's handmaiden, and I can only do what a woman can do."

"And what is that?" Sarah asked, genuinely curious now.

"Here we offer young girls a safe place to stay, if they need one. Many of them had been living on the streets or worse. Others lived with their families, but they still need to learn the skills that will make them productive wives and mothers, things like cooking and sewing and simple hygiene. You would be amazed at the squalor in which they live."

Sarah thought of the tenements where a single outside spigot or pump served a dozen families and no one had a bathtub. She thought of streets clogged with garbage and horse droppings because the city workers didn't want to go into that neighborhood to pick it up. If cleanliness was next to Godliness, for some it was nothing short of a miracle. "I'm a midwife, Mrs. Wells," Sarah explained. "I know it only too well. For most of them, it's not a choice, however. It's a matter of not having any means of keeping clean."

"You're right, of course," Mrs. Wells said. "But things will never change unless people know fhat they should. We simply try to educate the young women who come to us about what kind of change is necessary — and how to accomplish it."

Certainly a worthy goal, Sarah thought, admiring the woman even more. "I know many of the settlement houses teach young women the skills you mentioned, in addition to helping them learn to read and write," she offered. The ones she'd seen in New York had been modeled after Hull House in Chicago, founded by Jane Addams.

"The settlement houses do emphasize education. You would expect nothing less, since they are run by college women." Mrs. Wells said the phrase "college women" with just a hint of disdain.

"Don't you approve of the settlement houses?" Sarah asked in amazement.

"I'm sure they mean well, Mrs. Brandt," Mrs. Wells allowed, "but they emphasize the physical and ignore the spiritual. Saving someone's body is useless unless you save the soul as well."

Sarah certainly believed many of the souls in the Lower East Side — and in all parts of the city, for that matter — needed saving, but she knew that wasn't nearly enough. "Don't you teach your girls to read?"

"Of course we do." Mrs. Wells seemed surprised at the question. "They read the Bible and other uplifting literature. While we prepare them for heaven, we also teach them how to have a better life here on earth."

"My wife never . . ." Dennis began, then stopped when the women looked at him in surprise. Sarah had almost forgotten he was there, and Mrs. Wells seemed to have, also.

"Yes, Mr. Dennis?" Mrs. Wells prodded gently.

"I never knew my wife to be interested in . . . in religious things. I mean, she attended church regularly, of course. One does, but she never seemed overly concerned about . . ." He gestured vaguely, unable to find the correct word.

"I gathered as much," Mrs. Wells said. "When she first came here, she was a seeker. That's what I call them. People who have an emptiness inside and are looking for a way to fill it. As I remember, Mrs. Dennis seemed very unhappy when we first met."

Sarah could have groaned. This wasn't what

Richard needed to hear. He already felt guilty enough over his wife's death. "I believe Mrs. Dennis was looking for something meaningful to do with her time," Sarah tried in Hazel Dennis's defense. "Women in her position in life sometimes grow bored with society."

"She was also unhappy because she didn't have a child," Richard offered.

"I don't have a child either, Mr. Dennis," Mrs. Wells said, her tone still gentle and reasonable. "My daughter was taken from me when she was only three. At first I was angry and grief-stricken, but eventually, I came to understand and accept. God needed me for other work, so He freed me of the responsibility of my child. She's in heaven, with her father, and I'm not selfish enough to wish her back here in this veil of tears. She's happier there than she could ever be here, and I, in turn, found fulfillment in the work God gave me. Your wife did, too."

"She did?" he asked, leaning forward in his eagerness to hear something that would give him peace.

"She found her true calling, Mr. Dennis. She did work she loved, she found God's peace, and she died in a state of grace. We cannot ask for more in this life."

Obviously, these answers more than satisfied Mrs. Wells, but Sarah wasn't sure how much comfort they would give Richard. "Perhaps you could show us around the mission so Mr. Dennis can see what his wife did here," she suggested.

Once again Mrs. Wells studied Sarah in that odd way of hers. "Forgive me, Mrs. Brandt, but were you a friend of Mrs. Dennis?"

So that was it! Mrs. Wells was simply trying to figure out what Sarah's role was in all of this. "No, I regret to say I never knew Mrs. Dennis."

"Mrs. Brandt is a friend of *mine*," Richard quickly explained. "I asked her to accompany me today because of her familiarity with the neighborhood and the people in it."

Mrs. Wells hadn't taken her gaze from Sarah. "Oh, yes, you said you were a midwife, I believe."

Sarah heard the unspoken questions that Mrs. Wells was too well bred to ask. She would naturally think it odd a man in Richard's position would be well acquainted with a midwife. "My family and Mr. Dennis's have been friends for many years. After my husband's death, I chose to make my own living doing what I love. Much as you did, Mrs. Wells," she added.

Mrs. Wells nodded, silently acknowledging the bond between them. "I hope your work affords you as much satisfaction as mine does to me, Mrs. Brandt," she said. Then she turned to Richard. "I believe you wanted to see what we do here at the mission."

"Yes, if you wouldn't mind showing us around," he said, giving her one of his charming smiles. Sarah wouldn't have thought charm could influence Mrs. Wells, but she allowed herself to return his smile.

"I would be happy to, Mr. Dennis. I consider it my Christian duty to help you find the peace you're seeking." She turned to Sarah with an unasked question in her dark eyes. "And to help you find whatever it is *you* are seeking, Mrs. Brandt."

# 3

SARAH HARDLY HAD A MOMENT TO REGISTER THE implication before Mrs. Wells rose to lead them out into the hall. She hadn't been aware of any needs of her own in making this visit, but she couldn't help admiring the fulfillment Mrs. Wells seemed to feel. Perhaps Mrs. Wells had sensed something of which Sarah herself had been unaware.

"We don't work on Sunday, of course," Mrs. Wells was saying, "but I can let you see where we do our other activities during the rest of the week."

She took them to the room where the girls had been singing earlier. They sat in rows and were bowed over their Bibles now, struggling with various degrees of success to read them. They all looked up when their visitors entered. Sarah scanned the faces and saw they represented many nations of origin and ranged in age from about twelve to perhaps sixteen or seventeen. Girls much older than that were either safely married or hopelessly lost — either to prostitution or death. The choices in life for impoverished females were severely limited.

These girls were as well scrubbed as the hallway, their hair braided or pinned up, their clothes neat and clean, if not new or stylish. The blond girl who had met them at the door, Emilia, sat on a stool at the front of the room, and she smiled at them. Again Sarah noticed how the smile brightened her face.

"These are the girls who live here with us at the present time," Mrs. Wells explained. "They have no place else to go except back to lives of sin and abomination, but they are safe here with us."

Sarah winced at the fact that she'd said this in front of them, but if any of them minded, they gave no indication. Probably, they'd heard it before. Sarah had to admit it was also true. A ministry that saved destitute girls from the streets was a haven indeed.

Mrs. Wells then took her visitors through the kitchen, a large room as spotless as the rest of the house, and out to the small plot of ground behind the house that had been turned into a playground. Here a couple dozen children played on swings and slides and seesaws, things that existed no place else in this part of town. They weren't as clean or as well dressed as the girls inside. Obviously, they were children from the neighborhood who had come to this amazing refuge to enjoy a few hours of idyllic childhood. Then Sarah noticed other small faces pressed longingly against the slats on the other side of the fence, peering in at their fellows.

True, the yard was already swarming with children, but Sarah couldn't imagine locking others out and cheating them of this unique opportunity. "How do you decide who gets to come in to play and who doesn't?" Sarah asked, indicating the pathetic onlookers.

"We can't allow them all in at once, of course," Mrs. Wells explained, her gaze settling lovingly on the children. "If we did, none of them could enjoy the yard. So we let a group of them come in for an hour, and then we send them out and admit the next group. It's the only fair way."

Sarah looked at the older woman with admiration. She might be a bit rigid in her religious views, but she obviously cared deeply for the people in the neighborhood.

A few adult women stood around, watching over the children as they played, stepping in to settle disputes and helping the smaller children when they needed it. Their clothes identified them as belonging to a higher social class than the children they tended, so Sarah assumed they were volunteers. She imagined Hazel Dennis standing in this yard, doing the same thing. Had she found being with the children fulfilling or had they only reminded her of what she did not have? Surely, visiting the mission couldn't have been painful, or she wouldn't have continued to come.

Sarah glanced up at Richard and wondered what he was thinking as he watched the grubby children at their play. Could he imagine his wife finding joy and satisfaction here?

"Would you like to go upstairs and see the work rooms and the dormitory?" Mrs. Wells asked.

"Yes," Richard said, still deep in thought. "Yes, I would."

When they reentered the house, they found Emilia waiting for them. "The *bambini* are happy here," she said, the words almost a question, demanding they agree.

"They certainly appear to be," Sarah said. The girl seemed eager for their approval, and Sarah knew how much attention from outsiders could mean to someone in her position in life. "How long have you been here, Emilia?"

The girl's eyes widened in surprise that Sarah knew her name. "I am here five months," she said carefully, glancing at Mrs. Wells for confirmation. "I learn to sew."

"Emilia hopes to find a job making clothes," Mrs. Wells explained. "She's been doing very well."

"I'm sure she is," Sarah said with an encouraging smile. The girl beamed.

"Are the girls finished with their Bible study, Emilia?" Mrs. Wells asked.

"*Si,* they have gone to eat."

Sarah hoped Mrs. Wells would invite Emilia to join them upstairs, but she left the girl standing in the kitchen, staring longingly after them. Mrs. Wells didn't speak again until they reached the top of the stairs. Then she turned to face Sarah and Richard.

"Emilia is a perfect example of what we have been able to accomplish here," she said softly, so no one could overhear. "She was seduced by a wicked man who had no intention of marrying her. When her family found out, they disowned her for her wantonness. You can imagine what she had to do to survive. By the time she came to us, she was completely degraded, but I'm happy to say that she has since re-

pented both of her sins and of her popish ways. She
is now a true child of God."

Dennis nodded in approval, but Sarah couldn't
help wondering what her Irish friend Malloy would
have to say about Mrs. Wells's opinion of Roman
Catholics. Of course, the prejudice was practically
universal among Protestants, so Sarah couldn't single
the woman out for disapproval.

Upstairs they saw the workrooms where the girls
learned various skills. Mrs. Wells pointed out the two
sewing machines she'd been able to provide for the
girls to practice on. The attic had been converted into
a dormitory where the residents slept on rows of
identical cots under the sloping roof, all neatly made
up with identical blankets.

"What exactly did my wife do when she came
here?" Richard asked as they made their way back
down the stairs to the first floor.

"Let's see," Mrs. Wells said, considering. "It's
been a while, hasn't it? I'm not sure, but I believe she
led the singing. She had a fine voice, if I recall."

"Yes, she did," Richard confirmed eagerly. "Our
friends always enjoyed hearing her sing."

"I seem to remember she may also have taught
sewing. Did she do needlework?"

"She . . . I believe she did." He was less confident
of this.

They had reached the front hallway, and Mrs.
Wells turned to face them. "Mr. Dennis, what your
wife did here exactly really isn't important. The fact
that she came at all is what matters. The work she did
here helped to save young girls from the streets and
prepare them for heaven. You can comfort yourself
with knowing her life had meaning and purpose, even

if it was shorter than we might have wished. You may also comfort yourself that she is with God. I'm certain of that."

Her words transformed Richard, finally giving him the consolation he'd sought. "Thank you, Mrs. Wells," he said gratefully. "You've been very kind."

"Not at all, Mr. Dennis. I've simply told the truth," she said. "Do you have any other questions that I can answer?"

Richard glanced at Sarah, giving her the opportunity to respond. She couldn't think of any questions, but she did remember something else. "I brought a few things of mine that I thought your residents might be able to use," she said, indicating the bundle that still sat on the floor in the front parlor.

"Thank you very much, Mrs. Brandt. I know the girls will appreciate your generosity," Mrs. Wells said with her sweet smile.

"I didn't bring anything with me," Richard said, "but you will be receiving a donation from me very soon."

"That really isn't necessary, but we will accept it gratefully, in your wife's memory, Mr. Dennis," Mrs. Wells said. She could not have said anything that could have pleased Richard more, and to Sarah's amazement, her voice held no hint that she considered Richard's money any more important to her ministry than Sarah's old clothes.

As they walked back down Mulberry Street after taking their leave of Mrs. Wells, Sarah allowed Richard some time to reflect on what he had learned. The noise and activity in the neighborhood didn't allow for much conversation anyway, so he didn't really say anything until they were back in the relative quiet of the El station, waiting for the next train to arrive.

"I had no idea," he finally said. "What would happen to those girls if the mission wasn't there?"

"Many of them would probably become prostitutes," Sarah said. "And most of those would die young."

He frowned, probably not certain whether he should be shocked by the facts or by hearing Sarah say them aloud. Ladies of her class studiously avoided acknowledging that prostitution existed. "I still can't imagine Hazel in a place like that. I guess you're right, I didn't know her at all."

"I didn't say that," Sarah hastily reminded him. "Sometimes we hide things from the people we love. She might not have allowed you to see that side of her. Maybe she thought you'd disapprove."

"Or maybe she thought I just didn't care," he said with a sigh.

"Since we'll never know for certain, why don't we decide that you weren't as much to blame as you are trying to be," Sarah suggested with a small smile. "I think your grief over losing her is deep enough without punishing yourself with guilt that you might not even deserve."

"You're generous, Sarah," he said, returning her smile with a sad one of his own.

"I'm not generous at all," she corrected him. "I'm just being reasonable. I thought men appreciated that in a female."

"I'm learning to," Richard said with a smile as the train pulled into the station.

\* \* \*

Sarah had to stop and catch her breath for a moment before she could tell the nurse what she wanted. She'd practically run most of the way to Dr. Newton's office in an effort to get there in time for Brian's appointment to get his cast off. "Is Mr. Malloy still here?" she finally asked.

The nurse smiled in recognition. "Oh, yes, I remember now! You came in with Mr. Malloy the first time. They're still in with the doctor. Would you like to join them?"

"If it's all right."

"I'm sure it is." The nurse led her back to the examining room.

She opened the door to a strange tableau. Dr. David Newton was hunkered down with one knee on the floor. Malloy was in the same position, facing him and holding Brian, who was making pathetic whimpering sounds and struggling to get free. He was deaf, so he hadn't learned how to howl in his unhappiness.

Sarah saw at once that the cast was off his foot. There were some angry red lines where Dr. Newton's knife had cut in order to make the necessary repairs, but otherwise the foot seemed almost perfectly normal in size and shape.

Both men looked up when the door opened, and Dr. Newton instantly rose to his feet. "Sarah," he said in greeting. "How nice to see you. Mr. Malloy didn't think you were coming."

Sarah glanced at Malloy, who was rising more slowly since he had a squirming three-year-old to contend with. He avoided meeting her eye, and Sarah wondered why he looked so angry.

"I had a birth last night," she explained to David,

who had been an old friend of her husband's. "I got here as quickly as I could," she added for Malloy's benefit. Could he be angry because she was late?

Brian had finally noticed her arrival, and now he was reaching out for her, anxious to escape his father. Brian was particularly fond of Sarah because she often brought him presents.

"What have you been doing to the poor boy?" she scolded the men, gladly taking Brian's small body into her arms. He clung to her fiercely.

"We've been trying to get him to put his weight on his foot," David explained. "He's never walked, and his foot has been sore for a while, so naturally, he's reluctant."

Sarah turned to Malloy. "He's probably just stubborn, like his father," she said with a smile. He didn't smile back. Maybe he really *was* angry at her. Or maybe he was just upset about Brian and didn't want to show it. She didn't bother to wonder how she knew that about him.

Brian was still clinging to her tightly. "Let's see if we can give him a reason to walk," Sarah suggested. "Malloy, take him back."

"He'll throw a fit," Malloy protested.

"And he'll want to get back to me," Sarah said. "When he does, set him on his feet and let him go."

"Wonderful idea, Sarah," David said, moving out of the way to give them room.

Malloy's dark gaze was unfathomable as he reached out and wrenched Brian away from her. The boy did pitch a fit, arms and legs flailing as garbled sounds erupted from his throat. Malloy held him at arm's length until Sarah could step back a bit and stoop down, her long skirts pooling around her.

"All right," she said to Malloy, who slowly lowered the boy to the floor.

"Brian, come here," Sarah said, forgetting he couldn't hear her. He didn't need to hear to know what her outstretched arms meant, though. He tried to drop to his knees so he could crawl across the distance that separated them, but Malloy held him up, allowing his feet to touch the floor but letting him go no farther down.

His normal foot planted on the floor, but he kept drawing up the damaged one each time it touched.

"Come on, Brian!" Sarah urged him, beckoning him with her hands, her smile bright and encouraging. "You can do it!"

Malloy let him move forward a step when his damaged foot came down in front of the other one. The boy looked down in surprise and instantly drew the foot up again. This time, however, he stared at it, as if trying to figure out what it had done.

All the adults in the room held their breath as he tried to decide what to do next. After what seemed an hour, the boy gingerly lowered the damaged foot to the floor again, and this time Malloy quickly reached down and scooted his good foot forward, forcing him to take a step with his weight on the damaged foot. His knee buckled, but Malloy didn't let him fall.

Brian turned his angel blue eyes to Sarah beseechingly, but she just kept smiling and beckoning. "Come on, sweetheart! You can do it!" she insisted.

He looked down at his foot again and this time lifted it tentatively and placed it down a step ahead. Sarah clapped her hands, and Brian smiled when he looked up and saw it. He wanted desperately to please her. She pointed at his normal foot and motioned for him to move it forward.

His beautiful face screwed up with mingled apprehension and determination. He tried one more beseeching glance, but Sarah nodded and beckoned again. "That's right, you can do it!"

As quickly as he could, he threw his good foot forward a step, putting his weight on the damaged foot for only the briefest of seconds. But when he looked up, he saw Sarah was laughing and clapping again, cheering him on. Two more halting steps, and he had almost reached her. Frantically, he pried Malloy's fingers from his hips, then lunged forward on his own, walking unaided for the first time in his life, and collapsed into Sarah's arms.

She hugged him to her, fairly squealing with delight. David's strong hands helped her to stand upright, and she swung Brian around in joyous celebration.

"Never underestimate the power of a beautiful woman, Mr. Malloy," David was saying.

Sarah turned to Malloy to share this wonderful moment, but he wasn't smiling. Could he possibly be unhappy that Brian could finally walk? Instinctively, she knew she had to make him part of this. "Now I'll send him back to you, Malloy," she said.

She carefully untangled the boy's arms and legs from around her and turned him to face his father, then bent down and set him back on his feet. Malloy hesitated only an instant before going down on one knee again and reaching out for his son.

This time Brian knew what he was supposed to do. The damaged foot tentatively found the floor again, and when Malloy reached out, Brian began lurching

clumsily toward him. Sarah held on to keep him from
falling, but after a few steps, he impatiently pushed
her hands away. He wanted to do it himself!

She let him go, hands still hovering only inches
away, to catch him if he fell. But he didn't fall. He
staggered triumphantly into his father's arms. Malloy
enveloped him, burying his face in the sweet curve of
the boy's neck. Sarah felt the sting of tears as she
stepped back.

Brian could walk. The wonder of it washed over
her, leaving her weak with gratitude. "You've done a
miracle, David."

"All in a day's work," he demurred. "Bring Brian
into the office when you're ready, Mr. Malloy," he
added. Taking Sarah's elbow, he guided her into his
adjoining office and drew the connecting door almost
shut behind them, allowing Malloy a measure of privacy to deal with his emotions.

For herself, Sarah could hardly hold back her own,
and she couldn't even begin to imagine what Malloy
must be feeling. Brian would be able to walk. Soon
he could run and play in the street like other children.
His world would no longer be limited to the small flat
where he lived with his grandmother.

And he would never become another cripple begging on the streets for his livelihood.

"Anne is angry with you," David was saying as he
seated himself behind his desk. Anne was his wife
and a dear friend of Sarah's.

"I hated breaking our dinner engagement, but I
can't plan my schedule the way you can," she reminded him. "Babies come when they want to."

"I was instructed to tell you that we expect you for
dinner tomorrow evening, no excuses."

"I'll be there if you promise to allow me to come early so I can play with the children."

"I'm sure we would all be delighted," David assured her. They chatted for a few more minutes, and Sarah was grateful for the distraction. By the time Malloy brought Brian into the office, she had regained her composure.

But she almost lost it again when she saw that Brian was walking. Malloy held his hand and was giving him more than ordinary support, but he was taking his own steps, however uncertain. His small face was a study in determination and pride as he glanced up to see her reaction.

This time she didn't try to hold back the tears. Her eyes filled and overflowed even as she laughed in delight. "Oh, Malloy, isn't it wonderful?"

But when she looked up at him, his expression remained grim. "He's still deaf," he reminded her.

She felt as if he'd slapped her. She stared up at him, but he didn't even glance at her as he took the other chair and hoisted Brian into his lap.

David had been shocked, too, but he was too professional to let it to show. He explained to Malloy what to expect and answered his questions. All the while, Brian kept examining his new foot, tracing the scars with his finger and poking and prodding and wiggling his toes, then comparing his two feet and silently marveling at how alike they now were.

His wonder was enchanting, but Sarah still felt the sting of Malloy's rebuke. What was wrong with him? Why wasn't he overjoyed? And why on earth was he taking his anger out on her?

When David was finished and Malloy had no more questions, Malloy gathered Brian up and rose. He shook David's hand and thanked him. Then he turned to Sarah, nodded, and took his leave. Brian reached back longingly. Plainly, he wanted her to come along with them, but Malloy didn't even glance back.

"We'll see you tomorrow then," David said to Sarah, pretending not to notice how rude Malloy had been. "Come as early as you like. Anne will be glad for the company."

Sarah made her own escape as quickly as propriety would allow and hurried out into the street, hoping to catch up with Malloy and confront him. Luckily, the traffic had stopped them at the corner, so she was able to simply encounter them without resorting to any unseemly behavior, such as running after them or calling out.

Brian saw her first, and he squealed with joy and flung himself toward her. Caught by surprise, Malloy would have dropped him, but Sarah saved the boy from falling to the pavement and took him into her arms.

"I'm happy to see you, too, Brian," she said, settling him on her hip. He was touching her face and looking up at her new hat. He seemed to approve of it. "It seems the operation was a success," she tried on Malloy.

"My mother will be glad," he replied, not quite meeting her eye. "You didn't have to come today," he added gruffly.

"I told you I'd be here if I could," she reminded him.

"You've got better things to do than worry about the likes of us." His jaw was set in the stubborn line she'd seen too many times before.

She'd thought he was upset because she was late

for the appointment, but could he possibly be angry that she'd come at all? "If you didn't want me here, you should have said so," she said.

This time he looked straight at her, his eyes as dark as she'd ever seen them. "You should be with your own kind, Sarah."

At that moment, there was a break in the traffic, and he snatched Brian from her and hurried across the street. Brian's small arms were still reaching back for her when they disappeared behind the closing wall of carriages and hacks.

Stunned, Sarah could only stand there staring until the people walking by began to make remarks about her blocking the way. Then she started blindly down the street, walking in the opposite direction, as much to get away as to get to someplace else.

The worst part was that she didn't know whether to be angry or hurt. Other people had certainly advised her that she should confine herself to associations with people of her own social class. Her parents had done so many times, as had her old friends. Some were well meaning, and others were snobs. She had ignored them all and done what she pleased.

What she pleased was to continue the work that her husband Tom had begun, providing medical services to everyone who needed it, regardless of their ability to pay. Sarah wasn't a physician, but she could save the lives of mothers and their babies, so that's what she did.

In the six months she'd known Frank Malloy, she thought he'd come to respect her, and even to approve of her. The last thing she'd ever expected was to hear him say she should be with her "own kind." An hour ago, she would have said that Frank Malloy was her own kind! Now he was warning her away from him.

She had to admit it: he'd hurt her. She hadn't known until this moment how much she valued his opinion of her. When the people she loved most in the world begged her at every opportunity to turn her back on all that she found fulfilling in life, he had accepted her as a competent professional, someone whom he consulted on matters of importance. She'd even helped him solve a number of murders. Just last week, she'd kept an innocent person from being executed, and all on her own, she'd made sure her neighbor's son got to keep his position at the bank Richard Dennis owned. Even Malloy couldn't have influenced Richard the way she had!

The thought stopped her in her tracks and caused the gentleman behind her to nearly fall in his hasty effort to avoid colliding with her. She apologized profusely as he regained his balance and sidled around her, not certain what to make of a woman so lost in thought she was paying no attention to anything else.

Only then did she realize she was back on the corner where Malloy had left her. She'd made a complete circle of the block.

"Malloy, you're jealous!" she whispered to the spot where he had disappeared with Brian into the traffic. She really shouldn't have been surprised. He'd been quite upset when she told him she was going to the opera with Richard. She'd thought they had parted on good terms last Friday, but his behavior today proved she was wrong. Now all she had to do was figure out if he really did think she should stay with her own kind.

And if he did, what she should do about it.

*     *     *

Frank should have been pleased. A woman had been found dead in City Hall Park, and he'd been selected for the case because of his reputation for handling difficult situations with care. Nobody knew who the woman was, but she'd been well dressed. Nobody knew how she'd died, either, but if she'd been killed — in broad daylight on the doorstep of City Hall — nobody wanted a scandal. Unlike many of his colleagues, Frank could be counted upon not to offend the wrong people and not to let the press hear anything they shouldn't.

The Elevated Train ran right down to City Hall, so Frank got on at Bleeker Street. The morning rush was over, and he got a seat all to himself and a few minutes to collect his thoughts. Unfortunately, he didn't particularly want to collect his thoughts, because every time he did, Sarah Brandt turned up in them.

He hadn't admitted to himself how badly he'd wanted her there when Brian got his cast off. She'd gone to so much trouble to make sure her friend operated on his son, but it was more than that. He'd needed her there. He'd needed to share the anxiety and the joy with her. She was the only one who could truly understand.

Of course, he'd told her she didn't have to come. He didn't want her to feel any sense of obligation. Or pity. He and Brian were nothing to her, after all. Yet still he'd been hoping . . .

And then she'd come. Breathless from hurrying, her cheeks rosy and her eyes shining, she'd looked like a goddess. Brian had thrown himself into her arms, and Frank had longed to do the same. Jealous of his own son, jealous of the doctor whose friendship entitled him to call her Sarah, and jealous of Richard Dennis, whose position in life gave him the right to court her, Frank had hardly dared look her in the eye for fear he would betray the feelings to which he had no right.

As the train lurched to a stop at the next station and passengers began to come and go in the car, Frank rubbed his head. He hadn't gotten much sleep last night. Every time he closed his eyes, he'd see her face and the hurt in her eyes just before he'd snatched Brian from her arms and fled.

She'd never speak to him again, but that was as it should be. She never should have spoken to him in the first place. He never should have gotten to know her. He never should have allowed her to help him solve any murders. And he never should have let her help Brian.

But he had. She'd done him a favor, her good deed for the year. She'd been repaying him for the cases he'd solved for her, because she was the only one who cared if they ever were or not. They were even. Or at least she needn't feel she was in his debt.

But each time his son took a step, he realized he would be in her debt forever.

That probably also meant he'd remember her forever. It couldn't be any harder than losing Kathleen, he reasoned. He'd thought the pain of losing his wife would kill him, and here he was, three years later, alive and well. Of course, Kathleen had died, so he didn't have any choice about accepting that. He couldn't see her again, and she wasn't there somewhere in the city, living without him. He'd certainly never had to worry about meeting her accidentally and not knowing how he'd react if he did. He'd had no choice but to let Kathleen go.

Sarah Brandt was another story, at least until one of them was dead. Maybe then he'd be able to stop thinking about her. And wondering if things might have been different if . . . if everything about them had been different.

Finally, the train stopped at City Hall, and Frank rose wearily from his seat and made his way out of the station. Glad for the distraction from his own, painful thoughts, he let himself be caught up in the roar of the street. People of all descriptions milled and mingled in the shadow of the city's government. Each day, hundreds of them took the train or walked across the bridge from Brooklyn. Dozens of street vendors waited, ready to sell them whatever they might need. The crowds ebbed and flowed around the government buildings and those nearby on Newspaper Row, where the major papers had their offices.

City Hall itself sprawled for a block, its marble front gleaming in the morning sunlight. Wide steps led up to the columned portico, inviting all who were not too intimidated to enter and be heard.

For several years the politicians had been talking about building a new City Hall. This one was too small for such a large city, and the cheap brownstone they'd originally used on the back of the building was crumbling. Nearly a hundred years ago, no one had imagined the city growing northward beyond that point, so the back of the building hadn't seemed important. Now, of course, the city stretched northward for miles, and thousands of people saw the back of City Hall with its crumbling brownstone every day.

The report had said the dead woman had been

found in the park across from City Hall. Frank crossed the busy street and entered the relative sanctuary of the park. Recent rains had stripped most of the leaves from the trees, but the grass was still green, or at least what he could see of it beneath the leafy covering. He quickly spotted his destination. A small crowd had gathered and several uniformed officers were keeping them back, guarding the place where the body lay.

One of the officers had covered the woman with his coat. She was lying on the ground in front of a bench, as if she'd been sitting there, tried to rise, and fallen down dead. Frank saw no signs of a struggle. The leaves on the ground around her were undisturbed. He pushed his way into the circle the officers were maintaining.

"Detective Sergeant Frank Malloy," he told them, showing his badge.

The three young men seemed relieved to finally have someone in authority present.

"'Morning, sir," the one without a coat said. He was Jewish. Another one of Commissioner Roosevelt's innovations. Frank wasn't sure he'd ever get used to seeing Jews on the force, but he supposed as long as they did their job, it was all right. "I'm Eisenberg."

"Tell me what you know."

"Well, now, I was walking my beat this morning, just like usual, when this fellow comes up and says a woman is laying on the ground over here. I thought it might be a whore or something, passed out drunk. They don't like that kind of thing in the park, so I goes over to take a look." He glanced down at the body. "She was just laying there. Her face was all blue like. I knew she was dead. Couldn't be that color and still be alive, could you? Her eyes was open, too, just staring."

Frank glanced at the body again. "Had she been interfered with?"

Eisenberg glanced at the body, too. "I didn't look for that," he said, appalled.

Frank sighed. "I mean, were her skirts down like that when you found her?"

"Oh, yeah, I mean, yes, sir. She was just like that. We didn't touch her or anything. Just threw my coat over her, so people wouldn't be gawking." He gave the gathering crowd a derisive glance. "Didn't stop 'em, though."

"I sent for an ambulance to take her to the morgue," Frank said. "But I want to have a look at her before they get here."

"Wasn't a mark on her that I could see," Eisenberg reported as they stepped over to the body. Frank would have them sift through the leaves when the body was gone, to make sure nothing had been dropped or left behind.

"She was probably strangled," Frank said.

"I thought that, too, but like I said, didn't see no bruises on her neck or anything." Eisenberg gingerly lifted his coat from the body, which lay facedown in the leaves, the head turned away from him. "I never saw nobody turn that color blue when they was strangled, either."

Frank stared down at the woman for a long moment, his mind unable quite to comprehend what he was seeing. A woman. Blond hair. An ugly hat he knew well, lying nearby where it had been jarred loose when she fell. Brian had tried to pull that flower off the last time he'd seen it. Frank heard a strange roaring in his ears, as if the El were running right through his head.

"Sir? Are you all right?" Eisenberg's voice seemed to come from very far away.

Frank opened his mouth to reply, but no sound came out. He wasn't all right, and he would never be all right again.

The dead woman was Sarah Brandt.

# 4

"DETECTIVE?"

Frank forced himself to look away from the body and back at Officer Eisenberg. "Turn her over," he said, his voice strangely hoarse.

"Yes, sir." But when Eisenberg reached down, Frank realized he didn't want a stranger touching her.

"*Wait*, I'll do it," he said sharply, startling Eisenberg, who quickly jumped out of the way.

She'd been wearing that hat when he'd kissed her only a few days ago. This suit, too. He'd seen her wear it a dozen times. Gently he put his hands on her shoulder and her hip to turn her. She wasn't stiff, which meant she'd been dead for only a couple of hours at most. The coldness of death had seeped through her clothing, though, a chill unlike any other. A chill that could never be warmed.

He'd been a fool. He should have told her how he

felt. He should have kissed her again. He should never have let her die without at least trying.

The pain was like a vise around his heart, and he could hardly breathe as he forced his hands to move. Ever so slowly he eased her over, hating the indignity of it, hating that she was lying on the ground, dried leaves clinging to her clothing and her hair, hating that total strangers were staring at her, people who had no right to even speak her name.

He got her over far enough that her own weight carried her onto her back. She landed with a soft rustle in the leaves, and Frank stared down at the face, slack jawed in death, the skin stained an odd, bluish color. The empty eyes stared back at him, holding a secret the blue lips could never reveal.

"Sir, what is it?" one of the other officers asked. The tone in his voice was kind, the way he'd talk to someone who was very ill.

"I just . . ." Frank had to clear his throat. "I thought I knew her." It was the eyes. They were brown, not blue. Not Sarah's eyes at all, thank God. And not her face, either, no matter how death might alter it. He drew a breath and felt the vise of pain around his heart release, leaving him weak.

It wasn't Sarah. Sarah wasn't dead.

But someone else was, someone who was wearing Sarah's ugly hat. Someone who was wearing Sarah's clothing.

"You don't recognize her then?" Eisenberg asked.

"No, but I know someone who might." He sighed with resignation. Or was it relief? Once again fate would take him back to Sarah Brandt.

*     *     *

Sarah had been taking advantage of having no babies to deliver this morning to do her often-neglected housework. She had just finished sweeping the last of the dirt from her kitchen out the back door when she heard someone pounding on the front door. She glanced down at her housedress in dismay. At least she could tell from the urgency of the pounding that it was a summons to service and not a social call, so it didn't matter what she was wearing. Whoever had come to fetch her would wait while she changed into something more presentable.

Before she could put the broom away, her visitor was pounding again. They were always like that when a baby was on the way. Nobody seemed to remember that most babies took their own sweet time. Untying her apron, she made her way through the front room, which had been converted into a medical office, to the front door.

She hung the apron on the coatrack nearby and gave her hair a cursory pat before opening the door.

"Malloy!" she exclaimed in surprise. She wasn't sure which was more shocking, his presence here at all or the expression on his face. He looked almost *desperate*. "What is it?" she demanded, growing desperate herself. "Is something wrong? Is it Brian?" she added as the new fear blossomed.

She stepped back instinctively as he came into the house without waiting for an invitation. Only then did she realize how intensely he was looking at her. His gaze swept over her, taking in her appearance from head to toe. Self-consciously, she touched her hand to her bodice, making sure all her buttons were fastened.

"Malloy, what —?" was all she managed to say be-

fore his arms came around her and he crushed her to
his chest.

A thousand sensations collided in her brain. Her
cheek against the rough fabric of his suit, his masculine scent engulfing her, his arms locked fiercely
around her, his breath harsh and rasping in her ear.
What felt like a shudder wracked his large frame, and
then, as suddenly as he had embraced her, he let her
go.

Robbed of his support, she nearly lost her balance,
and he caught her arm to steady her, then quickly
dropped his hand again. She stared up at him, trying
to get control of her scrambled senses. Before she
could, he said, "You're alive."

"Yes, I am," she agreed, a little breathless and still
unable to make any sense of this. "Was there ever any
doubt?"

She'd expected him to smile the way he did whenever she said something sarcastic. But he didn't
smile, and the hand he raised to his head was trembling. *Malloy was trembling!*

"Come in and sit down," she urged him, convinced
now that he must be ill. Nothing else could explain
such bizarre behavior. She took his arm, and he let
her lead him to the upholstered chairs that sat by her
front window. "Can I get you something?" she asked
when he was seated in one of them.

"No," he said, still looking at her strangely. "No,
just . . . just sit down here where I can see you."

Now Sarah really was worried. She did as he'd instructed her, taking the other chair. "It's not Brian, is
it? Nothing's happened to him?"

"He's fine," he said. "Everything's fine now. It's
just . . . a little while ago, I thought you were dead."

*"Dead?"* she repeated incredulously. "What made you think I was dead?"

He drew a deep breath and let it out in a shaky sigh as he rubbed a large hand over his face. Then he gave her a crooked smile. "Because I saw your dead body."

"Malloy, stop this!" she cried. "You're frightening me."

"Then we're even. I had a few bad minutes myself when I saw you lying dead in City Hall Park this morning."

"I haven't been near City Hall in weeks," she insisted.

"Well, someone was near there. A woman with blond hair who was wearing your clothes and your hat, and she was dead."

"That's impossible! What made you think they were my clothes?"

"I recognized them. How could anybody forget that hat? It's the ugliest thing any woman ever put on her head. There couldn't be two like it in the city."

"There's absolutely nothing ugly about my hat," she informed him indignantly, "and there's also no way anyone else could be wearing it or . . ."

"Or what?" he prodded when her voice trailed off on that thought.

"Oh, dear," she said, remembering. "Someone else *could* have been wearing my hat. I gave it away!"

"Who did you give it to?"

"I took it to the mission. The Prodigal Son Mission. I took a whole bundle of clothes down there on Sunday afternoon."

He looked askance at the shabby dress she was

wearing. "Did you take a vow of poverty or something?"

"This is a housedress, Malloy," she said, indignant again. "I was cleaning when you came. I gave my other clothes away because I got some new ones. From my mother."

"Did your mother take a vow of poverty?"

Sarah almost smiled. This was the old Malloy. Whatever had been wrong with him, he was feeling better now. "I needed something to wear to the opera last Saturday, so I went to my parents' house to borrow a dress."

At the mention of the opera, he frowned, confirming Sarah's opinion that he was jealous of Richard Dennis. She pretended not to notice.

"While I was there, she insisted that I take several other things as well. My mother has excellent taste, and my new clothes are so much more fashionable than the old ones, I decided I didn't need them anymore."

"So you took them to this mission," Malloy guessed. "The Prodigal Son? Isn't that the one on Mulberry Street, down by Police Headquarters?"

"Yes, do you know anything about it?"

He shrugged, which either meant that he didn't know anything or that he didn't want to say. "So who did you give the clothes to at the mission?"

She opened her mouth to say she'd given them to Mrs. Wells, when the real meaning of his question hit her. "The dead woman must be someone from the mission!"

"Or at least they'll know who they gave your clothes to," he said.

Sarah felt a sickness in the pit of her stomach. "Did you say the dead woman had blond hair?"

He winced a little, reminding her that he'd thought the body was hers at first. "Yes. She had brown eyes. Younger than you, but about the same size."

Sarah groaned and closed her eyes.

"Do you know who it is?" he asked.

"I think . . . I'd have to see her, of course, but one of the girls at the mission fits that description. An Italian girl."

"This girl was blond," he reminded her.

"She must have been from Northern Italy. Her name was Emilia."

"Emilia what?"

"I don't know. They'll know her at the mission, I suppose. If it really is her. They might have given the clothes to someone else," she added hopefully. Maybe it would turn out to be someone she didn't know at all.

Malloy sighed again. "I'll get someone from the mission to identify the body then."

Sarah remembered the girl she'd met who'd been so full of life and hope. She was learning to sew so she could make an honest living and overcome her unfortunate past.

"I could identify her," she offered. "If it is Emilia, that would save someone who really knew her from having to go."

"The city morgue isn't a very pleasant place," he warned her.

"That's why I'd like to save someone else from making the trip. I only met her once, so seeing her in a place like that won't be as painful for me as it would for someone who cared about her."

Malloy didn't want to take her there. She could see it in every line of his face.

"I can go without you," she reminded him.

"And what if it isn't her?"

"Then we can go to the mission and tell them what happened. They'll send someone to find out who it really is."

This was a perfectly logical plan, but Malloy didn't like it at all. She wasn't sure what part of it bothered him until he said, "I guess you won't want me to go with you."

"Why not?" she asked without thinking. He didn't reply, giving her a chance to figure it out for herself. "Oh," she said after a moment. "Because you were so rude to me yesterday."

He didn't confirm or deny it. He just sat there, stubborn as always.

"I've been meaning to ask you about that," she said. "Were you angry at me for being late?"

His lips tightened. "I told you, you didn't have to come. I didn't really expect you'd come at all."

She suspected that wasn't true, but she said, "Then you must be mad because I *did* come."

He sighed. "I'm not mad about anything."

She wanted to ask if he was jealous, but she decided that would be a waste of time. He'd deny it, and she'd look silly. She decided on another tactic. "Then are you going to explain why you were so rude to me?"

He gave her one of the looks he reserved for uncooperative criminals. "I wasn't being rude, Mrs. Brandt. I was just stating a fact."

His look didn't bother her one bit. "Then I won't expect an apology," she retorted pleasantly.

She thought he might be grinding his teeth. "Do you want me to go with you to the morgue or not?" he asked finally.

She wasn't going to fall into that trap. "You'll need to know if I recognize the dead woman, so you might as well go with me," she said, trumping him. "I'll need to change my clothes first. I won't be long."

Sarah took her time changing and redoing her hair. Perversely, she wanted to look her best for this awful task. She distracted herself from thinking about what lay ahead by thinking about the way Malloy had embraced her when he came into the house. The act in itself was shocking. Even more shocking was the fact that he hadn't apologized for taking such a liberty. She wasn't sure what that meant, but she wasn't going to ask him about it. The mood he was in, she couldn't imagine what he'd have to say on the matter, and she thought perhaps they were both better off pretending it hadn't happened.

Until she was ready to mention it again, of course.

One thing was certain, however: he'd been very happy to find her alive and well, happier than he felt he had a right to be.

The question was, did Sarah think he had a right to be? She remembered how he'd kissed her that night last week when he'd thought she wouldn't remember. She remembered how she'd felt in his arms a short while ago. She remembered how her parents had warned her about Malloy. And she remembered how Malloy had warned her about Malloy. Too many things to remember, she decided as she slid her foot-long hat pin carefully into her new hat. The sturdy pin would hold it in place through the force of a hurricane.

Sarah thought she looked very attractive in the stylish suit her mother had insisted she couldn't possibly wear again because it was a year old. Malloy didn't look impressed, however. His eyes narrowed, and she realized he was staring at her hat.

"Don't tell me you think *this* hat is ugly, too," she challenged.

"I remember now. You were wearing this one yesterday."

Which meant the dead woman had been wearing the old one. Sarah didn't want to think about that. "Let's go," she said.

They walked over to Sixth Avenue in silence, and Malloy hailed a Hansom cab to take them to the morgue.

Malloy's bulk made for close quarters in the cab. Sarah should have felt awkward, but the enforced intimacy came naturally to her now. In the months she'd known Malloy, they'd been through a lot together. A few recent, awkward moments couldn't make him an unfamiliar or uncomfortable presence.

"How is Brian doing?" she asked to break the silence. Traffic was moving slowly, as usual, so they'd have a lot of time to fill before they reached their destination.

He carefully didn't look at her. "He's driving my mother crazy. All he wants to do is walk on his new foot. He even tries to get out every time somebody opens the door to the flat."

"It's cruel to keep him inside," she pointed out.

"He doesn't have shoes yet," Malloy reminded her. "Ma won't let him out without shoes."

"What did she say when she saw he could walk?"

Malloy did look at her then. "She crossed herself and said a Hail Mary."

Sarah could easily imagine Mrs. Malloy doing just that. She wouldn't dare express joy, for fear of attracting bad fortune to her loved ones.

When he offered nothing else, she let a few minutes pass before she said, "What do you know about the Prodigal Son Mission?"

"I know they don't allow any prodigal sons in."

"What do you mean?"

"It's for prodigal daughters only. I thought you said you visited them. You didn't see any boys around, did you?"

"There were boys playing in the yard," she said.

"The old woman lets them in the yard, but no further."

"But that's good," Sarah argued. "The girls she takes in probably need to be protected from men."

"Then she should call the mission something else," Malloy argued back.

He still hadn't answered her question. "Do you know Mrs. Wells, the lady who runs it?"

"Not very well. Everybody knew her husband. He preached on street corners for years."

"What was he like?"

"A fanatic, like all of them."

"Like all of who?" she challenged. "Protestants?"

He gave her another of his looks. "Evangelists," he corrected her. "At least the kind who think they're called to save the poor."

"Don't you think that's a worthy calling?"

"Depends on what you're saving them from."

"I imagine they're trying to save them from hell," she said.

"There are lots of kinds of hell," he reminded her. "And you can find all of them on the Lower East Side."

"Mrs. Wells is saving girls from that, too," Sarah pointed out. "Emilia, the girl I was telling you about, was a prostitute when Mrs. Wells took her in."

"You didn't ask me what I thought of Mrs. Wells. You asked me what I thought of her husband."

That was true. "And you haven't really told me."

Malloy gave her a put-upon look. "He was enthusiastic but . . . weak," he said, finally settling on a word.

"Weak in what way?" Sarah thought he might mean physically, since she knew Mr. Wells had died young.

"I'm not sure weak is the right word, but he just never accomplished anything important. He preached for years, and he still never had a congregation or many followers. He tried to help people, but he never had much success."

"How did he get the mission?"

"Some rich woman gave him the money, or at least that's what I heard. He bought the house, and then he got sick and died."

"And his wife took over his ministry," Sarah said. "She seems to have been stronger than he was."

"She's more successful, at least."

"But you don't seem to think much of her, either."

"She doesn't have any use for Papists, Mrs. Brandt."

Sarah recalled that Mrs. Wells had been pleased that Emilia had renounced her Catholic faith. "Does she force people to convert?"

"I'm not sure you'd call it forcing. She just doesn't help anyone who doesn't."

"Oh," was all Sarah could think to say. She tried to imagine turning away someone in need because she didn't agree with the way they worshipped God. Mrs. Wells seemed too kind to do something like that, but she *was* deeply religious and convinced her faith was the only correct one.

As if tired of the subject, Malloy asked if she'd seen Webster Prescott, the newspaper reporter who had been injured during their last investigation. Sarah informed him of Prescott's improving condition, and they discussed the young man's situation for the rest of the trip.

When the cab reached the morgue, Sarah began to regret her decision to come. The building seemed to loom over her, casting a shadow across the sun of this pleasant day. Malloy paid the cab driver, then offered her a hand down. A small part of her wanted to tell him she'd changed her mind, but pride controlled the larger part of her. She took his hand and stepped out of the cab.

His fingers were strong, but he released her as soon as she was safely on the pavement and stepped back, as if anxious to keep a safe distance between them now that they were out of the confines of the cab.

"You don't have to do this," he reminded her, as if sensing her doubts.

"Yes, I do," she said. He shook his head, but he led her inside.

For some reason, she had expected more ceremony around the viewing of a body. The unidentified dead were kept in a basement room, their bodies lying on tables and covered with sheets. The place reeked of chemicals and death. She fought an urge to put her handkerchief over her nose. She didn't want to betray any weakness before Malloy.

The attendant was a scrawny young man with a pockmarked face who acted annoyed at being disturbed.

"This is the one," he said, leading them to one of the tables after consulting his list. "Came in this morning." Sarah followed him and stood beside the table holding the shrouded body he'd indicated. He went to the other side of the table and casually drew back the sheet, revealing the dead woman's face and bare shoulders. They had already removed her clothing, the last indignity of death.

Someone had closed her eyes, but no one would imagine she slept. Her skin was blue, her lips almost purple. Still, Sarah recognized her instantly, and the sadness was like a weight in her chest. "It's Emilia," she informed Malloy who stood off a ways, waiting for her verdict. "How did she die?" she asked the attendant.

He shrugged.

"Her cheek is all red. Did someone beat her?" she asked.

"No, that's from the blood," he explained importantly. "She was laying on her face when they found her. The blood settles to the lowest point." Sarah looked more closely and realized he was right.

"She's blue," she told Malloy this time. "That means she must have suffocated."

"Coroner says not," the attendant said, now with an air of superiority. "Her eyes ain't bloodshot, like she would be if somebody smothered her."

To the attendant's surprise, Sarah reached out and raised the dead girl's eyelid. He was right. Then she leaned closer, examining the girl's neck for signs she was choked. "There aren't any bruises on her throat, either."

"What are you, lady, some kind of doctor?" the attendant asked, giving Malloy a questioning glance.

"I'm a trained nurse," she informed him. A nurse who had seen death many times and witnessed dying far too often. She turned to Malloy. "What does the coroner think killed her?"

"He don't know," the attendant replied, obviously taking great pleasure in knowing more than either of them. "There ain't a mark on her anyplace."

"Well, something made her stop breathing against her will," Sarah said impatiently. "Maybe she was poisoned."

"You know of a poison makes people stop breathing like that?" he replied in challenge.

Sarah supposed there could be, but she wasn't exactly an expert on poisons. She turned to Malloy, who was looking even more annoyed than he had before. "Could I examine her myself? Maybe I can find something they missed."

"They ain't done an autopsy yet," the attendant said with a small smirk, "but if you think you can save 'em the trouble, go ahead." With a flick of his wrist, he jerked the sheet off the body, leaving the poor girl lying there naked and completely exposed.

"You ghoul!" Sarah shouted in outrage, but Malloy was faster. He slammed the attendant against the wall.

"You jackass!" Malloy was saying, his forearm pressed against the fellow's throat in a very threatening way. "Haynes will hear about this. Now get out of here, before I put you on one of these slabs."

The attendant had undergone a complete transformation. Stricken with terror over what Malloy might do to him, he'd suddenly found his manners. "I . . . I'm sorry, ma'am," he stammered when Malloy released him and gave him a shove toward the door. "I didn't mean no harm. Please don't say nothing to Doc Haynes," he added as he backed out of the room.

Sarah was too busy gathering up the sheet and spreading it over Emilia again to respond. Malloy made a move, as if to go after the fellow, and he scampered away, slamming the door behind him.

"I'm sorry for that," Malloy said when he was gone. "This kind of work . . . Well, the best people don't choose a job like this."

Sarah could imagine. "This poor girl had little enough dignity in life. I hate the thought of that . . . that creature looking at her now."

"He won't be looking at anything around here anymore. I'll see to that."

She looked up from arranging the sheet and gave Malloy a grateful smile. "Do you think it would be all right if I examined her?"

"You don't have to. Haynes will be doing an autopsy, like that idiot said. He'll figure it out."

Sarah sighed. "It's just . . . I feel responsible somehow."

"Because she was wearing your clothes?" he asked with a frown.

"I don't know why. I just do. Please, I'll only need a minute."

He sighed in resignation. "Take as long as you need." He walked to the other side of the room and sat down in the attendant's chair. She noticed he carefully turned his back, giving the girl some privacy even in death, and she smiled at his consideration.

Without really knowing what she was doing, Sarah carefully examined every inch of Emilia's body. Except for more of the red marks on her arm and hip and knee, from where the blood had pooled when she'd been lying dead in the park, she found nothing unusual. Covering her with the sheet again, she called, "Malloy, could you help me turn her over?"

He wasn't happy about it, but he did, lifting the slight girl as if she'd been a straw dummy and placing her gently on her stomach. "You're wasting your time," he said as she pulled the sheet down to check the skin of the girl's back. "Haynes will probably find out she had some disease and just picked this morning to drop dead."

"She didn't look sick when I saw her," Sarah argued.

The girl's hair had come undone and was in a hopeless tangle around her shoulders, bits of dead leaves clinging to it. From this angle, Sarah realized with a start why Malloy had thought Sarah's was the dead body lying in the park. Emilia's hair was almost the same color as hers.

A wave of pity washed over her, bringing tears to her eyes. She wanted to go back in time. She wanted to change things so that Emilia would still be alive, a young girl full of hope, perhaps for the first time in her life.

Tenderly, she touched the tangle of golden hair in a feeble attempt to smooth it. She found a stray hairpin and pulled it out. As if of their own accord, her fingers began searching for others, combing through the silken locks and pulling out the bits of leaf and dead grass, the way she would have if it had been her own hair.

When she'd done what she could, she twisted the mass back into the semblance of a bun and began securing it with the pins she'd salvaged. She didn't realize she was crying until a tear dropped onto Emilia's shoulder, but she didn't bother to wipe her eyes until she'd finished with her futile task.

Only when Emilia's hair was tidy again — or as tidy as it could be under the circumstances, did Sarah reach for the handkerchief that all well-bred ladies carried tucked into their sleeves. Emilia's image blurred, but Sarah resolutely blotted away her tears, until she could see the girl clearly again.

"You can leave her for Dr. Haynes now," Malloy said quietly, gently. She couldn't remember ever hearing that tone in his voice. She wanted to look up and see the expression on his face, but something else had caught her attention.

"What's that?" she asked of no one in particular, leaning down to peer more closely at the hollow on the back of the girl's neck that was now exposed.

"What's what?" Malloy asked, but she didn't answer. She was tracing the small mark with her finger.

"Look, there's a little dried blood here," she said, pointing at a spot just at the base of the girl's skull, where her hair almost hid it.

Malloy examined the spot she'd found. He wasn't impressed. "You don't die from a scratch on the neck."

"It's more than a scratch," she insisted. "It looks as if someone stuck something in there. See, the skin closed over it because the wound is so small."

He looked again. "Could a wound like that kill someone?"

Sarah tried to remember her anatomy classes, and what she remembered alarmed her. "The brain is just inches from this spot. If the knife or whatever it was went straight in, it would sever the spinal cord. If it went upward at an angle, it would plunge right into the brain."

Malloy still wasn't convinced. "I thought you said she suffocated."

"I said she stopped breathing against her will. We don't know much about how the brain works, but we do know that injuries to it can stop various bodily functions."

"Like breathing?"

"Like breathing," she confirmed.

Malloy stepped back from the table, thumbs hooked into his vest pockets, and considered her theory. "Wouldn't there have been a lot of blood?"

Sarah couldn't imagine they'd missed blood on the girl's clothing when they'd removed it. "Where are her things?" she asked, looking around.

Malloy found them under the table, in a sack. Sarah removed each item carefully, trying not to remember that some of these things had touched her own body so recently. She didn't recognize the shoes and the undergarments. They would have belonged to Emilia. Then she pulled out the jacket of the suit she'd bought at Lord & Taylor just a few short months ago. They'd been having a sale, and she'd been pleased to improve her wardrobe for the reasonable sum of seven dollars. Carefully, hating the very feel of the fabric, she turned the jacket and examined the neckline. She saw no trace of blood.

"I don't see anything, but a deep puncture wound probably wouldn't have bled very much," she said, handing it to Malloy and reaching into the bag for something else. She pulled out the hat she'd worn for so long that she'd stopped noticing it. Malloy had called it ugly, and indeed it was. She tried to imagine anyone being pleased to receive such a worn and shabby thing or wearing it proudly, as Emilia must have done. The thought was too painful to bear.

"What's this?" Malloy asked and showed her the jacket again. Sarah took it and looked closely at the spot he indicated. She'd missed it because it blended with the dark color of the material, but there, about halfway down, below where the right shoulder blade would have been, was a curiously shaped stain.

"Is it blood?" she asked.

"Looks like it."

Sarah stared more closely, holding it up to the feeble light. "It's not from a wound," she said.

"No," he said grimly.

"What is it, then?"

"She must have been stabbed with something thin, right?"

"Right."

"The killer pulled it out and wiped the blood off on her back before he walked away."

Sarah shuddered in horror. "Dear heaven," she murmured. "What could they have used to kill her?"

"You said she was Italian?" he asked.

"Yes, I'm sure she was."

"I'd say it was a stiletto."

# 5

"A STILETTO?" SHE REPEATED, AS IF SHE'D NEVER heard the word before. Maybe she hadn't, Frank thought.

"It's a long, thin-bladed knife. The Italians like it, for some reason. Probably because it goes in so easily."

She flinched at the image, and he instantly regretted drawing it for her. "Here, let's put her clothes back in the bag. I'll tell Haynes your theory. He can check to see exactly what happened."

He took the jacket from her and began stuffing it into the bag, but she made a sound of protest and snatched both of them away from him. Probably, she didn't think he was showing enough respect. She carefully folded the jacket and placed it into the bag along with the rest of her things. When everything was tucked away, she gently pulled the sheet back up over the dead girl, preserving what little was left of her privacy. Her hand lingered for a moment, smoothing the girl's hair one last time.

"Come on," he said, his voice sounding a little gravelly to his own ears. "Let's get some fresh air."

"Aren't you going to speak to the coroner first?"

"He's not here right now. I'll come back later."

He took her arm when she hesitated. He certainly didn't mind touching her, and she didn't resist when he led her to the door and out into the hallway and up the stairs. When they emerged into the crisp, sunny afternoon, they stopped as if by mutual consent to take a deep breath.

Malloy looked down at her. At least she wasn't crying anymore. He'd never seen her cry before. They'd been through a lot together, including several attempts on her life, and none of those adventures had brought her even close to tears. Who would have guessed the death of a girl she hardly knew would do it? He certainly hoped he'd never have to witness such a sight again. It had nearly unmanned him. "Are you all right?" he asked.

"No," she replied, looking up at him. "I'm furious." She looked it, too.

Greatly relieved, he asked, "At who?"

"At whoever killed that girl. Do you think it was the Black Hand?"

"How do you know about the Black Hand?" he challenged.

"Everyone knows about the Black Hand. They're the most despicable creatures on earth. Imagine blackmailing your own kind, people who are slaving away just to make a living."

The members of this secret society sold "protection" to their fellows. The police did pretty much the same thing, except if you didn't pay the police, you were simply at the mercy of the laws you were already breaking. The Black Hand sold you protection from themselves. If you didn't pay, they'd beat you or damage your business or burn it to the ground. Sometimes they even used bombs, if they wanted to make a particular example of someone. Killing people also set an example, although you couldn't collect money from a dead person, so murder was only used as a last resort. A very nasty bunch.

"Why would the Black Hand want to kill this girl?" he asked, taking her elbow again to encourage her on her way.

"I have no idea. That's what we have to find out."

And *that's* what he'd been afraid of. "I can't help thinking that if Commissioner Roosevelt had appointed you to the police department, it would have been in all the newspapers."

She gave him a look that told him she didn't appreciate his attempt at humor. "Do you really think you'll find out anything useful from the girls at the mission? They'll be too frightened of you to say a word."

"I'm sure those girls have seen much worse things than a police detective, Mrs. Brandt. Don't forget where they came from before they got to the mission."

She was glaring at him now, her blue eyes flashing fire. For a moment he thought of Kathleen. If she'd even *thought* about crying, her eyes and nose would turn beet red for hours. Sarah Brandt's fair complexion showed no trace of the tears she'd shed over the dead girl. He wondered vaguely if that was because she'd been born rich.

"Malloy, you know I can help you with this," she argued.

"Nobody can help me if it's the Black Hand. Even if somebody knows who killed her, they'll never tell. They're all too scared . . . and they should be."

"That's terrible! How will they ever be free of those devils if no one speaks against them?"

"How will somebody ever speak against them if they're dead?" he replied quite reasonably, if she'd just admit it.

She wouldn't. "The police should do something then!"

"Like what? Arrest everybody in Little Italy?"

"You must have an idea who the ring leaders are," she insisted.

"Even if we did — and didn't anybody tell you that it's a *secret* society?— what would we do with them?"

"Put them on trial!"

"For what? And who would testify against them? You can't just lock somebody up because you think they deserve it. If you could, this world would be a better place."

Even she didn't have an answer for that. Or at least he didn't think she did. He was busy looking for a Hansom cab to take her home when she said, "*I* wouldn't be afraid to testify against them. That's why you should let me help you with this case."

He turned on her the look that made hardened criminals tremble in their chairs. "And that's exactly why I'm *not* going to let you anywhere near this case."

His glare had no effect on her whatsoever. "Then how will you ever solve it?"

"I won't solve it. Nobody will. Sarah, listen to me," he said, forgetting not to use her first name. "You told me yourself this girl was a prostitute."

"She *had been* once, but she wasn't anymore, not since she went to live at the mission!"

As if that made a difference. "Her family disowned her. They won't care that she's dead. No one will care. She'll be just one of the hundreds of people who die in this city every year without being noticed."

"I'll notice! I'll care!"

She'd claimed she was furious a few minutes ago, but she'd only been getting started then. She was really amazing when she got good and mad. "Enough to get yourself killed by asking the wrong people the wrong questions?"

"I'm not going to do that!" she insisted.

"You've done it before," he reminded her.

This time she gave him a murderous glare that almost made him smile, because it meant that for once she didn't have an answer.

"You can't just go waltzing down to Mulberry Bend and start asking people who killed this girl," he said, prepared to be reasonable now that she was silenced. "No one will trust you, so no one will tell you anything. And if you get too annoying, somebody will stick a knife into you, too. I really *will* find you dead, and if you ever put me through that again," he threatened, shaking a finger in her face, "I'll *kill* you!"

She blinked in surprise, and only when she grinned did he realize how ridiculous his threat was. Whatever ground he had gained vanished, evaporating in the blaze of her smile. "Malloy, you always amaze me."

From the corner of his eye, he saw his salvation. A Hansom cab was coming toward them. He held up a hand to flag it down.

"Where are we going?" she asked when she realized what he was doing.

"*You* are going home, where you'll be safe."

She didn't like that a bit. "You can't just let this girl's killer go free!"

Frank supposed being rich gave you a completely different way of thinking. It wasn't a very good way, either. "I told you," he said, trying to be patient when he really wanted to start shouting at her. "Nobody will care that this girl is dead."

"You mean nobody will pay a reward to find her killer," she said, knowing full well how angry this would make him. Everybody knew the police solved crimes only when a reward was involved or when someone in power demanded it. Frank hated that it was true, but it was the only way he could support his family, since no one could be expected to live on the meager salaries the police department paid.

He managed to hold his temper and say quite reasonably, "I mean nobody will give me any information, so it won't matter if there's a reward or not." If she offered to give him a reward to solve the case, he really would kill her.

Fortunately, she knew better than that. "Aren't you even going to try?" she asked, which made him even madder than if she'd offered him a reward.

"I'm going down to the mission now to tell them she's dead and find out what her last name was," he said, trying hard not to grit his teeth or sound angry. "Then I'll try to locate her family and tell them."

"But . . ." she began to protest. He held up his hand to stop her.

"I will also ask them questions and try to find out who might've killed her. My guess is they'll swear she didn't have an enemy in the world and they don't have any idea who could've done it. If I'm wrong," he continued when she would have interrupted him again, "and they tell me they think a lover killed her or some jealous wife, then I'll investigate. But don't count on it," he added.

He'd expected another argument, but she seemed pleased with this promise. "So if you get some information, you'll investigate?" she asked.

"Yes, I will." Now he *was* gritting his teeth. He couldn't help it. "Do you want me to take a blood oath or something?"

"Don't be silly," she said with one of her smiles. "Your word is good enough for me."

The cab had finally managed to pull over to the curb, and the driver was waiting for his passenger.

"Now swear to me you'll go straight home," he said as he handed her into the cab.

"Of course I will," she said, holding up her hand as if to take an oath.

Frank frowned as he gave the driver the address on Bank Street. She'd given in far too easily. She was up to something. He just hoped to God it didn't get her killed.

Sarah settled back into her seat and tried not to remember how poor Emilia had looked lying there so cold and dead in the morgue. She couldn't help thinking that she somehow could have prevented the girl's death, even though she knew that was ridiculous. She didn't even know why Emilia had been killed, so how could she have prevented it? Logic didn't prevent her from wanting to weep again, however. She couldn't explain her tears back there at the morgue, but she knew they had come partly from a sense of helplessness. No matter how hard she tried, she couldn't stop evil from triumphing. And heaven knew, she wasn't really trying very hard most of the time.

She thought of Mrs. Wells. Now *she* was trying. And she was succeeding. Sarah might not share her religious fervor, but she had to respect the woman. Look at all those young girls who were safe at the mission, probably for the first time in their lives. They were learning how to take care of themselves, earn an honest living, and have self-respect. Compared to that, Sarah had never accomplished anything worthwhile.

Oh, she knew that saving babies and their mothers from dying in childbirth was important, but what happened to them after that? Perhaps she'd saved them for a life of misery. She had never considered this possibility, and she didn't like the thought at all. Was it possible for her to do the kind of lasting good that Mrs. Wells did at the mission? She didn't know. Certainly, not many people could accomplish what Mrs. Wells had. Not many people would have had the courage and dedication to even try.

But if Sarah couldn't do that work herself, perhaps she could at least help those who did. Mrs. Wells needed volunteers and supporters. She remembered what Richard had said about his wife. Hazel Dennis had first gotten involved when a friend had been asked to make a donation to the mission. Mrs. Wells probably had to work very hard to keep contributions coming from wealthy people like the Dennises. Cultivating wealthy donors would take a lot of time and energy away from the real work she was doing. She would probably greatly appreciate some help in that area, and Sarah was certainly in a position to give it to her.

She reached up and knocked on the roof of the cab to get the driver's attention.

"Yes, miss?" he called down.

"I've changed my mind," she said. "Could you take me to West Fifty-seventh Street instead, please?"

"I sure can," he replied happily. The longer distance would mean a higher fare. Sarah sat back and began to plan what she was going to say to her mother.

Elizabeth and Felix Decker lived in a townhouse right off Fifth Avenue, not too far from Marble Row, where millionaires flaunted their wealth with marble-fronted homes. The Deckers were more modest about their wealth, but they were probably even richer than anyone on Marble Row.

The maid recognized her instantly and admitted her at once, greeting her by name. Sarah couldn't help remembering that this same girl had almost turned her away a few short months ago as unworthy to enter. Her long estrangement from her parents had made her a stranger to their household.

"Mrs. Decker is in her salon, Mrs. Brandt," the girl told her. "I'm sure she'll be glad to see you. Shall I tell her you're here?"

"I'll go with you and save you a trip," Sarah offered, certain her mother would be "at home" to her.

Her mother was writing letters at her desk, a delicately carved work of art. She looked up in surprise when the maid announced her daughter, and a smile brightened her lovely face.

"Sarah, my dear, I hope you've come to tell me what a wonderful time you had at the opera with Richard," she exclaimed, rising from her chair and hurrying over to give her daughter a kiss.

Sarah felt a twinge of guilt. She probably should have come over much sooner to give her mother a report on her first outing with the very eligible Mr. Dennis. She also felt guilty that wasn't her reason for being here today, either. Still, her mother never had to know it. "I did have a wonderful time, Mother," she said, taking a seat beside her mother on an exquisite brocaded sofa. "Do you want to hear about every thrilling aria and all the glorious costumes?"

"Of course not," her mother said. "I want to know how you and Richard got along." She folded her hands expectantly.

Sarah didn't want to disappoint her mother. Mrs. Decker had been hoping to see her daughter married to someone she considered suitable ever since the day Tom Brandt had died. Both of her daughters had married men she considered unworthy of them. That decision had cost Sarah's sister Maggie her life. Sarah's choice had given her three joyous years followed by three years of mourning after Tom's death. She couldn't blame her mother for wanting to see her settled again. Unfortunately, she'd never see her settled with Richard Dennis. Sarah couldn't bear to tell her that, however. At least not so soon.

"We got along very well," Sarah said quite truthfully. "He's a very charming man."

Mrs. Decker frowned. "You don't like him."

"I like him very much," Sarah protested, wondering how her mother could have come to such a conclusion.

*"Very charming?"* Mrs. Decker said, mocking Sarah's words. "I could say that about my footmen. In fact, I consider it a qualification of employment for them."

"What should I have said?" Sarah asked contritely.

Mrs. Decker sighed in mock dismay. "You should have said he was handsome and exciting and the most fascinating man you've ever met."

"But we hardly know each other," she protested good-naturedly.

"Which is exactly why you could have found him fascinating. Fascination seldom survives long acquaintance, as I'm sure you know."

Sarah didn't bother to hide her smile. "I'm sorry to be such a constant source of disappointment to you, Mother."

Mrs. Decker waved her disappointment away. "I'm growing used to it now, Sarah. I've despaired of ever finding a man who will suit you."

For some reason, Sarah thought of Frank Malloy. No one would consider him suitable for her, least of all Frank Malloy, but she had to admit the idea was intriguing. She didn't mention it to her mother, however.

"I'm afraid Richard isn't ready to remarry either," she confessed.

Mrs. Decker was surprised at that. "Hazel has been gone at least four years now."

"Five, I think. But he's still married to her in his mind. In fact, I don't think he would have invited me to the opera if he thought I was seriously interested in a relationship with him."

"Why else would he have invited you, then?" her mother asked in amazement.

Sarah couldn't believe how easily she had brought the subject up. "He wanted me to help him understand his wife better."

"But you didn't even know her."

"No, but I do have some understanding of the work she was doing when she died."

"*Work?*" Her mother said the word as if it were slightly distasteful.

"Yes, Hazel Dennis was helping at the Prodigal Son Mission down by Mulberry Bend in Little Italy."

Mrs. Decker absorbed this astonishing piece of information. "She hardly seemed the type, from what I remember of her. What is this place like? What kind of work do they do there?"

"They help young girls. Some of them have been abandoned by their families and others have run away from theirs because things were so bad for them there. They have no place to go and no honest way to make a living. The mission gives them a place to live and food to eat and an education. They also teach them how to operate a sewing machine and other skills they can use to get a job."

Her mother was frowning again. "How do *you* know so much about it?"

"Because Richard and I went there on Sunday afternoon for a visit."

She brightened instantly. "You went there together?"

"He asked me to accompany him. He wanted to find out why Hazel had been so interested in their work."

"That was kind of you, Sarah."

"I'm a kind person, Mother," she reminded her with a grin.

"Of course you are," Mrs. Decker said with a grin of her own. "And a lovely one."

"At any rate, Richard was pleased with what he saw at the mission, and so was I. In fact, I was just thinking on the way over here today that I'd like to do something to help them myself."

Mrs. Decker surprised her by frowning yet again. This frown looked worried. "That's an admirable sentiment, Sarah, but I must warn you, it's very difficult to compete with a ghost."

For a moment, Sarah had no idea what her mother was talking about, but then it hit her. "I have no intention of competing with Hazel Dennis," Sarah assured her.

"That's the spirit," Mrs. Decker said, making Sarah want to roll her eyes.

"I mean it, Mother," she insisted. "I'm not interested in taking Hazel's place in Richard's life."

"You would be foolish to even try."

Sarah was beginning to think her mother was deliberately misunderstanding her, but she didn't want to take the time to find out. She had a more important task to accomplish today.

"I do, however, want to help the mission, if I can."

"Are you going to offer to deliver babies for them?" her mother asked doubtfully.

Sarah almost laughed at the notion. "I think the

idea of the mission is to *prevent* them from having babies. No, I had something more practical in mind."

Her mother was an intelligent woman. She guessed instantly. "And you want me to help."

"Yes, I want you to have a party."

"For the people at the mission?" She was horrified at the very thought.

"No, for your rich friends, so we can ask them to make a donation to the mission."

Sarah didn't know what reaction she'd expected, but her mother had heard only one word in that sentence. *"We?"*

She'd said that by accident, but it had turned out to be the magic word. "Well, I haven't actually asked him, but I'd like Richard to help host the party. He already said he was going to make a donation himself, in Hazel's memory. I'm sure he wouldn't mind asking others to do the same."

"How could he possibly refuse?" her mother asked. "We'll ask *everyone* to make a donation in Hazel's memory."

Sarah could see she was already mentally composing a guest list. "How soon can you arrange it?"

"I'll have to check my calendar, but I think a week should be enough time. I'll have my secretary start making out the invitations this afternoon. As soon as I hear from you that Richard has agreed to participate," she added shrewdly.

Her mother drove a hard bargain. "I'll stop by his office on the way home and ask him."

Sarah was probably being cruel, getting her mother's hopes up like this. Still, she knew perfectly well Richard Dennis wasn't any more interested in marriage than she was. Sarah would never have to refuse a marriage proposal she hadn't received, and her mother would have a few weeks of happiness, imagining her daughter marrying her way back into Society's Four Hundred.

Frank was only too familiar with the Prodigal Son Mission. He'd watched its transformation from a rundown boardinghouse into its present incarnation when Reverend Wells first took possession of it. He'd also watched a parade of young girls going through there during the past several years. Some had gone on to find respectable jobs and even to marry. Others had escaped back into the world they'd originally fled, managing to find men to mistreat and abuse them and make their lives even more miserable than before. He'd long since ceased to wonder why some chose one path and others another.

The girl who answered his knock was Irish, all gangly limbs, frizzy red hair, and enormous eyes that stared up at him apprehensively. People always knew he was a cop, even though he dressed just like every other man in the city. Nobody liked cops, and most people feared them.

A swear word escaped her young lips before she could stop it, and she quickly covered her mouth in horror at the slip. Probably, they frowned on swearing at the mission.

"Is Mrs. Wells here?" he asked as kindly as he could, hoping to reassure her.

"She ain't done nothing. Nobody here done nothing!" she argued.

"I didn't say they did," he reminded her. "Now if you don't want to get Mrs. Wells, I guess I'll have to come in and find her myself."

That prospect frightened the girl even more. "I'll get her," she cried, but she slammed the door in his face instead of inviting him in, as she should have. The lapse in etiquette didn't bother Frank. As soon as her footsteps clattered away, he opened the door and stepped inside anyway.

The place fairly echoed with emptiness. The sparse furniture, bare wooden floors, and religious pictures made him think this was what a convent would look like. He doubted Mrs. Wells would appreciate the comparison.

He could hear the sounds of activity from upstairs, and after a few more minutes, a woman he recognized as Mrs. Wells came down the staircase. She moved slowly, her hand resting gently on the rail, her back rigidly straight, her face calmly expressionless. She was in no hurry to see him, nor was she reluctant. She had nothing to fear from the police.

"Mrs. Wells," he said, removing his bowler hat as she reached the bottom of the stairs. "I'm Detective Sergeant Frank Malloy. I'm afraid I have some bad news for you."

"And what would that be?" she asked, not at all concerned about whatever he might have to say to her.

Frank glanced up the stairs and saw several young faces peering over the railing above, straining to hear what he was saying.

"Is there someplace we can talk privately?"

"I don't pay protection money to the police," she warned him. "Our heavenly Father protects us."

Frank decided to ignore the provocation. "I have some news about one of your . . ." He gestured helplessly, not certain what to call the girls who lived here.

"Guests?" she supplied.

"Yeah, one of your *guests*," he agreed, glancing up the stairs again. More faces were staring down at them now. All sounds of activity upstairs had stopped.

She glanced up, too, and instantly the faces vanished. The sound of scurrying footsteps was followed by the slamming of a door, and all was quiet. She turned back to Frank.

"Very well," she said. "Please step into the parlor."

He followed her into a shabbily furnished room. She didn't bother to close the doors — or maybe she didn't trust him enough to close the doors. She turned to face him, neither offering him a seat nor taking one herself.

"What is it?" she asked, making it clear she still didn't think his visit was important.

"Did you have a girl named Emilia living here?"

Finally, he saw the apprehension he would have expected, although she was trying hard not to let it show. "A girl named Emilia lives here, yes," she said cautiously.

"Blond hair, brown eyes?"

"Yes," she said, clearly reluctant to admit it. "Why are you asking about Emilia? What's happened?"

"She was found dead this morning in City Hall Park."

She took a moment to absorb the shock. "That's impossible," she finally said. People always denied death at first.

"Why? Is she here now?"

Mrs. Wells's apprehension was slowly giving way

to anxiety. "No, but . . ." She glanced out the doorway, as if expecting to see the girl standing there. "She was going out this morning to look for work. She hasn't come back yet, but I expect her any moment."

"She won't be coming back, Mrs. Wells. She's dead."

She shook her head slightly in silent denial. "I can't . . . There must be some mistake."

"There isn't. She was identified at the morgue."

Mrs. Wells was beginning to look noticeably agitated. "Who could have identified her?"

"Mrs. Sarah Brandt."

"Who . . . ?" she began, but then she remembered. And frowned with what might have been disapproval. "Oh, yes, Mr. Dennis's friend."

Frank felt as if he'd been punched. *Dennis's friend!* Sarah had said she came here on Sunday. Had Dennis come with her? If so, she'd been with him on Saturday night and on Sunday, too. She'd only known him for a week! He felt something burning in his chest, as bitter as gall.

"Detective?" Mrs. Wells said sharply. "I asked you a question."

"What was it?" he asked, forcing himself to concentrate on the task at hand.

"I asked you how Mrs. Brandt came to identify Emilia's body."

"She was wearing Mrs. Brandt's clothing. I thought she might know who the girl was, so I asked her to come to the morgue."

Mrs. Wells was completely bewildered. "How did you know she was wearing Mrs. Brandt's clothing?"

"Because Mrs. Brandt is a friend of mine, too," he said with a small sense of satisfaction.

Fortunately, Elizabeth Decker had suggested Sarah telephone to make sure Richard would be in his office this afternoon. He'd planned to go out, but he changed his plans immediately when he learned Sarah needed to see him. After Sarah had luncheon with her mother, she'd been delivered to Richard's bank in the Decker family carriage, complete with its charming footmen.

Now she was being escorted directly into his private office by an obsequious little man whose plump body had been stuffed into a suit that was too small for him. When she entered his office, Richard rose from behind his desk and came out to greet her, taking her hand in both of his.

"To what do I owe this pleasure?" he asked in his very charming way as he led her to one of the chairs in front of his desk. Instead of returning to his place behind it, he sat in the other chair beside her. She had his full attention.

"I'm afraid our visit to the mission on Sunday had a profound effect on me," she began, debating whether to tell him about Emilia's murder. No use in starting out on such a tragic topic. She'd wait and see if she could work it naturally into her explanation.

"What kind of an effect?" he asked, his brow furrowing with concern.

"I've had a . . . a reawakening, I suppose you'd call it. I suddenly feel as if my life doesn't have much meaning, and that I'm not doing anything important."

"What nonsense," he said gallantly. "Your work must be very important."

She chose not to notice that he really wasn't certain it was. "You're right, of course. I do save lives," she added, in case he hadn't realized it. "But Mrs. Wells *changes* lives. I don't think I could do the kind of work she does, but I could help her. I've asked my mother if she'd give a party and ask her friends to make a donation to the mission . . . in Hazel's memory."

She'd touched him deeply. For a moment, he couldn't speak. "Sarah," he finally said. "I think that's the kindest thing anyone has ever done for me."

"I'm not being kind, Richard," she assured him. "I'm being selfish. I want to feel better about myself by doing something good."

"I'm sure that's the basic motivation for all charitable acts," he said with an understanding smile.

"Perhaps it is. I hope it doesn't matter what the motivation is, so long as the act itself is good," she added.

"I'm sure you're right."

"Would you come to the party?" she asked.

He seemed surprised. "Of course. I mean, I assumed you wouldn't have told me about it if you weren't going to invite me."

Had he forgotten that he blamed the people at the mission for giving Hazel her fatal illness? If so, Sarah wasn't going to remind him. "We want to do more than simply invite you. We were hoping you'd agree to help host. Perhaps you could also speak about Hazel's work at the mission."

"I don't know what I could say, but I'll be happy to play host. I've been to a number of this type of event. We should ask Mrs. Wells to come and speak about her work. She's the one who knows the most."

"I hadn't thought of that. What a good idea."

"She'll probably also bring a couple of the girls along, to show the guests some examples of her success."

Sarah almost winced when she thought of Emilia. "You haven't asked me what inspired my sudden desire to help the mission."

"I assumed it was a result of our visit there."

Sarah took a deep breath and let it out with a sigh. "I wish that were all. I had a very unpleasant experience today. Do you remember that girl Emilia whom we met at the mission?"

He frowned in concentration. "I'm afraid I don't remember any of the girls in particular."

"She was the one who answered the door. Mrs. Wells said she'd been seduced by a man who refused to marry her and her family had disowned her."

Plainly, he hadn't seen any reason to remember the incident. "Has she approached you for help?"

"No, not exactly. She was found dead in City Hall Park this morning."

"*Dead?*" he echoed in surprise. "A young girl like that? What happened?"

"She was murdered."

An expression of distaste crossed his handsome face. "How unfortunate. But I suppose you can't be too surprised with that kind of girl."

Sarah wanted to demand to know what he meant by "that kind of girl," but she refrained. She had little hope of changing Richard Dennis's prejudices. She'd settle for getting his help in changing other people's lives. "She was wearing my clothes when she died."

"*Your* clothes?" he echoed, obviously confused.

"The clothes I donated to the mission on Sunday. That made me think, 'There but for the grace of God go I.' I don't want any other girls to die like that."

He nodded, his expression grave with understanding, although Sarah suspected he couldn't even begin to understand. "Certainly not. And don't worry, I'll do everything I can to help. Would your mother like for me to give her a list of Hazel's particular friends?"

"I'm sure she'd appreciate that. I can't thank you enough for helping with this."

"I'm glad to do it, but I'm afraid I will have to have a favor in return," he added with a smile.

"What kind of favor?" she asked, intrigued.

"Some friends of mine are giving a party on Halloween. I was hoping you would accompany me."

Sarah's mother would be so pleased. "Of course," she said.

# 6

Sarah thought enough time had passed since Malloy had put her into the Hansom cab. He would have long since been to the mission and gone, so it was now safe for her to go there herself and speak with Mrs. Wells about her plans. If she also happened to learn more about Emilia while she was there, she'd certainly be happy to share that information with Detective Sergeant Frank Malloy.

The girl who opened the door to her had red hair and freckles, and she looked at Sarah suspiciously. News of Emilia's death would certainly have upset everyone in the house and made them wary. Sarah asked to speak with Mrs. Wells and was admitted and instructed to wait in the parlor.

Mrs. Wells appeared a few minutes later. Her expression was somber, her smile of greeting sad. "Mrs. Brandt," she said. "How good of you to come. Won't you sit down?" She directed Sarah to the horsehair sofa and took a seat beside her, her back still rigidly straight, her hands folded tightly in her lap. Like most women, she had been taught to put on a good face in public, no matter what her private pain might be.

"I'm terribly sorry about Emilia," Sarah said.

"So are we," Mrs. Wells said. "She had struggled for a long time against the forces of evil. At least we can take comfort that she is at peace now."

Sarah thought that an odd thing to say about someone so young and healthy as Emilia had been, but she knew her view of life and death was different from Mrs. Wells's.

"I was surprised," Mrs. Wells continued, not waiting for Sarah to respond, "that you had been asked to identify Emilia's body."

Sarah heard the unspoken question. She wondered how Malloy had explained it to her. "Detective Sergeant Malloy recognized the hat Emilia was wearing as one he'd seen me wear."

"He must know you very well," Mrs. Wells observed. "Few men would remember a lady's hat."

Sarah wasn't sure if she heard a note of disapproval in Mrs. Wells's voice or not. Few people would think it proper for her to be on intimate terms with a policeman, since the police were considered as corrupt as the criminals they arrested. She reminded herself that her own mother disapproved of her acquaintance with Malloy. "I have been able to assist Mr. Malloy on several of his cases — cases that involved people with whom I was acquainted," she added when Mrs. Wells's eyebrows rose a notch.

Her eyebrows rose even higher, but she said, "I suppose as a midwife, you must encounter all sorts of people." Obviously, she wouldn't have expected Sarah to meet people who got themselves murdered in the ordinary course of her life.

"Just as you do, in *your* work," Sarah pointed out.

"I'm sorry if I seem overly curious about your personal affairs, Mrs. Brandt, but I don't believe I've ever known the police to be particularly vigilant about solving crimes involving people like Emilia. But Mr. Malloy has made an extraordinary effort, and I was wondering why."

Sarah couldn't take offense at that. Mrs. Wells was absolutely correct. "You'll be happy to know that Mr. Malloy is unusually conscientious. He has also promised to do everything he can to find out who killed Emilia so brutally and bring her killer to justice."

The blood seemed to drain from the other woman's face, and she pressed a handkerchief to her lips. Sarah instantly regretted reminding her so coldly of Emilia's death.

"Are you ill?" Sarah asked in concern, leaning forward and ready to catch her if she fainted.

"No, I'm fine," she said, a little weakly. She drew a deep breath and forced herself to look up at Sarah as if to prove her assessment of her own condition. "That poor, dear girl. It's just been very difficult . . ."

"I'm sure it has. The other girls must be terribly upset."

"I've tried to set a good example, of course," Mrs. Wells explained. "We must not grieve for those who have gone to be with the Lord. They are much happier than we can ever imagine."

Sarah supposed this was a good way to deal with grief. She liked to think of Tom as living happily in the hereafter. It had never been enough to make her content to live without him, however. "I suppose Emilia had a very unhappy life before she came here," she ventured, hoping to allow Mrs. Wells an opportunity to tell her about the girl in whom she had invested so much effort. As Sarah knew, talking about the deceased helped ease the pain of loss. Not to mention, she might reveal some useful information in the process.

"Her family was no worse than most, I suppose," Mrs. Wells said, not looking at Sarah. She seemed to be speaking more to herself, lost in her own memories. "The Italians are of an emotional temperament, as I'm sure you know. Emilia was a sensitive girl. She suffered more than most under her parents' inability to control themselves. I'm afraid that made her easy prey for the wrong kind of man."

"You mentioned that she had been seduced by a man who wouldn't marry her," Sarah reminded her.

"Emilia wasn't his first conquest, I'm afraid. He promised her marriage, but he had no intention of keeping that promise. Why should he when Emilia had already granted him every privilege of marriage without it?"

Sarah had heard this same story many times, innocent girls betrayed by faithless lovers.

"How did she come to the mission?" Sarah asked.

Mrs. Wells sighed. "The first time she was desperate. When her lover refused to marry her, she had enough self-respect left to leave him, but her parents refused to take her back. She'd disgraced them, they said. As if people like that had any honor to begin with."

Her contempt was probably well deserved, Sarah

thought. People who turned a child away were despicable. "So she came to the mission?" Sarah guessed.

"Not then," Mrs. Wells said with a sigh. "She allowed herself to be deceived by yet another man who was even worse than the first one. This one forced her to . . . to sell herself in the streets."

Sarah winced. Too many girls ended up in this situation, never to escape. "How did she manage to get away from him?"

"She became ill, and he threw her out. She wandered the streets and ended up on our doorstep."

"She was fortunate."

Mrs. Wells gave her a sad smile. "I only wish she had realized it. As soon as she was well, she left us."

"She went back to her pimp?" Sarah asked in amazement.

"At least it wasn't that bad," Mrs. Wells said. "She returned to the man who had originally seduced her. She still loved him, and she was grateful he still wanted her after what she'd done."

"Did he promise to marry her this time?"

Mrs. Wells shook her head. "She didn't care. She just wanted someone to love her, she said. And someone who wouldn't make her walk the streets again."

Sarah's heart ached for a girl so desperate for love that she would believe any lie and endure any humiliation. "What brought her back to the mission?"

"She found herself with child. She begged her lover to marry her, for the sake of the baby, but he refused. He said he couldn't even be sure the child was his. Then he beat her until she lost the baby."

Sarah couldn't hold back a low moan. She could feel Emilia's pain and the despair she must have endured after losing her baby. "So that brought her back here," she guessed.

"I'm afraid so. God works in mysterious ways, Mrs. Brandt, and all things work together for good. We cannot question why evil things happen if they lead us to Him."

Sarah had long since stopped trying to understand why evil things happened. "She seemed very happy when I saw her on Sunday."

"She was very pleased when I gave her the clothing you brought. She said that now she would look like a lady." Mrs. Wells smiled sadly at the memory. "She was going to find work today."

Sarah could just imagine how excited the girl must have been, setting out in her "new" outfit to start a new life. What had taken her to the park this morning, instead, and who had killed her?

"Do you know where she was going?"

"She was going to look for a job in one of the factories nearby, making clothes. She had developed into a fine seamstress."

"Why would she have been down by City Hall?"

"I . . . I can't imagine," she said. "I don't want to believe she lied about where she was going." Plainly, the thought pained her.

"Could she have gone to meet someone?" Sarah asked.

Mrs. Wells winced slightly. "Your friend, Mr. Malloy, asked me the same thing," she said. "I told him I didn't know. I'm sure if Emilia was meeting a lover, she wouldn't have let anyone here know it."

That did seem reasonable. "I guess you couldn't blame her if she wanted someone she knew to see her all dressed up," Sarah said.

Mrs. Wells lowered her gaze, studying her folded hands for a long moment. "She did say . . ." she began, then caught herself.

"What did she say?" Sarah asked. "It might be a clue to who killed her."

Plainly, Mrs. Wells did not want to tell her. "One of the girls told me . . . You must understand, I'm sure Emilia was just talking when she said it."

Sarah nodded encouragingly.

"She said she wished Ugo could see her. That is the man who beat her."

Sarah tried not to let her excitement show. This could be a clue as to who killed Emilia, but she didn't want to alarm Mrs. Wells or frighten her. "It would be perfectly natural for her to want him see how beautiful she is and to regret losing her," she said.

" 'Favor is deceitful and beauty is vain,' " she quoted with a hint of despair in her voice. "In Emilia's case, I'm afraid it may also have killed her."

"Do you think that's what she did? Meet her lover to let him see what he'd lost or even to make him want to take her back?"

"It's possible. Heaven knows, I've seen girls do things even more foolish. And this Ugo *is* prone to violence, as he proved before."

"Did you tell this to Mr. Malloy?" Sarah asked.

Mrs. Wells shook her head. "I'm afraid I didn't think of it. He asked me the name of her family, of course. And I also told him her lover was named Ugo. I never heard his last name."

"I'm sure her family will know it," Sarah said. "Malloy should know that she might have gone to meet him this morning, though."

"Would you have the opportunity to tell him?"

Mrs. Wells asked. "I'm afraid I'd rather not discuss it any further. It's rather painful, and I . . . Well, I'd really rather not deal with the police anymore."

"Of course. I'll be glad to tell him," Sarah said. No one ever wanted to deal with the police.

"Thank you, Mrs. Brandt," she said, preparing to rise. Sarah knew this was a signal their visit was over, but Sarah hadn't yet told her why she'd really come.

"Mrs. Wells, I was wondering if you would allow me and Mr. Dennis to hold a party to raise money on behalf of the mission."

Mrs. Wells stared at her with that intense gaze she had noticed on her previous visit, as if she were trying to look into Sarah's soul and read what was written there. "That would be very kind of you," she said, her voice carefully neutral. She wouldn't want to appear too eager, of course. That would make her look greedy.

"My parents would actually host the party, at their home. My father is Felix Decker," she added, knowing this would overcome Mrs. Wells's wariness.

As self-contained as she usually was, Mrs. Wells could not conceal her surprise. She had obviously underestimated Sarah Brandt. "Mrs. Brandt, I . . . We would be honored."

"Mr. Dennis suggested that perhaps you would like to attend the party yourself and speak about the work you are doing here. He thought it might also help if you brought a few of the girls with you, to actually show the success you're having."

"I'm sure we can do whatever you think would be most appropriate. We never have enough of anything here at the mission. Raising funds is a constant struggle."

"I was certain that was true," Sarah said. "Which is why I want to help. I'd like to think that Emilia's death can bring some good."

Mrs. Wells smiled sadly. "I'd like to think that, too, Mrs. Brandt."

When Emilia Donato left home, she hadn't gone too far, Frank observed. Her parents lived only a few blocks from the mission, where Mulberry Street made a sharp turn between Park and Bayard Streets. Known as the Bend, the area had long been the location of the most notorious slums in the city. A couple decades earlier, it had been the juncture of five streets. The Five Points area had been so dangerous that even the police never went there except in large groups. Five Points crime had been cleaned up, but the poverty and squalor remained.

Thousands of Jewish and Italian immigrants were now crammed into crumbling tenements and rotting houses left over from the original Dutch settlers. The city had recently decided to tear down the worst of them and build a park on the west side of Mulberry Street, but the work was just beginning. The people who lived here now were still trapped in their poverty and misery, and in addition to the criminals that plagued the entire city, they were also terrorized by the more subtle members of the Black Hand.

Frank had waited until evening to call on the Donato family, figuring the father and brother were more likely to be home at that time of day. Frank was assuming, of course, that they had jobs. From the way Mrs. Wells had spoken of them, he would not have been surprised to find them lying in a drunken stupor in their flat at nine o'clock in the morning.

This part of the Bend was inhabited primarily by Italian immigrants, most of them recent arrivals. The people were dressed in bright colors, and everyone spoke in Italian. Except for the buildings surrounding it, the street might have been in any village in Italy. Peddlers' carts lined both curbs, and even at this hour, transactions were taking place with much shouting and gesturing as housewives negotiated for the ingredients of their evening meals. Even the doorways of the buildings had been commandeered for commerce. Boards were stretched across the openings and merchandise displayed upon them. Each merchant stood inside the tiny lobby of the building, as if it were his shop, and conducted his business on this makeshift counter. Tenants of the buildings had broken holes in the back walls of the lobbies, and they used those improvised entrances so as not to disturb the transactions taking place in the official doorways.

Everyone on the streets looked suspiciously at an Irish policeman. Conversation died as Frank approached each group and picked up again noisily as soon as he was past. Their fear and distrust were like a miasma through which he walked until he reached the alley that led to the Donatos' tenement.

Most of the windows in the surrounding buildings were open, even though the day was cool and getting colder, and the residents who weren't outside were hanging out of the windows, conversing with those below. The Italians liked the outdoors, even if that meant city streets without a tree or a blade of grass for miles. They'd appreciate the park, when it was finally built . . . if they managed to find cheap lodging nearby after these buildings were torn down.

Frank passed an old hag selling stale bread from a

sack made of filthy bed ticking and found his way into one of the many twisting alleys in the neighborhood to the rear tenement where Mrs. Wells had said the Donato family lived.

A woman had just begun climbing the stairs in the pitch-dark hallway when Frank entered. A red bandanna covered her hair, and the darkness shadowed her face, but her weary step and hunched shoulders told of years of suffering. She carried a market basket over one arm.

"Donato?" Frank called, hoping for some direction to the proper flat.

She looked up in surprise.

"Do you know where the Donatos live?" he asked, hoping she spoke some English.

"What you want?" she asked suspiciously.

"I want to see them. Which flat is theirs?"

"We no do nothing wrong," the woman said, the fear thick in her voice.

"Are you Mrs. Donato?" he asked, coming closer.

She cringed away. "We no do nothing wrong," she insisted.

"I need to talk to you, about your daughter Emilia."

"*Emilia!*" she echoed scornfully. "I have no daughter. Go away."

She certainly didn't have a daughter any longer, but Frank didn't want to break the news to her in the hallway, no matter how angry she might be with the girl.

"Is your husband at home?" Frank asked.

Now that his eyes were used to the darkness, he could make out her features more clearly. She wasn't as old as her plodding gait had suggested, but the years hadn't been kind to her. "He no here," she claimed almost desperately. "Come back later."

"Maybe I'll just wait here for him," Frank suggested. "Or go get the landlord to help me find him."

This put the fear of God into her. Landlords didn't like tenants who brought the police snooping around. "What you want?"

"I told you, I want to talk to you about your daughter Emilia," he said patiently. His experience had been that most of the Italians avoided trouble whenever possible and were terrified of dealing with the police. Apparently, law enforcement in their native country was even more corrupt than it was in New York City. "I won't keep you very long, but it's not something I want to talk about here," he added meaningfully.

She hated him. He could see it in her eyes, along with the fear. But she said, "Come," and started up the stairs again. She was a short woman, but not small. Her breasts and hips were full and round. They were sagging now, but she'd probably had an appealing figure as a young girl, before the years and childbirth had taken their toll.

Fortunately, the Donato flat was only on the third floor in this five-floor walk-up. Frank found it difficult to question someone when he was completely winded.

The Donato flat was exactly like a million others in the city. A few pieces of furniture might have been carried from the old country, but the rest had been purchased here, as cheaply as possible, or scrounged from the trash heaps. Brightly colored curtains hung from the front window, and scarves were draped here and there to brighten up the place, but nothing could help the back rooms where sunlight never reached.

The door opened into the kitchen of the flat, and

Mrs. Donato set her basket on the table, which was no more than planks laid over some wooden crates. Frank saw that tonight's dinner would be some dried-up potatoes and turnips. What appeared to be dead weeds would probably become a salad. Beneath the recently purchased food, he could see a few paper flowers, and the kitchen table held the makings for more. Probably the woman made and sold them for extra money, as many wives in the tenements did.

"Tell me quick, before Antonio come home," she advised him. "He want to help if she in trouble, so I no tell. We no help her. I have no daughter."

Frank was beginning to wonder if that could be true. He could see now that her hair beneath the scarf was black, only slightly tinged with gray, and her complexion was the dark olive he would have expected. He wondered if Mr. Donato was blond. Sarah had said that Emilia must be from Northern Italy because of her blond hair, but her mother certainly wasn't. "Your daughter was found dead this morning," he said baldly, since she'd already informed him she didn't care about the girl.

"Dead?" she repeated as if she wasn't sure what the word meant. *"Guasto?"*

"Yeah, *guasto*," he replied, nodding so she'd understand.

"Emilia?" Was she trying to deny it, as most mothers would, or was she just trying to make sure?

"She had yellow hair," Frank said. "She'd been living at the mission. She had a lover named Ugo."

*"Sì,* Emilia," she confirmed with a sigh, sinking down into one of the mismatched chairs. She set her elbow on the table and rested her forehead on her clenched fist.

"I'm sorry," Frank said, interpreting the gesture as grief.

But when she looked up, her dark eyes were blazing with fury. "She trouble, all a time, trouble. Is good she dead. No more trouble."

Frank had seen reactions like this before, but usually it was because the deceased was a son who'd gone bad. Rarely did a mother react this way to the death of a daughter. Of course, he'd never had to inform a prostitute's mother that she was dead. With women like that, nobody even knew who their mothers were.

Frank heard the sound of footsteps climbing the stairs. It could have been anyone, but Mrs. Donato must have recognized them. She jumped to her feet. "You go now," she said urgently. "I have no daughter. You go."

But Frank hadn't quite finished his business here. He wanted to get a look at Emilia's father, just to satisfy his curiosity. He stepped out onto the landing and waited. Mrs. Donato hovered anxiously in the doorway. Frank figured her husband might not be as glad as she was that the girl was dead. He wondered why.

The man who emerged from the gloom of the stairway was a little shorter than average height, his body stocky and muscular from heavy labor. His swarthy face had been darkened even further by the sun, and beneath his workman's cap, his hair was as black as his wife's. He stopped in alarm when he saw Frank standing there and glanced at his wife with a silent question.

"*Polizia,*" she said as a warning. "*È venuta dirci che Emilia fosse guasto.*"

Frank wasn't certain exactly what she'd said but recognized enough words to know she'd warned him

Frank was from the police and Emilia was dead. The man showed the shock his wife had not.

"Emilia?" He didn't want to believe it, and he looked to Frank for confirmation.

"Someone stabbed her to death this morning in City Hall Park," he said.

*"No,"* he said desperately. "No true!"

"I'm afraid it is. Someone who knows her already identified the body."

"Who?" he challenged.

Sarah's name would mean nothing to them. "A lady who met her at the mission."

*"Mission,"* Mrs. Donato repeated and spat on the floor to show her contempt. Donato's shoulders sank in defeat, and he looked as if he might pass out.

This wasn't going the way Frank had expected. The man of the house was shocked senseless and his wife was spitting on the floor. "Sit down, Mr. Donato," he tried, guiding the man into the flat and pulling out a chair for him. He sank down as his wife had, but he was suffering from grief, or something very like it. Frank still wasn't sure.

Donato rubbed a calloused hand over his face. When he looked up, Frank saw strong emotions but none he could identify. "You say she stab?"

"Probably with a stiletto," Frank said, watching for a reaction.

Donato frowned, and his wife started muttering invectives in Italian.

"Do you know anyone who might have wanted to kill Emilia?" Frank asked.

"We no see her, long time," Mrs. Donato said firmly.

"What about her brother? Has he seen her?"

"No," Mrs. Donato said firmly. Her husband said nothing.

"Maybe I should ask him myself. When will he be home?"

She crossed her arms beneath her heavy breasts and just glared at him.

"What about Ugo?" Frank asked casually. "You wouldn't mind if he went to jail, would you?"

Frank expected Mrs. Donato to spit on the floor again, but she just continued to glare at him furiously. He looked down at Donato and gave the leg of his chair a slight nudge.

Donato made a squeak of surprise and looked up, terrified.

"What's this Ugo's last name and where does he live?" Frank asked.

"Ianuzzi," Mrs. Donato hastily offered and added an address farther down Mulberry Street. "He bad," she added helpfully. "He kill sure."

"Was he angry at Emilia for leaving him?" Frank tried.

"*Si*, he hate Emilia. He kill, you see." She was much too certain, as if she were trying to convince herself, too.

Frank looked at Donato. He wasn't saying anything, just staring at the table. Frank would have to catch him without his wife. He'd need to see the son, too. They had no intention of telling the police anything. They thought they were well rid of Emilia and her "trouble," and they weren't going to let any other family member get dragged down with her.

"I'll be back," he warned them and took his leave. Making his way carefully down the dark stairwell, he silently cursed Sarah Brandt. Only she could have compelled him to make such a ridiculous promise. No one was going to be able to find Emilia's killer. Not only didn't these people speak English, they were too terrified to tell the truth to the police. They'd also lie to protect each other, even if they were innocent.

He could probably beat a confession out of someone, but he made a point of saving that tactic for people he knew were guilty. In this case, he'd be lucky to find someone who even knew she'd be in the park this morning. On the other hand, she *must* have been killed by someone she knew. She'd had nothing of value, so she hadn't been robbed, and she hadn't been molested, either. Someone who had wanted her dead and knew exactly what he was doing had stabbed her quickly and neatly and walked calmly away, leaving her to fall to the ground and die.

How many enemies so cold-blooded could a girl like that have? And although she'd obviously had at least one, how on earth was Frank ever going to find him when her own mother thought he'd done them a favor?

Sarah could tell by the way Frank Malloy was pounding on her door the next morning that he hadn't liked getting a message from her at Police Headquarters. She opened the door and said, "My only other choice was to go by your flat and leave a message with your mother," before he could even open his mouth.

Whatever angry words he'd been about to say died on his lips, but his glare was still fierce. "At least my mother wouldn't have laughed," he informed her grimly.

She could only imagine how much teasing he endured each time she contacted him there. "I'm sorry, Malloy, but I didn't know how else to get you over here. You made it very clear you didn't want me to get involved in the case, so I knew you weren't going to drop by to consult with me." She stepped back and allowed him to enter.

He pulled off his hat and hung it up without waiting for an invitation to stay. "Don't think for a minute that I'm here to *consult* you," he warned. "You aren't getting involved in this, and that's final."

"Of course," she agreed cheerfully. "I'm sure you'll find Emilia's killer all by yourself in a day or two, so I won't even have time to get involved. I just wanted you to know one thing that Mrs. Wells forgot to tell you."

This time he looked so angry that Sarah began to feel a little uneasy.

"When did you see Mrs. Wells?" he asked her in a voice that raised the hair on her arms.

"I went to see her yesterday afternoon," she said, refusing to be cowed. "I had to tell her that my mother offered to hold a party to raise funds for the mission."

He needed a minute to absorb this information. "Your *mother*?" he repeated incredulously. "What does you mother have to do with this?"

"Nothing at all. I just thought I'd like to do something to help Mrs. Wells with her work at the mission. Places like that always need money, and my mother knows lots of rich people."

"Does you mother know she's giving a party for the mission?" he asked suspiciously.

"Of course she does!" Sarah replied huffily. "She was only too happy to do it."

"What about Richard Dennis?"

"What about him?"

"Does he know about this party, too?"

Sarah knew Malloy had no love for Richard Dennis, but the expression in his voice when he said the man's name went far beyond simple dislike. She remembered her suspicion that Malloy was jealous of Richard, but she didn't dwell on it. She didn't need to, because now she was certain of it. "Mr. Dennis's wife worked as a volunteer at the mission before her death. He is also very interested in helping them."

"Was he with you on Sunday when you visited the mission?"

He was acting as if he had a right to question her like this! She could, of course, point out that it was none of his business, but she said, "Mr. Dennis asked me to accompany him so he could see what kind of work they do there."

She gave him a moment to digest this, but before he could come up with another intrusive question, she said, "Would you like some coffee?" Without waiting for his answer, she turned and walked off toward the kitchen, perfectly confident that he would follow.

He did.

"Have a seat," she offered, busying herself with finding some cups. The pot was still warm from breakfast, so she poured them each a cup and set them on the kitchen table. Only then did he deign to sit, and once again she spoke before he could.

"Mrs. Wells told me that Emilia was very proud of her new outfit. The one I'd donated to the mission," she added, knowing full well he already knew which outfit Emilia had been wearing. "One of the other girls heard Emilia say that she wished Ugo could see her. Ugo was her lover, the one who beat her and threw her out."

"I know who he is," he snapped.

"Have you talked to him already?" she asked.

"He wasn't home when I called," Malloy said sourly.

"That's good. You probably needed to know this information before you question him."

"*What* information?"

"That Emilia was thinking about showing Ugo how beautiful she looked," Sarah said, amazed he couldn't figure that out. "It's a normal, feminine reaction. She's feeling confident and irresistible, so she seeks out the man who rejected her."

"Why? So he'll take her back and beat her up again?"

He really was in a bad mood. She couldn't help wondering how much of it was due to Richard Dennis. "I'm sure she wasn't thinking about him beating her up. She was probably thinking about him falling in love with her and *wanting* her back. Then she could reject him and have her revenge."

"Italians get real excited over revenge," he observed, taking a sip of his coffee.

"I don't think you're taking this seriously, Malloy."

"Okay, let's think about this seriously," he suggested. "The girl gets all dressed up, looks in the mirror, and decides she wants her old lover to see her and regret throwing her out. Even though she hasn't seen him in months, she goes straight down to City Hall Park, where she meets up with him. They have a fight, he pulls out a stiletto and shoves it in her neck.

Then he walks away. Is that about how you figured it happened?"

When he said it like that, it didn't sound very convincing, but Sarah wasn't going to give in without a fight. "I hadn't thought about it. Maybe she'd seen him around before that day. Or maybe someone had told her he'd be in the park that morning. She'd probably known about the clothes since Sunday, when I dropped them off. Why did she wait to go out looking for work? Maybe she'd arranged to meet him that morning and only told Mrs. Wells she'd be looking for work so she wouldn't get suspicious."

There, that was plausible! She watched him drinking his coffee and trying to figure out what was wrong with her theory. "Okay, then why did he kill her? And why did he kill her *like that*?"

A very good question. "He . . . She made him angry," Sarah improvised.

"Why didn't he just walk away then? Or hit her and walk away?"

"He didn't want to cause a scene or draw attention to himself. The park is a busy place."

"Not that busy. A girl got killed without anybody noticing," he reminded her.

"Which is why he stabbed her instead of hitting her."

"Yeah, he killed her so he wouldn't draw attention to himself by slapping her. That makes sense." Sarah glared at him but he ignored it. "So why did he stab her there?"

"There? You mean in the park?" she asked in confusion.

"No, in the neck. And by the way, Dr. Haynes, the coroner, agreed with you. The girl was killed by being stabbed the way you thought. But why there? I've seen lots of people get stabbed in lots of places, but never in the back of the neck."

Sarah hadn't thought about this aspect of the case. "That is strange. Whoever stabbed her must have known it would kill her."

"How many people would know a thing like that? Would you?"

"I . . . I knew it when I saw where she'd been stabbed, or at least I knew a wound there could have damaged the brain. But I don't think I ever would have thought of it as a way to kill someone."

"Would a doctor know it?"

Sarah shook her head. "He'd know how dangerous it is to injure the brain, but I can't imagine *anyone* choosing it as a method of murder. In any case, it couldn't have been a crime of passion. Whoever did it had planned it." Then she thought of something else. "Maybe this is a traditional way the Black Hand kills people!"

"They usually like to kill people in very dramatic ways — like blowing up their store or something. They only kill as a last resort. You can't collect money from a dead man, so they do it to make an example, to scare everybody else into submission."

"But don't they assassinate people, too? This could be one of those things they brought over with them from the Old Country."

He shrugged. Sarah figured he knew she was right but couldn't bear to agree with her. "What else did you find out from Mrs. Wells that I didn't?" he asked, without much apparent interest.

"I'm not sure. Did she tell you Emilia had a pimp?"

He frowned. Malloy wouldn't approve of a lady knowing about pimps. "She claimed she didn't know his name."

"Did you ask her parents? Maybe they know."

"The subject didn't come up. What color hair do your parents have?" he asked suddenly.

Sarah stared at him in surprise. What did that have to do with anything? "My mother's is blond, like mine. My father's is brown."

"Emilia's parents both have black hair."

Sarah needed a moment to recognize the significance of this. "And hers was blond. That's unusual, but not unheard of, I suspect."

"I didn't see any other blond girls in that neighborhood. Everybody is from Southern Italy, like the Donatos. They're all dark."

"What are you saying?"

"I'm not saying anything. I'm just telling you what I saw."

Sarah considered this information. "Do you think Emilia wasn't really their daughter?"

"The old woman — her mother — kept saying she didn't have a daughter."

"Are you sure you were talking to the right people?"

"Oh, yeah, they were her family. The father acted the way he should have, shocked and sad. The mother was just mad. She hated the girl. Sounded like she'd disowned her. When she first saw me, she thought Emilia was just in trouble with the police, and she didn't want me to tell her husband because he'd help her."

"That's strange," Sarah mused. "Usually, it's the mother who tries to protect the child, and the father who gets angry and wants to disown her. Does Emilia have sisters?"

"Just a brother, according to Mrs. Wells. He wasn't home."

"Is he older or younger?"

"I don't know yet. Look," he said, growing solemn and setting his coffee cup down firmly, "they aren't going to let me spend much time on this. I can only give it another day or two, not even that long if somebody upstairs realizes nobody cares about this girl."

"Then you'll need my help," Sarah said, certain that's what he was getting at.

"No," he said impatiently, "you don't understand. I'll question this Ugo and try to find the pimp and her brother. After that, if I haven't found out what happened, I'll have to close the case. Nobody will ever find out who killed her."

"But you can't —"

"Yes, I can," he corrected her firmly. "You are not going down to Mulberry Bend and start asking questions about the Black Hand. This isn't like the other cases you were involved in. These aren't respectable killers who made a bad mistake. These people are pure evil. I don't want to see *your* body on a slab in the morgue. Do you understand?"

She'd never seen anyone look so angry and so vulnerable at the same time. She swallowed. "Yes, I understand."

# 7

SARAH SHIFTED THE BASKET FROM HER LEFT ARM TO her right. She'd been a little overgenerous in filling it, and now she was paying the price. Not only was the basket heavy, but carrying it along crowded sidewalks was difficult. She kept bumping people with it, earning irritated looks and even more irritated curses as she made her way down Mulberry Street.

When Mrs. Wells had described where Emilia's family lived, Sarah had immediately recognized the area. She'd delivered several babies in these tenements. Few of those babies lived to celebrate their first birthdays, but at least they'd arrived alive and well into the world.

The fall weather was holding, and today was even warmer than yesterday, with the sun shining brightly. All the residents of Mulberry Bend seemed to be out in the street, standing on their fire escapes or leaning out their windows, shouting back and forth to each other. Women of every age sat lined up on the curbs and stoops, some nursing babies, some screaming at children who had wandered too far away, others just talking and gossiping.

Sarah's basket bumped a young mother carrying an infant in a sling. "Excuse me," she apologized.

The woman smiled. "*Signora* Brandt?" she asked.

Sarah looked more closely. "Maria?" Sarah had delivered the baby who slept so peacefully at his mother's breast. "How is your baby doing?"

Maria was carrying some vegetables in her apron, but using her free hand, she obligingly shifted the fabric of the sling to reveal the child. He looked healthy and fat.

"*Buono,*" Sarah said with an approving smile, using one of her few Italian words. She stroked the baby's thick, dark curls.

"*Sì, è bello,*" Maria agreed, smiling back. "He is fat like pig!"

"That proves your milk is good," Sarah said. "You're a good mother."

Maria beamed with pride. "You here . . . more baby?" she asked.

"No, I'm visiting the Donato family. Do you know them?"

Maria nodded, and her smile faded. "I know Emilia, before she go away."

"Have you heard what happened to her?"

Maria shook her head warily.

"Someone murdered her."

Maria's eyes widened in surprise. She crossed herself quickly and murmured what might have been a prayer or a blessing.

"I'm sorry," Sarah said. "Were you good friends?"

Maria shrugged one shoulder. "I know her. That is all. Who kill her? Lucca?"

"Who is Lucca?" Sarah asked, trying not to sound too eager.

Maria glanced around nervously, afraid someone would overhear. "He bad man," she said.

Sarah knew there had been two bad men in Emilia's life. One of them had been named Ugo. "Was he her pimp?" Sarah whispered, wondering how she would explain this if Maria wasn't familiar with the word.

Maria's dark eyes grew wide again. Sarah supposed she was surprised Sarah knew the word. "*Sì*," she said, nodding vigorously. "Very bad man."

"Do you know his last name?"

She shook her head. "He just Lucca. *Very bad man*," she repeated firmly, as if afraid Sarah hadn't quite understood.

"Thank you, Maria. I'll be careful."

"*Sì*, careful," Maria agreed. "*Molta attenta*."

Sarah smiled to reassure the girl. "Could you show me the alley where the Donatos live? I brought them a basket of food from the mission."

Maria didn't smile back. "*Signora* Donato, she not be sad Emilia dead," she warned.

Sarah was actually counting on that. She hoped the woman's anger at her dead daughter would loosen her tongue. "I know."

Maria studied her face for a moment, making sure Sarah wasn't going to waiver in her mission of mercy, before saying, "Come, I show you."

"Do you know Emilia's brother, too?" Sarah asked as Maria fell in beside her.

"*Sì*, Georgio. He play . . . organ?" She wasn't sure she'd chosen the correct word.

For a moment Sarah pictured a man in a tuxedo playing a pipe organ in an enormous cathedral. Then she noticed Maria moving her hand in a cranking motion. "He's an organ grinder," she guessed.

"*Sì*." Maria was pleased she had made Sarah understand. "He . . . no foot," she said, gesturing vaguely toward the ground.

"He lost his foot?" This would explain his organ grinding. He wouldn't be able to hold a regular laboring job.

"No, he . . . born, no foot."

Sarah nodded her understanding. She thought of Brian Malloy's misshapen foot and wondered if Malloy knew how lucky his son had been, even in his misfortune. At least Georgio Donato had managed to find a profession of sorts, even if it was nothing more than glorified begging.

"Does he play around here?" Sarah asked.

Maria grinned at Sarah's naiveté. "No, he play Macy's," she said, naming the popular department store on Sixth Avenue.

Of course, Sarah should have realized an organ grinder would have to go where people had enough money to give him coins for the entertainment he provided. She'd seen various musicians lining the streets in those neighborhoods, looking for alms from the passing throngs, but she'd hardly ever paid attention to them.

Maria had led her down one of the twisting alleys and now she stopped and pointed at the next building. "There," she said. "*Tre* steps." She held up three fingers and pointed up. Sarah understood the Donatos lived on the third floor.

She thanked Maria, wished her well, and insisted she take one of the small cakes from her basket as a reward. When the girl had gone, Sarah drew a fortifying breath and continued with her objective. By the time she had reached the third floor of the Donatos' building, she was *extremely* sorry she'd filled the basket so full. She only hoped the Donatos were grateful enough to accept her offerings, because she had no intention of carrying them back down again.

The doors to some of the flats stood open to catch the breeze from the stairwell. This allowed some feeble light to guide her in the windowless area. When she reached the third floor, she saw a woman in one of the flats. She was sitting at her kitchen table. The makings of paper flowers lay on the table before her. Many families in the tenements made flowers or other crafts to sell in the street, putting children to the task as soon as they were old enough to do the work. This woman was simply staring blankly at the wall today. Sarah thought she looked like someone who had just lost her daughter.

"Mrs. Donato?" she tried.

The woman looked around slowly, squinting to make out who was standing in the shadows. Sarah stepped into the doorway. "Are you Mrs. Donato?"

"We pay rent," the woman said defensively.

Sarah tried a reassuring smile. "I'm Sarah Brandt," she said, too late realizing Malloy might have told them she was the one who had identified Emilia's body. "I met Emilia at the mission," she hurried on. "I was very sorry to hear what happened, and I brought some things I thought you might be able to use."

Mrs. Donato gave no indication she'd ever heard Sarah's name before. Count on Malloy to be discreet. When Mrs. Donato also didn't offer any objection, Sarah pulled back the cloth covering the basket to reveal an assortment of delicacies she'd purchased at the bakery near her house. She'd been careful not to choose anything that might look like charity or indicate she thought the family couldn't provide regular meals for themselves. "For the funeral," she said. They would need something special to serve the mourners after the service.

Mrs. Donato's round face darkened. "No funeral," she said bitterly. "She no Catholic no more. She . . . mission." She said the word as if it were a curse.

Sarah remembered what Mrs. Wells had said about Emilia giving up her "popish" ways. She knew how important their faith was to Catholics. No wonder Mrs. Donato sounded bitter. Sarah stood there for a moment, wondering what on earth she could say. That was when she really looked at the other woman and saw what a trained nurse should have seen immediately.

"Mrs. Donato, when was the last time you had something to eat?"

Mrs. Donato's eyes narrowed suspiciously. "We have food. No need charity."

"I'm sure you don't," Sarah agreed, "but when was the last time you ate any of your food? You look as if you might be a little dehydrated."

"No sick," she protested, probably not recognizing the word. Few people would, even if they spoke fluent English.

"You *will* be sick if you don't eat something soon," Sarah warned. "I'm a nurse and a midwife. I delivered Maria Fortunato's baby," she added, hoping that would give her some credibility. "I just saw her down on the street, and she showed me where you lived."

Mrs. Donato made a sound in her throat. Sarah didn't know what it meant, but she chose to interpret it positively. She saw a coffeepot on the stove and stepped over to see if it was still warm. The kitchen was small enough, she only needed to take one step.

Warm enough, she decided, and took a cup down from the shelf and filled it. On second thought, she poured a second one. Sarah would sit down with her and force the woman to see her as a guest. With any luck, Mrs. Donato would feel obligated to treat her with some small bit of hospitality. She set the cups on the table, then got a plate from the shelf, too. Digging in the basket, she found some cookies and a sugar cake. She set them on the plate, breaking the cake in half. Then she sat down at the table, too.

"Please," she said, "eat just a little to be polite."

Mrs. Donato looked up at her in surprise, and Sarah smiled encouragingly.

"It really is delicious," she added, breaking off a small piece of the cake and popping it into her mouth to demonstrate.

Slowly, almost grudgingly, the other woman reached out and did the same, bringing the morsel cautiously to her lips.

"Isn't it good?" Sarah asked, but she didn't wait for an answer. "I didn't know Emilia very well. I only met her once. Someone asked me to visit the mission to see the kind of work they do there, and that's when I saw her. She seemed like a lovely girl."

Mrs. Donato wasn't gratified at the compliment as most mothers would have been. "Emilia . . . mistake," she said after searching for the correct word.

"I know she made mistakes," Sarah commiserated. "But many young girls get fooled by evil men. She was trying to change, though. She'd learned how to sew, so she could get honest work."

The eyes that stared back at her were full of suppressed rage. "No," she said slowly and deliberately, trying to make sure Sarah understood. "*She* mistake, from before born!"

"Because she was a girl?" Sarah asked, not really certain what the other woman meant. She knew many people, especially the foreign born, preferred sons.

"No, because she *is*!"

Now Sarah thought she understood. "You didn't want another child after . . . I know your son is crippled."

But that wasn't it either. She leaned forward, desperate for Sarah to comprehend. "Emilia child of *Devil*!"

Sarah couldn't let Mrs. Donato remember her daughter only for the tragic mistakes she'd made in her short life. "No child is born evil," she tried.

Mrs. Donato made a growling sound in her throat. "She child of *Devil*," she repeated. "On ship to America, I get lost one day. Sailors find me." The pain in her eyes left no doubt as to what the sailors had done to her. Sarah instinctively reached out, laying a hand on the other woman's arm in comfort. She didn't even seem to notice. "I never tell what they do. I too ashamed. I never tell. Then I get baby."

How horrible that must have been for her! She hadn't been able to share the pain of being raped, and then to get pregnant from it. If the child was the result of the rape, she'd be a constant reminder of it for the rest of her life. "She could have been your husband's child," Sarah tried.

"I pray it is so. I do not know until I see her. I afraid, all a time afraid. Then I see her, and I know. One sailor, yellow hair. Baby with yellow hair. I *know*. Child of Devil."

No wonder Emilia had felt unloved. Her own mother had seen her as a symbol of shame and degradation. "Did your husband know, too?"

She shook her head vehemently. "I never tell. Never tell no one until now. Now you know. She not good. Child of Devil."

Poor Emilia. The shame of her conception had destined her, in her mother's eyes at least, to a life of disgrace. Then she had fulfilled her mother's expectations in the worst possible way. "She was trying to change," Sarah offered.

"She never change," her mother insisted. "Better dead."

Sarah managed not to wince. She'd seen too many women express such a sentiment. Only the rich could afford the luxury of cherishing their children. A baby born to a poor family was a burden, another mouth to feed that wouldn't be able to contribute to its support for many years. Worse, it might get sick and further drain the family's resources.

Many times the babies Sarah delivered were considered a curse, not a blessing. No wonder so many women drank noxious potions to abort their pregnancies. No wonder abortionists grew fat and wealthy. No wonder babies were left in alleys to die. No wonder thousands of homeless children roamed the streets, scrounging and thieving and prostituting themselves just to stay alive. At least the Donatos had raised Emilia instead of turning her out. That was probably Mr. Donato's doing, since he had no reason to suspect she wasn't his child. As loveless as her home was, she'd had one, which was more than far too many children could claim.

"Mrs. Donato, do you have any idea who might have killed Emilia?"

The other woman narrowed her eyes in suspicion again. "No. We no see her, long time."

Sarah decided to take a chance. "What about Ugo or Lucca?"

Mrs. Donato reared back as if Sarah had slapped her and muttered what might have been a curse in Italian. "Get out my house," she said, pushing herself to her feet. Her face had paled, but Sarah judged she was more angry than shocked. "You go now."

Sarah wanted to bite her tongue. What had she been thinking to mention those names to Emilia's mother? "I'm sorry if I offended you . . ."

"You go now. I tell you nothing."

Sarah rose to her feet. "Let me leave these things for you," she said, reaching into the basket and setting another cake onto the table.

"We no need nothing," she insisted, her voice rising along with her color.

"I know you don't, but please accept it as a gift." Remembering her pledge not to carry these things back with her, she relentlessly continued to empty the basket, setting the things out on the crude kitchen table as quickly as she could before Mrs. Donato threw her out physically.

She hadn't quite finished, but she could see from

the way the other woman was breathing that she was working herself up to an emotional outburst. Sarah quickly gathered her basket and said, "I'm very sorry about Emilia. If I can do anything, please let me know."

An empty platitude, if ever she'd uttered one. Mrs. Donato would have no way of contacting her except through the mission. Sarah figured the woman would starve to death before contacting the mission about anything.

When she reached the door with her basket over her arm, Sarah looked back to take her leave. For an instant she thought she saw tears standing in Mrs. Donato's eyes, but she couldn't be sure in the poor light. "Please, try to eat something," she said lamely before making her hasty departure.

As she groped her way down the dark stairs, she sent up a silent prayer that Malloy would never find out about this visit. Not only hadn't she learned anything useful, but she'd alienated Mrs. Donato, which meant she'd never be able to go back again.

As she left the building, she had to pause a moment to allow her eyes to adjust to the bright sunlight. A group of ragged children were playing stickball in the alley, shouting and running and screaming at each other for not performing as well as they might have. All of them, she noted, had dark hair, just as Malloy had observed. Emilia must have felt very strange growing up in this neighborhood.

Sarah remembered the goodies left in her basket, the ones Mrs. Donato hadn't given her time to unpack. She strolled over to the group and asked if they wanted something to eat. When they saw what she had, greedy hands quickly relieved her of every last crumb.

A few mumbled *"grazies"* trailed after the children as they darted away, disappearing into nooks and crannies with their treats, lest she change her mind. Watching them running away so nimbly made her think of Brian and wonder if he would soon be able to run like that. Which made her think of Emilia's brother Georgio, who had never been able even to walk.

Maria had said he played his organ outside of Macy's. How difficult would it be to find an Italian organ grinder with one foot? Sarah wasn't sure what he would be able to tell her, but she really couldn't know any less than she already did about Emilia. If nothing else, she'd be able to tell Malloy where to find him.

The Canal Street Station of the El wasn't too far. She took the train to Fourteenth Street and walked over to Sixth Avenue. The sidewalks were crowded with the buxom wives of successful businessmen who were doing their duty by spending the money their husbands earned.

As she walked along, Sarah realized she'd never really paid much attention to the people who came here for the purpose of earning their daily bread by performing for the passing crowd. Everyone understood that they were beggars, but if they juggled or played a musical instrument or performed in some other way, people could maintain the fiction that they were earning a living. No one wanted to see real beggars on the sidewalks.

Macy's occupied the entire block between Thirteenth and Fourteenth Streets, so Sarah had a lot of ground to cover as she circled the building. She was just starting to feel silly for having thought she could locate Georgio so easily when she found him on the corner of Sixth and Thirteenth. Actually, she'd noticed the little girl first, not even registering who was making the music to which she danced.

The child was adorable. She was probably about four or five years old and as dainty as a fairy in her bright red dress. Her dark hair hung in curls that fell to her shoulders and bounced delightfully as her tiny bare feet formed intricate patterns on the pavement. Her enormous brown eyes glittered with happiness at the attention she had attracted. Sarah wasn't the only passerby who had stopped to watch, entranced. Then the song ended, and the gathered crowd applauded. The girl bobbed a curtsey and looked around expectantly. In a moment, coins appeared, fished from pockets and purses and offered in tribute. The coins disappeared again as if by magic, spirited away by little fingers as nimble as the little feet had been and deposited into the pocket of her dress.

While the crowd disbursed, the girl turned and hurried back to the man who had produced the music. That was when Sarah recalled her purpose in being here. The child was emptying her pocket and giving the coins to a handsome youth who sat on a small stool with his back against the building. He held the organ between his knees, resting on a small stand. He wore a dark shirt and trousers and had a red bandanna tied rakishly at his throat. He looked so perfect that Sarah almost didn't notice the wooden crutches tucked discreetly between his stool and the wall. Finally, she saw the pant leg pinned up at the ankle.

She'd never expected Georgio to have a child,

which was why she'd been so slow to realize she'd found him. Taking advantage of this lull, she stepped over to where the man and the girl were conversing in Italian. There seemed to be some question about whether she'd given him all the coins she'd collected.

"Georgio?" Sarah tried.

He looked up from beneath the bill of his small cap. His eyes were dark and liquid, his smile big and bright and charming. "*Sì, Signorina,* do you want to see the little one dance?" His English was very good, probably honed from conversing with his customers.

"No, although she dances very well," Sarah added, giving the child an approving smile, in case she didn't understand the compliment. "I wanted to ask you about your sister Emilia."

His charming smile vanished, and the dark eyes grew wary. "She is dead," he said very carefully.

"I know. I'm very sorry."

"Who are you and what do you want?" he asked suspiciously. When he frowned, Sarah realized how much he looked like his mother.

"My name is Sarah Brandt, and I met Emilia at the Prodigal Son Mission." His expression hardened from wariness into anger. Plainly, none of the Donato family had any love for the mission. "She was such a lovely girl, and she was trying very hard to become a respectable young woman," Sarah hurried on, wishing she had some idea how Georgio felt about his sister.

Seeing that the grown-ups were going to talk a bit, the little girl sank down onto the pavement with a weary sigh and leaned back against the wall. Sarah wondered vaguely how many times she had to perform in a day. She probably had a right to be tired.

"Emilia is whore," he said baldly. "Now she dead. Why you care? Why anybody care?"

"She was learning to sew," Sarah tried. "She wanted to earn an honest living. She wanted to change."

"She go to mission before, then she go back with Ugo," Georgio said. "She never change. Just pretend. She want clothes and food and place to live. Easy life for a while. Then she go back."

Sarah wondered if that could be true. She'd hardly known Emilia. Mrs. Wells had been convinced that Emilia had changed, however, and after her years of experience working at the mission, she wouldn't be easily fooled. "This time she really meant it," Sarah argued. "She was going to get a job. In fact, that's what she was going to do the morning she was killed."

The eyes that stared back at her were unmoved. He knew his sister better than Sarah, and he didn't believe anything good about her. Sarah glanced at the child to remind herself that Georgio was a father himself. Maybe she could reach him that way.

"Your daughter is asleep," she observed, half in wonder at the way children could just drop off any time and any place. She looked like a brightly clad porcelain doll sitting there.

Georgio looked down and struck out with his whole foot, catching her on the hip. Jolted awake, she yelped in pain and outrage as Sarah cried out in protest. He ignored Sarah and gave the girl a sharp command in Italian. She rose sullenly, rubbing her hip.

*"Sorriso!"* he commanded, and she twisted her face into the parody of a smile. He started to turn the

crank and coax music from the box. The girl's tiny feet began to move, sketching out the steps so lightly they hardly seemed to touch the ground. She twirled, making her colorful skirt float out around her brown legs. People began to stop and watch. Soon a crowd formed. Georgio relentlessly ignored Sarah. He didn't want to hear what she had to say about his sister. A man who would kick his own child on a public street to get her to dance wouldn't care about a sister who'd disgraced her family by selling herself. She was wasting her time here.

Another failure she didn't want to report to Malloy, especially when he'd expressly forbidden her to do any investigation at all in this case.

Frank knew better than to go exploring the alleys of Mulberry Bend alone at night. The sun had dropped far enough in the sky to cast these rear tenement buildings into darkness, even though it was still daylight in the rest of the city. He'd gathered up a couple of the beat cops to accompany him now that he had learned where Ugo Ianuzzi made his living.

"You know which one it is?" one of the cops asked as they made their way, stepping over the trash and the tramps lying in the alley.

"No," Frank said. Ianuzzi's landlady hadn't been specific. "Just that it's in one of these buildings."

"There must be a dozen dives back here," the other cop complained.

"Then we'll look in each one until we find him," Frank replied irritably. He'd much rather be home, enjoying his mother's cooking and his son's company, than searching stale beer dives for a man he didn't consider good enough to spit on.

The early hour ensured the crowds would be small in these establishments that were very distant cousins to saloons. Located in any available basement or cubbyhole, the dive consisted of a few tables and chairs and a keg of stale beer. The proprietor would have stolen the keg from a sidewalk in front of a legitimate saloon, where the flat beer from the night before was set out each morning for the breweries to pick up the kegs and refill them. The dive keeper would doctor the flat beer with chemicals to put some foam back into it and sell it for pennies to the homeless beggars who worked their trade all day just to afford the privilege. In exchange for their purchases, they would be allowed to stay in the dive all night, sleeping in a chair or on the floor in drunken oblivion. Ugo Ianuzzi had made his fortune by running such a place.

One of the officers kicked open the door of the first dive they came to. The room was the dank cellar of a ramshackle frame tenement house. The walls were covered with years of grime. The dirt floor consisted of a layer of crawling bugs feeding on the filth beneath. An ancient hag clad in garments so dirty, their original color was indistinguishable, was filling a tomato can — which passed for a glass — from the keg that sat in the center of the room on the remains of a broken chair. She and her customer, a pockmarked young man with crossed eyes and no front teeth, looked up in terror at the intrusion. Usually, a raid by the police would mean six months "on the island" for the proprietor and her customers.

"Don't worry. We ain't looking for you," one of the cops said. He turned to Frank. "What's the name?"

"Ugo Ianuzzi," Frank said. "Where is he?"

The old woman made a pretense of refusing to co-operate, but the cops only needed to threaten her with their nightsticks to encourage cooperation. She probably wouldn't have survived an actual blow from the locust wood clubs. She very quickly gave them directions in broken English to a place two buildings down.

"If you're lying, we'll be back," one of the cops warned her.

They passed several more of the dives on their way, and Frank realized the reformers were right: the only way to clean out The Bend was to tear it down. So long as this rabbit warren of decay existed, evil would breed here like cockroaches.

When they reached the place the old woman had described, one of the cops opened the door with the heel of his boot. It slammed back against the wall, startling the early arrivals. This room was bigger than most of the dives. Ugo had commandeered a space almost twenty feet square and furnished it with a mismatched assortment of chairs and makeshift tables made of odd pieces of lumber laid over broken barrels. The requisite keg rested in its place of honor at the center of the room. Several dozen empty tin cans sat on the floor in front of it, awaiting customers.

"Ianuzzi?" Frank shouted, looking around.

A burly man with a cigar clenched in his teeth came forward. He appeared to be in his thirties, and he was far more respectable looking than the hag who ran the first dive they'd checked. In his shirtsleeves, he wore a vest with a watch chain stretched across it. His lush mustache was neatly trimmed, and his dark hair lavishly pomaded. He shouted something in Italian to his customers, who rose as one and made for the door. Some hunched their shoulders and ducked their heads in anticipation of blows from the coppers' locusts, but no one paid them any mind.

"I want to ask you some questions, Ugo," Frank said in a tone that brooked no argument.

"No 'stand," Ugo tried with an elaborate shrug.

"Maybe you'll understand this," Frank said. "I want to talk to you about Emilia Donato."

Ugo's expression hardened. "Emilia is whore," he declared. "I no see her, long time."

"Then you won't mind answering a few questions about her."

"I know nothing. I no see her. She run away, long time."

'I know all about why she ran away from you, Ugo," Frank said pleasantly. "And just so you know, I don't think much of men who beat women, especially when they're expecting a child."

"She lie, all a time, lie. No believe her," Ugo advised, gesturing with his hands. "She run away, go to pimp. I no see, long time."

"It's a real shame about your memory being so bad," Frank said. "I'll bet it gets a whole lot better after a couple hours at Police Headquarters."

Ugo protested vigorously, but a few well-placed blows from the locusts changed his mind. Eventually, he agreed to accompany them up the street to Headquarters.

"They steal all my beer," he complained when they dragged him out of his dive, leaving his keg unattended.

"Then you'll just have to steal some more to replace it," Frank pointed out. He hadn't ever really considered how profitable such a dive could be. The stolen beer was free, and Ugo certainly didn't pay any rent for his basement space. Except for a few cents' worth of chemicals to give "life" to the flat beer, he had no expenses at all. Each night he'd take in the entire day's earnings of dozens of beggars, and it would be pure profit.

Frank gave Ugo an hour in the airless cellar cells at Headquarters to consider his predicament before moving him into a basement interrogation room. When Frank joined him, he looked a little less arrogant but a lot more annoyed.

"Nice business you've got there, Ugo," he remarked as he sat down across the scarred table from his prisoner. The table and a few chairs were the only furnishings in the room. A single window high on one wall provided a little light during the day and none at night. A gas jet on the wall cast eerie shadows. "Is that where you met Emilia?"

Ugo was still being tough. He just glared at Frank, refusing to answer.

"How long since you've seen her, Ugo?" Frank waited. No answer.

"I think you saw her yesterday, Ugo," Frank said, still pleasant. "I think you met her at City Hall Park. She wanted to show you her new dress."

Ugo was getting uneasy, but he still wasn't going to say anything.

"I think you met her in the park, and she wanted you to marry her. You refused, and she got mad. You had a fight, and then you killed her."

Ugo's swagger evaporated. "No kill nobody!" he insisted, terror widening his eyes and draining the color from his face.

"I can't blame you," Frank said reasonably. "You must have been tired of her asking you to marry her."

"I no can marry her," Ugo said. "Have wife already, and children."

This was a surprise, although Frank didn't let on. "Where are they?"

"In Italy. Three children," he said, holding up three fingers. "No marry Emilia. Have wife already."

"That didn't stop you from seducing her, though," Frank pointed out.

Ugo frowned. "See-deuce?" he repeated uncertainly.

Frank made a gesture with his hands that overcame the language barrier. Ugo's face lit with understanding.

"I no see-deuce. She do it. She think I marry her then."

Frank thought it unlikely that a girl like Emilia would have traded her virginity for anything less than a promise of marriage, but he let Ugo's lie pass for now.

"And when you refused, she left you?" Frank guessed.

"She go to pimp," Ugo said, aggrieved. "I tell you, she whore."

"Is that why you killed her? Because she became a whore?"

"I no kill nobody!"

"I think you got mad at Emilia. You didn't want her bothering you anymore. You didn't want her begging you to marry her. But she kept coming back, so you decided to stick a knife into her and be done with it."

"No! I no see Emilia, long time. I no kill!"

"Is that how the Black Hand kills someone, Ugo? The way you killed Emilia?"

Ugo was looking around wildly, as if searching for a means of escape. "I no kill Emilia!" he insisted. Frank was discouraged. He was acting far too much like an innocent man. Frank wanted Ugo to be guilty so he could close the case, but it looked as if he wasn't.

"Somebody killed her, Ugo," Frank said. "And here you are. If you confess, I don't have to look for anybody else."

Ugo obviously knew that the police routinely beat confessions out of innocent men in order to close difficult cases. Or even easy ones, if they didn't feel like working too hard.

"I no kill Emilia!" he cried frantically.

"Then start answering my questions, Ugo," Frank advised him.

"I answer! I answer!"

"Good." Frank folded his hands expectantly on the table. "Now tell me about the Black Hand."

# 8

SARAH WAS BONE WEARY AS SHE MADE HER WAY down Bank Street late Saturday morning. She wasn't sure how much of her fatigue had been caused by the middle-of-the-night call to deliver a baby and how much by her depression over not being able to help find out who'd killed Emilia Donato. At least the earlier rain had stopped, but the gray sky matched her mood perfectly.

As usual, her next-door neighbor was out sweeping her front steps, or pretending to, even though the porch would have been washed clean by the morning rain. In reality, she was waiting to welcome Sarah home and find out how her delivery had gone.

"Good morning, Mrs. Ellsworth," Sarah called when she was within hailing distance.

"Good morning, Mrs. Brandt. Were you on a delivery?"

"Yes, a little boy. He's doing fine, and so is his mother."

"That's a blessing."

Sarah thought of all the unwanted children in the world, children like Emilia Donato. Were they blessings? Sarah didn't think she wanted to know right now. "Mrs. Ellsworth, would you come in for some tea? I'd like to ask your advice about something."

Since Sarah had never asked Mrs. Ellsworth for anything at all, the older woman looked startled for a second. In the next second, however, she looked extremely pleased. "I'd be happy to help in any way I can, my dear. Just give me a moment to take off my apron!"

Sarah went into her house, and after removing her cape and opening her umbrella and setting it on the floor so it could dry thoroughly, she went to the kitchen to start a fire in the stove. It was burning well by the time she heard Mrs. Ellsworth's knock.

Mrs. Ellsworth must have been even more impressed by her request than Sarah had thought for her to be using the front door, as if this were a formal visit. She usually came to the kitchen door.

When Sarah admitted her, she saw the rain had started up again, and Mrs. Ellsworth was half-hidden beneath an enormous black umbrella. The old woman closed it and shook it out on the front stoop, then came inside.

"We can set it here by mine to dry," Sarah offered, reaching for the umbrella. Mrs. Ellsworth made a strangled sound of alarm, pointing in wordless horror.

Sarah looked where she was pointing, expecting to see that a poisonous snake had somehow crawled into her foyer. Instead all she saw was her own umbrella dripping quietly onto the floor.

"You can't open an umbrella in the house!" Mrs. Ellsworth informed her, appalled. She hastily dropped her own onto the floor and snatched up Sarah's to close it. "What were you thinking?"

She'd been thinking it would dry more quickly if it were opened, but of course she didn't say that to Mrs. Ellsworth. "I suppose that's bad luck," she guessed. Mrs. Ellsworth's superstitions were legion.

"It certainly is," she said, clutching the offending object to her as if she could shelter it from the evil spirits that might be ready to descend.

"I had no idea," Sarah admitted apologetically. "I'll be more careful in the future." Then she reached down to pick up the umbrella that Mrs. Ellsworth had dropped in her haste to rescue Sarah's.

"Don't touch that!" Mrs. Ellsworth cried, startling Sarah all over again. She jumped and hastily straightened, holding both hands up to prove she had obeyed the command.

"It can't be bad luck just to pick up an umbrella, can it?" she asked in amazement.

"It's bad luck to let someone else pick up an umbrella you've dropped," she explained as if to a child, bending to pick up it up herself. "Of course, now that I remember, the bad luck is that you'll become a spinster for the rest of your life. Since I'm not in any danger of becoming a spinster, I suppose it's all right after all," she added in amusement.

"I suppose so," Sarah agreed, taking both umbrellas from her and setting them in the umbrella stand beside the door. When Mrs. Ellsworth made no further protest, Sarah assumed this was a safe way to deal with them. "Come into the kitchen. I was just going to put the kettle on."

"I must say I'm intrigued," Mrs. Ellsworth said as she followed Sarah through her front office and into the back of the house. "I can't imagine what you might need *my* advice about."

Sarah put the kettle on, and the two women seated themselves at Sarah's kitchen table. "Remember I went to visit the Prodigal Son Mission last Sunday?" she began.

"Oh, yes," Mrs. Ellsworth said with elaborate casualness. "With Mr. Dennis, I believe," she added expectantly.

Sarah bit back a smile. She wasn't going to explain her relationship with Richard to the mother of one of Richard's employees. "Yes, he accompanied me there." She proceeded to tell her neighbor about meeting Emilia at the mission and then how Malloy had found her body in the park wearing Sarah's clothing.

"That poor man! It must have been a shock to him, thinking you were dead," she observed.

Such a shock that he actually hugged Sarah the next time he saw her, but she didn't mention that to her neighbor. Mrs. Ellsworth already had too many romantic notions about Detective Sergeant Frank Malloy. "No one knew who she was, so he came here to find out how she might have gotten my clothes. I was able to identify her."

"Do they have any idea who might have killed her?"

"Emilia had been involved with several disreputable men before she went to live at the mission, but I really don't know what Malloy has found out about them. You see, he was so . . ." Sarah searched for the proper word. " . . . distressed by seeing the dead girl in my clothing that he forbade me from having anything to do with the investigation."

"He's right, you know. Those Italians are dangerous people." She pronounced it *Eye-talians*. "You know about the evil eye! They can kill a baby in its mother's womb with it."

Sarah seriously doubted that, but she simply nodded her understanding. "Do you know anything about the Black Hand?"

"Only what I read in the newspapers. I don't know what this world is coming to! We should never allow people like that into our country."

"Mrs. Ellsworth, everyone in our country came from someplace else at one time or another," Sarah reminded her gently.

"I know that!" Mrs. Ellsworth said, a little indignant. "I just meant we shouldn't allow *foreigners* in!"

Sarah was beginning to wonder why she'd thought Mrs. Ellsworth could help her with her dilemma. Mercifully, she noticed the water was boiling, so she got up and fixed the tea. By the time she'd filled the pot and set it and the cups on the table, she figured enough time had passed so she could broach the subject she really wanted to discuss.

"Malloy has forbidden me to help him in this investigation, but I still feel like I need to do something to help," she began while they waited for the tea to steep. "Because I feel so guilty."

"Guilty? What on earth for?" Mrs. Ellsworth asked in amazement.

"I'm not sure. Ever since I visited the mission, I've

had this feeling that I'm not doing anything important with my life."

"That's nonsense! I'm sure there are hundreds of mothers in the city who think you're doing something extremely important."

Sarah frowned. "Bringing babies into the world alive is just the beginning. Think about how many infants are abandoned or killed and how many children end up living on the streets because their families throw them out."

"You can't save them all, my dear. One person can only do so much."

"That's just it. I don't feel that I'm doing anything at all."

"What could you possibly do?"

This was what Sarah had been fretting about and why she'd asked her neighbor to come over. "I was thinking perhaps I should volunteer to help out at the mission, the way Mr. Dennis's wife did."

The older woman frowned, considering. "What did Mrs. Dennis do there?"

"I'm not sure. I think she may have taught the girls needlework or something like that."

"Do you do needlework?"

"Heavens, no, but I could teach them something I do know. Like hygiene, how to keep themselves and their homes clean and free of disease. Things like that."

"Don't their mothers teach them those things?" Mrs. Ellsworth asked in all sincerity.

"Many of them don't have mothers," Sarah said tactfully. She didn't want to explain all the reasons the poor lived in squalor. Mrs. Ellsworth's opinion of "foreigners" was already low enough.

"In that case, I'm sure they would appreciate knowing such things. In fact, I'm surprised they don't already have someone teaching those things at the mission."

"Perhaps they do. I guess I'll find out when I offer my services."

"Is that what you wanted my advice about?" Mrs. Ellsworth asked. "Because if it was, I don't think I was much help!"

"You were a tremendous help," Sarah assured her. "I think I just needed to hear someone else say it was a good idea."

"My dear Mrs. Brandt, I'm sure you've never had a bad idea in your life," Mrs. Ellsworth said with a smile as Sarah picked up the pot and began to pour their tea.

Thinking of the ideas she'd had yesterday, about visiting Emilia's family members to find out who might have killed her, she smiled in return. "I've had my share, I promise you."

"Oh, look," Mrs. Ellsworth said, pointing at the tea leaf floating on the surface of Sarah's cup. "That means you're going to have a visitor."

"Can you read my tea leaves to find out who it will be?" Sarah asked good-naturedly.

Mrs. Ellsworth closed her eyes and pretended to go into a trance. "I see a man who asks a lot of questions. He's a man who puts criminals in jail. And I also see that he is very fond of you." She opened one eye and peered at Sarah slyly. "And you, I think, are very fond of him."

"I think," Sarah said, "that from now on, I will only serve you coffee."

\* \* \*

Frank was getting tired of Mulberry Bend. Once again he came in the early evening, just as the sun was setting. He'd spent most of last night with Ugo Ianuzzi and learned enough to know the Black Hand probably had nothing to do with Emilia Donato's death. Except for the weapon used — a thin-bladed stiletto — nothing else pointed to this group.

Emilia's father was a laborer on the garbage scows, men who were known as rag pickers. They'd acquired this nickname because while their job was to level the loads of refuse as it was loaded onto the barges that would carry it out to be dumped into the sea, they were also allowed to pick through it for anything that might be of value to keep and sell. Most of what they found was rags, which could be cleaned and fashioned into rugs or stuffed into furniture or mattresses. The "cleaning," of course, usually consisted of merely hanging the rags on clotheslines and letting the rain and sun do their work. Men who did this kind of labor owed their jobs to *padroni,* men who had managed to get the contract from the city and hired laborers to do the work. Mr. Donato, as a lowly laborer, was hardly powerful enough to arouse the interest of the Black Hand, much less inspire them to murder his daughter in some vendetta.

From what he'd learned of Emilia's brother, he was a crippled beggar, likewise unlikely to have been involved with the Secret Society. Emilia's lover Ugo, while a bit more successful, paid his protection money and kept in the Black Hand's good graces. Even if he didn't, killing his discarded mistress would hardly intimidate him.

That left the pimp who had exploited Emilia. Ugo had said his name was Lucca. Nobody seemed to know his last name. He wasn't industrious or successful enough to keep a brothel. He exerted himself only to seduce young women and coerce them into prostituting themselves. Then he was content to live off the earnings of his latest victim.

Lucca had a tiny flat in one of the old Dutch houses, according to Ugo. Frank found the place easily enough. The elements had scoured the wooden siding clean of paint years ago, and the planks were now warped and rotting. Some of the windows hung crooked in their frames, the glass threatening to slide out with the slightest encouragement. Lucca rented part of the attic, which meant Frank had to trudge up the filthy, rickety stairs to the third floor. Halfway up the final flight, he could hear an argument going on above.

A woman was pleading and crying while a man was shouting and threatening. Frank could tell this easily, even though he didn't understand a word of the language in which they conversed. He'd heard countless arguments just like it in many languages, and they were always the same. He quickened his step, hoping to interrupt it before its inevitable conclusion, but he wasn't fast enough. The sound of flesh striking flesh, followed by a cry of pain and hysterical weeping, came to him just as he reached the top of the stairs.

The man's voice rose to be heard above her weeping, shouting a warning and another threat. Frank reached the door and pounded on it before he could strike another blow.

"Open up," he shouted. "Police."

The door opened immediately, and the man stared back at him defiantly. He wore dirty trousers with the suspenders hanging down around his hips, and a yellowed undershirt. Although slight of stature, he'd planted himself squarely in the doorway and glared at Frank as if daring him to make trouble for what was obviously nobody else's business.

"Lucca?" Frank asked and saw the instant of surprise register on the man's face before he could collect himself.

"Not here," he claimed, lifting his chin impudently. He was vaguely handsome, the way a snake can be called beautiful, no matter how dangerous it might be. The woman was still sobbing pitifully in the background.

"Maybe the lady knows where he is," Frank suggested mildly, tilting his head to look over Lucca's shoulder. He could see her sitting on the bed, cradling her cheek in one hand and rocking back and forth to comfort herself.

"She know nothing," Lucca insisted. "Not here. Come back later."

Frank looked him up and down. He wasn't a big man, and what weight he had was soft. "I don't want to come back later," Frank said, still not raising his voice. That was why Lucca wasn't prepared when Frank lunged at him. In one swift move, he threw the man off balance, caught his arm, and twisted it around his back. He propelled Lucca across the small room and slammed him face-first into the wall.

The woman screamed. Frank spared her a glance and was surprised to see she was no more than a girl, probably only fourteen at most. She stared at Frank, eyes filled with terror, her tears forgotten. "Get out of here," he told her.

She blinked, either too frightened to understand or

else she didn't speak English. "Tell her to get out," he said to Lucca, twisting his arm a little higher to encourage his cooperation.

Lucca howled with pain, but he said something to the girl in Italian, his voice high and strained.

She started to protest, but he cut her off sharply. Even though she wasn't dressed for the street, she snatched up a jacket and hurried out. Her footsteps echoed lightly down the stairs and faded away.

"What you want?" Lucca asked. His voice was a little muffled because his face was still smashed against the wall.

"I want to know why you killed Emilia Donato," Frank said.

"Who?" he asked.

Frank didn't like people who tried to be coy with him. He gave Lucca's arm another twist. When he'd stopped screaming, Frank said, "Emilia Donato," very deliberately.

"Who is this girl?" he asked quickly, before Frank could encourage him again. "I do not know her!"

Was it possible Frank had found the wrong man? "Yellow hair. Emilia. She got sick, and you threw her out," he tried.

"Oh, *sì*, yes, I know her now!" he assured Frank hastily. "She not here long. I forget!"

Frank wanted to smash his head right through the wall. Couldn't he at least have the decency to remember their names? "Tell me about her, Lucca," he suggested instead, his voice dangerously low.

"She lazy girl. No work."

"You mean she wouldn't walk the streets?"

"She cry. Say she sick. No go out."

"So you slapped her around like you did that girl just now?" Frank asked.

"Lazy girl," he defended himself. "No work. Must work, get money."

"So you made her go out to make money for you," Frank offered.

"She go but no make money. Stay out all night. Afraid come home. Afraid I mad. Stay out all night in rain. Get sick." He shrugged. "What I do? She no can work. I send her away."

"When was the last time you saw her?"

"Long time. Can't tell. Long, long time!" he insisted. "She nothing to me. Why you come here?"

"Because somebody killed her two days ago."

Now the seriousness of his situation was finally sinking in. "Why I kill her?" he cried. "She nothing to me!"

"Because she met you on Thursday morning. She wanted you to see her new dress. She wanted you to see how pretty she was and make you sorry you threw her out. She made you angry, so you stabbed her to death."

"No!" he cried frantically. "I no see her, long time! She nothing to me. She go to mission. I no see no more. I think she die. I no kill. Why I kill? She nothing to me!"

Either he was a better liar than he had a right to be or he was telling the truth. Frank was afraid he was telling the truth. Coming here had been a long shot in any case, but he'd run out of suspects. No one, it seemed, had any reason to want Emilia Donato dead.

Maybe if he had some more time, he could figure it out, but they'd told him yesterday at Headquarters to close the case. Emilia's parents weren't going to offer a reward or pressure the police to do anything. Even they didn't care that she was dead. No one cared.

No one except Sarah Brandt.

Frank didn't ask himself why he was walking down Bank Street. If he didn't ask himself, he wouldn't have to make up a lie to satisfy his pride. The truth was, he only needed the slightest excuse to come here, and this time his excuse was pretty substantial.

Darkness had fallen on the city, even though the hour wasn't particularly late. The days were growing shorter as October wound to a close. As soon as he'd turned the corner, he'd seen a light on in Sarah's front room. There was always a chance she'd be out on a call, but his luck seemed to be holding. The darkness would keep Mrs. Ellsworth inside, too, since even the busiest of busybodies couldn't sweep her front steps in the pitch dark. He didn't feel much like answering her questions tonight, no matter how well intentioned they were.

Sarah Brandt opened the door at his knock. She said, "Malloy," but she didn't smile the way she usually did. She looked worried, maybe even a little nervous. "Is something wrong?"

So that was it. She was worried about Brian. "No, nothing's wrong, except that I haven't found your murderer."

That seemed to reassure her. "Come in. Would you like some coffee? Have you eaten?"

"Just some coffee," he said, hanging his hat in her hallway the way he always did. He followed her into the kitchen, admiring the shape of her body in the worn housedress. Apparently, she hadn't given *all* of her old clothes to the mission.

For an instant he remembered the way she had felt in his arms in that emotional moment he'd forgotten himself at finding her alive and well. The memory brought the heat to his face and to other parts of him, too, so he quickly banished it. Still, he wondered if she thought about it and how she felt when she did. She'd certainly never mentioned it, thank God. If she was willing to pretend it hadn't happened, so was he.

"Sit down," she said, pointing to the kitchen table, and began making the coffee.

He watched her work, enjoying these few stolen minutes of false intimacy when he could pretend he belonged here, with her. Too soon she was finished, and she sat down across from him at the table. Her eyes were guarded, as if she was afraid to hope too much.

"What did you find out?" she asked when he didn't speak.

"That nobody had any reason to kill Emilia."

"Did you find her lover?"

"Yeah, and her pimp, too. She wasn't a very good prostitute. Even when this fellow Lucca beat her, she wouldn't earn any money for him."

"Wouldn't that give him a reason to kill her?"

"Not months after he'd thrown her out, and he'd found a new girl. He didn't even remember her name."

"How awful!"

"Pimps aren't usually known for their social graces," Frank reminded her.

"What about that Ugo, the man who seduced her in the first place?"

"He was finished with her, too. I took him down to Headquarters and let him sit in a cell for a while. He was pretty scared, so I'm fairly certain he didn't kill her either. Neither of them had seen her recently, not since she went to the mission, at least."

"What about our theory that she wanted one of them to take her back?"

"If she met a man in the park that morning, it wasn't either one of them."

She frowned. She didn't like this one bit. "It must have been the Black Hand, then. They're the ones who use stilettos," she decided.

"I did some research into the Black Hand. Her family is too poor to attract their attention. Besides, every Italian man in New York owns a stiletto."

She wasn't going to let it rest. "What about her family then? Did you talk to her father and her brother?"

"I didn't see her brother, but why would her family want her dead?"

"They're Catholics," she reminded him. "Emilia had left her faith."

Frank didn't know whether to laugh or take offense. "I know you Protestants think Catholics eat babies for communion, but we don't kill people just for leaving the church."

He was gratified to see her instant contrition. "I'm sorry! I didn't mean to sound so . . . so bigoted," she said. "I just . . . I thought maybe . . . Her mother, at least, didn't seem to care about Emilia at all."

"If they didn't like her, all the more reason why they wouldn't have killed her for leaving the church," Frank said before the real import of her words struck him. "Wait a minute, when did you meet Emilia's mother?" he asked suspiciously.

She would have been a terrible failure as a criminal. Her guilt was as obvious as a scarlet brand on her forehead. "I . . . That is . . . one of my patients told me. I deliver a lot of babies in that neighborhood and —"

"You went to the Donatos' flat even after I told you how dangerous it was to get involved in this!" he accused her furiously.

"I just took her mother some food for the funeral. It was the Christian thing to do," she added hastily when he clenched his fists on the table. "I also found out some very interesting information."

"Then you wasted your time. It doesn't matter what you found out, because the case is closed," he told her, somehow managing to restrain his impulse to reach across the table and shake some sense into her.

"You mean you found the killer? I thought you said —"

"I said I didn't find the killer, and I'm not going to," he snapped. "Headquarters ordered me to close the case."

"But what about the person who murdered Emilia? Does he just go free?" she demanded, horrified.

"Like hundreds of others do every year," he said. "There isn't much justice in the world, Mrs. Brandt, and hardly any at all in New York City. You should know that by now."

The coffee was boiling, splashing out of the spout to sputter on the stovetop. She jumped up to save it. He waited, trying to rein in his anger while she filled two cups and carried them to the table.

She was angry, too, if he could judge by the way she set the cups down. Coffee sloshed over the sides into the saucers. She didn't even notice. "Somebody wanted her dead," she reminded him, planting her hands on her hips. "Because she *is* dead. And it wasn't a robbery because she wasn't robbed, and it wasn't an assault, because she wasn't assaulted. Someone killed her deliberately and efficiently, and that person had probably planned it carefully ahead of time."

"Fine," he replied. "Tell me who it was, and I'll arrest him."

She looked like she wanted to spit nails, but she sat back down in her chair instead. "It had to have been someone who knew her."

"She probably knew a lot of people. People in her neighborhood, people in the mission . . ."

She perked up at that. "I hadn't thought about the mission. She probably met lots of unsavory people there."

"Unsavory people do seem to be their specialty," Frank observed, earning a black look for his efforts.

"I'm serious, Malloy. She could have made an enemy of someone who came to the mission but didn't reform."

He nodded. "Yeah, a girl who also happened to be a doctor or a nurse and knew that stabbing somebody in the back of the head would kill them without making a mess."

"Other people could know that, too," she argued, undaunted. Her persistence was amazing.

"Like who?"

"I don't know. Someone who worked in a slaughterhouse or maybe a butcher . . ."

"I guess a lot of those girls at the mission used to be butchers."

"Malloy, if you aren't careful, I'm going to pour the next cup of coffee in your lap!"

He managed not to grin because she just might do it if he provoked her any more. He decided to try reason. "I'm just trying to point out that none of these theories make sense. Is this the important information you got when you visited Mrs. Donato?"

"Of course not!" In an instant, her anger was gone. He'd never known a woman who calmed down so quickly. But then, he'd never known any women like Sarah Brandt before. "I found out that Emilia wasn't Mr. Donato's daughter."

He wasn't sure what difference this could possibly make, but he'd humor her. "Who was her father then?"

"Her mother was . . . attacked by some sailors on the ship coming over. That's why she had blond hair. She was only half Italian."

That explained a lot about Mrs. Donato's attitude toward her daughter. "I'm surprised Donato agreed to keep the girl."

"He didn't know. Mrs. Donato never told anyone about the attack."

"He must've thought it was funny she had light hair."

"I'm sure lots of people did, but Mrs. Donato claims he never suspected. She couldn't bring herself to love Emilia, though. I'm sure that made life hard for her. No wonder she was deceived by the first man to pay her any attention."

"That Ugo fellow has a wife and three kids back in

Italy," Malloy said, in case she was going to put any of the blame on Emilia.

"*What?* That cad!" she exclaimed, outraged.

"He didn't marry Emilia because he didn't want to be a bigamist."

"How very noble of him," she said acidly. "He should be horsewhipped."

"At least," Frank agreed.

"Maybe Emilia found out about his wife and threatened to expose him," she said. "That would give him a reason to kill her."

"Only if he *cared* that his wife back in Italy knew he had a mistress. I don't think Ugo is too worried about things like that."

She frowned. She knew he was right and didn't want to admit it. "Her brother is an organ grinder," she offered after a moment.

"Is he?" Frank wasn't sure why this was important.

"He plays outside of Macy's."

"Do you think *he* killed Emilia?" Frank asked, trying hard not to sound sarcastic.

Apparently, he succeeded because she didn't take offense. "He's a cripple. He was . . . he was born without a foot."

Frank couldn't help flinching a bit. He'd instantly thought of Brian and the future he'd once imagined for his crippled, simple-minded son. Because of Sarah, Brian was no longer a cripple, and now Frank knew he was deaf, and not simple at all. He'd never be sitting on the pavement outside of Macy's, begging for coins.

"That's how I know he didn't kill Emilia," she

went on. "He never could have come up behind her and stabbed her because he walks with crutches."

Frank glared at her. "When did you meet *him*?"

She didn't quite meet his eye, which was a good thing because the look he was giving her would've curled her hair. "I . . . I told you, he plays outside of Macy's. I had some shopping to do, so I looked for him. He has a little daughter who dances for him."

Frank decided it was a waste of energy to be angry at this bit of foolishness. At least she hadn't been in any danger on a public street. "Are you sure she's his daughter?"

"What do you mean?"

"A lot of those beggars don't have children of their own or children the right size or that are cute enough, so they hire one."

"How awful!"

"Not really. At least the kid isn't working in a tenement sweatshop. She probably earns more money dancing than she would making cigars or paper flowers anyway."

She frowned. "I guess that's why he wasn't very nice to her. She was so tired, she fell asleep sitting on the sidewalk, and he kicked her and made her get up and dance some more."

"That doesn't prove she's not his daughter," Frank pointed out. They'd both seen natural parents do far worse than that to their children.

"I suppose you're right." She sighed and studied her coffee for a moment. Then she looked up. "Mrs. Donato makes paper flowers." Her eyes lit up. "Do you suppose she sells them in City Hall Park?"

"Do you think *she* killed the girl?" he asked skeptically. "Because she acted pretty innocent when I questioned her."

She sighed again. "No, I guess I don't think she did it."

She looked tired. He figured she'd been delivering babies and hadn't been getting enough sleep. Why did babies always come in the middle of the night?

"You aren't going to find out who killed Emilia Donato," he warned her. "Nobody is going to find out. Sometimes we can't solve these cases. Most times, in fact. Girls like that, they take up with a stranger, and they end up dead. Maybe the girl herself didn't know who he was."

"But she wasn't taking up with strangers anymore," she reminded him. "She was going to get a job."

"That's what she told the woman at the mission. We don't know what she did when she left there. And nobody knows why she was in the park that morning. She couldn't have been there to look for a job."

"Her killer knows why she was there," she argued.

"Maybe. Maybe not. But you've got to accept the fact that sometimes there just isn't an answer and some murders don't get solved."

"It's not fair, Malloy."

"No, it's not. But you've got to accept it, and you've got to forget about Emilia Donato, Sarah."

He waited for her to agree, but she never did.

# 9

SARAH PURPOSELY DIDN'T GLANCE OVER WHEN SHE
walked past Police Headquarters on Mulberry Street.
She was half afraid she'd see Malloy if she did. Of
course, he didn't have any right to stop her from what
she was doing. Nobody did, come to that. Still, she
didn't feel like having an argument with him about it
in the middle of the street, and she knew him well
enough to know he'd want to argue if he saw her
heading toward the Prodigal Son Mission.

She'd wanted to come yesterday, but she knew
Sunday wasn't a typical day at the mission. Besides,
she'd had a baby to deliver, and by the time she was
finished, it was too late. Yes, Monday morning was
better anyway. The beginning of a new week would
be the perfect time to offer her services as an instruc-
tor. Volunteering her help was just what she needed to

make her feel her life was serving an important purpose.

And if she found out more about Emilia Donato's murder, too, well, that would be extremely fortunate.

A very small girl opened the door to her knock. She looked up at Sarah with big brown eyes, her expression solemn, and didn't utter a single word. Sarah couldn't help smiling.

"Is Mrs. Wells at home?" she asked.

The little girl nodded her head and didn't move.

"Could I come in to see her?" Sarah asked.

The girl had to think it over. Apparently, she decided Sarah was acceptable, because she stepped back after a few moments and opened the door wide enough for her visitor to enter. The red-haired girl who had answered the door the last time was hurrying down the hallway from the kitchen. "Aggie, I told you not to open the door!" she scolded the child.

The little one looked up at Sarah, gave her a mischievous grin, and scurried away, dodging the older girl to scramble up the staircase and out of sight.

"I'm sorry, miss," the red-haired girl said, a little breathless from her rush. "Aggie don't pay much mind to anybody but Mrs. Wells. Can I help you?"

"I came to see Mrs. Wells, if she's available. Would you tell her Mrs. Brandt is here?"

"Mrs. Brandt, how good to see you," Mrs. Wells said.

Sarah and the girl looked up in surprise to see her descending the stairs.

"Aggie told me I had a visitor." She gave the red-haired girl a look that appeared only mildly disapproving, but the girl paled noticeably, and her eyes widened with apprehension.

"I'm that sorry, Mrs. Wells, truly I am!" she said anxiously. "She don't pay me no mind when I tell her not to do something."

"Doesn't," Mrs. Wells said, correcting her. "She doesn't pay you *any* mind, Maeve. In that case, you need to watch her more closely, don't you?"

"Yes, ma'am," she agreed eagerly and bobbed a curtsey. "I'll do that, I will." She hurried off up the stairs, presumably to find Aggie and watch her closely.

"One does try to teach them manners," Mrs. Wells explained apologetically. "One isn't always successful. Would you come in and sit down, Mrs. Brandt? I presume you're here to discuss the party." Sarah's mother had scheduled the party to benefit the mission for Thursday evening.

Sarah followed her hostess into the parlor and took a seat on the worn sofa once more. "I'll be glad to discuss the party, if you wish," she began, "but I really came here to volunteer my services to you."

Mrs. Wells was so self-contained that Sarah had a difficult time reading her reaction. She'd had one, of course, but it was so slight it might have been anything from pleasure to distaste. Sarah had no way of judging. "You said you are a midwife," Mrs. Wells said, and Sarah heard the unspoken question.

"I'm sure you don't have a need for a midwife at the mission, but I'm also a trained nurse. I was very impressed with the work you're doing here, Mrs. Wells, and I haven't been able to stop thinking about the mission. I want to help you in whatever way I can."

"You're already helping quite a bit by raising funds for our ministry here," she reminded her.

Sarah folded her hands and leaned forward to show her sincerity. "I want to do more than that. I'd like to work directly with the girls."

The expression on Mrs. Wells's face looked almost like suspicion. "Doing what?"

"I could teach them a class in hygiene," Sarah offered, glad she'd taken the time to think this through. "So many illnesses can be prevented by the simple application of soap and water, and you mentioned yourself how ignorant the people in the tenements are about the importance of cleanliness."

"You're right, of course," she said, her voice carefully expressionless.

Sarah hadn't really thought about what reaction she might get from her offer, but she'd certainly never imagined disapproval. "On the other hand," Sarah said quickly, "if you have something else in mind, something you think would be more valuable, I would be happy to do whatever would help you the most."

"My dear Mrs. Brandt, please don't think I'm ungrateful for your offer," she assured Sarah with one of her sweet smiles. "I didn't mean to give that impression. I'm afraid . . . Well, quite frankly, people are often inspired when they see the work we do here and enthusiastically offer to help. Their enthusiasm seldom survives a few additional visits to the mission, however. You see, the idea of helping the poor is far more appealing than actually doing the work. The poor aren't especially anxious to be helped, and they are seldom grateful."

Now Sarah understood. She wasn't the first upper-class woman to impulsively offer her assistance. "I'm not as innocent as you imagine, Mrs. Wells," Sarah assured her. "My husband was a physician who worked with the poor, and I've delivered many babies right here in this neighborhood myself."

"In that case, you understand the situation. I'm also reluctant to introduce someone new to the girls who might not ever return. If that happens frequently, the girls begin to believe they are repulsive in some way. God's creatures should be humble, Mrs. Brandt, but not humiliated."

Sarah nodded her understanding. "I promise you, I won't disappear after one visit."

This time Mrs. Wells folded her hands and leaned forward, her eyes dark with the soul-searching intensity Sarah had noticed before. "Mrs. Brandt, why are you doing this?"

Sarah thought she'd already explained herself. "I want to do something important with my life."

"Why?"

Sarah hadn't expected to be challenged, and she was surprised to realize she didn't really have an answer to that question. "I . . . I guess it's because of Emilia."

"Because of her death?" Mrs. Wells asked.

Sarah knew this was a large part of her motivation. "Yes, that's it. It's difficult to accept that such a young girl with so much promise will never get the chance to fulfill her destiny."

Mrs. Wells smiled kindly. "On the other hand, she'll never fall back into a life of debauchery again either. If you are going to mourn for what might have been, you should know how few girls succeed in fulfilling the goals you had for Emilia."

"But she was determined to have a decent life," Sarah argued.

"They all are, when they arrive here. For every girl who stays pure, a dozen more backslide, and a thousand never come to us at all. Emilia had already failed once, and she might well have failed again. This time at least she was fortunate that she died in a state of grace and will spend eternity in heaven."

"Are you saying her death was a blessing?" Sarah asked in amazement.

"Death *can* be a blessing, Mrs. Brandt. We should trust the Lord's judgment."

"But the Lord didn't kill her," Sarah pointed out. "A human being took matters into his own hands."

"Then we must trust the Lord to be the judge of that, too."

"I'm afraid I can't be as forgiving as you, Mrs. Wells," Sarah said. "I'd like to see justice done."

" 'Vengeance is mine; I will repay, saith the Lord,' " she quoted.

Sarah would have to be sure to tell Malloy that he and Mrs. Wells agreed about the necessity of catching Emilia's killer. "I suppose I'm going to have to learn to accept your point of view."

"Because you've seen the wisdom of it?"

"No, because the police have closed the investigation into Emilia's death."

"Closed it?" Mrs. Wells echoed as if she didn't understand.

"Yes, they aren't particularly interested in who killed her or why, and since no one else is either, they're not going to waste any more time on it."

Mrs. Wells was staring intently at Sarah. "Your friend Mr. Malloy seemed very determined to solve the case, and you were certain he would."

"He was ordered to stop the investigation," Sarah

said, trying not to sound bitter. "I'm very much afraid no one will ever find out who killed Emilia."

Mrs. Wells closed her eyes as a spasm of pain twisted her features. It was the first strong emotion Sarah had seen her display, and it lasted only a moment. Then she lowered her head, and Sarah realized she must be praying. Even though she hadn't betrayed her grief at Emilia's death, Sarah now knew she had been concealing her true emotions, holding them tightly in check as well-bred females were expected to do. Perhaps she had been hurt so many times, she could no longer allow herself to feel the true depths of anguish and loss at all. Even still, losing Emilia was a blow, and her grief was just as real as if she'd collapsed on the floor in hysterics.

When she raised her head, Sarah saw how fragile was her self-control and how strained the smile she managed. Her eyes were moist with unshed tears. "We must accept God's will," she said softly, as if trying to convince herself. Obviously, she wasn't as resigned to Emilia's death as she'd wanted Sarah to believe.

"The question is, will you accept me?" Sarah asked. "I couldn't do anything for Emilia, but perhaps I can help the next girl. I'd like the chance to try."

"Certainly, Mrs. Brandt," she said, shedding her grief by force of will. "We would be honored to have you here."

Frank shouldn't have felt guilty. He didn't have any reason to feel guilty. Nobody could find Emilia Donato's killer. Even if someone knew something, the Italians didn't trust the police. They'd carry a secret like that to their graves before sharing it with the cops. All things considered, the killer had probably spared the girl a life of misery anyway. Not that he approved of murder, of course, but some deaths were more tragic than others. This girl's was less tragic than most.

And it wasn't that he'd just given up or anything. He'd been *ordered* to close the case. He could lose his job if he disobeyed. Which was why he didn't feel guilty, not a bit.

He just wished he could forget the expression on Sarah Brandt's face when he'd told her they'd never find Emilia's killer.

So now he was back in the alley where he'd found the mysterious Danny, the boy who supposedly knew who'd killed Sarah's husband. This time he'd brought some help, though. He'd had to hunt down these two cops from the night watch and wake them up. When things were quiet, the beat cops found a safe hidey-hole and nodded off. They weren't too happy about being disturbed, but since he could've reported them for sleeping on duty and Commissioner Teddy Roosevelt had been cracking down on malingerers on the force, they weren't complaining too much.

"You sure he's back? I ain't seen him around," one of the cops asked as they groped their way through the alley to the rear of the tenements.

"He's back," Frank said with more confidence than he had a right to feel. What he knew for sure was that *somebody* was living in the hovel where he'd found Danny the last time. An empty space where no one would charge rent, no matter how humble, wouldn't stay vacant for long. Probably the most he could hope for was that someone inside would know where to find Danny now. A slim possibility, to be sure, but the only one he had.

Frank cursed as he tripped over a drunk sleeping it off in the alley. "Light your lantern," he told one of the cops irritably. "We'll need to see who's in the house."

After some fumbling and some more cursing, the cop got the lantern lit. It made an eerie glow in the shadowy courtyard, revealing more sleeping forms on the ground here and there, drunks taking advantage of the relative shelter.

Frank sent one of the cops around behind the shanty in case someone tried to create a new exit through the rear wall when the trouble started. Then he stationed the other cop on one side of the crude doorway, holding the lantern up to illuminate the inmates, and he took the other side himself. When they were in position, he nodded to the cop with the lantern. The fellow raised his nightstick and pounded on the door, nearly shattering the flimsy structure with the force of his blow.

"Police!" he shouted. "Everybody out!"

The other cop began pounding on the back wall of the structure to hurry the evacuation process along.

The place came alive like a disturbed beehive. Shouts and screams and the sounds of bodies thudding against walls and each other erupted from within. In another second, the door swung open and small forms spewed out, arms covering heads to ward off blows from the dreaded locusts. They ran in every direction, disappearing into the darkness.

Frank waited like a patient fisherman, letting the little ones go. Finally, a larger figure emerged. The cop brought down his locust, and the taller boy fell to his knees with a cry of pain. He wasn't Danny, but Frank grabbed him and dragged him out of the way, holding on to the limp form in case he was only faking injury. They watched until the last of the children had vanished, but Danny didn't come out. Frank sent the cop with the lantern inside to make sure no one else was lingering, then he jerked his prisoner to his feet and slammed him up against the wall of the hovel.

The cop shone the lantern light directly in the boy's face. He squinted in pain, but Frank recognized him as the one who had sliced his arm so Danny could escape. "Do you remember me, b'hoyo?" Frank asked menacingly.

The boy blinked, trying to focus, but having little success. He stank of beer, among other things, and the blow from the cop's locust had scattered whatever brains he'd had left.

"Let's take him down to Headquarters so he can think about his situation for a little while," Frank suggested and turned him over to the two cops. They each took an arm and began dragging the protesting boy toward the alley that led to the street.

Frank followed, absently rubbing the cut on his arm. The stitches still itched like crazy. His mother said that was a good sign, but it didn't feel good. It just made him angry. This kid would bear the brunt of his anger. Frank couldn't help hoping the boy didn't betray Danny too quickly.

Mrs. Wells had scheduled Sarah's first class for Tuesday morning. The girls had entered the classroom quietly, almost hesitantly. She could see their wariness and suspicion. Like stray dogs who had been kicked too many times, they trusted no one. The red-haired girl, Maeve, was the worst of all. She glared at Sarah with undisguised animosity.

Sarah forced herself to keep smiling, as if she sensed nothing amiss. At least they were paying attention, she thought, painfully aware of their unblinking stares as she began her lesson. At first they seemed to be afraid to react, but then Sarah said something especially silly, just to test them. Someone in the back giggled, quickly slapping a hand over her mouth as if afraid of being reprimanded, but Sarah laughed, too, and soon they were all laughing. All except Maeve, who continued to glare.

Slowly, Sarah won them over. By the end of the class, they were interrupting each other with questions, raising their hands and waving them to capture her attention, if only for a few moments. When the class was finished and she dismissed them, they jostled each other, pushing and shoving, as they all tried to gather around her at once.

Their faces revealed a variety of ethnic backgrounds, the tongues a babble of different accents, but the eyes were all exactly alike. Every pair held an eager desperation for Sarah's attention and approval. This, she knew, was why she'd come. Here was her chance to touch these girls' lives and show them they had other alternatives than the ones they saw around them. She wanted to help them choose the right path so they didn't end up selling themselves in the streets or worse.

Finally, the bell summoned the girls to their noon meal, and they reluctantly took their leave of her after extracting numerous promises that she would return. Only then did she notice the red-haired girl, Maeve, still lingering. She hadn't joined the group that had surrounded Sarah but had hung back. When they were alone, she came forward.

"Did you have a question, Maeve?" Sarah asked kindly, hoping to break through the animosity.

Only then did she correctly identify the expression in Maeve's brown eyes. She was defiant and . . . and *haughty*. Sarah could think of no other word to describe her. She came right up, looked Sarah straight in the eye, then turned and walked out of the room. Clearly, she wanted Sarah to know she didn't need her attention the way the other girls did. She didn't even *want* it. Sarah couldn't help wondering why she had felt compelled to inform her of that.

After gathering her things, Sarah went to find Mrs. Wells to take her leave. Everyone was in the dining room. Plank tables had been set up there, and girls of all sizes and shapes lined the benches on either side of them.

"Won't you join us, Mrs. Brandt?" Mrs. Wells asked before Sarah could say a thing. If she still harbored any reservations about Sarah's motivations for being there, she hid them well. Her smile was warm and friendly.

"I don't want to . . ." Sarah gestured helplessly. "Impose."

"You mean take food out of the children's mouths?" Mrs. Wells guessed. "Nonsense. We're just having soup and bread. One serving of each won't make any difference at all. Please, have a seat."

She indicated an empty place at the end of one of the tables, across from Maeve and the child Aggie. Maeve didn't look pleased by Sarah's choice of seats, but Aggie glanced up when Sarah sat down across from her. Her expression was still solemn, but her eyes danced with mischief.

"Aggie, behave," Maeve warned sternly, giving Sarah a look that accused her of encouraging bad behavior.

"Maeve, please get Mrs. Brandt some luncheon," Mrs. Wells said.

Maeve's expression changed instantly. She smiled, practically beaming with pleasure as she looked up at Mrs. Wells. "Yes, ma'am," she said, rising so quickly she would have knocked over the bench if the other girls' weight hadn't been holding it in place.

"I can serve myself," Sarah protested, but Maeve didn't even glance at her. She took her orders from Mrs. Wells and sought only to please her.

"You're our guest," Mrs. Wells said, sliding into the bench beside her. She had, Sarah noticed, gotten her own bowl of soup.

"Aggie seems young to be here," Sarah observed, noticing the next youngest of the girls was at least several years older than the child. Aggie couldn't be more than five and perhaps as young as three.

"She's a foundling," Mrs. Wells explained, giving Aggie a small smile which the child did not return. "We found her sleeping in our doorway one morning several months ago. She was painfully thin and filthy and dressed in rags, and she wouldn't speak. We tried to find her family, but no one in the neighborhood knew who she was — or at least no one admitted it."

"She's still very quiet," Sarah said, then smiled at Aggie. "Do you like living here, Aggie?"

The little girl did not return the smile, but she nodded slowly, deliberately, proving she'd understood Sarah's question. Sarah had wondered if the child might be deaf, which would explain her being mute, but apparently, she could hear just fine.

"She still doesn't speak," Mrs. Wells explained. "And we don't really know her name, of course. I named her Agnes, after my mother."

"Sometimes children stop speaking when they are badly frightened by something," Sarah said as Maeve returned with her soup and a slice of bread. Sarah didn't even want to imagine what a child like Aggie might have seen to scare her speechless.

Maeve carried the soup carefully, not allowing so much as a drop to spill. She set it in front of Sarah with the air of one delivering a precious gift, then looked at Mrs. Wells for approval. She didn't care if Sarah was pleased or not.

"Thank you, Maeve," Mrs. Wells said, and the girl fairly beamed with pride.

Squaring her narrow shoulders, she took her own seat again, bumping Aggie slightly but deliberately in the process. The smaller girl cast Maeve an annoyed glance, but she didn't make a fuss. Once again Sarah saw the mischievous gleam in her eyes.

Aggie got up from her place, walked around to where Mrs. Wells sat, and gently tugged at the woman's sleeve. Mrs. Wells looked down.

"What is it, Aggie?"

The child gave her a beseeching look and held out her arms. No one could have resisted such an appeal. She reached down and lifted the child into her lap. "You haven't finished your soup," she said and pulled the child's bowl over so she could feed her.

Sarah happened to glance over at Maeve and caught a look of sheer loathing in the girl's honey brown eyes. Jealousy was an ugly thing, Sarah thought, looking to see if the other girls shared this emotion. To her surprise, she saw that most of them were staring at the cozy couple with unabashed envy. When she looked back at Aggie, she caught the little one giving the rest of them a superior smirk that Mrs. Wells couldn't see.

The hair on Sarah's arms rose as a chill raced over her. So much for her illusions that the mission was a haven from the evils of the world. If she'd thought of this as Eden, it was an Eden where the serpent operated freely.

Did Mrs. Wells suspect the petty rivalries that existed? Did she realize she was sowing seeds of discord among her charges simply by favoring one who appeared to be weaker and more helpless than the others? Surely not, Sarah decided. Someone as caring as Mrs. Wells wouldn't consciously foster such rivalries, and she certainly wouldn't let the rivalries continue if she knew about them. But no wonder so many of the girls backslid, as Mrs. Wells had lamented. They'd come here seeking acceptance and found only more of the rejection they'd known outside.

Sarah was wondering how she could tactfully point out what was happening when Mrs. Wells asked, "How is your soup, Mrs. Brandt?"

"It's delicious," Sarah lied, then took her first spoonful. Fortunately, it was tasty enough that she didn't have to retract her praise.

"We are fortunate that several of the grocers supply us at a very reasonable cost, and my father was a butcher," she said, feeding Aggie another spoonful of soup. "He always sold the better cuts of meat to his customers, so I learned early in life how to use the parts no one else wanted. We pinch every penny we receive in donations."

"You must be sure to mention that on Thursday night," Sarah said. "Which girls will you be bringing with you to the party?"

Instantly, Sarah regretted the question. Although Mrs. Wells seemed unaware of it, Sarah could literally feel the wave of reaction that swept through the room. The eyes of every girl had turned to her. Obviously, they'd known nothing about a party or the prospect of attending. Their desperate longing to be chosen was palpable — and not very pleasant to behold. These were children who very recently would have sold their bodies or even their souls for a crust of bread. What might they do for such an honor as this?

Looking at the desire burning in those eyes, Sarah could almost imagine they might do murder.

"No, Mrs. Brandt," Mrs. Wells replied, still engrossed in feeding Aggie her soup. "I haven't made up my mind yet."

Frank stifled a yawn as he finished up his report on the warehouse robbery he'd just solved. The hour was late, and he was the last detective still working at Police Headquarters, but Frank had to admit that was the only inconvenience involved. If real business ran as smoothly as criminal business did in the city, Millionaires' Row would be a hundred miles long, he thought, recalling how easily he'd put this case to rest. The Short Tail Gang had robbed a warehouse of a shipment of dry goods, and the owners had summoned the police. Frank let it be known among his informants that he'd been assigned to the case, and the next day a member of the gang approached him. After some negotiating, they'd settled on the amount of the reward, and he'd notified the owners, who had duly posted it. Then Frank had been able to locate the missing goods exactly where the gang member told him they would be. The owners paid Frank the reward, he gave the gang their share, and everyone was happy. Except, of course, the poor folks who had to pay more for their dry goods to cover the cost of the reward.

Why couldn't all crimes be solved in such a civilized manner? Frank's job would be so much easier, and he'd be able to make captain a lot sooner. Making the rank of captain had always been his goal, because of the financial security that came with it. Captains received a percentage of all bribes paid to the men in their command, and they retired as wealthy men. Ever since Brian was born, Frank had believed the child would never be able to earn a living and would need to be supported the rest of his life. A mere policeman or even a detective sergeant couldn't hope to leave a legacy large enough for that. A captain could, though, even after paying the $14,000 bribe necessary to obtain the appointment.

Brian's recent operation had taken some of Frank's "captain" savings, but it had also reduced the possibility that Brian would require the kind of care Frank had once envisioned. The boy was still deaf, but even that might not be much of a handicap. Educators he'd spoken with assured Frank that the boy could learn a trade and make a living. So maybe making captain wasn't so important after all. Maybe, instead, he had a totally different kind of obligation to his son.

And to Sarah Brandt.

He stacked the reports neatly and filed them. Then he sighed and made his way back down the stairs to the lobby of the building. The offices were mostly empty at this time of night, and the rest of the building was quiet. No one had brought in any prisoners for a while, and those who were already in custody had been locked away two floors below in the dank dungeon that passed for a jail.

Frank wearily headed down the stairs to the cells. The stench of unwashed bodies, vomit, and human waste was like a miasma in this airless, windowless hole. The night guard slept in his chair, snoring loudly, as did many of the inmates who were curled on filthy mattresses or on the even filthier floor. Others sat, sleepless, staring into the constant darkness with haunted eyes.

Frank picked up the guard's locust and poked it through the bars to prod a body that sat huddled against them, trembling even in sleep. He started awake, coming to his feet instantly, ready to ward off whatever attack was imminent. His crazed gaze finally settled on Frank, standing patiently outside the bars.

"Hello, Billy boy," Frank said cheerfully. "How are you feeling? Are they taking good care of you down here?"

Billy was the boy Frank had found living in Danny's hovel. Almost twenty-four hours had passed since Frank had brought him in, but he'd steadfastly refused to betray his friend. Frank could have charged him with assaulting a police officer — for cutting his arm the day he'd tried to arrest Danny — but that would have meant transferring him to the city jail. In spite of its nickname, The Tombs was a palace compared to this lockup. Frank figured Billy would never betray his friend once he'd settled in over there in relative comfort.

Frank had begun to doubt he would break even here, but seeing him now, he realized the fight had finally gone out of the boy. Stronger men than he had broken in this place.

"Get me out of here," the boy pleaded in a broken whisper.

"I'll be glad to, just as soon as you tell me what I want to know," Frank said pleasantly.

"I'll tell you anything. *Please,*" he added, his youthful face twisting with the effort of begging.

Frank told the guard to let Billy out, and he had the boy taken to an interrogation room on the floor above. He smelled pretty bad, Frank noted when he closed the door to the room behind him. He wore only a ragged pair of pants and an equally disreputable shirt, all he'd had time to grab on his dash out of the hovel after the raid. Shoeless and coatless, he'd suffered from the chill of the cellar in addition to all the other discomforts. A stocky young man, he'd been quite formidable when Frank met him the first time. Now he sat with shoulders hunched and eyes lowered to the table.

He looked up warily, showing a black eye and bruised face beneath a layer of grime. Frank had administered some of the bruises, while others were courtesy of his cell mates. The other men would have subjected him to additional indignities as well, unspeakable things he'd never tell a soul for as long as he lived. Frank had tried to warn him last night, but the boy had to learn the hard way.

Frank pulled out the other chair, and the boy jumped at the noise. He eyed Frank as a cornered rat would have eyed a dog. "Are you hungry, Billy?" Frank asked.

The boy nodded quickly.

"I'll bet you'd appreciate a square meal and a clean bed."

The boy nodded again, more slowly this time, as if sensing a trick.

"You know," Frank said thoughtfully, "you ruined a perfectly good suit when you cut my arm. I get mad whenever I think about it."

"I don't know where Danny is," Billy said.

Frank started to rise.

"But I've got some ideas where you could find him," the boy added hastily.

Frank took his seat again and waited.

"What'll I get if I tell you?" the boy asked.

Frank smiled. "You're in no position to bargain, Billy boy," he reminded him. "What you'll get if you *don't* tell me is to rot right here. I can hold out as long as you can, but every day that passes gives Danny a chance to hide better and gives you less of a chance of giving me information that will help me find him."

"What did he do that you want to find him?"

"You can ask him that yourself when you see him in The Tombs," Frank replied, losing his patience. "Now are you going to talk or do I send you back downstairs?" He started to rise again, but the boy stopped him.

"All right, all right!" he cried, motioning for Frank to sit back down. "I'll tell you everything I know. Like I said, he might not be in any of the places, but maybe somebody there'll know where he is."

Frank reached into his coat pocket and pulled out his notebook and a pencil. Wetting the tip of the lead on his tongue, he said, "Start talking."

A half an hour later, Frank had only had to cuff the boy a couple times to remind him not to lie. Satisfied he'd gotten all he could for now, he said, "I'll call the guard."

"I'm going to The Tombs now, right?" Billy said hopefully.

Frank called the guard and stood back as two burly men came in. "Take him back downstairs," he said.

"No!" Billy cried and began swearing and fighting as the guards jerked him to his feet. Several blows from the locust sticks subdued him enough to allow the guards to drag him out without too much trouble. He still cursed Frank roundly as his voice faded down the hallway.

Frank looked at the list of locations Billy had given him. None of them were places he could go alone at night, and some would be risky even during the day. He'd need to get some patrolmen to go with him, but that would have to wait until tomorrow. Billy would have to spend another night in the cellar, but he certainly deserved it. And if he'd lied, he'd be even more anxious to make amends tomorrow.

Frank tucked his notes back into his coat pocket and made his way upstairs and out into the street. He'd get an early start tomorrow. Tonight he'd go back to his flat and spend a few minutes watching his son sleep to remind himself why this was all worthwhile.

Sarah had spent the day delivering twins to a family who already had five more children than they could feed. The mother was so sickly, Sarah doubted she'd be able to nourish two babies adequately. The babies would doubtless die, and the effort might kill the mother, too. Tomorrow she would return to check on everyone and suggest an orphanage for the infants. They might even be adopted if they were healthy, which meant any delay in placing them would lower their chances.

Convincing the family was often difficult, however. For some reason, people thought it cruel to put an infant in an orphanage, but thought nothing of turning a five-year-old out into the streets to fend for itself. If this woman died, her husband would probably be unable to keep the family together and all of the children would be on the streets. No one wanted to imagine themselves being that desperately cruel in the future, however, so people were reluctant to take steps to prevent it.

Sarah knew of a few good orphanages in the city, but she couldn't help wondering if Mrs. Wells had contacts someplace. If Sarah could assure the family of the babies' care, convincing them might be easier. As she left the family's tenement, she turned her steps toward Mulberry Street.

The weather was unseasonably warm, teasing in its promise of spring. But soon the winter wind would whistle through the city streets, stealing men's hats and freezing the unfortunates whose only home was a sheltered doorway. As Sarah reached the mission, she heard the sound of shouting coming from inside. Even stranger, the shouter was a man.

Thinking Mrs. Wells might need assistance, she hurried up the front steps and let herself in without knocking.

Once inside, she realized the shouting was also in Italian.

"Please, Mr. Donato," Mrs. Wells was saying very calmly and patiently. "I can't understand you unless you speak English."

*Mr. Donato!* Could it be Emilia's father? The doors to the parlor were open, and Sarah saw a middle-aged man dressed as a laborer confronting Mrs. Wells. He stood only a few inches taller than she, but his body was thickened by years of hard labor. He was shaking his fist in her face, but miraculously, Mrs. Wells didn't seem the least bit concerned for her safety.

"You have money," Donato was saying. "Give money for bury Emilia!"

"I told you, we're all very sorry about Emilia's death, but the mission simply doesn't have money to spare for something like that. I dearly wish we could help, but I'm afraid you'll have to take care of her yourself."

"No have money to bury!" Donato informed her. "You have money. You bury!"

Mrs. Wells still betrayed no hint of apprehension. She stared Donato straight in the eye. "I cannot help you," she said loudly. Many people believed they could make those who didn't speak English understand them if they shouted. "And if you don't leave, I'm afraid I shall have to summon the police."

He may not have understood much else, but he knew the word "police." He stiffened in alarm and muttered something unpleasant in Italian. Then he turned on his heel and hurried from the room. Sarah stepped out of the way just in time to avoid being run over. He hardly spared her a glance.

"Mrs. Brandt," Mrs. Wells exclaimed in surprise. They both winced as Donato slammed the door behind him. Then Mrs. Wells managed a small smile. "I didn't hear you come in."

"It's no wonder," Sarah said, coming into the room. "You were otherwise engaged. Are you all right?"

"Yes, of course," she said, although she did look a bit pale. "That was Emilia's father. He's naturally upset. It seems he inquired about her body at the city morgue and was told she'd be put in a pauper's grave unless he claimed the body."

"I gather he can't afford to bury her himself."

"No, and he just wouldn't accept the fact that the mission doesn't have money for that sort of thing, either." Mrs. Wells sighed and sat down in one of the chairs. Obviously, the encounter had upset her more than she wanted to admit. "I'd like nothing better than to give Emilia a Christian burial, but it just isn't possible."

"Funerals are more for the living, I've always believed," Sarah said by way of comfort. "The dead certainly don't need them, but it helps the mourners accept the loss better."

"We did have a memorial service for her with the other girls," Mrs. Wells said. "That was all I could do, since her family is Catholic and wouldn't attend a service here anyway."

"Then you mustn't feel guilty," Sarah said. "You've done what you could."

"Thank you for your encouragement, Mrs. Brandt." Mrs. Wells smiled her sweet smile. "Now, was there some reason you stopped by or were you just sent by an angel to rescue me from Mr. Donato?"

Sarah began to tell her about the twin babies and their family, but even as she spoke, she was thinking about Emilia being buried in a pauper's grave. Sarah didn't want that either, and she was certain she could figure out some way to help her family.

# 10

Sarah hoped Mr. Donato had returned to his home after his encounter with Mrs. Wells. If not, she'd have no idea how to locate him. Searching the saloons in the neighborhood would probably be fruitful, but that was a task Sarah wasn't prepared to handle.

Mulberry Street was crowded with men returning home after their day's work. The street vendors were doing their last rush of business, selling what remained of their foodstuffs for the evening meals. Housewives bartered in loud voices for the best deal, and children ran and shouted, glad for a few more moments of freedom before being called in for the evening.

Sarah took the winding alley that led to the rear tenement where the Donatos lived. She looked up, trying to find their windows and judge whether anyone could be at home. It wasn't dark enough yet for anyone to be wasting a candle or gaslight, so she had no clue. Her only option was to trudge up the stairs and find out for herself. She only hoped Mrs. Donato wasn't there alone. She wasn't quite sure what her welcome would be under those circumstances.

When she reached the third-floor landing, she could hear two men arguing in Italian. One of the voices sounded like it might be Mr. Donato's. Sarah crept up more quietly, in case she decided she didn't want the men to see her. But when she reached the top of the stairs, she saw that Mr. Donato was arguing with his son, Georgio.

Georgio's organ rested on the kitchen table, and he sat in one of the chairs, his crutches on the floor beside him. Mr. Donato was pacing the small kitchen, gesturing angrily. Mrs. Donato was nowhere in sight. Sarah took a deep breath, walked up to the open doorway, and knocked loudly on the door frame.

Donato broke off in mid-sentence, and both men turned to her in surprise.

"Excuse me for intruding," she said with the polite smile her mother had taught her years ago. "I'm Mrs. Brandt, and I was a friend of Emilia's."

Both men recognized her from their earlier encounters and pointed, shouting accusations she couldn't understand. She clutched her medical bag in front of her and kept smiling until they paused for breath.

"I understand you'd like to give Emilia a decent burial," she said into the first moment of silence. "I thought perhaps I could help."

"Why you want to help?" Georgio asked suspiciously.

"I told you, I met Emilia at the mission. I was

also . . . well, the police asked me to identify her body." Sarah's voice caught at the memory, but she forced herself to go on. "I can't forget how she looked, lying there, and I'd like to see her put to rest properly."

"Mission lady no pay," Mr. Donato reported. "You pay?"

"I'll certainly help as much as I can. Have you spoken with anyone about making arrangements?"

Mr. Donato exploded into a babble of furious Italian punctuated by violent hand motions. Sarah listened with a frown, trying to pick up a word here and there that might give her a clue as to what had made him so angry, but when he was finished, she was as baffled as ever. She looked at Georgio questioningly.

"Mama go to priest," he said. He said the word "priest" as if it left a bad taste in his mouth.

"I hadn't thought of that," Sarah said. "Maybe the church can help."

Donato said something in Italian and spit on the floor.

Sarah jumped, unable to check her reaction. This time she looked at Georgio in wide-eyed amazement.

"Priest no bury a Dago whore," he explained bitterly.

"But Emilia had changed. She wasn't —"

"No," Georgio interrupted her impatiently. "Priest no care. No bury Dago. Hate Dago."

This didn't seem right to Sarah. "But you're Catholics, aren't you? Wouldn't the priest do something for *you*, if not for Emilia?"

"No, he hate Dagos," Georgio repeated angrily.

"Then why don't you go to another church?" she asked, horrified.

"All priests Irish. All hate Dagos," Georgio explained impatiently. "You understand now?"

Sarah was afraid she did, only too well. "Would the priest bury Emilia if he was paid?"

Georgio shrugged. "She still whore," he reminded her.

"Whore," his father spat, then muttered something in Italian.

His son's face grew scarlet with fury, and he lunged to his feet, nearly forgetting he couldn't support himself. Grasping the table to keep from falling, he shouted something about his mother.

Donato grabbed his head with both hands, babbling something and howling in anguish. His face was almost purple.

"Mr. Donato, you must calm down," Sarah cried in alarm.

Neither man even seemed aware of her presence. Donato was frantically trying to explain something to his furious son, who was screaming invectives at him. Then, as Sarah had feared, Donato made a strangled sound and pitched over. Georgio instinctively reached out to grab him, but with only one foot to balance him, he merely succeeded in breaking his father's fall as they both collapsed onto the floor.

Sarah was beside them in an instant, rolling Mr. Donato on his back and helping Georgio untangle himself from his father.

"What is wrong?" Georgio demanded as Sarah checked the older man's pulse.

"I don't know yet. It could be anything." She threw open her medical bag and dragged out the stethoscope.

"What is that?" Georgio demanded, but Sarah didn't take time to explain.

She fitted in the ear pieces and pressed the bell to Donato's chest. Miraculously, his heartbeat was strong and regular, although much too rapid. "His heart seems fine," she reported, then lifted his eyelids to check his eyes. Before she could do more, he moaned and his eyes fluttered open.

"Papa?" Georgio asked, leaning closer from where he knelt beside Sarah.

"Georgio?" Donato replied weakly and tried to push himself up.

"Don't move," Sarah warned him. "Lie still for a few minutes."

Donato looked at her as if he'd never seen her before.

"You had a fall," Sarah explained. "I'm a nurse. You need to rest for a while, until we're sure you're all right." She looked at Georgio. "Make sure he understands what I'm saying."

Georgio translated, and the older man groaned again and closed his eyes. He was only resting this time, though.

"Did he hurt you when he fell?" she asked Georgio.

He shook his head, not taking his eyes off his father.

"What was he saying when he collapsed?"

Georgio gave her a look that said it was none of her business.

"I need to know if he was . . ." She'd started to say incoherent, but realized Georgio probably wouldn't recognize the word. "Was he talking crazy? I need to know if something is wrong with his brain . . . his head," she added, pointing to her own.

Georgio's frown was puzzled. "He say Mama is a whore, too, and this is why Emilia is bad."

This obviously made no sense to Georgio, but Sarah understood it. Somehow Mr. Donato had guessed that he wasn't Emilia's father and he had decided his wife had been unfaithful. Or so she assumed, but Mr. Donato was groaning again and muttering, "No, no."

"Not Mama," he insisted. "*Emilia's* mama."

Now Sarah was growing more alarmed. The man may have had a stroke. She'd have to get him to a hospital right away, although even that wouldn't help him very much if he was paralyzed. She took his hands in hers. "Can you squeeze my hands, Mr. Donato?"

He did, with a grip so powerful it made her cry out. "*Emilia's* mama is whore!" he cried, his gaze boring into hers, desperate to make her understand he wasn't crazy.

She exchanged a glace with Georgio, who only shrugged.

"Mr. Donato, don't excite yourself. I'll send for a —"

"No, Emilia not our baby. Midwife bring. Our baby die."

Now she was sure he was confused. "I didn't bring a baby," she told him gently, thinking he was talking about her.

"No, when Emilia born! Our baby born, but he die. Mama so sad, all a time, sad. I think she die if baby die. Midwife have baby of whore. No want baby. She take away. I tell her we keep baby. She take dead baby away. Mama never know."

"Are you saying Emilia wasn't your child at all?" Sarah asked incredulously.

"Child of whore. She whore, like mother. No good."

"She have yellow hair," Georgio murmured, as if finally solving an old mystery.

"*Sì,*" his father confirmed. "Yellow hair, like whore."

All these years, Mrs. Donato had thought her daughter was the child of her rapist. Sarah finally understood. Mrs. Donato hadn't been able to love her daughter because she'd believed her to be the result of her greatest shame. Mr. Donato had carried the guilt of an act of kindness that still hadn't made his wife happy. Emilia had known only that she wasn't loved and had sought that love from men who destroyed her.

Mr. Donato was weeping, and Sarah and Georgio helped him sit up. After determining that he was recovered from his faint, they got him into a chair. Sarah checked his pulse and his heart again, and found them normal. His color was good, and he seemed no worse for his experience.

"You should rest for a day or two, just to be sure you're all right," Sarah suggested.

He waved away the idea. "I work tomorrow, same as always."

She glanced at Georgio, who shrugged again, promising nothing.

"I'll go down to the morgue and see what I can find out about burying Emilia. I won't let them put her into a pauper's grave," she promised. From the look Georgio was giving her, Sarah figured he felt no further obligation toward the woman he'd believed to be his sister. From what Sarah knew, Mrs. Donato probably wouldn't either when she found out the truth about Emilia's birth. "Do you want me to let you know . . . ?" she began, but Georgio was already shaking his head.

"You go," he said. "No come back."

Sarah was only too glad to oblige.

By the time Sarah got home, she had decided what she must do for Emilia, but she didn't have a chance to act on that decision. A message awaited her that one of her patients had gone into labor. The baby, the first for this mother, took his time arriving, and she didn't get back home until almost noon the next day. Since she had to attend the party at her mother's house that evening, she spent the rest of the afternoon napping.

Sarah wasn't to learn which girls Mrs. Wells had chosen to accompany her to the party until the event itself. Perhaps the woman just had difficulty making the decision. Sarah hoped that was the reason. Or perhaps Mrs. Wells understood the intense rivalry among the girls and didn't want to give anyone a reason to gloat any sooner than necessary. The only other possibility was that she was making the girls compete for the honor up to the very last minute. Whatever her real reason, Sarah was afraid the effect was the latter. She could just imagine how the girls would be preening and fawning, not to mention undermining each other, to win attention.

"You're very quiet, my dear," her mother observed as they checked the third-floor ballroom one last time. The gaslights cast the room in a warm glow that was reflected in the large mirrors, and vases of fresh flowers filled it with a sweet perfume. The wooden floor shone like glass, and the gilt chairs were grouped conveniently around the room for those who wanted to sit and chat or those who were too old or too fat to do anything *but* sit and chat. At one end of the room, a "light" buffet supper was being laid, which included enough food to feed the entire population of Mulberry Bend for a week. At the other end, a piano player and harpist were tuning up. "Are you worried about how the evening will go?"

Sarah gave her mother a reassuring smile. "How could I be? You're the perfect hostess, Mother."

"I don't have any control over this Mrs. Wells, however," she said. "Are you sure she'll give a good account of herself?"

"I'm certain of it. She's the most self-possessed female I've ever met."

"In her own world, she may be, but what will happen when she's faced with a crowd of her . . ." She caught herself just in time. She'd almost said "her betters," and Sarah would have had to reprove her for it. Chagrined by Sarah's frown, she said, "You know what I mean, dear. Our friends can be very intimidating to others who are . . . less fortunate."

"I doubt that Mrs. Wells considers herself less fortunate than your friends, Mother. She may not be wealthy in worldly terms, but she believes herself the equal of anyone on this earth."

Her mother was not reassured by this information. "We should go downstairs. Our guests will be arriving soon."

When they reached the front foyer, they found

Felix Decker talking with Richard Dennis, who had just arrived. He greeted Sarah warmly, although she could see he was a bit nervous.

"I'm sure your wife would have been pleased at what you're doing this evening," she said to him when her parents were distracted by a question from one of the servants.

Richard's smile was wan. "I hope so. I never really concerned myself with what would please her when she was alive, so I can't be sure."

"You must stop feeling guilty, Richard. We can't change the past. We can only do better in the future."

Was that what she was trying to do herself? Was that what had motivated her work at the mission? She hadn't been aware of any guilt, but perhaps she felt some for her privileged upbringing. Did she feel some sort of debt that must be repaid? Or was it all about Emilia and her senseless death?

She didn't have time to figure it out just then, because her mother was giving them instructions. "Your father and I will greet people here at the door. Why don't you and Richard go upstairs and circulate among the guests?"

Richard followed her upstairs, his step heavy and his shoulders hunched against some invisible burden. She began to regret asking him to participate, but then the guests began to arrive, and she forgot to feel sorry for him. To his credit, he quickly assumed the role of host with the ease of long practice, and no one would have suspected he had any qualms about the event.

Sarah greeted many of her old friends and people she hadn't seen in many years. The crowd included a sprinkling of Astors and Vanderbilts, along with some of the less famous but no less wealthy names from the social register. Then a tall woman came in whom Sarah didn't recognize.

For all her expensive finery, she was very plain and somewhat awkward, as if uncomfortable in her own body. She looked as if she might be much more at home on horseback, riding with the hunt, than mingling with the idle rich. The man with her was a head shorter than she and almost as round as he was tall. His bald head shone in the reflected gaslight. Richard Dennis greeted them both with genuine affection and motioned Sarah over to meet them.

"Sarah, this is Opal and Charles Graves. Opal was Hazel's dearest friend." Sarah remembered that Richard had given her mother their names to add to the guest list.

"Oh, yes," Sarah said, shaking both their hands. "I'm so glad you could come."

"And we're glad you've agreed to accompany Richard to our party on Saturday night," Opal Graves said. "I hope he warned you that you must wear a costume."

Sarah managed not to wince. Richard had said nothing about a costume, although she should have guessed it would be expected at a Halloween party. "I'm looking forward to it," she managed.

"So are we." Mrs. Graves gave Richard a glance that said her true enjoyment would be seeing him with a female.

Sarah decided a change of subject was in order. "I suppose you already know all about the work of the mission."

"Yes," Opal Graves agreed. "I've supported their work for many years, since they first began in fact."

"I'm sure Mrs. Wells will be happy to see a familiar face in the crowd," Sarah said.

Mrs. Graves frowned ever so slightly. "I'm afraid I'm not well acquainted with Mrs. Wells. Her late husband was the one who first approached Charles and me about his dreams of starting a ministry."

"He must have been an extraordinary man," Sarah said.

"Hardly," Charles Graves said with a chuckle. "He'd still be preaching on street corners if his wife hadn't pushed him."

"Now, darling, you mustn't speak ill of the dead," his wife chided him fondly. "Reverend Wells was a dedicated man of God. What he lacked in ambition, he more than made up for in his zeal to minister to others."

"And his wife more than made up for his lack of ambition," he chided right back, looking up at her with an adoring twinkle in his eyes. For all the difference in their physical appearances, they obviously shared a mutual affection that Sarah couldn't help but envy.

"I understand you were the one who first introduced Mrs. Dennis to the work at the mission," Sarah said, deciding she'd ask Mrs. Graves some more about Mrs. Wells when she could get her alone.

"Yes, I was," she said with a rueful glance at Richard.

"She did enjoy her work there," Richard assured her quickly. However much he might blame the mission for Hazel's death, he held no grudge against his friends.

"And she is very kindly remembered there," Sarah added.

"I'm not surprised," Mrs. Graves said. "Hazel was an exceptional person."

Some more guests were arriving who needed Sarah's attention, but she said to Mrs. Graves, "I'd love to hear more about how you became involved with the mission. Could we talk later?"

"Certainly," Mrs. Graves said. "I'd be happy to tell you everything I know about it."

Mr. and Mrs. Graves went off to mingle and greet acquaintances while Sarah and Richard finished their duties. A short time later, Sarah's parents joined the party, which meant that all the guests had arrived. Mrs. Wells was scheduled to make her appearance a little later in the evening, after the guests had a chance to sample the food and wine the Deckers had provided for them and were in a more generous mood.

Sarah found Opal Graves sitting in a corner, entertaining an elderly lady who could hardly hear a word she was saying. Sarah rescued her, taking her out into the corridor where they could speak without being overheard.

"I wanted to thank you for coming," Sarah began.

"And I wanted to thank you for inviting us. It's good to see Richard taking an interest in society again. He's been far too solitary since Hazel died. I suppose we have you to thank for that, Mrs. Brandt," she added with a twinkle.

"I don't want to disappoint you, but Richard and I are merely friends," Sarah said. "He knew that my work often takes me to the Lower East Side, and he asked me to go with him to the mission so he could find out what his wife had done there."

"Forgive me if I sound like a hopeless romantic,

but love has grown in rockier soil than that," she said. "Now don't look so panicked," she added with a large grin. "I'm only teasing you."

Sarah managed a smile in return. "It would take more than that to panic me," she assured her companion. "I *am* grateful to Richard for introducing me to the mission, however. I've started volunteering there myself."

"You mentioned your work takes you to that neighborhood. What type of work do you do?"

"I'm a midwife," she said, fully expecting to see the frown of disapproval or even distaste that usually followed this admission, but Mrs. Graves simply looked intrigued. "Of course I don't deliver babies at the mission," Sarah assured her. "I've begun teaching the girls about hygiene and how to protect themselves against disease."

"Mrs. Brandt, you astonish me! How did you ever escape the clutches of your adoring family to pursue such a career?"

"I married well," Sarah said, her smile genuine this time. "And when my husband died, I continued his work. He was a physician."

"I see. So you've decided to help Mrs. Wells save the souls of those poor, miserable girls."

"I don't know about their souls. That's Mrs. Wells's job. I'm only trying to save their bodies."

"A worthy goal, and one that is far easier to attain," Mrs. Graves said with sincere approval.

"You said you didn't know Mrs. Wells very well, but I was wondering what you thought of her," Sarah asked.

"What do you mean?" she asked.

"I'm not asking you to gossip," Sarah hastily assured her. "I'd just like your opinion on her methods. Have they been successful? I saw a few things at the mission that concerned me, and I'd like to have someone else's view of the situation."

"As I told you, I don't know Mrs. Wells very well. We've continued to support the mission out of respect for Mr. Wells and his vision, and because we honestly believe it serves a useful purpose. I'm ashamed to admit we haven't been as involved as we should have been, however, since Hazel died. I've been — well, going there brought back too many memories of her. What have you seen that disturbed you?"

"Nothing untoward," Sarah said. "I'm sure Mrs. Wells isn't even aware of it, but I saw a lot of rivalry among the girls for her affections."

"I would expect them to be jealous of each other, under the circumstances. Our children are jealous of each other. It's only natural for them to want all the attention for themselves."

"I wish it were that type of jealousy, but I had a sister, and I know the difference," Sarah said. "At the mission, they are much more fierce."

"Don't forget you aren't dealing with a finishing school here, Mrs. Brandt," Mrs. Graves reminded her. "You would know even better than I what those girls have been through. They may have seen people beaten to death out of jealousy or stabbed for a scrap of food. They've probably never even seen *friendly* competition."

"I suppose you're right. I hadn't thought of it that way, but I still don't think it's a good situation. The girls behave almost as if they were romantic rivals."

Mrs. Graves raised her eyebrows as the meaning

of Sarah's words sank in. "I suppose they are, in a way," she agreed. "They must be desperate for love, and Mrs. Wells offers them the promise of unconditional acceptance — from God but mostly from herself, as his messenger on earth."

"I thought you said you didn't know her well," Sarah said.

"I don't, but this seems like the approach she would take," she explained. "And it would certainly be effective. The girls know they must repent their evil ways in order to win Mrs. Wells's acceptance, and along the way, they seek God's acceptance as well."

"That seems almost . . . dishonest," Sarah admitted reluctantly.

"Tricking someone into the Kingdom of God? Perhaps you're right, but who are we to judge?"

Sarah had no answer to that question.

"Mrs. Brandt, although I haven't been to the mission in a long time, I do know how much Hazel loved her work there," Mrs. Graves said. "She found . . . I'm not sure how to describe it. Perhaps it was peace she found. I'd never seen her so contented, and she credited Mrs. Wells for helping her achieve that peace. This is why we've continued to support the work there."

"Would you like to go down with me sometime to see it again?"

Mrs. Graves considered the offer for a moment. "Yes, after what you've told me, I think I'd like to see what's going on there."

Sarah smiled, glad that she would have an unbiased observer to help her make sense of what she'd seen there. "I'll be going tomorrow, if you're free."

"I'll make a point of it," she said thoughtfully.

Someone touched Sarah's arm. She turned to see one of the maids, who said, "Mrs. Wells is here, ma'am."

Frank was getting tired of searching through the rat holes of the slums in the dark of night, but he supposed if he was hunting rats, he'd have to go where they were. He and his cohorts had spent the better part of two days seeking out the locations Billy had given him. Finding Danny during the daylight hours was more than he'd hoped for, and his expectations had been met. The young man was most likely out keeping an eye on his young charges while they worked the streets. The children who stole for him would require constant supervision, Frank supposed. Children could be unreliable.

Of all the places Billy had mentioned, Frank had thought the shanty under the bridge would be their best bet, and he'd been right. The earlier rain shower had driven everyone to shelter, and when they arrived after full dark, a fire still smoldered in front of the open doorway. A small child was making his way through the trash and debris carrying a growler of beer toward it. He would have purchased the tin pail of liquid refreshment at a nearby stale beer dive for a few cents. Children wouldn't be welcome to remain in such places, so one of them would make a purchase and bring it back for the rest of them to share. When their weariness and loneliness and fear had been deadened by the alcohol, the children would sleep under the protection of their mentor.

A shout from the hovel announced the arrival of the child with the beer, and those inside spilled out to meet him, waving their tin cups eagerly. Frank watched from the shadows, waiting for the tallest figure to emerge. From this distance, Frank could tell only that the figure was the right size to be Danny. He couldn't hear what was said, but the children fell silent and waited while he took the first ration from the growler. When he'd finished, the rest of them crowded around, jostling to be next and hardly bothering to step away before downing their portions.

Frank felt a pain and realized he was clenching his jaws in anger at the spectacle. He couldn't have said at whom his anger was directed. Not Danny, for all he might deserve it. The boy did protect the children as well as he could, Frank supposed. And the lot of them were merely trying to survive in a world where the adults who should have cherished them had abandoned them to die. Maybe he was angry at a world where children must seek help and comfort from each other because no one cared for or about them.

"Let's go," he told the cops with him. He'd brought four this time, taking no chances of losing his quarry. As previously arranged, they stole away into the darkness to make a circle around the hovel. Whichever way Danny ran, someone would be there to intercept him.

The children were quarreling now over who got the dregs of beer. Some were coming to blows, while others were shrieking and pushing. The taller figure merely stood by, looking on but taking no part in the squabbling. Frank could imagine he was smiling at the confusion. He wouldn't be smiling for long.

When he judged the other cops had had time to reach their positions, he gave the signal. "Police!" he shouted.

The children needed no other warning. Without a second's hesitation, they fled into the night. Frank kept his eye on the tall figure, who ducked and ran in the opposite direction from his voice. Frank hurried after him, taking care not to fall over the rubble in the darkness. "He's heading uptown," he shouted, in case the others hadn't seen him. The river on one side would limit the directions he could go.

"I see him!" someone shouted, and Frank turned toward the voice. By the time he got to the other side of the shanty, he could hear the sounds of a scuffle and then the familiar thump of locust wood against human flesh. The scuffle ceased.

Now, if Danny's brains hadn't been knocked loose, Frank would finally get some answers.

Sarah went downstairs to greet her guest. Mrs. Wells was waiting in the foyer with two girls. Sarah wasn't surprised to see the glow of Maeve's red hair in the light from the chandelier. She recognized the other girl, Gina, from her class. Both of them were dressed in white with pale blue sashes tied around their waists, making Sarah think of sacrificial virgins. They were looking around wide-eyed and slack-jawed, taking in the luxury of the Deckers' home with an air of disbelief.

Mrs. Wells betrayed no hint that she was impressed by her surroundings. She simply waited patiently, her expression serene. Apparently, Sarah's mother's theory that Mrs. Wells would be intimidated by her "betters" was unfounded.

"Mrs. Wells, I'm so glad you're here," Sarah said. "Maeve and Gina, you both look lovely."

The girls smiled tentatively, gratified at the compliment but still nervous and unsure of themselves.

"We appreciate your invitation, Mrs. Brandt," Mrs. Wells said. "Although you didn't have to send a carriage for us."

"My mother insisted," Sarah said. "The weather forecast was for showers, and besides, she doesn't like the idea of ladies traveling unaccompanied in the city at night." Sarah was aware of the irony, since she herself frequently traveled unaccompanied in the city at night. "Please come upstairs. Everyone is anxious to meet you."

"Come along, girls," Mrs. Wells said encouragingly when they hesitated to follow her and Sarah up the grand staircase. They exchanged an anxious glance before obeying.

When they reached the ballroom, Sarah's parents greeted them. After introductions had been made, Mrs. Decker took charge of Mrs. Wells and proceeded to introduce her to other guests, leaving the two girls standing alone in stunned silence as they took in the grand room and the sumptuously clad guests.

"Would you girls like something to eat?" Sarah asked.

They nodded, perhaps too frightened to speak aloud, and Sarah escorted them over to the buffet table. Gina came eagerly, but Maeve displayed her usual reluctance to trust Sarah.

"Who is all this food for?" Gina asked in a whisper.

Sarah realized they'd probably never seen this much food all in one place in their lives. "It's for the guests," Sarah explained.

Gina glanced at the crowd and back at the table again. "They must be real hungry."

Sarah bit back a smile and handed each of the girls a plate. "Just tell the servers what you'd like and they'll put it on your plate for you," she instructed.

By the time the girls had reached the end of the table, their plates were heaping with far more food than they could ever hope to eat. The servants were frowning in disapproval, but they didn't say anything because Sarah kept giving them warning looks behind the girls' backs. Sarah seated them at one of the small tables that had been set up at the end of the room, and took the liberty of joining them while they ate.

Mrs. Wells had taught them table manners, if not restraint, so at least they didn't disgrace themselves. Sarah gave them a few minutes to sample their delicacies before striking up a conversation.

"Did you enjoy the carriage ride?" she asked.

Maeve looked at her suspiciously. Plainly, she was remembering how she'd snubbed Sarah at the mission, but she knew she needed to be polite to her here. She was probably trying to decide if Sarah's friendliness was genuine or a ploy to get her in some kind of trouble as revenge.

Gina didn't have any reason to be suspicious. "It was fancy," she said. "And so big!" Her thick, dark hair hung in a single braid down her back, and her dark eyes were lovely in her olive-skinned face. While Maeve was bony and angular, Gina's curves were soft and rounded.

"The driver wasn't very nice," Maeve reported sourly.

"He was, too!" Gina said. "He opened the door for us!"

"He kept his nose up in the air," Maeve said. "You could see he didn't like us."

"Coachmen are trained to act like that," Sarah explained. "They're not supposed to stare at their passengers."

"He helped us down when we got out, too," Gina reminded Maeve. "He took my hand so I wouldn't fall. I thought he was handsome."

"He was ugly as a toad," Maeve insisted.

Since the Deckers' coachman was neither, Sarah had to smile.

"I'm just glad we come in a coach," Gina said. "I never was in one before, and neither was you, Maeve, so don't pretend you was!"

Maeve wasn't going to argue the point, especially in front of Sarah, so she just glared at Gina. Sarah remembered what Opal Graves had said about sisters arguing, and had to agree the girls were behaving just like siblings. Perhaps she'd been mistaken in thinking the rivalry at the mission was more than that.

"We wanted to be sure you were safe coming here tonight," Sarah said, deciding to raise the subject she really wanted to discuss, "after what happened to Emilia."

Gina frowned and glanced around uneasily, as if checking to make sure no one had overheard this reference to the dead girl.

Maeve didn't seem the least bit disturbed, however. "That won't happen to us," she said confidently.

"You seem very sure," Sarah said.

"Emilia was stupid," Maeve said.

"You just didn't like her because she was Mrs. Wells's favorite," Gina accused.

"No, she wasn't," Maeve insisted. "Mrs. Wells just felt sorry for her!"

"Then she must feel sorry for you, too, because she gave you all of her jobs!"

"You're just jealous because she didn't give them to you!"

"I don't want to watch Aggie," Gina claimed disdainfully. "That little brat can run out in the street and get herself trampled to a lump for all I care!"

"I guess Mrs. Wells don't know how much you hate Aggie," Maeve observed with a sly grin, and Gina blushed scarlet.

"Everybody hates Aggie, and that includes you!" Gina claimed.

"What other jobs did Emilia have?" Sarah asked quickly, before the two girls came to blows. "Besides watching Aggie, that is."

Maeve obviously had no intention of answering, but Gina said, "She was in charge of making all the girls get up and dressed in the morning, then she looked after them all day, so they went to their classes and to meals and didn't sneak out. Then she checked to make sure everybody was in bed at night."

"All that in addition to looking after Aggie," Sarah said in amazement. "That's a lot of responsibility. And now you do it all, Maeve?"

Somewhat mollified by the implied respect, Maeve said, "Yes, ma'am, I do everything."

"So now all the girls hate her instead of Emilia," Gina said smugly.

Wanting to head off another argument, Sarah said,

"You said Emilia was stupid, Maeve. It sounds like she had to be smart to do all those jobs, though."

"She went places she shouldn't go," Maeve said. "Like that park where she got killed. That was stupid."

"City Hall Park isn't really a bad place," Sarah said. "In fact, it's a very nice park. Courting couples meet there all the time. But of course we don't know why she went there that morning. Did she say anything to either of you about it?"

"She was always doing things she shouldn't do," Maeve insisted. Her eyes narrowed. "And she was stupid with men. That's why she got herself killed."

"Was she going to meet a man that morning?" Sarah asked, remembering Mrs. Wells had said one of the girls heard Emilia say she wanted Ugo to see how nice she looked. Perhaps Emilia had said more than that.

"No, she was going to get a job," Gina said. "She told everybody who would listen. We was sick of hearing about it."

"That and her new dress," Maeve recalled with a frown. "It wasn't new at all. Somebody gave it for charity, and it was an ugly old thing! Mrs. Wells offered it to me first, but I wouldn't take it."

"She did not," Gina said. "You're a liar! Everybody knows she always gave the best things to Emilia. And I heard you begging Mrs. Wells for that hat Emilia was wearing."

"So you don't think Emilia was going to meet a lover that morning?" Sarah pressed, trying not to remember the hat and dress in question had been hers.

"Not likely," Gina said, taking a bite of caviar then

quickly spitting it out. "Ew, what was that awful stuff?"

"Fish eggs," Sarah said with a smile. "I've never cared for them either."

Gina looked more closely at the brown glop. "Fish don't lay eggs," she informed Sarah. "*Chickens* lay eggs. You're teasing me."

Sarah could have argued, but she didn't want to get distracted. "You're right, I am," she agreed. "Why wouldn't Emilia have been meeting a lover?"

"She said she didn't have no use for men after what happened to her," Gina said. "She swore she'd never so much as speak to one again."

"She must've changed her mind," Maeve said with an unpleasant grin, "or she wouldn't be dead, would she?"

"Did either of you hear her say she wished Ugo could see her in her new outfit?" Sarah asked.

Both girls just gave her a blank look.

Sarah opened her mouth to ask another question when she heard her father calling for everyone's attention.

"Is it time for Mrs. Wells?" Maeve asked in alarm.

"I guess it is," Sarah replied, and the girls were gone in an instant, hurrying to take their places beside her. Sarah rose and made her way more slowly to the other end of the ballroom so she could have a good view of the proceedings.

# II

DANNY HADN'T FARED WELL DURING THE TRIP BACK to Mulberry Street. He insisted on trying to escape, which meant the officers had to keep using their locusts on him. Frank was beginning to wonder if there'd be anything left to question. By the time he got the boy into an interrogation room, he was bloodied and more than a little groggy.

"Do you remember me, b'hoyo?" Frank asked him. "Your friend Billy cut me up so you could escape the last time we met."

Danny gave him a pained grin, still cocky in spite of his condition. "You gave me whiskey the last time," he remembered.

"Tell me what I want to know, and you could get some tonight, too."

"I don't know much," he tried.

"I think you do. You started telling me about Dr.

Tom Brandt. And don't pretend you don't know who I'm talking about."

"I don't gotta pretend," the boy said. Even with the bruises, he managed to look innocent.

"The doctor who was murdered three years ago. You were telling me how somebody hired you to fetch the good doctor. Who was it?"

Danny no longer looked quite so cocky. He glanced over at the cop still holding his locust at the ready and measured his chances. He didn't want to anger Frank, but he was afraid of someone else, too. "He finds out I ratted on him, he'll kill me."

"How could he find out?"

"You start asking him questions, what else he gonna think? Then he finds me and kills me."

"Maybe you should be more worried about me right now," Frank suggested.

But Danny wasn't fooled. "You might beat me up, but you ain't gonna kill me."

"I'll put him in jail and then he'll meet up with Old Sparky," Frank said, using the nickname for New York's brand new electric chair. "You won't have to worry about him again."

Danny shook his head, his expression grim. "Swells like him don't go to jail. You even talk to him, he'll have your job."

"Nobody's that important," Frank tried, knowing perfectly well it was a lie. "But if you're that afraid, I'll see you get out of the city safely. You can go someplace else, where you can start a new life."

"Why would I want to get out of the city?" he asked in amazement. "This is the only place I've ever lived. This is where all my friends are."

Frank sighed. He wasn't getting anywhere with

kindness. He could beat the boy, but Frank had an idea he'd hold up pretty well against brute force. He'd been taking beatings all his life, and he was right when he said Frank wouldn't kill him. How else was he going to find out who killed Tom Brandt?

"I guess I'll just keep you here overnight, then," he said, rising.

"I could give you a nice reward for letting me go," the boy offered.

Frank glared at him. "Now you've gone and made me mad, Danny." He motioned for the guard to take him away.

Danny gave him no trouble, and Frank led them down to the cellar cells.

The night guard woke up at the sound of their footsteps. "You got another birdie for the cage, Detective Sergeant?" he asked sleepily.

"Yeah, but I want you to let one prisoner out and put this one in."

Frank noticed Danny's swagger had vanished at the sight of the cells and their inhabitants. He was still trying to put up a good front, but Frank could see the growing apprehension in his eyes.

"Who do you want to let out?" the night guard asked.

Frank pointed to the huddled figure in the corner of the nearest cell. Billy hadn't moved, although Frank could see his eyes staring blankly at them.

The guard went in and pulled him to his feet, prodding him with his locust to get him to leave the cell. Frank had once seen some boys torture a dog to death. Billy's expression reminded him of that dog.

"What's the matter, Danny? Don't you recognize

your friend?" Frank asked, shoving Danny until the two were face to face.

He watched Danny's eyes widen in recognition. Billy seemed incapable of a change of expression.

"What're you doing here?" Danny demanded of his friend. "What happened to you?"

Billy just stared, as if he didn't even comprehend the question.

"You'll have to excuse Billy," Frank said. "He's been here for a while, and he's not feeling too good right now."

"Billy, say something!" Danny begged, his voice high with fear.

Frank figured the two had been through a lot together, but Danny had never seen his friend like this. It was an ugly thing to witness.

Billy's mouth was moving, but it took him a minute to find his voice. "Danny?" he croaked.

"Billy! What happened to you? What're you doing here?"

Billy couldn't answer, and Frank decided Danny had seen enough. "Put him in the cell," he told the guard.

Danny put up a fight this time, but he stood no chance against the burly guards. When the cell door slammed shut, Frank looked at Billy, who didn't seem to comprehend what was happening.

"You can't leave me here!" Danny was yelling. "I'll tell you what you want to know! I'll tell you everything!"

Frank ignored him. He knew better than to believe promises made in panic. "I'll be back tomorrow, Danny," he said. "We'll have a long talk then."

He took Billy's arm. "Come on, b'hoyo."

Billy went meekly, eyes lowered, steps shuffling. He stumbled on the stairs, and Frank had to hold his arm to keep him from falling.

If Frank had wanted revenge for being attacked by this boy, he would be savoring this moment. Instead he felt disgusted.

He took the boy upstairs to the lobby and out the front door. "You can go now," Frank told him.

Billy's blank gaze rose to him, not comprehending. "Go?"

"Yeah, go home, or wherever it is you go."

"I thought . . ."

"You thought I'd send you to The Tombs," Frank supplied. "You're not worth the trouble. Get out of here, and if I ever arrest you again, you'll wish I'd killed you tonight."

For a second, the boy didn't move. Maybe he thought it was a trick, that Frank would knock him down if he moved. So Frank stepped back and waited, slipping his fingers into his vest pockets.

Billy's Adam's apple bobbed as he swallowed, and Frank could see him gathering himself.

Before he could blink, the boy was gone, running as if for his life and disappearing into the darkness.

Frank rubbed his arm, which still itched, and walked off in the other direction.

Sarah's mother introduced Richard Dennis who told briefly about his wife's devotion to the mission and the work they did. Obviously ill at ease, he still made a moving speech, then introduced Mrs. Wells, who began to speak with a poise that must have impressed even the Deckers.

Sarah found herself mesmerized by Mrs. Wells's

presentation, even though she thought she'd already been thoroughly impressed by the work they were doing at the mission. She'd meant to watch the reactions of the other guests, but she forgot, caught up in the images Mrs. Wells painted of the lost children of the tenements.

Maeve and Gina stood beside her looking young and vulnerable, like the sacrificial virgins Sarah had imagined them to be earlier in the evening. They listened with rapt attention, their young faces fairly glowing with their devotion to the woman who had saved them.

Mrs. Wells told stories of some of the girls she had known. She gave no names, so Sarah could only guess which story was whose. But she had no trouble at all identifying the subject of her final story.

"I wish I could tell you we succeed with all of our girls. The truth is that some of them yield to temptation again when they leave us. One young woman came to us to escape a life of shame and degradation. She was ill and desperate, and we believed she had found a home with us and hope for the future.

"We were wrong, however. She stayed only until her health returned. When she was strong again, she left us, turning her back on God's love and ours. We continued to pray for her. We pray for every girl who comes through our doors, in the hope that God will protect her and perhaps even bring her back before she is totally lost.

"The girl of whom I speak returned to the man who had first ruined her, believing his lies and trusting one who was unworthy of that trust. The next time we saw her, she was bruised and broken, beaten

nearly to death for the sin of loving an evil man."
Several women in the crowd murmured in sympathy.

"We could have turned her away," Mrs. Wells continued. "We could have reminded her that she had betrayed our faith in her. But we followed Christ's
admonition to forgive seventy times seven times, and
we once more offered her a haven. And once again
she grew strong. We prayed for her, and she began to
change. We saw her accept God's love. We saw her
reject the temptations of this world. She worked hard
and learned skills that would help her earn her living
honestly. One morning, she set out to start her new
life, full of hope and promise. It was a promise she
would not live to keep. She was only sixteen when
she died." Some of the guests gasped.

"Most of us would consider her sudden death a
tragedy," Mrs. Wells went on. "Had she never come
to the mission, had she died without knowing God's
love, her death *would* have been tragic. But she did
come to the mission. She did know God's love, and
now she is in paradise. 'O death where is thy sting?
O grave where is thy victory?'" she added, quoting
the Bible.

Several women dabbed at their eyes with lace
handkerchiefs, and Sarah felt the sting of tears herself.

"The tenements hold hundreds of girls like this.
We'd like to reach every one of them, but we can't do
that without your support." Mrs. Wells continued
with a moving appeal, and then she closed, offering
to speak to people individually if they had questions
about the mission.

A crowd quickly formed around her. Most of them
were female and deeply concerned about the plight of

young women in the city. Sarah stood back and watched Mrs. Wells answer their questions for a moment, until she noticed Gina and Maeve had been edged out and were standing alone. Sarah decided to rescue them again.

This time even Maeve looked glad to see her. Sarah ushered them away and got them a plate of sweets to nibble while they waited for Mrs. Wells to finish her business.

"I didn't know she was gonna talk about Emilia," Gina said to Maeve after she'd sampled a few of the different cakes. "She never did before."

"Emilia wasn't dead before," Maeve reminded her impatiently. "She wasn't nothing to talk about until she was dead."

"Mrs. Wells probably thinks her story will touch people's hearts," Sarah said.

"You mean make them sad?" Gina asked with a frown.

"That's right," Sarah said.

Gina still didn't understand. "Why would they care? They didn't even know her."

"And the ones who did know her are *glad* she's dead," Maeve informed Sarah importantly.

"I'm not glad," Gina protested.

"You said you was," Maeve reminded her. "Everybody was."

"Just like they'll all be glad when you're dead," Gina taunted.

Sarah tried not to let them see how they'd shocked her. But, she reminded herself, the young didn't really comprehend death, not the way older people did. They saw it only as a solution to a problem. If they hadn't liked Emilia because she bossed them around and was Mrs. Wells's favorite, they'd simply be glad she was gone.

Or maybe one of them had decided to solve the problem herself.

Sarah recalled what she had been discussing with the girls earlier, about Emilia going out to show someone her dress. Perhaps someone had invented that story, someone who wanted to cast suspicion on another. "Girls, would you do me a favor?"

They both looked up. Gina was curious and Maeve, suspicious.

"Mrs. Wells said one of the girls heard Emilia say she wanted Ugo to see her in her new dress. Ugo was her former lover."

"The one who beat her up, we know," Maeve said in disgust.

"Could you find out which girl it was?" Sarah asked.

Maeve just frowned, but Gina was still eager to please her. "Sure," she agreed.

Sarah had arranged to meet Opal Graves at the mission at one o'clock the next afternoon so she would have time to accomplish her other goals that morning. She'd debated asking Malloy to help her with her first errand, but she knew he'd just be angry that she was still involved in Emilia's death. Since she wasn't in the mood for a lecture, she found the small Catholic church herself. The building was nestled between the tenements a few blocks from Mulberry Street.

St. John's was well kept, in spite of the poverty of its parishioners. She passed an elderly Irish woman coming out and held the door for her. The woman looked at her curiously, as if she could tell just by looking that Sarah wasn't a Catholic. Or maybe that was Sarah's overactive imagination.

The interior of the church was cold and quiet and dim. Paneled in dark wood, the room was lit by a few candles in a rack at the rear of the church and whatever sunlight seeped through the tiny stained glass windows. Her footsteps echoed on the hardwood floor as she walked down the aisle, looking for someone who could help her. She should have asked the old woman, she realized, then she heard a sound to her right.

The door to what appeared to be a closet opened and another old woman came out. She said, "Thank you, Father," and carefully closed the door.

Could the priest be in the closet? Sarah started toward the door as the old woman hobbled away, but before she reached it, another door just beside it opened, and a priest emerged. He was young, his light brown hair plastered down so he would look more dignified, but it didn't help.

"Excuse me, Father," she called before he could walk away.

He looked up in surprise. "I'm sorry, I didn't know anyone else was waiting." He turned and started back into his closet.

"Could I ask you something before you go?" she called to stop him.

He turned back and frowned. "Didn't you want me to hear your confession?"

For a moment she didn't know what he was talking about, and then she remembered what little she knew about the Catholic faith. "Oh, no," she said with an apologetic smile as she finally reached him.

"I'm not even Catholic. I've come to ask you about one of your parishioners."

"Which one?"

"Emilia Donato."

His frown deepened. Sarah sensed his disapproval and hastily defended the girl.

"I know she'd behaved shamefully, but she repented in the end. She was a fine Christian girl when she died, and it would be a great comfort to her family to give her a decent burial," she added, painfully aware she was lying in church. Sarah and the residents of the mission were the only ones likely to be comforted.

"Maybe you'd better talk to Father O'Brien," he suggested. "Come."

Sarah followed him out a side door into what appeared to be the priests' private area. He took her to an office door and told her to wait while he went inside. In a moment, he returned and directed her into the room. An older priest rose from behind his desk. He was a large man whose face gave evidence of the years he'd spent bearing other people's burdens.

"How can I help you, Mrs. — ?"

"Mrs. Brandt," Sarah said. "I'm pleased to meet you, Father O'Brien."

He offered her a seat in one of two comfortable wing chairs by a window. The window overlooked an alley, but at least it let in some natural light. The young priest waited by the door, as if ready to rush to Father O'Brien's aid if necessary.

"Father Ahearn said you'd come about some Italian girl?" the old priest began when he had seated himself in the other chair.

She didn't like the way he said "Italian," but she said, "Emilia Donato. She was murdered last week."

The priest nodded. "Oh, yes. Her mother was here. She's the girl who went to the mission," he explained to Father Ahearn. Their disapproval was obvious.

"The mission can't afford to bury her," Sarah quickly explained, "and neither can her parents. Since her family is Catholic, I know they would be very grateful if the church would see that she was buried properly."

"Mrs. Brandt," the old priest explained patiently, "you must understand. We don't even allow the Italians to worship in the sanctuary."

Sarah could hardly believe what she was hearing. This was even worse than Georgio Donato had said. "Why on earth not?" she demanded.

"They are very different from us, my dear lady. Their customs and even their saints are different from ours. They celebrate different feast days and different holy days. They don't even speak the same language."

"But they worship the same God, don't they?" she challenged, unable to conceal her contempt for such bigotry. She couldn't believe that the Irish, who had been the victims of prejudice for so long themselves, would practice it on others.

"We allow them their own place to worship," Father Ahearn said defensively.

"Where, in the basement?" Sarah asked sarcastically.

"*Downstairs,*" he corrected her primly. "It's a very nice room."

Sarah could only gape at them, unable to conceive of so-called men of God relegating fellow Christians to the cellar to worship. "Do you at least allow them Christian charity?" Sarah asked, unable to keep the anger from her voice.

"All of our parishioners live in poverty," Father O'Brien said. "We do what we can for them."

"Do you bury those who can't afford it?"

Father O'Brien's expression was sad, although Sarah couldn't help doubting his sincerity. "The city buries them, Mrs. Brandt. We try to reserve our resources for the living."

"Unless they happen to be Italian," Sarah said before she remembered her manners.

Father O'Brien wasn't easily offended. "My answer would be the same if the girl was Irish."

"I'll have to take your word for that, won't I?" Sarah snapped and started to rise.

"Are you closely involved with the mission, Mrs. Brandt?" he asked before she could take her leave.

Something about the tone of his question disturbed her. "I just recently began to volunteer there," she said warily.

"Then you don't know very much about them," he guessed.

"I know they have converted some Catholic girls," Sarah said, "and I'm sure that must make them some sort of competition for you."

"God's work isn't a competition," he said with a small smile. "Although I can understand you might think we're jealous or resentful of the way Mrs. Wells is leading young girls away from their faith."

"I'm sure she would argue that she's leading them *to* faith," Sarah defended her.

"I'm sure she would. I just wonder what she would say about the girls who have simply been led away."

"What do you mean?"

"I mean, Mrs. Brandt, that you should ask Mrs. Wells what becomes of the girls who go to her mission and are never seen again."

He was jealous. That's the only explanation Sarah could think of to explain the priest's horrible accusation. No one knew anything about girls disappearing from the mission. Or at least she hadn't heard anyone say anything about it. She had no doubt that girls did leave. Emilia herself had returned to her old life after her first visit. Surely, others had done so, too. If no one ever heard from them again, it was probably because they had disappeared into a prostitute's life and early grave. She certainly wasn't going to give any credence to a rumor started by a priest who wouldn't even minister to people just because they spoke another language.

At least she knew she couldn't count on charity from the church to get Emilia decently buried. That meant she would have to figure out something herself. Such an expense would be a small fortune to people as poor as the Donatos, but surely, she could manage the cost of a simple casket and a burial plot herself. If not, she'd borrow money from her parents. Somehow, she would make sure that Emilia didn't end up in an unmarked grave.

Her next stop was a grim visit to the morgue to let them know she was going to see that Emilia was properly buried. Sarah was gratified to see a new attendant on duty. He was respectful both to Sarah and to Emilia's body.

When she'd explained her purpose, he gave her papers to fill out and sign. Then he said, "You better look at her clothes and see if they're fit to bury her in."

"They are," Sarah said, wanting to avoid looking at her old suit again with Emilia's blood smeared on the back.

"Then you better make sure everything's still there. Sometimes things disappear around here," he said kindly. "Some folks think it ain't much of a crime to steal from the dead."

Reluctantly, Sarah opened the bag and pulled out each item of clothing. When she pulled out the hat she'd worn for so long, the attendant said, "Might as well take that away. We don't bury people in hats. Shoes neither, so you can take them, too."

Sarah didn't want to take any of it, but she realized someone at the mission could probably use the shoes, at least. She dug them out of the bag and found a hat pin as well. A pretty metal flower adorned the end. She hadn't donated any hat pins, so it must have come from the mission. The foot-long pin was a bit rusty, but a girl with a new hat wouldn't mind cleaning it off and using it again. She laid it aside with the shoes and hat.

The attendant wrapped the items in brown paper, and Sarah took them with her. If she hurried, she would be just in time to meet Opal Graves at the mission. On the way, she stopped and bought a meat pie from a street vendor so she wouldn't have to eat at the mission. No matter what Mrs. Wells said, Sarah just couldn't bear to use anything that might benefit one of the girls.

When she arrived at the mission, Opal was already there. Sarah knew because her carriage was waiting for her at the curb and causing quite a sensation among the neighborhood children. They kept wanting to climb up and get inside. The driver was having quite a time scaring them away. Sarah found Opal inside, chatting with Mrs. Wells. Sarah greeted them both.

"I was just telling Mrs. Wells how well she did last night. I don't think anyone who heard her could refuse to support her work here," Opal said.

"You flatter me, Mrs. Graves," Mrs. Wells said. "And I assure you, many people refuse to support our work. But the Lord has always provided for us, and I have faith He always will."

"After last night, He'll have a lot of help," Opal said with a smile.

"I'm glad to hear our guests were generous," Sarah said. "My mother will be happy she was able to help."

"I was just about to show Mrs. Graves around, Mrs. Brandt. Would you like to accompany us?" Mrs. Wells asked.

"Thank you, but I promised the girls I would talk with them again today, if you don't mind. They had a lot of questions after our first class."

"They're upstairs sewing," Mrs. Wells said with a knowing smile. "I'm sure they'd be happy for an interruption. After we've finished our tour, we'll all have tea in the parlor."

Mrs. Wells escorted Opal to tour the downstairs and the yard while Sarah went upstairs. To her surprise, the girls squealed with delight when she walked into the room. She conducted an impromptu class in female health concerns, answering questions that would have shocked most women of her social status. The girls repeatedly told her how grateful they were for her willingness to discuss such sensitive topics. Probably no one else had ever done so with them.

Sarah discreetly ended the discussion when she heard Mrs. Wells bringing Opal up the stairs. Mrs. Wells introduced her guest to them as one of their benefactors and began explaining to Opal the training the girls were receiving. Sarah stepped out into the hallway, and Gina followed her.

"Mrs. Brandt, can I talk to you?" she asked quietly. She looked over her shoulder anxiously, probably checking to see if Maeve was going to stop her from speaking with Sarah. Fortunately, Maeve was busy showing off for their guest.

"Certainly, let's go back downstairs."

Gina followed her. As they walked into the parlor, Sarah realized she had left the package she'd brought from the morgue lying on a chair there. She'd have to remember to give it to Mrs. Wells before she left.

"What did you want to talk about?" Sarah asked her when they were alone.

"I did what you told me to do."

"What was that?" Sarah asked, trying to recall. So much had happened since last night, she was having trouble.

"You wanted to know which one of the girls heard Emilia say she wanted Ugo to see her all dressed up."

"Oh, yes." Sarah had completely forgotten. "Who was it?"

"It wasn't anybody."

"What do you mean?"

"I mean nobody heard her say that. I asked everybody, even Aggie."

"I thought Aggie doesn't speak."

"She don't, but she can hear. I asked her did she

hear Emilia say that, and she shook her head no. No-body heard her say nothing about Ugo. All she said was she wanted to get a job."

This was just what Sarah had feared. One of the girls had lied to Mrs. Wells, hoping to throw suspicion onto Ugo. All Sarah needed to do now was find out which girl had invented the lie. She would have to ask Mrs. Wells.

"What's that?" Gina asked, pointing at the parcel.

Sarah glanced at it. "I brought back the shoes and the hat Emilia was wearing when she died."

Gina looked at it longingly. "What are you going to do with them?"

Sarah realized that Gina would probably appreciate having Emilia's things. Perhaps she should consult with Mrs. Wells before making a gift of them, but she remembered what Gina had said last night about Emilia getting all the nice things when she'd been the girl in charge. Maeve would probably receive them now, if Mrs. Wells were making the choice, but Gina had earned a reward for trying to help Sarah.

"Would you like to have them?" she asked Gina.

The girl looked almost reluctant to admit that she did. Finally, she nodded tentatively.

With a smile, Sarah handed the package to her.

Gina glanced apprehensively in the direction of the door, as if afraid someone might come in and stop her, but seeing no one, she quickly tore open the package. Almost reverently, she picked up the hat that Sarah had considered throwing away and set it on her head. Her dark eyes shone with happiness and gratitude. "Maeve'll be so jealous!" she whispered with glee. Then she kicked off the worn slippers she wore and sat down to put the almost-new boots on her feet.

She was laughing with pleasure now, and when the hat slipped off and fell onto the floor, Sarah laughed, too.

"There's a hat pin in there, too. Do you know how to use it?"

"Oh, yes," Gina assured her happily. "All well-bred young ladies know how to use a hat pin!"

She picked up the hat with one hand and located the hat pin with the other. "No wonder Emilia wanted her mother to see her wearing this," she said as she stuck the hat on her head.

Sarah wasn't sure she'd heard her correctly. "Her mother?" she asked, but Gina wasn't paying attention.

She was staring at the pin. "What's all over it?"

"It's rusty," Sarah said. "It will come off if you —"

"That's not rust," Gina said, peering more closely. She ran a finger along the shaft and it came off brown and smooth, not gritty like rust.

Sarah looked more closely, too. In the dim light of the morgue, she hadn't paid much attention. She'd simply made an assumption, but now, seeing it in the light . . .

She had a vision of the brown stains on the back of Emilia's jacket — Sarah's old jacket. Malloy had said her killer had wiped the blood off his knife — a long, thin-bladed knife — and walked away.

Sarah felt as if the room were tilting, but she forced her hand to move. She snatched the pin out of Gina's hand. "I'll get you another one," she said. Her voice sounded as if it were coming from very far away. Gorge rose in her throat, but she swallowed it down.

"What is it?" Gina asked in alarm. "Your face is all white!"

"Nothing, I'm fine," Sarah insisted. She snatched up the discarded wrapping paper and quickly wrapped it around the pin.

They could hear Mrs. Wells and Opal coming down the stairs. Gina glanced in that direction and jerked the hat from her head. "Thank you," she whispered, gathering her discarded slippers, and darted out of the room. Sarah realized she was afraid Mrs. Wells would take away her gifts if she saw them, and once again she felt a niggling unease at the way the woman showed favoritism among the girls.

By the time Opal and Mrs. Wells entered the parlor, Sarah had drawn a couple deep breaths and managed to regain most of her composure. She tried not to think about the fact that she was holding in her hand the weapon that had killed Emilia.

"Mrs. Brandt, is something wrong?" Mrs. Wells asked the instant they came in.

Sarah tried to smile. "No, why do you ask?"

"You look quite pale," Opal said, echoing Gina.

"Do I?" Sarah decided to take advantage of their concern. "I was feeling a bit light-headed. Perhaps I should go home. I know you were planning tea, but —"

"Don't be silly," Opal said. "Of course you should go if you're not feeling well. I have my carriage outside, and I'll be happy to see you safely home. Mrs. Wells, I'm sorry to cut our visit short, but —"

"Of course, you're absolutely right," Mrs. Wells said. "Mrs. Brandt should go right home. Please feel free to return at any time, Mrs. Graves, and thank you for your support."

Sarah managed to say the correct things and allow Opal to escort her out of the mission. When her driver had handed them into the carriage, and they were settled, Opal noticed the package Sarah carried.

"What have you got there?" she asked.

Sarah looked down at the paper-wrapped hat pin. "I'm not sure you'll want to know."

# 12

"NOW YOU *MUST* TELL ME," OPAL INSISTED. "DOES IT have something to do with why you were suddenly taken ill?"

"Yes," Sarah said, laying the object on the seat beside her so she no longer had to touch it. "It gave me a bit of a shock."

"More than a bit of one," Opal said. "I thought you were going to faint."

Sarah sighed, grateful for the privacy of the carriage, even though Opal had been ostentatious to bring it into the neighborhood. "I didn't tell you the real reason I became interested in the mission," she began, and explained to her about Emilia and how she came to be wearing Sarah's clothes when she was killed in the park. "They didn't have any idea who the girl was and probably never would have found out, but one of the police detectives recognized the clothes. He asked me to identify the body, if I could."

"How horrible!" Opal exclaimed. "And how on earth would a *policeman* recognize your clothes?"

Sarah managed not to feel defensive. "I had met him several months ago when he was investigating another murder. I helped him solve the case."

Opal wasn't the least bit satisfied with this explanation. "Are you telling me this policeman remembered your clothes for several months and then recognized them on the dead girl?"

"I think it was the hat he remembered, and no, he didn't remember it for several months. He'd seen it recently. We . . . I've helped him with several other murder cases since then as well."

Sarah had expected to see disapproval or even disdain, but Opal simply looked intrigued. "You must tell me all about this policeman and how you got involved in solving murders," she insisted. "I don't believe I've ever heard of anything so interesting!"

Sarah supposed it *was* interesting, but just then she realized they were passing Police Headquarters. "Could you ask your driver to stop here for a moment?" she asked anxiously. "I need to leave Detective Sergeant Malloy a message while we're here."

Opal looked out the window at the imposing four-story, marble-fronted building with the fanlight over the arched doorway that read NEW YORK POLICE HEADQUARTERS.

"Oh, my," she said with a smile, signaling her driver to stop. "I really will have something amazing to tell Charles tonight when he asks me how my day was."

\* \* \*

Frank tried to remember back to the time before he'd met Sarah Brandt. Surely, he hadn't been angry all the time then. He would've had apoplexy long before now if he had been. No, he was sure he had never been this angry for this long in his entire life. And he was definitely going to have to forbid her to leave him any more messages at Mulberry Street, or he'd have to quit the force and become a street cleaner. As it was, nobody there could look at him without smirking.

Could a man be henpecked when he wasn't married? Frank didn't think he wanted to know.

As if things weren't bad enough, Mrs. Ellsworth was out on her porch as he came down Bank Street. She waved to get his attention, just in case he hadn't noticed her there. He waved back.

"Good evening, Mrs. Ellsworth. I hope you're keeping well," he said as pleasantly as he could considering how furious he was with Sarah Brandt.

"I'm fine, thank you, Mr. Malloy. I knew you'd be calling tonight — either you or Mr. Dennis. I dropped a knife at dinner. Knife falls, gentleman calls, or at least that's what they say."

Frank didn't ask who "they" were. He was too busy gritting his teeth at the thought of Richard Dennis calling on Sarah. "Is Mrs. Brandt at home?"

"Oh, my, yes. She arrived in a fancy carriage a few hours ago. We've seen a lot of carriages calling for her lately. Much different from the people who usually come running down the street to fetch her for a birth, I must say."

A fancy carriage. She'd probably been out somewhere with Dennis again. He tried reminding himself it was none of his concern, but he still felt like somebody had cut out a large chunk of his insides with a dull knife. "How is Nelson getting on?" he asked to change the subject. Mrs. Ellsworth's son had recently been accused of murder, and Frank and Sarah had helped exonerate him.

"He's working very hard, even harder than he did before," she said proudly. "I expect he wants to prove to Mr. Dennis that he made the right decision not to dismiss him."

"Knowing Nelson, he'll have Dennis's job before the year is out," Frank said, making Mrs. Ellsworth smile. Since Dennis owned the bank, they both knew that was unlikely.

"He'll be satisfied to become a vice president."

"Don't be so sure," Frank teased her. He climbed the steps to Sarah's door and knocked more loudly than he'd intended.

Mrs. Ellsworth bade him good night as the door opened.

"Malloy," Sarah said with the welcoming smile she hadn't given him the last few times he'd come here. "You must've gotten my message very quickly."

He refused to return that smile and went inside at her silent invitation. "You've got to stop leaving me messages at Headquarters," he said sternly, determined to get this settled.

She didn't seem the least bit intimidated. "Are you worried about my reputation or your own?" she asked in amusement.

"It's not funny. You should hear what they say about you."

"Why don't you tell them Commissioner Roosevelt has made me an honorary detective?" she suggested. "Then you'd have an excuse to consult with me."

"Maybe I'll ask him to do that," Frank said, reluctantly allowing his anger to cool a bit. She always had that effect on him. Until the next time she made him angry.

Which would probably be in about sixty seconds.

"Come into the kitchen. I've got a lot of things to tell you," she said.

Frank followed obediently, leaving his hat hanging in the hallway, as usual.

She'd already made coffee, and a pie sat on the table.

"Did Mrs. Ellsworth make the pie?" he asked.

"Of course. She said she knew you were coming. Something about a knife falling on the floor." She began to cut the pie.

"She told me she wasn't sure if it was me or Richard Dennis," he said, unable to keep the edge out of his voice as he took his seat at the table.

"She only said that to make you jealous," she said, setting a piece of apple pie in front of him. Apple was his favorite.

He decided not to reply to that. "Does this have something to do with that Italian girl's death?" he asked instead, neatly cutting off the point of his pie and raising it to his mouth.

"Yes, I've found out a lot of important things since I saw you last. I even found the murder weapon."

Frank nearly choked on his pie. She quickly poured him a cup of coffee, but it was too hot and burned his tongue. By the time he'd stopped coughing, he was good and mad again. "Didn't I tell you not to get involved with this?" he growled.

"You told me not to get involved with the Black Hand, and then you told me the Black Hand didn't have anything to do with Emilia's death. Besides," she added quickly, when he would have started shouting, "I wasn't investigating the murder. I just went down to the Mission to volunteer to help."

"What do you mean, *volunteer*?" He did shout this time.

She didn't even blink. "I decided they could use some help, so I offered it."

"Do they need a lot of babies delivered down there?"

She just ignored his sarcasm. "I'm teaching the girls how to avoid disease," she said self-righteously. "And last night my mother had a party to help Mrs. Wells raise money for the mission. I already told you about that."

Frank had to take a deep breath so he wouldn't shout again. "I thought Dennis was giving the party." He couldn't understand why he insisted on mentioning Dennis. It was like rubbing salt in an open wound.

"He helped us host it and invited some of his wife's friends," she said, setting her own coffee down on the table beside her piece of the pie and taking a seat opposite him. "I got to talk to two of the girls from the mission last night. I've noticed some strange things going on in that house."

"Like what?" Frank asked skeptically, knowing she'd tell him anyway but willing to do his part. He did enjoy pointing out the holes in her theories, and after what she'd done, she deserved it.

"First of all, Mrs. Wells tends to play favorites among the girls. Emilia was her latest favorite, and that made the other girls very jealous."

"You think one of them stabbed her to death because she was jealous?" he asked. The pie — now that he finally got to swallow some of it — was delicious, as usual.

"Don't make fun, Malloy," she warned him. "And don't forget where these girls came from. Some of them have lived on the streets. All of them have seen violence firsthand, and they know life is cheap. The mission is the best place they've ever been. They have food and clothes and a clean, safe place to sleep. They're treated with respect, and they want Mrs. Wells to love them. I think if one of them felt threatened, she wouldn't hesitate to kill a rival."

"You make it sound like a lovers' quarrel," he scoffed.

"It's more like a large family, with a mother who loves some of her children more than others. Mrs. Wells chooses one favorite girl. That girl is entrusted with big responsibilities, mainly being in charge of all the other girls. She also gets material rewards. Emilia got the clothes I donated. And she got special attention from Mrs. Wells, too. All that made the other girls hate her."

"How do you know?"

"They told me, or at least two of them did. One of them is the current favorite. She actually said she's glad Emilia died, and that others are, too."

"That's not surprising. Most brothers and sisters wish the others would die so they'd be the only child. That doesn't mean she stuck a knife in Emilia's neck." She was making this entirely too easy.

She got up. He thought maybe she was going to get him another piece of pie, but instead she picked up something wrapped in wrinkled paper that had been lying on top of her ice box and slapped it down on the table in front of him.

"What's this?" he asked suspiciously.

"Open it."

Gingerly, he peeled back the paper and saw . . . a hat pin.

"I told you," she said. "I found the murder weapon."

He looked up in surprise, but she seemed perfectly serious. He looked at the pin again. "How could this be the murder weapon?"

"Because," she said, sitting down again, "this is the hat pin that Emilia was wearing the morning she was killed. It was in the bag with the rest of her clothing at the morgue."

*The morgue?* Frank got a very uneasy feeling. "How did you get it?"

"I went down to the morgue to make arrangements to have her buried," she said, as if that was the most natural thing in the world for her to do.

*"What?"* he shouted again.

She didn't blink again. "Her family certainly can't afford to do it. You know that as well as I do. I even asked her priest if the church would pay for it, but he refused. Did you know that the Irish priests don't even allow the Italians to worship in the sanctuary? They make them go to the basement!"

Frank hadn't been in a church since Kathleen died, but he wouldn't doubt this was true. Nobody liked the Italians. He had to run a hand over his face to clear his mind. "Let me understand this. You went to a priest and asked him to pay to have Emilia buried?"

"Yes, and when he wouldn't, I decided I'd pay for it myself. I went down to the morgue to tell them so they wouldn't put her in a pauper's grave before I could make the arrangements."

He had to run a hand over his face again and take a deep breath so that he wouldn't raise his voice. Yelling at her for going to the morgue now wouldn't make any difference, since she'd already done it. "Now tell me again what this hat pin has to do with anything."

"The attendant at the morgue — and by the way, that horrible man wasn't there anymore — told me I could take the hat and the shoes Emilia was wearing, because they don't bury people in hats and shoes. I thought someone at the mission might want them, so I took them, and the hat pin, too. When I looked at it, I thought it must be rusty, because it was brown. But when I gave it to Gina, I realized it wasn't rusty at all."

"Who's Gina?"

"One of the girls at the mission. Look at the pin, Malloy," she said impatiently. "What do you see?"

Frank picked up the pin, holding it by the end that was shaped like a flower. He saw the brown residue near the base. He rubbed it with a finger and realized she was right. It wasn't rust.

"Remember we thought Emilia was stabbed with a stiletto because that was the thinnest blade we could think of?" she asked. "But she wasn't stabbed with a knife at all. Someone came up behind her, pulled the pin out of her hat, and used that to kill her."

Frank stared at the pin, easily picturing what must have happened. The sharp end of the sturdy pin would have gone in easily and neatly, and the shaft was more than long enough to do terrible damage once inside the girl's head. As much as he hated to admit it, Sarah was probably right. "Her hat was off when we found her," Frank murmured. "I thought it must've gotten knocked off when she fell."

"But it came off because someone took the pin out," Sarah said. He knew that tone. She was excited because she was right.

"Then the killer wiped the worst of the blood off of it on her back and dropped it," he said. "We found the pin in the leaves beside her body. Nobody even noticed the blood." He hated making a mistake like that.

"Nobody knew she'd been stabbed then," she reminded him, trying to make him feel better, he knew. "Besides, a man would never even consider a hat pin a weapon."

*A man would never consider a hat pin a weapon.* The truth of the words seemed to echo in his head. *He* certainly wouldn't have.

"Would a woman consider it a weapon?" he asked.

"Of course! I've used it myself on the train, when some masher thinks he can take advantage of a crowded car to press a little too close. A woman with a hat pin is never defenseless."

Frank laid the pin down carefully on the paper while he considered what she'd told him.

"Malloy, do you know what this means?" she asked when he didn't say anything.

He looked up. "Yeah, it means we were looking in the wrong direction."

"That's right. We figured Emilia had been stabbed by one of the men she'd been involved with."

"Because they're Italians and because we thought she'd been stabbed with a stiletto," he said.

"But it wasn't a stiletto, which means it probably also wasn't a man."

He hated being wrong, but he hated her being right more. At least she wasn't gloating yet.

"The girls also told me they're sure Emilia wouldn't have gone to meet a man that morning," she continued. "They said Emilia hated men, especially Ugo, for what he did to her."

"Not only wouldn't a man have thought of stabbing someone with a hat pin, he also wouldn't have bothered to wipe off the blood."

Her eyes widened. "I hadn't thought of that! It seemed such a natural thing to do, or at least *I* thought it was natural."

"Because you're a woman." He stared at her for a moment. "So what woman wanted her dead?"

She didn't want to say the words, even though she knew they were true. "It had to be one of the girls at the mission."

"Do you have any idea which one?"

"No, but I know how to find out."

"*No!*" he said, slamming his fist onto the table and making her jump. "You're not going to confront somebody who might be a killer."

Her smile was sad. "I don't have to confront anybody. All I have to do is ask Mrs. Wells which one of the girls said Emilia wanted Ugo to see her new dress. She's the one who was creating an alibi for herself because she's the one who killed Emilia."

Frank had to resist the urge to storm the Prodigal Son Mission as he walked down Mulberry Street on his way back to Police Headquarters. It was only a few more blocks away, and he knew Emilia Donato's killer was inside. The problem was that he couldn't just go barging into the mission asking questions, and certainly not this late in the evening. Mrs. Wells wouldn't like being disturbed by the police, and she especially wouldn't like him accusing her little angels of murder. She'd complain to his superiors, and Frank would draw their wrath for that and for continuing to investigate the case when he'd been ordered to stop. Besides, he couldn't possibly expect to get the kind of cooperation from Mrs. Wells that he'd need to identify the killer. As much as he hated to admit it, only Sarah Brandt could do that.

So Frank had reluctantly agreed to let her ask her questions and then notify Frank of what she learned. At least she had sense enough to agree with him that she shouldn't try confronting the killer herself — especially not a killer who could turn a harmless hat pin into an instrument of death. A girl who killed just for the opportunity to get a new dress or a little additional attention was dangerous indeed.

Trying not to think about that, Frank climbed the narrow steps to Headquarters. He had a prisoner to question.

Twenty-four hours in the cellar cells had softened Danny considerably. He wasn't completely broken yet, but Frank hoped he was smart enough to realize he soon would be if he didn't tell Frank what he wanted to know.

He had the guards bring the boy into an interrogation room. Frank pulled a small loaf of stale braided bread he had bought from an old Italian woman on the corner out of his pocket and laid it on the table in front of the boy. Danny looked up warily, afraid to trust an apparent act of kindness.

"Go ahead, eat it," Frank said, taking the chair opposite him.

The boy hesitated another second, then grabbed it up and tore into it like a starving dog. Frank let him finish it, waiting patiently. He noticed the boy had a few new bruises on his face since yesterday. Probably, he'd gotten them fighting to keep his ration of food from the other prisoners. That happened a lot.

Judging from the way he ate the bread, he'd lost those fights, too.

When he'd swallowed the last of the bread, the boy looked up at Frank again. His expression was cocky — probably out of habit — but his eyes held the haunted fear of despair.

"Just tell me what I want to know, and I'll let you go," Frank said reasonably.

"He'll kill me," the boy argued, but Frank could see he now feared Frank as much as the other man.

"Maybe he would and maybe he wouldn't, but I can kill you for sure," Frank said with a smile. "All I have to do is put you back down in that hole and forget you're there. You saw your friend Billy, and he'd only been down there a couple days."

"Oh, God," he moaned, covering his face with his hands.

Frank waited, giving him time to decide.

At last the boy looked up. "I don't know much," he said, his voice a pleading whine. "Not enough to be any help."

"Let me be the judge of that," Frank said. "And don't annoy me. It's been a long day and I'm tired. If I have to start slapping you around, I'm going to get very angry."

The boy swallowed. "He was a swell."

"Yeah, I know, a rich man. You told me that before," Frank reminded him sternly.

"He didn't tell me his name. He just said he wanted me to fetch this doctor. Tell him somebody was sick and needed him right away."

"Where were you supposed to take him?"

"Down by the river. I can show you the place," he added hopefully.

"Maybe later," Frank said. "Then what were you supposed to do?"

"I was supposed to leave him there and run."

"But you didn't, did you, Danny? A bright boy like you, you would've stayed around to listen. Never miss a trick, do you? Maybe you'll hear something useful, something that'll get you more money out of the rich swell."

Danny was shaking his head frantically, but Frank could see from his eyes that he was right.

"What did you hear, Danny?" he asked in the tone that usually got him the correct answer.

"Nothing that made any sense," he insisted.

"Tell me anyway," Frank suggested.

The boy swallowed again, his fear palpable. "I took him down this alley. It was dark, so he didn't see the swell at first. The swell just says, 'Hello, Tom,' and the doc stops and says, 'What're you doing here?' Then the swell tells me to go, so I do."

"But you don't go far, do you? You wait to see what's going to happen."

"I knew about the doc," he said in an effort to justify himself. "He never turned anybody away, even if they couldn't pay. I thought maybe he'd need help or something, so I waited, just in case."

Frank wasn't fooled, but he let Danny get away with the lie. "What did you hear?"

"Not much at first, until they started shouting. The swell, he says something about what the doc did to his daughter. The doc says he saved her or something like that. Then I hears a noise, like somebody getting hit. After a bit, the swell comes out of the alley. I'm sure he's gonna see me, but he's going too fast, and I'm in a doorway, hiding, and it's dark. I wait, but the doc don't come out, so I goes in to see, and he's just laying there, his head all smashed in. The swell, he had this cane with a big silver knob. I figure he hit the doc with it."

"Why didn't you call for help?"

Danny looked at him like he was crazy. "They'd think I done it! Besides, the doc is dead. Anybody can see that. Nothing's gonna help him now. So I run."

"You didn't tell me everything, Danny," Frank prodded.

"Yes, I did. I swear to God!" His voice was shrill with the terror of being thrown back into the cellar.

"The swell called the doc by name. What did the doc call him?"

"Nothing, I swear! He just called him 'you.'"

"I need a name, Danny," Frank said. "You must've heard Dr. Brandt say a name."

"Just one, when they was shouting. That's all."

"And what was the name?"

Danny's face blanched. "Decker."

Sarah heard the city clocks chiming two the next afternoon as she hurried down Mulberry Street toward the mission. She'd spent her morning dealing with the twins she'd delivered several days ago. She'd been summoned early that morning because the mother was ill, and she'd died only a few hours later. The babies were literally starving, and the father had thrust them on her, begging her to take them away. He couldn't even begin to care for the five children he already had, and he didn't want to watch the babies die.

Sarah couldn't help thinking of the midwife who had taken the baby who grew up to be Emilia Donato. She must have believed she had done a good deed and ensured the child would have a good life with a loving family. As Sarah had arranged for these two babies to be placed in an orphanage, she only hoped they would fare better than Emilia had.

When Sarah finally reached the mission, she was already exhausted, and she still had the costume party tonight. The city would be alive with ghosts and goblins as soon as the sun set. Sarah hoped she'd have time for a short nap before Richard called to pick her up. At least her mother had been able to supply her with a costume, so she hadn't had to worry about that.

Sarah's knock was answered by Maeve, who didn't look pleased to see her. "Mrs. Wells is busy," she informed Sarah.

"I'll wait then," Sarah said, undaunted. Whatever Maeve may think, Sarah knew that no matter how busy Mrs. Wells might be, she wouldn't refuse to see someone who had provided so much financial support for the mission. "I have something very important to discuss with her. Would you please tell her I'm here?" she added, managing to insinuate herself into the house without actually knocking Maeve over in the process.

Sarah heard a giggle and looked over to see Aggie sitting on the stairs, watching with amusement.

"What are you laughing at, you little brat?" Maeve asked her.

Aggie didn't even flinch. She knew she had nothing to fear from Maeve.

"I'll wait in the parlor," Sarah informed the girl, who should have already invited her to do so.

Maeve went off in a huff. Watching her go, Sarah had a horrible thought. What if Maeve was the killer? She'd admitted she was glad Emilia was dead, and she had no love for anyone at the mission except Mrs. Wells. And if she wasn't the killer, someone else here undoubtedly was.

Suddenly, annoying Maeve didn't seem like a wise move. Sarah would certainly have to be careful from now on.

The sound of another giggle distracted her, and she saw Aggie still sitting on the stairs, watching her. "Would you like to keep me company while I wait for Mrs. Wells?" she asked the girl.

Aggie nodded and followed Sarah into the parlor. The girl wore a shabby dress that was too big for her, but it was perfectly clean and neatly patched. Her brown hair had been carefully braided, and her face scrubbed until it fairly glowed.

Sarah set down her medical bag and took a seat on the sofa, inviting Aggie to sit beside her. Instead, the girl crawled into her lap, which suited Sarah just fine.

"You look very nice today, Aggie," Sarah said, settling the child more comfortably. "Who fixed your hair?"

The little girl smiled, showing her tiny teeth, but didn't answer, of course.

"Did Maeve fix your hair?"

The smile vanished and the little head shook no.

"Did Mrs. Wells?"

She nodded.

They proceeded like this for a while in a strange, one-sided conversation. Sarah learned that Aggie liked Emilia and missed her, but she didn't like Maeve at all. She enjoyed playing in the yard with the other children from the neighborhood, and she liked living at the mission. Sarah also discovered that whoever had left Aggie at the mission wasn't her mother or her father. When Sarah asked her what had become of her parents, her answer was a shrug and no indication of any emotion. She didn't know where they were and apparently had no memory of them.

"You're a very lucky girl to have come here," Sarah told her.

"She certainly is," Mrs. Wells said as she came into the room. "I hope you haven't been bothering Mrs. Brandt, Aggie."

"Oh, no," Sarah assured her. "We've been having a lovely visit, haven't we, Aggie?"

The child nodded vigorously, making Sarah smile. But when she looked up, Mrs. Wells was frowning. Before Sarah could wonder why, her expression lightened again.

"Maeve said you had something important to discuss with me," she said. "I hope nothing is wrong."

Sarah wanted to remind her that one of her girls had been murdered and nothing could be more wrong than that, but Aggie was there. Besides, it would be rude. Instead she said, "Perhaps we should close the doors . . . and send Aggie out to play."

Intrigued and concerned, Mrs. Wells lifted Aggie from Sarah's lap and stood her on her feet. "Run along outside now with the other children," she told the child, shooing her out. "I mean it," she added. "Remember what I told you about listening at doors." She waited until Aggie's footsteps died away, then pulled the parlor doors shut and turned back to Sarah. "You said nothing was wrong."

"Nothing new," Sarah said. "It's just . . . Detective Sergeant Malloy and I were discussing Emilia's murder, and he had a question I couldn't answer. I was hoping you could."

Mrs. Wells had grown appropriately solemn. "I thought Mr. Malloy was no longer investigating Emilia's death."

"He's not, but I'm still concerned, naturally. We were just discussing the facts we knew, and I recalled you said one of the girls heard Emilia say she wished Ugo could see her in her new outfit."

For a moment, Sarah thought she would deny it, but then she appeared to remember. "Oh, yes, I'd almost forgotten," she said cautiously. Sarah couldn't blame her for being cautious when they were discussing her girls.

"Do you remember which girl it was?"

She didn't answer right away. After a moment, she asked, "Do you believe this Ugo killed Emilia?"

"It's certainly a possibility," Sarah said tactfully. "We just thought it might be a clue."

"How could it be a clue?"

Sarah always got into trouble when she lied. "We think . . . that is, I don't believe Emilia actually said that."

Now Mrs. Wells was really confused. "Why not?"

"Because from what the other girls have told me, Emilia hated Ugo and wouldn't have wanted to see him."

Mrs. Wells gave her a pitying smile. "Mrs. Brandt, women who have been abused often profess to hate their abusers. Unfortunately, and for reasons I shall never understand, they also seem irresistibly drawn to them. Emilia herself went back to Ugo a second time, even after he mistreated her. If he had professed a renewed desire to have her, I'm afraid she might have returned to him yet again."

Sarah herself knew this to be true. "We do know,

however, that Ugo didn't kill Emilia," she explained. "In fact . . . Well, I'm not quite sure how to say this. I know it will be difficult for you to believe, but . . . we think Emilia was killed by a woman."

"A woman?" she echoed, apparently stunned.

"Or a girl," Sarah clarified. "I'm so sorry, but we think one of the girls here at the mission killed her."

The blood had drained from Mrs. Wells's face, and Sarah hurried to her side. "Are you all right? I've got some smelling salts in my bag, if you —"

"No, please," she said, stiffening her back and lifting her chin. She took a few deep breaths and the color slowly returned to her cheeks. "Really, I'm fine. It's just . . . such a shock."

"I know," Sarah agreed, sitting back down on the sofa. "I didn't want to believe it myself, but there seems to be no other explanation."

"I'm afraid I don't understand what led you to this conclusion. I can't believe . . . It's impossible!"

Sarah told her about the hat pin and how it had been used to kill Emilia.

"But how would someone know that would kill her?" Mrs. Wells asked. "How would a *girl* know it?"

"When we find the killer, we can ask her," Sarah said.

"And how will you find her? I'm sure no one is going to simply admit it."

"She won't have to. I think *you* know who the killer is, Mrs. Wells."

Mrs. Wells's expression collapsed into despair. "I?"

"Yes. Remember I asked you about the girl who told you Emilia wanted Ugo to see her new dress? I think she made that story up so when you told it to the police, they would think Ugo was the killer. I think that girl is the killer, Mrs. Wells, and you're the one who knows who she is. Who told you that story?"

Sarah watched the play of emotions across her face as she struggled with her desire to protect the living and her duty to find justice for the dead. "I thought . . . but you say it had to be a woman," she murmured, absently rubbing her temple as if to ward off a headache. "I'm trying to remember exactly . . . But it couldn't have been Maeve," she insisted finally.

"Was Maeve the one who told you?" Sarah asked, feeling a chill.

"Yes, but she couldn't have killed Emilia. She was here at the mission. She couldn't have left without anyone knowing!" Before Sarah realized what she was doing, Mrs. Wells rose and threw open the parlor door and called, "Maeve!"

Instinctively, Sarah rose to her feet, ready for whatever might happen.

"Maeve, come here at once!" Mrs. Wells called again, and Sarah could hear the patter of running feet.

Maeve skidded to a halt in the parlor doorway, and Mrs. Wells pulled her inside and slammed the door shut behind her. "Did you tell me that Emilia wanted Ugo to see her in her new dress the morning she was killed?"

Maeve looked terrified, her eyes so wide Sarah could see a rim of white all the way around. "I . . . no, ma'am, I never." She glared at Sarah. "I told Gina that when she asked me, too."

Fortunately, Mrs. Wells didn't ask what she meant by that. "But you did tell me she was going to see her lover, didn't you?" she pressed.

Maeve looked at her uncertainly, obviously wanting to please her but uncertain exactly how she could do that. "I . . . no, not her *lover*. Her mother. She wanted her mother to see her dressed up fine."

*Of course!* Now Sarah remembered that Gina had said something to that effect just before she'd noticed the blood on the hat pin. The shock had driven it completely from Sarah's mind. "But why would she have gone to the park to see her mother?" Sarah asked. "She only lives down the street."

Mrs. Wells turned to Sarah. Her face looked as if it were carved from stone. "Her mother sells paper flowers there."

Sarah felt as if all the air had been sucked out of the room.

"Mrs. Brandt, are you all right?" Mrs. Wells asked in alarm. "Surely, you don't think . . . her own mother?"

Sarah remembered Emilia's mother and how much she had hated the baby girl she believed had been spawned by rape. Had Emilia sought her out in the park that morning to flaunt her new respectability? Had old hatreds overwhelmed her? "I don't know," she lied. The idea made too much sense and explained all the strange details of the case. "But I'll have to tell Mr. Malloy. If she did, he'll find out."

"God help her," Mrs. Wells said.

# 13

Sarah had to leave yet another message for Malloy at Headquarters, but this time, at least, he wouldn't be angry. He wasn't likely to get it until Monday, though, so she would have to go to his flat tomorrow and leave one for him there, too. That would give her a good reason to visit Brian, which she'd been wanting to do anyway. She would've gone there right away except she had to get home to dress for the Halloween party she was attending with Richard Dennis. Why had she agreed to that? Probably, because she hadn't realized she would be so close to solving a murder at this particular time.

As it was, Sarah couldn't have felt less like socializing. She hadn't liked Mrs. Donato very much, but she didn't like learning she was a murderer, either. No matter how many times she was faced with evidence to the contrary, Sarah still wanted to believe mothers loved their children.

Sarah had to ask for Mrs. Ellsworth's help in getting into the costume her mother had loaned her. She'd thought modern clothes were cumbersome, but the French Queen Marie Antoinette had borne the added burden of an enormously elaborate hairstyle.

"My goodness," Mrs. Ellsworth exclaimed when she saw the wig. "Did women really put battle scenes in their hair back then?"

"The French had an odd notion of style, I suppose," Sarah said, examining the miniature naval battle depicted in a cavern constructed in the foot-high mound of the wig. The dress itself was bizarre enough, with its full skirt, tight lacing, and décolleté neckline. Her mother had also insisted she wear the beauty patch on her cheek.

Sarah picked up a comb to part her hair so she could start wrapping it tightly around her head to go under the wig, but Mrs. Ellsworth cried out a warning that startled her into dropping it on the floor.

"Good heavens," the old woman said, picking up the comb and placing it out of Sarah's reach. "You can't comb your hair at night. It's bad luck!"

Wasn't anything safe to do around Mrs. Ellsworth? "How am I supposed to get this wig on then?" Sarah asked in exasperation.

"You can use a brush, of course," Mrs. Ellsworth assured her. "That's why women only brush their hair at night. Here, let me help you."

Sarah agreed with a sigh, telling herself she was irritable only because she didn't want to go to a party.

By the time Mrs. Ellsworth had placed the wig on her head and helped her fasten it securely in place, she looked as if she'd escaped from a museum painting.

"I certainly hope Richard appreciates this," Sarah said in disgust.

"I'm sure you'll be the most beautiful lady at the party," Mrs. Ellsworth said. "You really should try to smile, though."

That did make Sarah smile. "Have I been terribly grumpy?"

"Just a bit," the old woman said tactfully. "If you really don't want to go, I'm sure Mr. Dennis would understand."

"It's not that. I'm just . . . Well, I've discovered who killed that girl, the one who was wearing my clothes."

"I'd expect that to make you happy," Mrs. Ellsworth said with a puzzled frown.

"I'd expect it, too," Sarah said with a sigh.

She was saved from explaining by a knock on the door.

"That will be Mr. Dennis," Mrs. Ellsworth said. "I'll let myself out the back door. Have a wonderful time!"

After thanking her neighbor for her help, Sarah carefully made her way to her front door, learning how to balance the contraption on her head and not knock anything over with her skirts at the same time. She opened the door to a tall Napoleon. He grinned broadly when he saw her. "You look magnificent."

"I won't if I fall on my face," she warned him. "You must promise to stay by my side all evening and hold me upright."

Richard raised his right hand as if taking an oath.

"Nothing could tear me away. Come, my queen, your carriage awaits."

The Graves family lived in a brownstone near Sarah's parents. The interior of their home had been furnished in excellent taste, with furniture obviously imported from England but notable for its simplicity. They might be quite wealthy, but they felt no need to make a show of it.

Opal and Charles were dressed as Anthony and Cleopatra. Opal exclaimed over Sarah's costume, then whispered how very glad she was to see Richard looking so happy again. Sarah ignored the provocation and allowed Opal to continue greeting her guests.

Opal found her later, enjoying a moment of solitude while Richard chatted with some business associates who were dressed as Knights of the Round Table.

"I've been dying to ask you how your investigation is going," she said, taking a seat beside Sarah at the edge of the large ballroom.

"I think we've found the killer," Sarah told her with a sigh.

"You don't look very happy about it," Opal said.

"That's because . . . I know it's hard to believe, but I think it may have been the girl's own mother."

"How awful! Of course, considering her background, I guess we shouldn't be too shocked. Her family are foreigners, aren't they?"

"Not all foreigners are murderers," Sarah reminded her sharply.

"Oh, dear, I guess that did sound patronizing, didn't it?" Opal said, chagrined. "I only meant . . . Well, I guess I did mean it badly, but . . . I can't help thinking that people in other countries aren't raised with the same sensitivities as we are. You must admit the Italians treat each other terribly."

Sarah had to agree with that when she thought of the Black Hand. "Even still, it's hard to think of a mother killing her child, although it happens with alarming frequency when people live in poverty."

Opal patted her hand in a gesture of comfort. "Does Mrs. Wells know yet?"

Sarah nodded. "We haven't arrested anyone though. I haven't been able to get in touch with Mr. Malloy since I found out who it was."

"That means she could escape," Opal said in horror. "Good heavens, what if she kills someone else?"

"We don't think that's likely. She killed Emilia in a fit of passion. She wouldn't have a reason to kill anyone else. As for escaping, she has no idea anyone even suspects her."

"Thank heaven for that. But poor Mrs. Wells, this will be so difficult for her, with a trial and all the publicity. She's already been through so much, and yet she has such strength. Did you know she lost a child in addition to her husband?"

"Yes, she told me."

"She was such a comfort to me when Hazel died. I know she was to Hazel, too. In fact, she was Hazel's last visitor. She told me they prayed together and that Hazel had finally found the peace she'd been seeking."

"That *would* be a comfort," Sarah agreed, thinking of Tom. How wonderful it would have been to know he'd found peace before he died.

"You ladies look entirely too serious," Charles

Graves informed them. "I'm afraid I must ask Mrs. Brandt to dance to cheer her up."

"That should do it," Opal said with a smile. "Dancing with Charles usually makes women laugh out loud."

Her husband wasn't the least bit offended. He took Sarah's hand with as much dignity as he could while dressed like an ancient Roman and led her to the dance floor. With her towering wig, she was even taller than Opal, but he was accustomed to the difference in height. By the time the dance was over, Sarah was indeed laughing at his clever teasing. She would think about killers tomorrow. That would be time enough.

Much later, Sarah turned to Richard as they rode home in his carriage. "I had a lovely time tonight. Thank you for inviting me."

"Thank you for accompanying me. I wouldn't have gone alone. I haven't been to a party like that since Hazel died."

"Then that explains why Opal was so happy to see me there."

"She and Charles have been good friends, although I suspect they've stuck by me mostly because of guilt."

"Why should they feel guilty?" Sarah asked.

"Because Opal was the one who got Hazel involved with the mission. I never blamed her," he hastened to explain. "But I think she may have blamed herself."

"She did tell me how much Hazel enjoyed working at the mission, and that she'd found the peace she'd been looking for."

"That's what Mrs. Wells told me, too. I'm afraid I

didn't take much comfort in that at the time, though. I was too angry."

"That's understandable."

"I also thought she was a bit of a . . . a fanatic, I guess."

"She does take her work very seriously."

"No, not about her work," Richard said. "It's the way she seems to think people are better off dead than alive."

"Where did you get that idea?" Sarah asked in surprise.

"From her." He sounded a little defensive.

"What did she say to make you think that?"

"She said Hazel was in a better place and she wouldn't be sad anymore, things like that."

"I'm sure she was just trying to make you feel better," Sarah argued. "Opal said Mrs. Wells was a great comfort to her."

"I'm glad she was a comfort to someone."

Sarah didn't know how to respond to that. Before she could think of anything, he said, "Didn't you say that one of the girls at the mission was murdered?"

"That's right."

"I wonder what she thinks about that." Sarah heard the bitterness in his voice.

"She did say she thought Emilia was at peace now. The girl had a very unhappy life," she added.

"Who's to say the rest of it wouldn't have been happy if she'd lived, though?" he challenged.

"I suppose we'll never know," Sarah said.

"Did they find out who killed her?"

"Yes," Sarah said reluctantly. "We believe it was her mother."

"Her *mother*?" he asked in amazement.

"Yes, she . . . She never liked the girl, and apparently, they quarreled."

"So she sent her to a better place?" Richard offered sarcastically when Sarah hesitated. "I suppose that's what Mrs. Wells thinks, at least."

"Richard, Mrs. Wells was devastated when Emilia died," she said gently.

He didn't seem to hear her. "Sometimes I think . . ."

"What do you think?" Sarah prodded, hoping it would help him to speak about the feelings he'd kept inside all these years.

"I think the woman is in love with death."

Richard's words haunted Sarah all night. She knew he had misinterpreted Mrs. Wells's faith, but she still couldn't shake the gloom he had invoked. Probably, she was just depressed because soon she would have to watch Malloy arrest a woman for killing her own daughter.

Wondering what the odds were of catching Malloy at home on a Sunday morning, Sarah was up earlier than was sensible after her late night. Since no trains ran east and west in the city and Hansom cab drivers were still recovering from their Saturday night jobs, Sarah had to walk all the way across town to Malloy's neighborhood in the Seventeenth Ward.

The streets were busy with the faithful on their way to or from church on this unseasonably warm morning. Everyone wore their finest clothes, and children hadn't yet had time to wear off the clean from their Saturday night baths. Sarah arrived just in time to see a sight she'd longed for. Mrs. Malloy and Brian were coming down the front stoop of their tenement, also dressed in their Sunday best. Mrs. Malloy held Brian's hand as he carefully negotiated the steps on his own two feet.

He was wearing obviously new shoes, and he couldn't seem to take his eyes off them. Or else he still felt the need to watch his feet when he walked. Whatever the reason, he didn't see Sarah until his grandmother yanked him to a stop before he reached the last step.

"Good morning, Mrs. Malloy," Sarah said with a warm smile, ignoring the old woman's disapproving glare.

Sensing her presence at last, the boy looked up. His face broke into a glorious smile, and he flung himself into Sarah's arms. She caught him with difficulty, somehow managing to pull him up so he could wrap his legs around her waist and his arms around her neck. She hugged him fiercely.

"It's so good to see you!" she exclaimed into the sweet curve of the child's neck. Then she pulled back and looked him in the face. "You're walking so well!" she exclaimed, freeing one hand and moving her first two fingers in a walking motion to illustrate her words.

He nodded enthusiastically and scrambled back down to his feet so he could show her. In a second he had ascended the front stoop and in another second he was back down again, his new shoes clumsy but effective. Sarah beamed and applauded his efforts when he looked up for her approval.

He started back up the steps again, still showing off, and Sarah looked at Mrs. Malloy to catch a reflection of anxiety in her eyes. Sarah knew what she feared, but reassuring the woman that she had no intention of taking Brian and Frank Malloy away from her wouldn't help. Instead she said, "You've done such a wonderful job with him."

Mrs. Malloy blinked in surprise. Had she expected to be insulted? "He's a good boy," she managed, not taking any credit for herself.

Brian had reached the bottom step again, and Sarah dutifully applauded him as required. When he turned to repeat his efforts, Sarah said to Mrs. Malloy, "I don't suppose your son is at home."

Mrs. Malloy didn't approve of Sarah chasing after her son, which was how she saw their relationship. "He never come home last night. Probably slept down at Mulberry Street, like he does when he works late," she informed Sarah with some satisfaction.

Sarah nodded, relieved. This meant he'd probably already gotten the message she'd left for him there. She had to stop and applaud Brian again. When he started back up the steps, she turned back to Mrs. Malloy. "When he gets home, would you tell him I called to say I got the information he wanted?"

The old woman wanted to ask what that information was, but she didn't want to look curious or nosy. She also didn't agree to Sarah's request, which would have given Sarah more respect than she thought she deserved. "I can't invite you in," she said instead. "We're on our way to Mass."

"Does Brian like church?" she asked, applauding yet another of his efforts on the steps.

"He can't hear it," she reminded Sarah unnecessarily. "He likes the candles and the windows, though. And seeing all the people."

"I'm sure he does." She waited until he reached the bottom step and clapped again.

"He'll keep that up till he drops if you let him," Mrs. Malloy said. "We're going to be late."

The next time Brian reached the bottom step, Sarah stooped down and gave him a big hug. "It was so nice to see you," she said with a smile. He couldn't understand the words, but he knew what the smile meant.

She looked up at Mrs. Malloy. "He'll start to cry if I leave now. Could I walk along with you to the church?"

Even Mrs. Malloy could see the wisdom of that. Brian was too big to drag, resisting, down the street. "If it suits you," she said.

They each took one of Brian's hands and directed him down the street. He looked up at both of them, beaming with pleasure.

"I can't believe how quickly he learned to walk," Sarah marveled.

"He's always been clever," Mrs. Malloy reminded her curtly.

They walked for a block in silence while Sarah tried to think of something to say that the other woman wouldn't interpret as an insult. Before she could think of anything, Mrs. Malloy spoke.

"Frances said I should thank you for helping Brian." She sounded like a child who had been ordered to apologize when she wasn't sorry.

Sarah managed not to smile at the thought. "I didn't do anything except tell Mr. Malloy about Dr. Newton. He's the one who does the miracles, not I."

Mrs. Malloy crossed herself quickly, as if Sarah had blasphemed, and gave her a black look. Sarah had a fleeting memory of Mrs. Ellsworth warning her about the evil eye. "Only God does miracles," the old woman informed her.

"Of course," Sarah agreed. "I didn't mean it that way. It does seem miraculous that Brian can walk, though, doesn't it? He must be wearing you out."

"I can manage," she said defensively, almost desperately.

Sarah had unwittingly touched another nerve, and she sighed in exasperation. "Mrs. Malloy, I have great respect for your son and great affection for your grandson, but surely Mr. Malloy has told you that he and I are merely friends and nothing more."

Mrs. Malloy looked over at Sarah. "I have eyes, don't I?" was all she said. Sarah had no idea what she meant by that and decided it would be foolish to ask.

Luckily, the church was on the next corner, and Mrs. Malloy managed to distract Brian while Sarah slipped away. She realized her trip here had been wasted if Malloy was at Police Headquarters. Or he might already be waiting for her at her house. But at least she'd gotten to see Brian and judge the progress he was making for herself.

As for seeing Malloy, she certainly hoped he would have a good idea for how to get Mrs. Donato to confess — an idea that didn't involve taking her down to Police Headquarters and giving her the third degree. If he could get a confession, maybe there wouldn't be a trial and all the accompanying scandal. The girls at the mission certainly didn't need any more trauma in their lives.

When Sarah turned the corner onto Bank Street, she saw a man sitting on her doorstep. For an instant, she thought it was Malloy and her heart leaped with an excitement she felt for nothing else in her life. Then the man stood up, and she realized it wasn't Malloy at all. She told herself not to be disappointed. A millionaire was waiting for her, after all, and he'd brought her a bouquet of flowers.

Richard Dennis hurried down the street to meet her. "Good morning," he said when he reached her. "I hope you don't mind my calling this early and waiting for you. Mrs. Ellsworth assured me it would be fine."

"I'm sure she did," Sarah said with a smile. She couldn't help noticing her neighbor had made herself scarce, too, for once. Probably, she was intimidated because Richard was her son's employer. "I hope you didn't have to wait long."

"Not at all," he assured her, falling into step with her to return to her house. "I felt I owed you an apology after the way I behaved last night."

"I told you, I had a wonderful time," she reminded him.

"Until I ruined it with my memories. I'm afraid I was feeling a little melancholy, in spite of the festivities."

"That's only natural. I'm sure being with your old friends reminded you of your wife. Won't you come in? I can make some coffee, and I have some pie."

He glanced down at the bouquet he still held. "Oh, and I guess I have some flowers for you. To prove my apology is sincere," he added, offering them to her.

"The flowers weren't necessary, but they are appreciated," Sarah said, accepting the gift. They were red roses, and she knew they must have cost a fortune and taken a monumental effort to procure. Flower shops would be closed on Sunday, and roses weren't blooming anywhere near the city on the first of November.

Without even thinking, Sarah settled Richard into one of the chairs in her front room, by the front window. She didn't ask herself why she hadn't invited him into the kitchen, as she always did with Malloy. Richard, she decided, just wasn't that type of man.

A short while later, she served the coffee and the remains of Mrs. Ellsworth's apple pie. They ate in companionable silence for a few minutes.

"I guess I owe you yet another apology, too," he said at last.

"For what?"

"For involving you in the mission. If I hadn't asked you to accompany me there, you never would have met the girl who was murdered."

"I've thought about that a lot," Sarah admitted. "Life would be simpler if we didn't get involved with other people, wouldn't it? On the other hand, if the girl hadn't been wearing my clothes, there's a good chance no one would even have known who she was. The people at the mission and"— Sarah had almost said her family —"and those who loved her would never have known what became of her, either."

"I hadn't thought of that," he admitted. "On the other hand, if she'd just disappeared, they could have imagined her alive and happy someplace else."

"That would be difficult," she said. "Girls like Emilia don't usually have happy lives, particularly if they just disappear into the streets."

"Or even if they find a home at the mission, apparently," he reminded her.

He frowned. "What did the mother say when she confessed? Did she explain why she did it?"

Suddenly, the sweet pie tasted like sawdust in her mouth. "She hasn't confessed yet," Sarah admitted. "She hasn't even been arrested."

"Then you don't know for sure she did it," he challenged.

"Well," Sarah hedged, "all the evidence points to her."

"What evidence?"

This was the most animated she'd ever seen him. How odd that he would suddenly be so concerned about this. "The way she was killed, for one thing. It's obvious a woman killed her." It did sound flimsy when she said it out loud like that.

"How was she killed?"

"With a hat pin."

Richard stared at her incredulously. "A *hat pin*?"

"There, you see," Sarah said with a small smile of triumph. "Men simply don't consider a hat pin a weapon. But think about it. A hat pin is as long and sturdy as a knife blade and sharp on the end. It could do as much damage as a stiletto."

"What do you know about stilettos, Sarah," he chided with amusement.

"Probably more than you," she chided right back. "And we found the hat pin the murdered girl was wearing. It had blood on it."

"Where was she stabbed with this deadly hat pin?" he asked, still not convinced.

Sarah explained, showing him on her own head how the pin went in.

Plainly, he was horrified at the mere thought. "How could that kill a person?" he asked in amazement.

"By damaging the brain somehow. She looked as

if she'd suffocated, so it must have affected her breathing."

He was going to ask a question, but just then Sarah saw a familiar figure pass by outside on the way to her front porch. "Malloy is here," she announced, jumping up to open the door for him.

Malloy wasn't smiling. "Didn't I tell you not to leave me any more messages?" he said before she could even open her mouth to greet him. "Sometimes I think you don't have the sense God gave a —" He stopped when he saw Richard, who had followed Sarah to the door, and his face got even redder than his anger justified.

"You know Mr. Dennis, don't you, Malloy?" she asked sweetly.

Richard looked outraged, and he probably was. A gentleman would never tell a lady she didn't have good sense, even if she didn't.

The two men glared at each other for a long moment. Neither offered to shake hands and neither spoke a word of greeting.

"I'm so glad you came, Malloy," Sarah said, pretending not to notice anything amiss. "Mrs. Wells and I were finally able to figure out who killed Emilia."

"It was her mother," Richard said with a satisfied smirk. Plainly, he wanted Malloy to know Sarah had confided in him first.

To his credit, Malloy didn't bat an eye. Instead, he drew a deep breath and let it out in a long sigh. "If you want me to come back at a more convenient time," he said to Sarah, with just a hint of sarcasm.

Sarah pretended not to hear the sarcasm. "I would hate to inconvenience you," she said with mock sincerity. "I know Richard will excuse us," she added with a smile. "I'm sorry to cut our visit short, but I'm sure you understand how important it is to see the killer arrested as soon as possible."

Richard's face turned so red, he looked as if he might explode. He hated the thought of leaving her alone with Malloy, but good breeding demanded that he obey her wishes. He needed a moment to regain control, and then he said, "I will forgive you if agree to dine with me tomorrow evening."

She didn't dare look at Malloy. "I'd be delighted," she said quite honestly.

"Good," Richard said with more satisfaction than was seemly. "I'll call for you at eight o'clock." He reached across Malloy and took his hat from where it hung by the door. Then he turned back and gave Sarah a small bow. "Until tomorrow then."

"Thank you for the flowers," Sarah said without thinking.

Richard smiled at this final triumph and took his leave. When Sarah closed the door and turned back to Malloy, he looked as if *he* might explode. "It was nice of you to come on a Sunday," she said as if she were oblivious to the drama they had just experienced.

She didn't invite him in. She knew he would follow her. She stopped to pick up the dirty dishes she and Richard had been using and put them back on the tray.

"I guess he ate all the pie, too," Malloy said sourly.

Sarah managed not to smile. "There's one piece left. Come into the kitchen."

He didn't say a word as she poured him some coffee and served him the pie, although she could feel his gaze on her every second. She was being silly to enjoy the small display of masculine rivalry over her, but she was going to enjoy it anyway.

She poured herself a second cup of coffee and took a seat across the table from him. He was still staring at her, his eyes narrowed. She couldn't read his expression.

"So today you think the girl's mother killed her," he said, feigning skepticism. "I suppose you've got a good reason for changing your mind."

"I went to the mission yesterday and asked Mrs. Wells which one of the girls had told her Emilia wanted Ugo to see her new dress. I was sure that girl was the killer and had been preparing Mrs. Wells to give that information to the police."

"And?" he prodded, not willing to offer any encouragement.

"And when I asked Mrs. Wells, she told me Maeve was the one who had said it, but Maeve couldn't be the killer because she hadn't left the mission all morning."

"She could've sneaked out," Malloy offered.

"I didn't think of that, but it doesn't matter. Mrs. Wells called her in and asked her why she'd said that about Ugo. That's when we realized Mrs. Wells had been mistaken. Maeve had told her that Emilia wanted her mother to see her looking so pretty."

"That doesn't make any sense," Malloy scoffed. "She didn't even like her mother."

"But she did love her," Sarah said. "Children always love their parents, no matter how badly they treat them. And children want their parents to love them back. Mrs. Donato never did because she believed Emilia was the result of the attack — oh, Malloy, I never had a chance to tell you! That isn't even true!"

"What isn't true?"

"Mrs. Donato thought Emilia was fathered by one of the sailors who attacked her because she had blond hair, but Mr. Donato told me his story, and that wasn't the reason at all."

"What story does Mr. Donato have?" Malloy asked in obvious confusion. "And why did he tell it to you?"

"He told it to me when I went over there to discuss Emilia's burial plans. You see, Emilia wasn't the Donatos' child at all! Their child died at birth. The midwife who delivered it had just delivered a baby to a prostitute. She was going to take it to an orphanage, but Mr. Donato decided to switch the babies, so Mrs. Donato wouldn't be upset because her baby died."

"And that's why the girl didn't look Italian," Malloy guessed.

"And why Mrs. Donato thought she'd been fathered by a sailor."

"And why Mr. Donato never questioned the girl's paternity," Malloy decided. "But it still doesn't mean Mrs. Donato killed her."

"Maeve said Emilia wanted her mother to see her in her new clothes. Mrs. Wells told me Mrs. Donato sells paper flowers in City Hall Park. Emilia would have known that. She went down there to see her mother. They must have gotten into an argument, and all of Mrs. Donato's anger made her finally kill the girl she'd always hated. You see, Malloy, this explains everything. Now it all makes sense — why she was in the park and why the killer used a hat pin. Everything makes sense."

She knew she was right, and Malloy knew it, too. She could tell by the way he was frowning. He hadn't even tasted the pie yet.

"Does she know Emilia wasn't her child?" he asked after a moment.

"I don't think so, unless Mr. Donato told her since I saw him, but I can't imagine why he would after all these years."

"I can use that, then," he said thoughtfully.

"Use it for what?"

"To break her and get her to confess."

# 14

FRANK SUPPOSED HE WAS GOING TO BE ANGRY every minute for the rest of his natural life. He didn't see any other possibility as long as he continued his acquaintance with Sarah Brandt. The worst part was that the thing he was angriest about was something he didn't have any right to even feel. That thing was, of course, jealousy of Richard Dennis.

Why should he be surprised to find Dennis at her house on a Sunday afternoon? He was exactly the kind of man she deserved — a man with money and social position and good manners. Frank supposed he should be grateful for the good manners. In Dennis's place, Frank would've thrown a scruffy police detective out into the street for speaking to Sarah the way Frank had spoken to her today. Not that she didn't deserve it, of course, but still, he'd been pretty rude.

On the other hand, Frank would have preferred

being beaten senseless to hearing Sarah accept Dennis's dinner invitation. The man might be well bred, but he knew how to inflict exquisite pain just the same. Frank would carry the bitter memory of her "delighted" acceptance for a long time to come. His mother would tell him he'd gotten no more than he deserved for trying to get above himself. Even worse, she'd be right.

Fortunately, Frank had the trip from Bank Street down to Mulberry Bend to get himself back under control again. He even managed to give some thought as to how he would approach Mrs. Donato. Remembering how dangerous the Italians could be with their knives — and their hat pins — Frank picked up a couple patrolmen at Headquarters to accompany him. He left one downstairs at the front door, and the other he instructed to wait in the hallway outside their flat.

When they had reached the top of the stairs, however, Frank saw that he needn't have worried. The door stood open, and Frank could see Mrs. Donato sitting alone at her kitchen table. The remains of the family's Sunday dinner still sat, untouched, and she was simply staring at nothing, oblivious even to her visitor.

"Mrs. Donato?" Frank said, startling her.

She looked up, not recognizing him at first. "We pay rent," she said, hardly able to work up any indignation.

"I'm Detective Sergeant Frank Malloy from the police," he said. Her eyes widened in alarm, but he hurried on, "I want to ask you some more questions about your daughter."

She seemed to shrink into herself at the mention of Emilia. "I know nothing. No can help you."

Frank went into the flat and pulled out a chair. He turned it and straddled it, resting his arms on the back and leaning in close to Mrs. Donato. He could see her eyes were bloodshot, as if she hadn't been sleeping, and her face was gray. She had been suffering the torment of the damned, but Frank was going to give her an opportunity to bare her blackened soul.

"You didn't like your daughter much, did you, Mrs. Donato?" he began.

She stiffened. True or not, such a thing would be difficult to admit. "She bad, all a time bad. No listen. No good."

"Maybe she just wanted her mother to love her," he suggested.

The woman drew back, eyeing him warily. He was dangerous. She could see that now. "She be good, I love then," she tried.

"She could never be good enough to make you forget the sailors, though, could she?" he prodded.

Even the gray drained out of her face, leaving her white. "How you know?" she demanded in an agonized whisper.

"You hated Emilia because of the sailors, because of what they did to you," he said ruthlessly. "You thought one of them was her father, because she had yellow hair."

She was staring at him as if he were a poisonous snake ready to strike. She couldn't stop him, so she simply braced herself for the pain.

"Poor Emilia, she never did anything wrong," Frank lamented. "She didn't know why you hated her, but you hated her from the minute she was born, didn't you?" He didn't wait for an answer. The woman was too terrified to speak. "Now that's the sad part. That's *really* sad, because there was something you didn't know about Emilia. Something your husband didn't tell you."

"Antonio know nothing!" she insisted.

"He knows Emilia isn't your baby," Frank said.

Her face wrinkled in confusion. "Emilia my baby."

Frank shook his head sadly. "Your baby died."

She shook her head frantically. She knew this couldn't be true.

"Your baby died," Frank repeated relentlessly. "But the midwife had another baby, a baby nobody wanted. She was going to take her to an orphanage, but Antonio took it instead."

She was shaking her head harder now. She didn't want it to be true.

"Antonio didn't want you to be sad because your baby died. He didn't know about the sailors. He didn't know you *wanted* the baby to die. So he took the baby girl that nobody wanted, and he gave her to you. The baby with yellow hair. Emilia."

"*Vi trovate!*" she cried. "Lies!"

"You know it's the truth. That's what Antonio would do, isn't it? He'd do anything to make you happy, even take a bastard child nobody wanted. Did he ever ask you why Emilia had yellow hair? Did he ever wonder? Did he ever suspect you had betrayed him?"

She was moaning and still shaking her head, but he could see the horror in her eyes. She knew it was true, and now she had to face what she had done to that poor child.

"You hated her for no reason. She was innocent, and all she wanted was her mother's love, but you hated her instead. You drove her out, and when she tried to come back, you killed her!"

She threw her arms over her head and screamed, slumping to the floor.

Behind him, Frank heard doors opening and feet running. He turned to see several women rushing to rescue their neighbor.

"Police," he announced loudly, stopping them instantly. They eyed him cautiously, torn between fear of him and a desire to help their friend.

Mrs. Donato was writhing on the floor, babbling in Italian.

"What's she saying?" he demanded, wondering if any of them spoke English.

They hesitated, afraid of him but afraid not to answer him, too.

"Something about Emilia," the youngest of them finally said. Then she looked at Frank in amazement. "She says she killed Emilia!"


Sarah couldn't believe she was back at The Tombs again so soon. Less than three weeks ago, she'd visited another woman here. Another woman who had confessed to murder. She still wasn't sure why she'd come today. When she received Malloy's message this morning that Mrs. Donato had confessed yesterday, she should have felt relieved. Emilia's murder was solved, and justice would be done. If Malloy was satisfied, she should be, too.

Except she wasn't. For some reason, she had to see the woman herself, just to make sure. Maybe she simply couldn't accept the idea of a woman killing her child. Even if Emilia wasn't really her flesh and blood, Mrs. Donato hadn't known it then. No matter how painful their relationship had been, murder was a drastic solution. Sarah supposed she needed to know exactly what had happened that morning to compel the woman to take her daughter's life.

Or maybe she was simply nosy. Too nosy for her own good, Malloy would have said.

The City Jail had been designed to look like an Egyptian tomb, hence its nickname. The interior was kept immaculate, although the stench from the sewers permeated the building no matter how clean it was. The women's section was just as she remembered. The female prisoners were free to leave their cells during the day, and they sat around the central courtyard area, visiting and doing needlework or knitting. A few enjoyed visits from family or friends, and others just sat and stared, perhaps contemplating their fates.

Sarah told the matron she was looking for Mrs. Donato, and the woman frowned.

"There's a priest with her right now," she said.

"A Catholic priest?" Sarah asked in amazement. Was it possible one of the Irish priests had overcome his prejudice enough to visit an Italian woman in prison?

"I expect that's the only kind there is," the matron told her humorlessly. She was a large woman with pitted skin and a hairy mole on her chin. "Better give 'em a few minutes. We had to send for him 'cause she almost died last night. She probably needs whatever mumbo-jumbo they do."

"Is she ill?" Sarah asked in alarm. "Does she need a doctor?"

"No, she ain't *ill*," the matron said mockingly. "She tried to hang herself. A lot of 'em do when they get in here and see what it's like. You ask me, they should've let her. Save Old Sparky the trouble," she added.

Sarah shouldn't have found the reference so distasteful. She'd been instrumental in getting Mrs. Donato arrested in the first place, after all. "If you don't mind, I'll wait until the priest is finished," Sarah said, moving off to find a place where she could wait without disturbing anyone. She tried to imagine the kind of despair that would cause someone to put a noose around her neck and choke herself to death. She imagined killing one's child could produce it.

Sarah had to wait only a few more minutes before she saw a black-clad figure emerge from the cell the matron had indicated. She recognized the young priest from St. John's, the one who had been so hostile to her request for money to bury Emilia. His expression was grave, and he started when he saw Sarah looking at him so expectantly.

Plainly, he couldn't place her.

"I'm Sarah Brandt," she reminded him. "I came to the church to ask for help to bury Emilia Donato." She saw the recognition in his eyes, but his expression didn't lighten. "How is Mrs. Donato?"

"She's alive," he said grimly.

"Did she really try to hang herself?"

He pressed his lips together. "She made a noose out of her undergarments. I guess she didn't realize that she wouldn't die instantly. Someone heard her choking, and they were able to cut her down. Thank God they did. Suicides can never see the face of God, Mrs. Brandt. They can't even be buried in consecrated ground."

The priest was acting as if Sarah were responsible

for this outrage. "Can murderers see the face of God?" she countered.

The color rose on his neck, but he managed to control his temper. "Repentant sinners can, and we are *all* sinners. But if you're referring to Mrs. Donato, she isn't a murderer."

"She told the police she killed her daughter," Sarah reminded him.

"No, she didn't."

Sarah stared at him in amazement. "She wouldn't be here if she hadn't confessed."

"I have no idea what happened when the police arrested her, or what they forced her to say, but she didn't kill her daughter."

"But she confessed!" Sarah insisted. She knew Malloy would have made sure of her guilt before he put the woman in jail.

The priest gave her a pitying look. "Not to me. I've heard many confessions in my life, Mrs. Brandt. People seldom lie to a priest — what would be the point? My job is to absolve them of their sins, and I can't do that unless I know what they are. People also know I can't reveal their secrets, and those who are dying are especially careful to bare their souls before facing the final judgment."

"Is Mrs. Donato dying?"

"She will most likely be executed for murder," he reminded her impatiently. "She was very anxious to confess after attempting suicide. As a priest, I can't reveal the secrets of the confessional, but I can tell you what she *didn't* say. She didn't confess to killing her daughter."

"She might be too ashamed to admit it," Sarah

tried, as dread formed a hot lump inside her. "And why else would she have tried to kill herself?"

"I don't speak Italian, so I didn't understand all of it, but she did something to the girl, treated her badly. I couldn't understand the reason, but she's sorry for it now. She blames herself because the girl is dead, but she didn't kill her. Although what that will matter now, I have no idea. The police have her, so they aren't likely to keep looking for the real killer. Why should they bother?"

"I need to speak with Mrs. Donato," Sarah said, knowing Malloy would bother if he knew Mrs. Donato was innocent.

"Why?" he asked, losing control of his temper at last. "So you can force her to say she's guilty?"

"Father . . . O'Hara, is it?"

"Ahearn," he corrected.

"Father Ahearn, I'm not interested in seeing an innocent person convicted of murder. I wanted justice for Emilia, and falsely accusing her mother won't accomplish that."

"And what good will it do if she does manage to convince you she didn't kill the girl?" he scoffed.

"It could get her out of jail, for one thing," Sarah snapped back, losing her own temper. "Have you forgotten I came to you for help — help you refused to give me? You've got no more right to judge me falsely than I do to judge Mrs. Donato. I'm surprised that you are here."

He sighed. "You judge me too harshly, Mrs. Brandt. As to Mrs. Donato, speak to her, then," he said, "for all the good it will do. I don't know what she can tell you that will save her. Everyone in this place claims to be innocent. Proving it is another matter entirely."

"I've had some experience doing that, Father," she informed him.

"Have you had experience convincing the police they've arrested the wrong person?" he challenged.

"As a matter of fact, I have."

She'd shocked him. He stared at her for a long moment, probably trying to judge whether she was lying or not. Apparently, he decided that she wasn't. "I wish you good fortune, then, Mrs. Brandt."

"Perhaps you should pray for me instead," she countered.

He nodded solemnly. "I will."

"And let me know if you learn anything that might help Mrs. Donato."

"You mean if the real killer confesses to me?" he asked with the ghost of a smile.

"I know you couldn't tell me that, but any other information you find, anything at all . . ."

"Of course," he promised. "I'll speak to Father O'Brien, too."

"Thank you."

He hesitated a second, and then he made the sign of the cross over her. "A blessing," he explained. "Now see what you can learn from Mrs. Donato."

Sarah felt a chill when she entered the narrow cell, which had been literally carved out of the stone. The single window high in the wall let in little light, and Sarah could barely make out the figure sitting huddled on the thin straw mattress covering the bed.

"Mrs. Donato?"

She was rocking back and forth, probably to comfort herself, and she gave no sign that she had heard.

"Mrs. Donato, I'm Sarah Brandt. I knew Emilia at the mission. I brought you some food after she died," she reminded her.

"Go away." The woman's voice was hoarse, but whether from weeping or from the near-hanging, Sarah didn't want to guess.

"I spoke to your priest outside, Father Ahearn. He asked me to help you." This wasn't exactly true, but Sarah figured the blessing would cover a few white lies.

Mrs. Donato didn't say a word, but at least she turned to look at Sarah. "Why you help?"

A fair question. "I don't want to see an innocent person punished, and I don't want to let a killer go free," she explained.

"Why you care?"

A better question. "Because I liked Emilia."

She was studying Sarah more closely. "I tell you about sailors," she remembered.

"Yes, you did. You told me that Emilia was the child of the devil."

Mrs. Donato closed her eyes and moaned, a sound drawn from deep in her soul. Almost instantly, the matron appeared in the doorway. She'd probably get in trouble if Mrs. Donato tried to harm herself again. Sarah gave the woman a reassuring wave, and she withdrew.

Mrs. Donato was rocking more vigorously now, her arms wrapped tightly around herself.

"That isn't true, Mrs. Donato," Sarah said. "Emilia wasn't your daughter at all."

She didn't speak for a long moment. Then she said, "*Poliziotto,* he say this. Then Antonio, he come, last night. He say my *bambino* die. He say midwife bring Emilia."

"That's right. Emilia wasn't your child. Your husband didn't want you to be sad because your baby died."

Tears were running down the older woman's face, but she didn't make a sound. She just kept rocking back and forth.

Finally, Sarah forced the issue. "Mrs. Donato, did you kill Emilia?"

"She die," she said bleakly. "My fault."

"Why was it your fault?" Sarah prodded.

"I no want. Never want. She run away. My fault."

"Where were you the morning Emilia was killed?"

"Sell flowers."

"Where?" Sarah asked. "Were you at the park?"

"*Sì*, park. Sell flowers."

"Did you see Emilia that day?"

"No, no see," she insisted.

"City Hall Park isn't that large," Sarah reminded her. "And she went there looking for you."

But Mrs. Donato was shaking her head. "No City Hall. Sell flowers, Washington Park."

"Washington Square?" Sarah asked.

"*Sì*, sell flowers. Washington. No City Hall. No there, long time."

"You sell your flowers in Washington Square now, but you used to sell them in City Hall Park?" Sarah asked.

Mrs. Donato nodded, obviously not understanding the significance of this.

"Why would Emilia have thought you'd be at City Hall Park that morning? Did she know you'd changed the place where you sell them?"

Mrs. Donato shrugged.

"Did anyone see you at Washington Square that morning?"

"Much people see," she said. A flower seller would have spoken to many potential customers, but how could any of them say they'd seen her on a particular day over a week ago?

"Would anyone remember seeing you on that day? Someone you know, maybe?"

"*Signora* Tomasetti. We go together. Always together."

The lump of dread in Sarah's stomach began to dissolve. "Where can I find Mrs. Tomasetti?"

Sarah was exhausted by the time she reached the mission that afternoon. Unwilling to subject Malloy to yet another round of harassment by leaving him a message at Police Headquarters, she had decided to ask one of the girls from the mission to take it over this time. She also felt obligated to update Mrs. Wells on what was happening. She must be getting anxious.

When she reached the front door of the mission, she heard the sounds of an argument coming from inside. She opened the door without knocking and hurried inside to find Maeve and Gina screaming at each other in the parlor. Maeve was wearing Sarah's old hat, the one Emilia had worn the morning she died.

"It's mine now!" Maeve was telling her. "You don't have any right to it!"

"The lady gave it to me!" Gina screamed back.

"Mrs. Wells would've given it to me! Ask her!"

"I don't have to ask her! It's mine!"

"I'll tell Mrs. Wells you stole it from me!"

"Give it back!" Gina screamed and lunged.

Maeve ducked out of reach and grabbed the hat. Or at least that's what Sarah thought she was going to do. Instead she jerked out the hat pin and raised it as if to strike.

*"No!"* Sarah shouted, and the girls jumped apart. Maeve dropped the hat pin and clutched the hat, which she was still holding in her other hand, to her thin chest.

"What do you think you're doing?" Sarah demanded, stooping to snatch the pin up from the floor.

"She took the hat you gave me," Gina complained.

But Sarah was looking at Maeve, who was glaring back, unrepentant. "I'm the top girl now. It should be mine!"

"I mean what were you doing with this?" She held up the pin.

Maeve looked only a bit chagrined. "I was going to stick her with it. I had to defend myself, didn't I?"

"What's going on here?" Mrs. Wells demanded as she appeared in the parlor doorway.

Sarah turned to face her, and Mrs. Wells blanched when she saw the hat pin in Sarah's hand. She quickly lowered it to her side. "The girls were arguing over this hat. I'd given it to Gina, but Maeve seems to think she deserves it instead."

With visible effort, Mrs. Wells turned her attention to the girls. "Maeve, I've spoken to you before about pride and selfishness. If Mrs. Brandt gave the hat to Gina, then it belongs to her."

Maeve had paled, too. She obviously hated being corrected by Mrs. Wells, especially in the presence of others. Grudgingly, she handed the hat to Gina, who snatched it eagerly and clutched it to her own chest, probably afraid it would be taken from her again.

"You girls have made a spectacle of yourselves in front of Mrs. Brandt. I think you owe her an apology."

The girls muttered something unintelligible, then hurried out. Maeve was scarlet with humiliation, while Gina glowed with triumph.

"I'm sorry you witnessed that," Mrs. Wells said. "We try so hard, but . . ."

"Don't worry about me," Sarah said, although she was still shaken from seeing Maeve with the hat pin. "I know girls argue. My sister and I fought all the time."

A slight movement caught Sarah's eye, and she saw Aggie peering at her around the door frame. "Hello, Aggie," she said, giving the child a reassuring smile.

Aggie returned the smile and rushed to Sarah, throwing her arms around her skirts. Sarah still held the hat pin in the folds of her skirts so as not to alarm Mrs. Wells, so she led Aggie over to the sofa and sat down. She laid the pin down on the seat and spread her skirt over it. Aggie climbed into her lap as she had before and settled in happily.

"Aggie seems very fond of you," Mrs. Wells said. Sarah couldn't tell if Mrs. Wells approved or not. She remembered how concerned Mrs. Wells had been that Sarah's interest in the mission was only temporary. Probably, she was concerned that Aggie would become too attached to Sarah, only to have her disappear from her life.

"I'm very fond of Aggie, too," Sarah assured her, earning another smile from Aggie.

"I'm glad to hear it," Mrs. Wells said, taking a seat

in one of the chairs. "We heard about poor Mrs. Donato."

"Do you know that she tried to . . . ?" Sarah glanced at Aggie and changed what she had intended to say. "Did you hear what happened last night? What she did to herself?"

"Yes, the entire neighborhood was buzzing with the news this morning. I understand they sent for a priest from St. John's for her."

"Father Ahearn. I saw him at the jail this morning."

"You visited the jail?" Mrs. Wells asked in surprise.

"I know it sounds strange, but I just had to see Mrs. Donato."

Mrs. Wells folded her hands in her lap and sighed. "I suppose I should go to see her, too. The Lord commands us to forgive whatever wrongs are done to us, and it's my duty to speak to her about her immortal soul. She still has the opportunity to save herself from the fires of hell." She looked up, her eyes bright with the fervor of her faith. "We should always be ready to face our judgment at any time. I trust you have made your own peace with God, Mrs. Brandt."

"I believe that I have," Sarah answered, unwilling to get into a discussion on the subject at the moment.

"I'm glad to hear it. Of course, Mrs. Donato's need is much more urgent. I suppose they'll execute her for Emilia's death."

"They will if she's guilty," Sarah said. "I have good reason to believe she isn't, however."

Mrs. Wells's face reflected understandable shock. "I understood that she had confessed."

"No, she didn't, and Father Ahearn and I believe she's innocent."

Now Mrs. Wells was truly confused. "But you were so certain when you left here . . . And then she confessed to the police . . ."

"I spoke with Mrs. Donato myself. She couldn't have killed Emilia. She was selling her flowers at Washington Square that day."

Mrs. Wells smiled sadly. "Mrs. Brandt, I can't believe you don't realize a woman like that would lie to protect herself. Of course she'd claim she was someplace else."

"I did think of that, but she has a friend who sells dolls, and they go to the park together. I spoke with the woman today, and she verified that they were both at Washington Square every day for the past several months."

Mrs. Wells considered this for a long moment. "What will this mean?" she asked finally. She looked crushed, as if she could not bear yet another disappointment.

Sarah hated to add to her burdens, but she had no choice. "I'm afraid it means we still haven't found the person who really killed Emilia."

Mrs. Wells lowered her head and rubbed her forehead with the tips of her fingers. The strain she was suffering must be awful. When she looked up again, her face was white. "Mrs. Brandt, I'm afraid we will never learn who took Emilia's life."

Sarah reached under the spread of her skirt and slid the hat pin out to rest on the sofa where Mrs. Wells could see it. The other woman's eyes grew wide as she stared at it.

"The last time I was here, I suggested that one of

the girls might have done it," Sarah said gently. "Just a moment ago, I caught Maeve trying to stab Gina."

Mrs. Wells was shaking her head in silent denial. "Maeve couldn't have done it," she said in a hoarse whisper.

"Someone did," Sarah pointed out.

Mrs. Wells sighed wearily. "This quest has caused so much pain, and nothing can bring Emilia back. Can't we just . . . let her rest in peace?" she tried.

"I'm afraid I'm not as forgiving as you, Mrs. Wells. *I* can't rest until Emilia's killer is caught."

Mrs. Wells sighed in resignation. "May God help you then, Mrs. Brandt."

# 15

IN THE END, SARAH HAD TO LEAVE THE MESSAGE FOR Malloy herself. She hadn't felt she could ask either Maeve or Gina to do an errand for her after breaking up their fight. And she certainly couldn't ask Mrs. Wells for a favor after informing the poor woman that one of her cherished girls was probably a killer. Knowing everyone at Headquarters would hear what her message had been, she'd simply asked Malloy to contact her immediately about something very important concerning Emilia Donato's death. She could tell the desk sergeant didn't believe her, but she didn't care if they thought she was chasing Frank Malloy.

Perhaps they should give in and pretend to be a courting couple. At least Malloy wouldn't suffer any more teasing as a result, and he might suffer less. She couldn't help smiling at the thought. Then she went home to wait.

By evening, Sarah had begun to regret accepting Richard's invitation to dinner. What if Malloy didn't arrive before Richard came for her? How could she enjoy an evening out when an innocent woman languished in jail for a murder she hadn't committed? And how could she live with herself if Maeve harmed someone else before Malloy could arrest her — assuming she was even the killer?

She changed her clothes into something appropriate for her scheduled engagement more to occupy herself than because she truly wished to look nice. Even still, the time dragged. Too distracted to read or sew or do anything constructive, Sarah simply sat by the front window, watching for Malloy by the light of the gas streetlamps.

The watch on her lapel said seven-thirty when she saw a familiar figure hurrying down the street, but not the one she'd been expecting. She rushed to the front door and threw it open.

"Gina!" she called, and the girl turned toward her voice.

"Oh, Mrs. Brandt, I'm so glad to see you!" she cried. She ran over and stumbled in her haste to climb Sarah's front steps. "I didn't think I'd ever find you."

"What are you doing here?" Sarah asked as she ushered the girl inside.

Gina needed a moment to catch her breath. "Mrs. Wells sent me. I've got a message for you." She searched in her pocket and produced a crumpled envelope. Her name had been scrawled on it. "Mrs. Wells told me you lived on Bank Street," she explained as Sarah tore it open. "She said to just go up

Seventh Avenue and ask people until I found the street. She said someone there would tell me which house was yours."

Sarah quickly scanned the note. It was from Father Ahearn. He said he'd found out who the killer was, and he needed her help. She remembered him saying he couldn't reveal the secrets of the confessional. Had the real killer confessed to him? Maeve was Irish and had most certainly been raised Catholic. She might have felt compelled to confess her guilt, if she was the killer. Father Ahearn certainly wouldn't be able to tell the police what he'd learned, but perhaps he hoped Sarah could help him convince the girl to surrender herself.

"How did you get this note?" Sarah asked her.

"Somebody brought it to Mrs. Wells. It's from a priest, she said. He didn't know how to find you, but he thought she would. What does he want?"

"I have to go meet him." The note urged her to come as soon as possible, since he was worried the killer might harm herself or someone else. "I'm expecting some visitors, though, so I need to leave them a message before I go."

Gina sat down to rest from her frantic mission while Sarah found paper and a pencil and began to compose her notes to Malloy and Richard. The one to Malloy was the most difficult. How could she explain in a few words that Mrs. Donato was innocent and someone else — she suspected it was Maeve but wasn't completely sure — was guilty and that she'd gone to see a priest about finding out for certain? She understood it all, and the story still sounded unbelievable to her. She could just imagine Malloy's reaction.

The note to Richard was easier. She apologized for her rudeness and explained she had to meet with someone to save an innocent woman's life. He might consider her foolish, but he'd forgive her.

When she had inserted the notes into envelopes and addressed them to each man, she was ready to leave. "How did you get here?" Sarah asked.

"I walked," Gina said. No wonder she was tired.

Sarah put on her hat and took her cape from the hook by the door. "Let's see if we can get a Hansom." She didn't think a cab would take them all the way to the mission, but they could probably get a lot closer than the El would take them. She stuck the notes in the door for the men to find and then led Gina down the street toward Seventh Avenue, where they would be most likely to find a cab.

Frank knew he should feel at least a little guilty, but he didn't, not one bit. Sarah had sent for him, so he had a perfectly legitimate reason to be calling on her. He'd happened to hear Richard Dennis make an engagement with her for eight o'clock this evening, and he knew she'd be home at this hour, waiting for him. He should have gone earlier, of course, so he wouldn't interfere with their plans. Unfortunately, he hadn't gotten her message until he returned to Headquarters after investigating a fatal knife fight in one of the neighborhood's stale beer dives. He could have waited until morning, of course, but she obviously thought her news too important to wait. He'd calculated that he had just enough time to reach her before Dennis carried her away in his carriage. And just enough time to interrupt Dennis's plans. Perhaps he could even spoil them altogether. He was smiling as he turned the corner onto Bank Street.

Even though the city clocks hadn't yet struck eight, Frank could see Dennis's carriage waiting outside Sarah's house. He quickened his pace. He didn't want to have to flag them down as they drove by. But as he approached, he saw Dennis standing beside the coach and no sign of Sarah. Dennis appeared to be reading something by the light of the coach lamp.

As Frank reached him, he looked up. His puzzled frown dissolved into recognition. "Mr. Malloy," he said. "Good evening. Mrs. Brandt has left you a message, too."

Frank glanced up and only then realized the lights were out in her flat. He saw what appeared to be an envelope stuck in the crack between the front door and its frame. He realized she must have gone out and left a similar note for Dennis, and that's what he had been reading.

Frank quickly retrieved his own message and carried it back to the coach light. His feeling of satisfaction had long since evaporated. Now he was uneasy and growing more so by the minute. By the time he'd finished the note, he was deeply troubled.

"What does she say?" Dennis asked anxiously. "If you can tell me," he added when Frank looked at him sharply.

"She's gone off to meet some priest," Frank said, wondering if he'd have any trouble getting Dennis to reveal her message to him. "What does she say to you?"

"She apologizes for canceling our engagement. We were going to have dinner together," he explained, either rubbing it in or having forgotten that

Frank knew their plans. Frank didn't bother to decide which it was. "She says she has to meet with someone who has information about that girl's murder. I thought you were going to settle all that yesterday."

Frank could have taken offense, but Dennis sounded genuinely concerned about Sarah, so he overlooked the provocation. "I arrested the girl's mother yesterday. She confessed, or at least it sounded like she did. She doesn't speak English very well. But Mrs. Brandt's note says she can prove the woman is innocent." The thought was difficult to contemplate. Even if the woman hadn't confessed, she hadn't protested her innocence either, not even when they locked her up. She'd behaved as if she was guilty. What was Frank supposed to think?

"If the mother isn't the killer, then who could it be?" Dennis asked.

A good question. "Mrs. Brandt thought it might be someone at the mission, or at least she did until it looked like the mother did it."

Frank could see that Dennis was trying to make sense of all this. "What priest is she going to meet?"

"She doesn't say, but I know she went to St. John's the other day to ask them to pay for the girl's funeral. That must be where she's gone."

"How would a priest know who the killer is, especially if it's someone at the mission?"

Frank had been trying to figure that out himself. "Maybe the killer made a confession to the priest. A lot of those girls are Catholic, or they were before Mrs. Wells got them. But priests aren't allowed to tell anyone what they hear in the confessional."

Dennis frowned as though something was bothering him. "Mrs. Brandt said that the murdered girl looked as if she'd suffocated. How would that make someone look?"

Frank considered the question. From the tone of Dennis's voice, he knew it wasn't idle curiosity. "The girl's skin was blue and her eyes were open real wide."

Something changed very slightly in Dennis's expression. He'd already been worried, but now he looked alarmed. "Would she have been gasping for breath before she died?"

Now Frank knew it wasn't idle curiosity. "I'm not sure, but it seems likely."

Dennis had unconsciously crumpled the note he still held as his hands closed into fists. "Sarah . . . Mrs. Brandt said the girl had been stabbed in the back of the neck."

"That's right," Frank said, watching the other man's face carefully.

"The wound . . . Did it bleed a lot?"

"Hardly at all. In fact, it was so small, we almost didn't notice it."

Dennis closed his eyes and sucked in his breath, as if he'd sustained a great shock and couldn't quite absorb it. "Mr. Malloy," he said in a strangled voice, "I think I may know who your killer is."

Gina had never ridden in a Hansom cab before, and she enjoyed it thoroughly. Fortunately, the traffic was much lighter at this hour than usual, and they traveled relatively quickly down Seventh Avenue. The driver refused to go into the tenement section of the city, however, so she and Gina were forced to walk the rest of the way. If Gina felt any apprehension at walking through the neighborhood after dark, she gave no indication. She was probably used to it, and Sarah certainly was, too.

After what seemed an eternity, they finally reached the mission. Sarah saw Gina safely inside, where Mrs. Wells anxiously awaited them, with Aggie clinging to her skirts. The little girl rushed to Sarah and threw her arms around her legs as usual. Sarah stooped and gave her a hug.

"It's nice to see you, too, Aggie," she told the child, who looked at her with such longing, she thought her heart might break. She knew Aggie was becoming too attached to her, but she couldn't bring herself to do anything about it.

"Thank you for finding Mrs. Brandt, Gina," Mrs. Wells was saying. "You did a good job." Gina fairly beamed with pleasure, reminding Sarah how desperate these girls were for approval of any kind. "Now you can go on upstairs with the other girls and get ready for bed." She glanced at the child Sarah still held. "And take Aggie, too, please."

Aggie struggled a bit, but a stern look from Mrs. Wells defeated her. As soon as they were gone, Mrs. Wells closed the parlor doors and asked, "What did the message say?"

"The priest thinks he knows who Emilia's killer is," she said. "I'm going to see him right now."

"Are you sure he can be trusted?" Mrs. Wells asked with a worried frown.

Sarah almost pointed out that the man was a priest, for heaven's sake, but then she realized that was probably exactly why Mrs. Wells wouldn't consider him trustworthy. "I believe so," she said instead. "I'm at least going to hear what he has to say."

"You're going tonight?" She seemed surprised.

"I think we need to learn the truth as soon as possible." Sarah didn't point out that she wanted to find the killer before anyone else was murdered, but she could see that Mrs. Wells understood just the same.

"I can go with you, if you'd like," Mrs. Wells offered tentatively. "Although they might not welcome me there."

"I'm sure I'll be fine," Sarah said. "I can't imagine any place safer than a church."

The city was settling down for the night. The hoards of people who congregated in the streets during the daylight hours had gone to seek their beds or some indoor entertainment. Saloons catering to every pocketbook would be crowded with patrons who had no place they'd rather be, while those fortunate enough to have a job would be at home in bed, in anticipation of another long workday.

St. John's sat forlornly on the corner, its steeple towering over the surrounding neighborhood. Only a feeble light from within illuminated the stained glass windows. Church, she realized, was a daylight activity. She was glad she'd chosen to come this evening, when Father Ahearn would be free to give her his full attention, and no one would be around to overhear what he was going to tell her.

The heavy front doors of the church were unlocked and moved silently on their hinges. Inside, she saw that one source of the light was a display of candles sitting in a wooden rack. They lit the foyer with a welcoming glow, and Sarah stepped inside. She moved forward, letting her eyes become accustomed to the shadows. Stopping behind the last pew, she scanned the sanctuary. She saw no sign of Father Ahearn, or anyone else, for that matter.

Of course, he couldn't have any idea how quickly she'd receive his message. He'd hardly be sitting here waiting for her. She'd have to find the door that led to the priests' private offices and see if he was there.

The church seemed cavernous in the semidarkness. The light from the candles in the foyer could not penetrate the depths of the sanctuary. Some solitary lights burned up near the altar, too, and Sarah used them to mark her progress down the long aisle. She was halfway to the door she was seeking when she heard a sound behind her.

"Father?" she called, turning. But the shadowy figure who had entered the door through which she'd come wasn't a priest.

Frank didn't like the idea of bringing Dennis along, but the man had offered the use of his carriage. Besides, Frank figured he wanted to see the confrontation that was coming. If Dennis was right in his theory about who the killer was, he certainly deserved the opportunity.

The carriage stopped in front of the mission, and the two men climbed out. Frank could see the driver looking around nervously, wondering how safe he'd be in this neighborhood. Curious eyes were probably already peering out at him from every building.

Frank climbed the front steps and pounded on the door. "Police, open up!" he shouted. The windows were dark, but he couldn't believe everyone inside was already asleep. Even if they were, he'd soon have them awake again. He needed to pound a few more times before someone finally unbolted the door and opened it a crack.

Without waiting for an invitation, Frank pushed it open, forcing whoever was behind it to back up or be knocked over. Once he was inside, he saw it was the same red-haired girl who had opened the door to him before. This must be Maeve, the girl Sarah suspected of being the killer. She wore a nightdress and carried a candle. "You can't come in here," she tried, but her voice trembled. Her face had gone so pale, her freckles looked almost black.

"Where's Mrs. Wells?" Frank demanded. Several other girls had come to see what the disturbance was about, and they stood on the stairs, staring down at him in wide-eyed terror.

"She's in her room, asleep," Maeve said. The candle she was carrying trembled.

"Then get her up," Frank said. "I need to speak to her."

For a second, he thought she might refuse, but then she obviously realized the futility of it. She nodded at a dark-haired girl, who took off running down the hallway, her bare feet slapping against the wooden floor.

"What do you want? Is something wrong?" the girl asked, but Frank just glared at her.

They stood like this for a minute or two. All the girls seemed to be holding their breath, sensing something awful but having no idea what it might be. Then they heard the sound of the girl's running feet returning. She stopped beside Maeve, her dark eyes wide with terror. "She ain't there."

Maeve turned on her in exasperation. "What do you mean she ain't there?"

"I mean, she ain't there. And she ain't in the kitchen. I looked."

"Where else could she be then?" Frank asked, his voice gruff and as frightening as he could make it without terrifying the girls into total silence.

"Nowhere," the dark-haired girl offered before Maeve could speak. "She told us all to go to bed, that she was going to her room to pray."

"When was this?" Frank asked.

"Just a little while ago," the dark-haired girl said. "Right after Mrs. Brandt left."

"Mrs. Brandt was *here*?" Frank nearly shouted, grabbing her by the arm.

Her eyes widened in terror and the color drained from her face. Instantly, Frank realized he'd made a tactical error. If the girl was too frightened, she wouldn't tell him a thing.

"There now," Dennis said calmly, coming to his rescue. "There's nothing to be afraid of. You're Gina, aren't you? I remember you were at the party the other night." Frank carefully released the girl's arm, allowing Dennis to use his charm. "Can you tell us why Mrs. Brandt was here?"

The girl started rubbing her arm where Frank had held her, but she was looking at Dennis now. Her face was still white, but she said, "She brought me home, and then she talked to Mrs. Wells —"

"What do you mean, she brought you home?" Frank asked too gruffly. The girl took a step back, but once again Dennis distracted her.

"Why did she bring you home, Gina?" he asked in his gentleman's voice.

"She wanted to see I got home safe." She glanced at Frank, but only for a second before looking back at

Dennis. "Then she talked to Mrs. Wells and left. I expect she went to see the priest."

"How did you know she was going to see the priest?" Frank asked, and this time he managed to keep his voice fairly gentle.

She might even have answered him, but Maeve beat her to it. "Because the priest sent Mrs. Brandt a note, except he didn't know where she lives, so he sent it here and asked Mrs. Wells to get it to her. Gina carried it."

Frank's mind was racing. Dear God, why hadn't he seen it before now? "Who brought the note here? Did anyone see the priest?" He looked up at the faces staring down at him. No one responded.

"Mrs. Wells said a boy brought it," Maeve offered after a moment.

"Did you see the boy?" She shook her head. "Did *anyone* see the boy?" Silence. "Did anyone even hear him knock?" More silence.

"Malloy, what is it?" Dennis asked frantically.

Frank turned to face him. "Mrs. Wells was the one who sent the note, and now she's gone after Sarah."

"Mrs. Wells, is that you?" Sarah called to the woman emerging from the shadows. "I told you that you didn't need to come with me."

"Oh, but I did need to come, Mrs. Brandt." Her voice sounded strange. It gave Sarah chills.

She knew she was only being fanciful. The eerie stillness of the church had spooked her. "I suppose you're as anxious as I am to find out who killed Emilia. I hope you won't be too disappointed if it turns out to be Maeve or one of the other girls."

"I won't be disappointed at all," Mrs. Wells assured her.

Sarah wished she could see the other woman's face, but it was too dark. The tone of her voice was frighteningly calm, even though Sarah knew she must be extremely upset. She wanted to send her home and spare her the pain of hearing the priest tell her what would surely be horrible news. But she couldn't spare her forever. "All right, then," Sarah said. "The priest's office is this way."

She turned and started to walk toward the front of the church again. Behind her, she heard the chillingly familiar rasp of a hat pin being pulled from a hat and then the patter of running feet coming up behind her, and in that instant, she understood everything.

Sarah threw herself into the nearest pew as Mrs. Wells dove for her. The woman stumbled, her momentum carrying her forward when she missed Sarah, so that she fell headlong to the floor.

Catching herself on the back of a pew, Sarah kept her feet and started for the opposite aisle as quickly as she could. The space between the benches was too narrow for real speed and her skirts kept trying to tangle with her feet, but she lurched on, knowing her attacker would be hindered the same way if she tried to follow.

She should scream. Someone would come if she screamed, but she didn't have the breath to do it. She'd have to concentrate on getting away instead.

She heard Mrs. Wells scrambling to her feet. Sarah risked a backward glance. The woman's hat was askew, and she held the hat pin like a knife, ready to plunge it into flesh. For a second Sarah thought the other woman was going to come after her, but then

she turned and started running back down the aisle,
toward the rear of the church. That's when Sarah realized she was planning to cut her off before she
could reach the door and make her escape.

Sarah's only chance was to beat her there. Terror
propelled her out from between the pews and into the
opposite aisle. Lifting her skirts with both hands, she
raced toward the rear of the church. Watching her ad-
versary out of the corner of her eye, she saw that she
stood a good chance. If she didn't fall, if she didn't
stumble, if she didn't slip . . .

Her breath gasping, she reached the last pew, and
she saw that she was going to make it. She was closer
to the door, and she would escape into the street and
then she would —

*"No!"* a shrill voice cried, and Sarah saw a tiny
wraith streak from shadows near the doors straight
for Mrs. Wells, who was running toward Sarah. The
woman caught herself just in time to keep from
sprawling over the tiny figure, who grabbed her
around the legs as she had done to Sarah only a short
time ago.

"Aggie, run!" Sarah cried, freezing in her tracks,
but she was too late. The child cried out in pain as
Mrs. Wells clutched a handful of her hair and held her
fast with one hand while she raised the hat pin threat-
eningly with the other. She looked up at Sarah in triumph. "Don't hurt her!" Sarah pleaded desperately.

"Why not?" Mrs. Wells asked, her voice icily
calm. "She'd be better off, just like the rest of them.
She'd be in heaven."

*Oh, dear God!* Sarah had to think, to plan. She had
to figure out how to save Aggie, so she had to keep
Mrs. Wells talking until she thought of something.

"Why?" she asked, her voice hoarse with terror. "Why did you do it?"

"I had to save them," she said, as if that made perfect sense. "Before the devil got them again." Aggie was whimpering softly, but thank heaven, she wasn't struggling.

"Were there others, before Emilia?" Sarah asked in an effort to distract her.

"Oh, yes. Once I realized how many of them would weaken and fall away, I knew I had to do something to save them."

Sarah's heart was pounding, and she felt the gorge rising in her throat, but she swallowed it down. "Please, let Aggie go."

Mrs. Wells considered the request. "All right," she said, and for a second Sarah's heart leaped with hope. "But *you* must stay."

"My life for hers, is that it?" Sarah asked unsteadily.

"I'm sorry, Mrs. Brandt, but I can't allow you to interfere. My work is too important. Those girls will go to hell unless I save them. I can't let anything stop me."

The woman wasn't thinking clearly at all, Sarah realized. She was bound to come under suspicion. But Sarah didn't think there was any chance of reasoning with her. She could never recall being so frightened. She could barely breathe, but she had to be strong for Aggie. The child kept trying to turn her little head to look at Sarah, but Mrs. Wells held her too tightly, the hat pin poised to strike if Sarah made a false move.

"It will be over quickly," Mrs. Wells promised. "You won't suffer."

Drawing a deep breath, Sarah somehow managed to keep her voice steady. "All right, Mrs. Wells. But you must let Aggie go."

"Not until . . . it's over," she said quite firmly. "I'm afraid I don't trust you to keep your part of the bargain if I release her. And she'll never be able to tell what happened, so it doesn't matter if she knows or not."

Sarah thought she heard something outside, but she was afraid to call for help. Mrs. Wells might panic and stab Aggie. She'd have to rely on her own wits and strength to save them both. She took a step toward the madwoman, and then another. Aggie was sobbing now. Another step, measuring, trying to decide how she could grab the hand that held the pin before —

*"Sarah!"*

The church doors slammed open, and Sarah instinctively looked to see Richard Dennis charging through them.

"She's got Aggie!" she cried and lunged for the other woman.

All Sarah could see was the hand holding the hat pin raised over Aggie's tiny neck. If she could grab it and stop it —

But Richard got there first. He snatched Aggie away just as the hat pin plunged downward. Someone else was calling Sarah's name, but she didn't have time to even look up. She was too busy wrestling Mrs. Wells, both of her hands wrapped around the fist that still clutched the hat pin.

Then suddenly someone was helping, overpowering Mrs. Wells and wrenching the hat pin from her fingers. A rough arm pushed Sarah away, and she rec-

ognized Malloy. He thrust the hat pin into Sarah's
hand and shoved Mrs. Wells to her knees, twisting
one of her arms behind her back. She cried out in
pain, but Malloy didn't release his grip.

"What's going on here!" an outraged voice
shouted. "Get out of here or I'll call the police!" Father Ahearn was running down the aisle toward them.
He wore only an undershirt and trousers and looked
very unpriestly.

"I *am* the police," Malloy shouted back. "This
woman is a murderer, and she's very dangerous. Get
me something to tie her up."

The startled priest stared at the tableau for only a
moment before hurrying to obey.

Malloy turned to Sarah. "What the hell were you
trying to do?" he demanded, but he didn't wait for an
answer. "Are you all right?"

"Yes, I'm fine. Take that other pin away from her!"
she added, suddenly horrified to realize Mrs. Wells
had another one still in her hat.

Malloy relieved the woman of that one, too, and
handed it to Sarah as well. Mrs. Wells's hat slipped
off and fell to the floor in front of her. Malloy continued to hold her firmly and painfully in place.

"Can you help me here?" Richard asked, his voice
oddly strained.

Sarah hurried to his aid. He lay on the floor where
he had fallen in the scuffle, and he held a terrified
Aggie to his chest. Still clutching the hat pins in her
left hand, Sarah reached out her right one and Aggie
grabbed it. Scrambling out of Richard's arms, the
child threw herself at Sarah and fairly climbed up her
body until her little arms were wrapped tightly
around Sarah's neck and her legs around Sarah's

waist. Sarah managed to stagger over to one of the pews and sit down, setting the hat pins on the seat beside her so she could hold the child with both arms. Her little body was trembling, and Sarah crooned meaningless words of comfort into the soft cloud of her hair.

Father Ahearn came running back with what appeared to be drapery cords. Malloy looked at them askance, but he used them to bind Mrs. Wells's hands securely behind her back. Then he hauled her roughly to her feet and shoved her down into the nearest pew.

Richard was a bit slow getting to his feet.

"Richard, are you all right?" Sarah asked in alarm when she noticed, remembering how Mrs. Wells had been wielding the hat pin.

But Richard wasn't listening. He was staring in horror at Mrs. Wells. "You killed Hazel, didn't you?"

Sarah gasped as Mrs. Wells looked up, her eyes bright with the fires of fanaticism. "She was very unhappy here, Mr. Dennis. I sent her to heaven."

Father Ahearn caught Richard when he would have attacked her and held him back.

"Let the law take care of her, Dennis," Malloy warned him. "She'll die for her crimes. There's nothing worse you can do to her."

Richard was shaking with fury, but after a moment, he allowed the priest to push him back a few steps.

"Father," Malloy said, "can you go to the nearest call box and have them send a wagon over for this woman?"

Father Ahearn nodded, probably only too glad to escape the nightmarish scene. Portly Father O'Brien came lumbering down the aisle, wheezing from the effort of running, just as Father Ahearn bolted away to do Malloy's bidding. He'd taken the time to put on his cassock, so he looked more professional than his young colleague. He recognized Mrs. Wells at once. "What are *you* doing here?" he demanded breathlessly.

"Trying to cause you some trouble, I expect, Father," Malloy said. "She's the one who killed Emilia Donato, and she just tried to kill Mrs. Brandt right here in the church."

Father O'Brien's gaze shifted back to where Mrs. Wells sat, bound and helpless. He stared at her as if the jaws of hell had suddenly opened up to reveal their horrors. "I *knew* something was wrong at that place," he murmured, and Sarah remembered his accusation about other missing girls. She didn't even want to think about how many others the woman had "sent to heaven." She hugged Aggie more tightly and was relieved to realize the child had stopped trembling.

Richard still glared at Mrs. Wells, but he seemed calmer now. Then Sarah noticed he was rubbing his chest.

"Richard, you *are* hurt!" she cried. "Did she stab you?"

"Just a little jab," he said. "It's not even bleeding."

Only a tiny drop of blood had stained his shirt beneath his vest, but Sarah remembered how Emilia's wound hadn't bled either. "Are you sure? How deep did the pin go in?"

"Not deep at all. I told you, it was just a jab."

Sarah knew even a shallow jab could become infected, and there was always a danger of lockjaw. He did seem pale, and he was sweating. "You should sit down. You look as if you're going to faint."

He took a seat in the pew in front of hers and half turned to face her. He was grinning boyishly, as if he'd done something a bit naughty and was proud of it. "I did do a bit of running to get here." He looked over at Malloy, who was still guarding Mrs. Wells. "In the end, I beat you here," he bragged.

Malloy frowned, but he didn't deny it. Then Sarah realized how amazing it was that they were here at all.

"How did you know I'd be in danger? And what are the two of you doing here together?" she demanded.

"I was on my way to your house, and we ran into each other," Malloy said unhelpfully.

Sarah turned to Richard expectantly.

"I'd just found your note and was reading it when Mr. Malloy arrived." His smile faded. "We started discussing that girl's murder, and I remembered something you'd said about how she looked after she died."

"You mean Emilia?" Sarah asked, still confused.

"Yes, you said she looked as if she'd suffocated. I asked Mr. Malloy to describe it and then I realized — that's the way Hazel looked. Mrs. Wells had come to visit her that last day, and when she left, we found Hazel gasping for breath. She died a short time later."

His gaze drifted to Mrs. Wells, who sat staring back at him, unrepentant.

"She went to heaven, Mr. Dennis," Mrs. Wells said. "That was her wish."

Richard looked as if he would have cheerfully broken her neck, but he managed to restrain himself.

"She'll be punished now," Sarah said, reaching up to pat his shoulder reassuringly. "And nothing you do to her can bring Hazel back."

He continued to glare at the woman, rubbing his chest absently.

Father Ahearn came running back into the church and reported that a police wagon was on its way and that a carriage had pulled up outside.

"A carriage?" Sarah echoed in amazement, looking at Richard for an explanation.

"We took my carriage from your house to the mission. Mr. Malloy was expecting to find Mrs. Wells there and accuse her of the murders. When she wasn't there . . . Well, that's when we realized she was the one who had sent you the note to lure you here. Mr. Malloy said it would be faster to go on foot, so we left Sydney to follow as best he could. It looks as if he found us," he added to Malloy.

Father O'Brien turned to Malloy. "Can someone tell me what happened here?"

Malloy looked at Sarah. "I received a note from Father Ahearn this evening," she began, but Ahearn interrupted her.

"I didn't send you a note!"

"I know that now," Sarah said. "Mrs. Wells sent it and claimed it had come from you. It said you had discovered who the killer was and asked me to come to the church as soon as possible."

"But you went to the mission first," Richard said.

"Gina, one of the girls there, had brought the message. I had to see her safely home and tell Mrs. Wells the good news," Sarah added bitterly.

Mrs. Wells refused to meet her gaze, but Malloy

said, "So that's how she knew exactly when you'd be at the church. Then she followed you over here."

"And Aggie must have followed *her*," Sarah said, looking down at the child, who had gone very still. Sarah realized with amazement she was asleep. "I can't imagine why. Look at her! She's in her night-dress and barefoot."

"She was trying to save you," Mrs. Wells informed her, although it gave her no pleasure. "She's a clever girl, and she understands more than you'd ever imagine."

"She understood that I was in danger, I guess," Sarah continued, "and she tried to stop Mrs. Wells from stabbing me with the hat pin. Mrs. Wells grabbed her and threatened to kill her if I didn't allow her to kill me instead."

Father O'Brien's expression was incredulous, but he couldn't seem to think of a question to ask that would shed any light on the unbelievable story. Father Ahearn wasn't quite as stunned. "How did you get the child away from her?"

"Mr. Dennis arrived. He snatched Aggie away, and Mr. Malloy and I disarmed her. That's when you got here."

The two priests just stared at her for a moment, and then Father O'Brien lowered himself into one of the pews, as if his legs had decided not to hold him anymore.

Sarah remembered her own questions about Emilia's death and looked at Mrs. Wells. "You killed Emilia in the park because you thought that's where her mother sold flowers, but you didn't know her mother hadn't been there in months."

She gazed back with guileless eyes. "You're

wrong. I *did* know it. Emilia didn't, though. She went there eagerly so her mother could see her new dress. But I wanted it to happen there so no one would recognize her. She would never be identified."

"Just like the others," Father O'Brien murmured, turning to Sarah in horror. "I told you other girls had disappeared. If no one knew who they were, they would never have been traced back to the mission."

"And no one would ever ask Mrs. Wells any embarrassing questions," Malloy added in disgust.

Sarah tried to make sense of this. How could this mild-mannered woman who quoted scripture be a heartless killer? "I should have known something was wrong when I caught you in a lie," she berated herself. "You said Emilia told one of the girls she wanted her lover to see her in her new dress, but she never said that. She really wanted her mother to see her. And you used that to murder her."

Sarah glared at her, but the eyes looking back held no hint of remorse. That was when she realized that even execution wasn't a great enough punishment for what the woman had done. If God was merciful, Mrs. Wells would burn in the hell from which she'd tried to save those poor girls.

Her heart aching, Sarah looked at Malloy again, and found him staring at her with a longing she easily recognized. She realized the fear he must have felt when he learned she had gone to meet the killer. The thought of him racing to her rescue touched her heart and brought the sting of tears to her eyes. Thank heaven they weren't alone, or Sarah was very much afraid she might have thrown her arms around Malloy and hugged him.

A policeman burst into the church. "Where's Malloy?" he shouted.

"Here," Malloy replied, "and show some respect. This is still a church."

The officer hurried toward him. "Sorry, sir. We've got a wagon outside, just like you wanted." He was looking around, probably trying to figure out which one was the criminal.

Malloy took Mrs. Wells's arm and jerked her roughly to her feet. "Come along, lady," he said. She gave him a withering glare, but he ignored it.

"That's who we're arresting?" the officer asked in astonishment. "Ain't she the lady from the mission?"

"Yeah, but don't let that fool you. She'll kill you quick as look at you," Malloy said.

Richard rose, too, and Sarah saw that he winced and grabbed at his chest.

"Malloy," she called in alarm, "Richard is badly hurt."

"I thought she just jabbed him," Malloy said, a question in his voice.

"It's nothing," Richard insisted, but Sarah picked up the hat pins that lay on the pew beside her and looked at them closely. The blood smear on one of them indicated far more than a jab.

"We need to get him to a hospital right away," she cried, although she was afraid even that wouldn't be enough. The wound must have been deep and may well have injured a lung, or even his heart.

"Don't be silly," Richard tried, but with less conviction than before.

Malloy turned to the police officer who was waiting to help with the prisoner. "That's his carriage outside. Help him get into it. Hurry!" he added when the man hesitated.

The officer rushed over and took one of Richard's arms. "It's really nothing," Richard protested, but his face was ashen.

Sarah looked around frantically for someone to take Aggie from her. "Father Ahearn? I'm a trained nurse. I should go with him. Can you —" she asked, and he understood instantly. He took the sleeping child and shifted her gently to his own shoulder.

"I'll take her back to the mission and get someone to stay with the girls tonight," he promised.

Sarah thanked him and ran to help the officer with Richard.

"Make your peace with God, Mr. Dennis," Mrs. Wells warned as they passed her.

Sarah would have slapped her if she hadn't been holding Richard upright.

Malloy muttered a curse and shoved her back down into her seat.

Richard's driver hurried to help them when they came out of the church, and somehow they got him into the carriage. The officer told the driver to take them to the nearest hospital, as Sarah helped Richard stretch out on one of the seats. Although it was much too short for him to recline, at least she could make him reasonably comfortable.

When the carriage lurched into motion, Sarah took a seat on the opposite side. After she'd covered Richard with the lap robe, she laid a hand on his chest and found his heartbeat slow and labored. Rage roared inside her. How could that woman have managed to stab him in the heart?

"She's killed me, too, hasn't she?" he asked quietly.

"Oh, Richard, we don't know that," she said, taking his hand in hers. "We'll get you to a doctor and —"

"No, that won't help," he said. Oddly, he didn't sound frightened or even upset. "I know I'm going to die, Sarah."

Sarah felt her eyes filling with tears and his image blurred. She blinked them away determinedly and squeezed his hand. "I'm so sorry, Richard."

"I'm just glad it wasn't you," he told her with a weak smile. "Or that child. I saved her, didn't I?"

She thought of how he'd thrown himself at Mrs. Wells to save Aggie. "Yes, Richard, you saved her life," she agreed. She would make sure everyone knew he'd died a hero. "Now you'll see Hazel, and you'll be able to tell her that you loved her."

His breathing was growing labored. "Yes," he said, his voice raspy. "And that I'm sorry."

"And that you brought her killer to justice," Sarah whispered as his eyes closed.

She held his hand tightly, tears rolling down her cheeks. His breaths became more and more shallow until a shudder wracked his body, and he finally lay still.

# Epilogue

THANK HEAVEN FOR TELEPHONES, SARAH THOUGHT. What had they ever done without them? She never would have been able to take care of so many crises all at once without this marvelous invention. She was beginning to think she might even get one herself.

She made her first telephone call from the hospital to Opal Graves. Opal was shocked and saddened by Richard's death and outraged by Mrs. Wells's perfidy, but she also realized the urgency of seeing to the needs of the girls at the mission. She promised to contact some of the volunteers from the mission at their homes and recruit women to stay with the girls until decisions could be made about what to do.

Sarah's second call was more difficult. While she was only calling her own parents, she had to ask them to notify Richard's family of his death. News like that shouldn't come over the telephone from someone

they didn't even know. Her parents were stunned by
Richard's death, but they agreed with her on the need
to break the news gently to his family.

Then came the most difficult task of all: waiting.
She simply couldn't leave Richard's body alone at
the hospital until his loved ones had come to claim
him. Besides, she knew they'd have questions about
what had happened, questions only she could answer.
She spent the hours until they came by preparing the
story she would tell, the story that would make
Richard a hero.

The hour was quite late by the time Richard's father had taken him away, and Sarah was free to go.
Her own father, who had accompanied Richard's, insisted she go home to get some rest and took her there
in his own carriage. Although she was exhausted and
emotionally drained, she slept fitfully. By midmorn-
ing, she was up and dressed and hurrying back to the
mission, where she might be desperately needed.

Mulberry Street was oddly quiet in these morning
hours. People milled on the sidewalks, as always, but
their conversation was muted and their expressions
solemn. Word of what had happened would have
spread like lightning through the community. Girls
who had sought refuge at the mission had been brutally murdered by the woman who should have been
their protector. A woman who claimed to have been
called by God had been a spawn of Satan. Even
among people who had known nothing but hardship
their entire lives, this would be devastating news.
And what would it do to their faith in the future?

When she passed Police Headquarters, Sarah
thought about stopping in to look for Malloy. She
wanted to see him, and she needed to talk to him, to

help her make whatever sense could made out of this whole mess. But she knew he probably wouldn't be there. He had taken Mrs. Wells to the city jail — The Tombs — and spent most of the night getting her confession. Then he would have gone home. He couldn't possibly be back this early.

The mission still looked exactly the same, even though everything had changed. When Sarah knocked, a woman she didn't recognize opened the door. Her clothes marked her as a resident of a much more prosperous part of the city. "I'm Sarah Brandt," she said. "Opal Graves contacted you at my request."

The woman's suspicious frown vanished, and she admitted Sarah immediately. "I'm so glad you've come, Mrs. Brandt. Some of the girls have been very concerned for your welfare."

"And I'm so glad *you've* come to help," Sarah replied. "We couldn't leave the girls here without an adult."

"I was glad to do it when Opal told me what Mrs. Wells had done. I still can't believe it!"

"Neither can I," Sarah assured her.

Sarah heard a small cry and then the clatter of little feet on the stairs. She looked up to see Aggie barreling down from upstairs at an alarming rate of speed. Sarah hurried over to the stairs to catch her. The child threw herself into Sarah's arms and clung to her neck as if she would never let her go.

Other girls came creeping out more cautiously, some from the parlor and others from upstairs. Most of them looked as if they'd been crying, and they all looked frightened.

Maeve was taking her role as "head girl" more seriously than ever. She stepped forward. "Is it true what they said, Mrs. Brandt? Did Mrs. Wells kill Emilia?"

"Yes," she told them. She wouldn't mention the others. Perhaps they'd never have to know the extent of Mrs. Wells's evil. "But you don't have to be afraid. She's in jail now, and she won't ever be free again."

Maeve and the others looked far from reassured, however. "Then what's going to happen to all of us?"

"Not a thing," Opal Graves informed them as she emerged from the kitchen. She was wearing an apron and her plain face had been transformed by a beatific smile. "You will stay here just as you've been doing. It may take us a little while, but we'll find someone to take Mrs. Wells's place — someone good," she added, just in case they were in doubt. "And meanwhile, my friends and I will take turns staying with you."

Sarah shot her a grateful look. She would thank her more profusely when they were alone.

"Will you stay here, too, Mrs. Brandt?" Gina asked anxiously.

"I can't stay all the time, but I'll certainly help as much as I can," she replied.

"Have you had anything to eat?" Opal asked her.

Sarah had been in a hurry to get here this morning. "No," she admitted.

"Come into the kitchen, and we'll fix you something," Opal said. "And bring your friend, too," she added with a nod at Aggie, who was still clinging fiercely to Sarah's neck.

The girls followed Sarah and gathered around where she sat at the small kitchen table. Aggie consented to sit on a chair beside her, but only if she could hold on to her skirt. The other girls stood or sat around the room, watching her eat the bread and jam Opal set before her. When she was finished, they started asking her questions, and she answered them as honestly as she could. At some point, Aggie climbed up into her lap and settled in comfortably.

Finally, Opal sensed Sarah's exhaustion and sent the girls off to do their lessons. When they protested, she explained that they needed something to occupy their minds. They all drifted out except Aggie, who refused to leave Sarah's side.

"I heard you yelling at Mrs. Wells last night," Sarah said to Aggie. Sarah looked up at Opal and said, "She yelled 'no' to stop her from coming after me with the hat pin."

Opal's eyes widened in surprise, but she wisely said nothing.

Sarah shared her wonder, but she didn't want to make too much of a fuss over Aggie and scare her out of ever speaking again.

"You were such a brave girl to help me," Sarah said, giving the child a hug. Aggie beamed with pride.

Finally, Opal and Sarah moved to the parlor. Aggie screamed when Opal tried to separate her from Sarah, and Sarah realized she needed someone warm to cuddle, so the child accompanied them, too. Sarah sat in the rocking chair and rocked Aggie until she fell asleep, still exhausted by the night's terrors. Then she answered Opal's questions about how Richard had died and why Mrs. Wells had murdered Emilia and other girls as well. Then she told her how Mrs. Wells had killed Hazel, too.

Sarah wept with her over her lost friend and listened while she vented her fury at the woman who had taken God's power of life and death into her own hands.

After everything had been told and the storm of emotion had passed, Opal said, "The best thing we can do now is keep the mission operating and try to make up for the evil that woman did. We'll have a difficult time of it, at least for a while. Three of the girls had already run off before I got here this morning."

"Oh dear!"

"I'm sure they were frightened when Richard and that detective came in shouting. Now that things have settled down, they'll probably come back. We can hope, at least."

Sarah sighed and looked down at Aggie's sweet face. "What should I do with Aggie?" she asked, wondering where the child normally slept so she could put her to bed.

"I think she should go to an orphanage," Opal said, misunderstanding the question. "This certainly isn't the right place for her, and a child that young deserves a chance to be adopted."

Sarah gaped at her in surprise. "I . . . I didn't mean that, but now that you say it . . . I realize you're right. These girls have so many problems themselves, they shouldn't be expected to look after a child. And neither should whomever you find to operate the mission."

"Some of the girls might also be a bad influence on her," Opal pointed out. "I'm sure Mrs. Wells kept her here out of selfishness, probably because she wanted a replacement for her daughter who died."

"She might not be adopted from an orphanage, though," Sarah said with a frown. "Many children aren't, and a child who doesn't speak isn't very likely to be chosen. I hate the thought of her growing up in an institution."

"If you feel that way, maybe you should keep her yourself," Opal suggested with a small smile. "She's very attached to you already. Come on, we'll take her upstairs and tuck her in."

But Sarah was looking down at the small face, so angelic in sleep. Opal had just been teasing, but Sarah didn't find the suggestion humorous at all. In fact, she found it terrifyingly compelling.

She couldn't raise a child, of course. She worked long hours and got called out in the middle of the night. Who would take care of Aggie when Sarah couldn't be home? The whole idea was insane.

"Sarah, you didn't fall asleep yourself, did you?" Opal called from the doorway.

"No, I'm coming," she said, lifting Aggie's delicate body in her arms. Yes, she would be crazy to take on the responsibility of a child. What had she been thinking?

For some reason, Frank hadn't expected the mission to look exactly the same as it always had. By rights, he supposed, it should have changed color or something, now that it was free of the Devil Woman who had run it.

While he'd been taking Mrs. Wells out to the police wagon, the old priest had accused her again of killing other girls in the past. To Frank's horror, she had admitted it, perversely proud that she had sent them to heaven while they were in what she called a state of grace — before they could backslide into evil once more. He still shuddered when he thought of the righteous expression on her face when she described robbing those young girls of their lives.

This morning, Frank only knew that he had to see Sarah Brandt and make sure she was truly all right. By the time he'd gotten Mrs. Wells legally incarcerated last night, it had been too late to seek her out. Now he was making his first stop at the mission, figuring she would have returned there at the first opportunity.

"Malloy," Sarah Brandt said with a smile when she opened the door to him. That smile brightened an already beautiful day.

"How are you this morning?" he asked, pulling off his bowler hat as he stepped into the foyer.

"A little bruised, but nothing that won't heal," she said with a rueful smile. She led him into the parlor and offered him a seat.

He chose one of the sturdier-looking chairs. She picked the rocker, as if she needed comfort.

"I'm sorry about Dennis," he said and watched her smile vanish.

"How did you know?"

"I checked with the hospital."

"She must have somehow managed to get the pin into his heart," she explained. Talking about it obviously pained her. "It had to have been an accident. I don't think she had time to plan it, and even if she did, the chances that she could pierce his clothing and slip the pin in between his ribs are very small. To hit his heart after all of that — well, as I said, it had to have been an accident."

"She might be the first woman to meet up with Old Sparky," he said. "Nobody cared about the poor girls she killed, but she won't get away with murdering Dennis and his wife."

"That's not much comfort," she said. "Her execution won't bring them back."

"At least it'll keep her from doing it again. The old priest was right — there were other girls before Emilia. God only knows how long she's been sending girls to heaven."

"How on earth did she decide that was her job?" she asked, outraged.

"I spent a lot of time with her last night. Seems like she decided when her husband was sick. She had a little girl who died years ago, and she kept telling herself the girl was better off in heaven. She nursed her husband for a long time, and then she started thinking he'd be better off in heaven, too."

"She killed her husband?" Sarah asked, her blue eyes wide with horror.

"Yeah. She thought she did him a favor, too."

"Did she kill him the same way she killed the girls?"

"Yeah, she said she'd learned it from her father, from killing animals."

"Oh, yes," Sarah remembered. "She said her father was a butcher." Why hadn't she realized the connection then?

"After she killed her husband," Malloy continued, "she started killing girls. She chose the ones she thought might go back to their evil ways if she didn't stop them."

"Emilia had already left the mission once and returned to her lover," she reminded him. "That's probably why she was killed."

"And she wanted to kill you because you weren't

going to stop until you found out who murdered Emilia. She couldn't take the chance that you'd figure out she did it. She picked the church as an insult to the priest there because he'd been so critical of her mission."

Just saying the words made Frank's blood run cold, and she shuddered, too.

"I'm so tired of death," she said, and a tear rolled down her cheek. The sight of it burned his soul like acid.

Frank thought of Tom Brandt and what he now knew about the good doctor's murder. Once he'd hoped to solve that mystery and give her peace and a touch of justice. That hope was gone. Telling her the truth would shatter the world she had built for herself, and he could never do that to her. His effort to repay her for all she'd done for his son had ended in ruin.

"What's going to happen to this place?" he asked to change the subject.

"Some of the women who've been supporting the mission are going to hire someone to run it. They think the work is too important to give up on it."

Frank nodded, figuring they had to do at least as well as Mrs. Wells had done.

"Malloy, I wanted to tell you," she said a little tentatively. "I told Richard's family that he died saving my life and Aggie's. I know you didn't think much of him," she added hastily, "but he was a good man."

And he'd certainly cared very deeply for Sarah, Frank knew. He'd been as desperate as Frank to save her from that madwoman. Frank shouldn't be surprised that she'd cared for Dennis in return. He had been everything Frank was not and would never be —

a man who could earn Sarah's love. "Yes," he agreed, "he was a good man."

She seemed relieved, perhaps even glad. He couldn't tell.

"I need to get back to work," he said, rising from his chair. If he didn't leave, he might say something that would embarrass them both.

"Thank you for coming. I needed to talk about what happened," she said.

When he turned to take his leave, he saw an expression on her face that he'd never seen before. Probably, she was thinking of Dennis.

"Will I see you soon?" she asked.

"Sure," he lied. He knew he couldn't ever see her again. He loved her too much, and knowing him was far too dangerous. Each time they met, she almost died, which meant she was only safe without him. It would take a miracle to bring them together again.

Or a murder.

# Author's Note

As the granddaughter of Italian immigrants, I've long been aware of the prejudice the Italians endured when they began coming to America in the late nineteenth and early twentieth centuries. I was fascinated to learn, however, that the Irish, who had been the most recent group of immigrants to endure persecution, were among those persecuting the Italians. Everyone, it seems, must have someone over whom to feel superior. In that respect, human beings haven't changed a bit in the last hundred years.

I'd like to thank my writer friends who helped me come up with the unique method of killing the victims in this book. In the nineteenth century, an Austrian empress actually was killed the same way Richard Dennis was, although the weapon was a thin-bladed knife and not a hat pin. Then I happened to see a display of antique hat pins while I was plotting this story, and I knew I'd found the murder weapon. Finally, thanks to Dr. Jim Hughes for explaining what would happen to someone when a hat pin was inserted into the base of her brain.

I hope you enjoyed this book. If you missed the earlier books in the Gaslight series, they are *Murder on Astor Place, Murder on St. Mark's Place, Murder on Gramercy Park,* and *Murder on Washington Square.*

If you send me an e-mail, I will send you a reminder when the next book in the series, *Murder on Marble Row,* comes out next year. You can contact me through my web page at www.victoriathompson.net.